| | |
|---|---|
| *Mr. Murder* | *The Vision* |
| *Dragon Tears* | *The Face of Fear* |
| *Hideaway* | *Night Chills* |
| *Cold Fire* | *Shattered* |
| *The Bad Place* | *The Voice of the Night* |
| *Midnight* | *The Servants of Twilight* |
| *Lightning* | *The House of Thunder* |
| *Watchers* | *The Key to Midnight* |
| *Strangers* | *Shadowfires* |
| *Twilight Eyes* | *Winter Moon* |
| *Darkfall* | *The Door to December* |
| *Phantoms* | *Dark Rivers of the Heart* |
| *Whispers* | *Icebound* |
| *The Mask* | *Strange Highways* |

# INTENSITY

# INTENSITY

A NOVEL BY

# DEAN KOONTZ

Alfred A. Knopf   NEW YORK   1996

THIS IS A BORZOI BOOK
PUBLISHED BY ALFRED A. KNOPF, INC.

Library of Congress Cataloging-in-Publication Data

Koontz, Dean R. (Dean Ray), [date]
Intensity : a novel / by Dean Koontz. — 1st ed.
p.    cm.
ISBN 0-679-42525-X
1. Young women—Crimes against—Fiction.
2. Psychopaths—Fiction.
I. Title.
PS3561.O55I58    1995b
813'.54—dc20               95-33591
CIP

Manufactured in the United States of America
First Trade Edition

*A signed first edition of this book has been privately
printed by The Franklin Library.*

This book is for Florence Koontz.

My mother. Long lost. My guardian.

*Hope is the destination that we seek.*

*Love is the road that leads to hope.*

*Courage is the motor that drives us.*

*We travel out of darkness into faith.*

—THE BOOK OF COUNTED SORROWS

# INTENSITY

1

The red sun balances on the highest ramparts of the mountains, and in its waning light, the foothills appear to be ablaze. A cool breeze blows down out of the sun and fans through the tall dry grass, which streams like waves of golden fire along the slopes toward the rich and shadowed valley.

In the knee-high grass, he stands with his hands in the pockets of his denim jacket, studying the vineyards below. The vines were pruned during the winter. The new growing season has just begun. The colorful wild mustard that flourished between the rows during the colder months has been chopped back and the stubble plowed under. The earth is dark and fertile.

The vineyards encircle a barn, outbuildings, and a bungalow for the caretaker. Except for the barn, the largest structure is the owners' Victorian house with its gables, dormers, decorative millwork under the eaves, and carved pediment over the front porch steps.

Paul and Sarah Templeton live in the house year-round, and their daughter, Laura, visits occasionally from San Francisco, where she attends university. She is supposed to be in residence throughout this weekend.

He dreamily contemplates a mental image of Laura's face, as detailed as a photograph. Curiously, the girl's perfect features engender thoughts of succulent, sugar-laden bunches of pinot noir and grenache with translucent purple skin. He can actually taste the phantom grapes as he imagines them bursting between his teeth.

As it slowly sinks behind the mountains, the sun sprays light so warmly colored and so mordant that, where touched, the darkening land appears to be wet with it and dyed forever. The grass grows red as well, no longer like a fireless burning but, instead, a red tide washing around his knees.

He turns his back on the house and the vineyards. Savoring the steadily intensifying taste of grapes, he walks westward into the shadows cast by the high forested ridges.

He can smell the small animals of the open meadows cowering in their burrows. He hears the whisper of feathers carving the wind as a hunting hawk circles hundreds of feet overhead, and he feels the cold glimmer of stars that are not yet visible.

In the strange sea of shimmering red light, the black shadows of overhanging trees flickered shark-swift across the windshield.

On the winding two-lane blacktop, Laura Templeton handled the Mustang with an expertise that Chyna admired, but she drove too fast. "You've got a heavy foot," Chyna said.

Laura grinned. "Better than a big butt."

"You'll get us killed."

"Mom has rules about being late for dinner."

"Being late is better than being *dead* for dinner."

"You've never met my mom. She's hell on rules."

"So is the highway patrol."

Laura laughed. "Sometimes you sound just like her."

"Who?"

"My mom."

Bracing herself as Laura took a curve too fast, Chyna said, "Well, one of us has to be a responsible adult."

"Sometimes I can't believe you're only three years older than me," Laura said affectionately. "Twenty-six, huh? You sure you're not a *hundred* and twenty-six?"

"I'm ancient," Chyna said.

They had left San Francisco under a hard blue sky, taking a four-day break from classes at the University of California, where, in the spring, they would earn master's degrees in psychology. Laura hadn't been delayed in her education by the need to earn her tuition and living expenses, but Chyna had spent the past ten years attending classes part time while working full time as a waitress, first in a Denny's, then in a unit of the Olive Garden chain, and most recently in an upscale restaurant with white tablecloths and cloth napkins and fresh flowers on the tables and customers—bless them—who routinely tipped fifteen or twenty percent. This visit to the Templetons' house in the Napa Valley would be the closest thing to a vacation that she'd had in a decade.

From San Francisco, Laura had followed Interstate 80 through Berkeley and across the eastern end of San Pablo Bay. Blue heron had stalked the shallows and leaped gracefully into flight: enormous, eerily prehistoric, beautiful against the cloudless heavens.

Now, in the gold-and-crimson sunset, scattered clouds burned in the sky, and the Napa Valley unrolled like a radiant tapestry. Laura had departed the main road in favor of a scenic route; however, she drove so fast that Chyna was seldom able to take her eyes off the highway to enjoy the scenery.

"Man, I love speed," Laura said.

"I hate it."

"I like to move, streak, *fly*. Hey, maybe I was a gazelle in a previous life. You think?"

Chyna looked at the speedometer and grimaced. "Yeah, maybe a gazelle—or a madwoman locked away in Bedlam."

"Or a cheetah. Cheetahs are really fast."

"Yeah, a cheetah, and one day you were chasing your prey and ran straight off the edge of a cliff at full tilt. You were the Wile E. Coyote of cheetahs."

"I'm a good driver, Chyna."

"I know."

"Then relax."

"I can't."

Laura sighed with fake exasperation. "Ever?"

"When I sleep," Chyna said, and she nearly jammed her feet through the floorboards as the Mustang took a wide curve at high speed.

Beyond the narrow graveled shoulder of the two-lane, the land sloped down through wild mustard and looping brambles to a row of tall black alders fringed with early-spring buds. Beyond the alders lay vineyards drenched with fierce red light, and Chyna was convinced that the car would slide off the blacktop, roll down the embankment, and crash into the trees, and that her blood would fertilize the nearest of the vines.

Instead, Laura effortlessly held the Mustang to the pavement. The car swept out of the curve and up a long incline.

Laura said, "I bet you even worry in your sleep."

"Well, sooner or later, in every dream there's a boogeyman. You've got to be on the lookout for him."

"I have lots of dreams without boogeymen," Laura said. "I have wonderful dreams."

"Getting shot out of a cannon?"

"That would be fun. No, but sometimes I dream that I can fly. I'm always naked and just floating or swooping along fifty feet above the ground, over telephone lines, across fields of bright flowers, over tree-tops. So free. People look up and smile and wave. They're so de-lighted to see that I can fly, so happy for me. And sometimes I'm with this beautiful guy, lean and muscular, with a mane of golden hair and lovely green eyes that look all the way *through* me to my soul, and we're making love in midair, drifting up there, and I'm having spec-tacular orgasms, one after another, floating through sunshine with flowers below and birds swooping overhead, birds with these gor-geous iridescent-blue wings and singing the most fantastic birdsongs you ever heard, and I feel as if I'm full of dazzling light, just a creature of light, and like I'm going to explode, such an energy, explode and form a whole new universe and *be* the universe and live forever. You ever have a dream like that?"

Chyna had finally taken her eyes off the onrushing blacktop. She stared in blank-faced astonishment at Laura. Finally she said, "No."

Glancing away from the two-lane, Laura said, "Really? You never had a dream like that?"

"Never."

"I have lots of dreams like that."

"Could you keep your eyes on the road, kiddo?"

Laura looked at the highway and said, "Don't you ever dream about sex?"

"Sometimes."

"And?"

"What?"

"*And?*"

Chyna shrugged. "It's bad."

Frowning, Laura said, "You dream about having bad sex? Listen, Chyna, you don't have to *dream* about that—there are lots of guys who can provide all the bad sex you want."

"Ho, ho. I mean these are nightmares, very threatening."

"Sex is threatening?"

"Because I'm always a little girl in the dreams—six or seven or eight—and I'm always hiding from this man, not quite sure what he wants, why he's looking for me, but I know he wants something from me that he shouldn't have, something terrible, and it's going to be like dying."

"Who's the man?"

"Different men."

"Some of the creeps your mother used to hang out with?"

Chyna had told Laura a great deal about her mother. She had never told anyone else. "Yeah. Them. I always got away from them in real life. They never touched me. And they never touch me in the dreams. But there's always a threat, always a possibility. . . ."

"So these aren't just dreams. They're memories too."

"I wish they *were* just dreams."

"What about when you're awake?" Laura asked.

"What do you mean?"

"Do you just turn all warm and fuzzy and let yourself go when a man makes love to you . . . or is the past always there?"

"What is this—analysis at eighty miles an hour?"

"Dodging the question?"

"You're a snoop."

"It's called friendship."

"It's called snoopery."

"Dodging the question?"

Chyna sighed. "All right. I like being with a man. I'm not inhibited. I'll admit that I've never felt as though I'm a creature of light going to explode into a new universe, but I've been fully satisfied, always had fun."

"Fully?"

"Fully."

Chyna had never actually been with a man until she was twenty-one; and her intimate relationships now totaled exactly two. Both had been gentle, kind, and decent men, and in each case Chyna had greatly enjoyed the lovemaking. One affair had lasted eleven months, the other thirteen, and neither lover had left her a single troubling memory. Nevertheless, neither man had helped her banish the vicious dreams, which continued to plague her periodically, and she'd been unable to achieve an emotional bond equal to the physical intimacy. To a man whom she loved, Chyna could give her body, but even for love, she could not entirely give her mind and heart. She was afraid to commit herself, to trust without reservation. No one in her life, with the possible exception of Laura Templeton—stunt driver and dream flier—had ever earned total trust.

Wind shrieked along the sides of the car. In the flickering shadows and fiery light, the long incline ahead of them seemed to be a ramp, as if they were going to be launched into space when they reached the top, vaulting across a dozen burning buses while a stadium full of thrill-seekers cheered.

"What if a tire blows?" Chyna asked.

"The tires won't blow," Laura said confidently.

"What if one does?"

Wrenching her face into an exaggerated, demonic grin, Laura said, "Then we're just girl jelly in a can. They won't even be able to separate the remains into two distinct bodies. A total amorphous mess. They won't even need coffins for us. They'll just pour our remains in a jug and put us in one grave, and the headstone will read: *Laura Chyna Templeton Shepherd. Only a Cuisinart Would Have Been More Thorough.*"

Chyna had hair so dark that it was virtually black, and Laura was a blue-eyed blonde, yet they were enough alike to be sisters. Both were five feet four and slender; they wore the same dress size. Each had high cheekbones and delicate features. Chyna had always felt that her mouth was too wide, but Laura, whose mouth was as wide as Chyna's, said it wasn't wide at all but merely "generous" enough to ensure an especially winning smile.

As Laura's love of speed proved, however, they were in some ways profoundly different people. The differences, perhaps more than the similarities, were what drew them to each other.

"You think your mom and dad will like me?" Chyna asked.

"I thought you were worried about a blown tire."

"I'm a multichannel worrier. Will they like me?"

"Of course they'll like you. You know what *I* worry about?" Laura asked as they raced toward the top of the incline.

"Apparently, not death."

"You. I worry about you," Laura said. She glanced at Chyna, and her expression was uncharacteristically serious.

"I can take care of myself," Chyna assured her.

"I don't doubt *that*. I know you too well to doubt *that*. But life isn't just about taking care of yourself, keeping your head down, getting through."

"Laura Templeton, girl philosopher."

"Life is about *living*."

"Deep," Chyna said sarcastically.

"Deeper than you think."

The Mustang crested the long hill, and there were no burning buses or cheering multitudes, but ahead of them was an older-model Buick, cruising well below the posted limit. Laura cut their speed by more than half, and they pulled behind the other car. Even in the fading light, Chyna could see that the round-shouldered driver was a white-haired, elderly man.

They were in a no-passing zone. The road rose and fell, turned left and right, rose again, and they could not see far ahead.

Laura switched on the Mustang headlights, hoping to encourage the driver of the Buick either to increase his speed or to ease over where the shoulder widened to let them pass.

"Take your own advice—relax, kiddo," Chyna said.

"Hate to be late for dinner."

"From everything you've said about her, I don't think your mom's the type to beat us with wire coat hangers."

"Mom's the best."

"So relax," Chyna said.

"But she has this disappointed look she gives you that's *worse* than wire coat hangers. Most people don't know this, but Mom is the reason the Cold War ended. Several years ago, the Pentagon sent her off to Moscow so she could give the whole damn Politburo the *Look*, and all those Soviet thugs just collapsed with remorse."

Ahead of them, the old man in the Buick checked his rearview mirror.

The white hair in the headlight beams, the angle of the man's head, and the mere suggestion of his eyes reflected in the mirror suddenly engendered in Chyna a powerful sense of déjà vu. For a moment, she didn't understand why a chill came over her—but then she was cast back in memory to an incident that she had long tried unsuccessfully to forget: another twilight, nineteen years ago, a lonely Florida highway.

"Oh, Jesus," she said.

Laura glanced at her. "What's wrong?"

Chyna closed her eyes.

"Chyna, you're as white as a ghost. What is it?"

"A long time ago . . . when I was just a little girl, seven years old . . . Maybe we were in the Everglades, maybe not . . . but the land was swampy like the 'glades. There weren't many trees, and the few you could see were hung with Spanish moss. Everything was flat as far as you could see, lots of sky and flatness, the sunlight red and fading like now, a back road somewhere, far away from anything, very rural, two narrow lanes, so damn empty and lonely. . . ."

Chyna had been with her mother and Jim Woltz, a Key West drug dealer and gunrunner with whom they had lived now and then, for a month or two at a time, during her childhood. They had been on a business trip and had been returning to the Keys in Woltz's vintage red Cadillac, one of those models with massive tailfins and with what seemed to be five tons of chrome grillwork. Woltz was driving fast on that straight highway, exceeding a hundred miles an hour at times. They hadn't encountered another car for almost fifteen minutes before they roared up behind the elderly couple in the tan Mercedes. The woman was driving. Birdlike. Close-cropped silver hair. Seventy-five if she was a day. She was doing forty miles an hour. Woltz could have pulled around the Mercedes; they were in a passing zone, and no traffic was in sight for miles on that dead-flat highway.

"But he was high on something," Chyna told Laura, eyes still closed, watching the memory with growing dread as it played like a movie on a screen behind her eyes. "He was most of the time high on something. Maybe it was cocaine that day. I don't know. Don't remember. He was drinking too. They were both drinking, him and my mother. They had a cooler full of ice. Bottles of grapefruit juice and vodka. The old lady in the Mercedes was driving really slow, and that incensed Woltz. He wasn't rational. What did it matter to him? He could've pulled around her. But the sight of her driving so slow on the wide-open highway infuriated him. Drugs and booze, that's all. So irrational. When he was angry . . . red-faced, arteries throbbing in his neck, jaw muscles bulging. No one could get angry quite as *totally* as Jim Woltz. His rage excited my mother. Always excited her. So she teased him, encouraged him. I was in the backseat, hanging on tight, pleading with her to stop, but she kept at him."

For a while, Woltz had hung close behind the other car, blowing his horn at the elderly couple, trying to force them to go faster. A few times he had nudged the rear bumper of the Mercedes with the front bumper of the Cadillac, metal kissing metal with a squeal. Eventually the old woman got rattled and began to swerve erratically, afraid to go faster with Woltz so close behind her but too frightened of him to pull off the road and let him pass by.

"Of course," Chyna said, "he wouldn't have gone past and left her alone. By then he was too psychotic. He would have stopped when she stopped. It still would have ended badly."

Woltz had pulled alongside the Mercedes a few times, driving in the wrong lane, shouting and shaking his fist at the white-haired couple, who first tried to ignore him and then stared back wide-eyed and fearful. Each time, rather than drive by and leave them in his dust, he had dropped behind again to play tag with their rear bumper. To Woltz, in his drug fever and alcoholic haze, this harassment was deadly serious business, with an importance and a meaning that could never be understood by anyone who was clean and sober. To Chyna's mother, Anne, it was all a game, an adventure, and it was she, in her ceaseless search for excitement, who said, *Why don't we give her a driving test?* Woltz said, *Test? I don't need to give the old bitch a test to see she can't drive for shit.* This time, as Woltz pulled beside the Mercedes, matching speeds with it, Anne said, *I mean, see if she can keep it on the road. Make it a challenge for her.*

To Laura, Chyna recalled, "There was a canal parallel to the road, one of those drainage channels you see along some Florida highways. Not deep but deep enough. Woltz used the Cadillac to crowd the Mercedes onto the shoulder of the road. The woman should have crowded him back, forced him the other way. She should have tramped the pedal to the floor and pegged the speedometer and gotten the hell out of there. The Mercedes would've outrun the Cadillac, no problem. But she was old and scared, and she'd never encountered anyone like this. I think she was just disbelieving, so unable to understand the kind of people she was up against, unable to grasp how far they'd go *even though she and her husband had done nothing to them.* Woltz forced her off the road. The Mercedes rolled into the canal."

Woltz had stopped, shifted the Cadillac into reverse, and backed up to where the Mercedes was swiftly sinking. He and Anne had gotten out of the car to watch. Chyna's mother had insisted that she watch too: *Come on, you little chicken. You don't want to miss this, baby. This is one to remember.* The passenger's side of the Mercedes was flat against the muddy bottom of the canal, and the driver's side was revealed to them as they stood on the embankment in the humid evening air. They were being bitten by hordes of mosquitoes but were hardly aware of them, mesmerized by the sight below them, gazing through the driver-side windows of the submerged vehicle.

"It was twilight," Chyna told Laura, putting into words the images behind her closed eyes, "so the headlights were on, still on even after the Mercedes sank, and there were lights inside the car. They had air-conditioning, so all the windows were closed, and neither the windshield nor the driver-side window had shattered when the car rolled. We could see inside, 'cause the windows were only a few inches under water. There was no sign of the husband. Maybe he was knocked unconscious when they rolled. But the old woman . . . her face was at the window. The car was flooded, but there was a big bubble of air against the inside of the glass, and she pressed her face into it so, she could breathe. We stood there looking down at her. Woltz could have helped. My mother could have helped. But they just watched. The old woman couldn't seem to get the window open, and the door must have been jammed, or maybe she was just too scared and too weak."

Chyna had tried to pull away, but her mother had held her, speaking urgently to her, the whispered words borne on a tide of breath sour with vodka and grapefruit juice. *We're different than other people, baby. No rules apply to us. You'll never understand what freedom really means if you don't watch this.* Chyna had closed her eyes, but she had still been able to hear the old woman screaming into the big air bubble inside the submerged car. Muffled screaming.

"Then gradually the screaming faded . . . finally stopped," Chyna told Laura. "When I opened my eyes, twilight had gone and night had come. There was still light in the Mercedes, and the woman's face was still pressed to the glass, but a breeze had risen, rippling the water in the canal, and her features were a blur. I knew she was dead. She and her husband. I started to cry. Woltz didn't like that. He threatened to drag me into the canal, open a door on the Mercedes, and shove me inside with the dead people. My mother made me drink some grapefruit juice with vodka. I was only seven. The rest of the way back to Key West, I lay on the backseat, dizzy from the vodka, half drunk and a little sick, still crying but quietly, so I wouldn't make Woltz angry, crying quietly until I fell asleep."

In Laura's Mustang, the only sounds were the soft rumble of the engine and the singing of the tires on the blacktop.

Chyna finally opened her eyes and came back from the memory of Florida, from the long-ago humid twilight to the Napa Valley, where most of the red light had gone out of the sky and darkness encroached on all sides.

The old man in the Buick was no longer in front of them. They were not driving as fast as before, and evidently he had gotten far ahead of them.

Laura said softly, "Dear God."

Chyna was shaking uncontrollably. She plucked a few Kleenex from the console box between the seats, blew her nose, and blotted her eyes. Over the past two years, she had shared part of her childhood with Laura, but every new revelation—and there was much still to reveal—was as difficult as the one before it. When she spoke of the past, she always burned with shame, as though she had been as guilty as her mother, as if every criminal act and spell of madness could be blamed on her, though she had been only a helpless child trapped in the insanity of others.

"Will you ever see her again?" Laura asked.

Recollection had left Chyna half numb with horror. "I don't know."

"Would you want to?"

Chyna hesitated. Her hands were curled into fists, the damp Kleenex wadded in the right one. "Maybe."

"For God's sake why?"

"To ask her why. To try to understand. To settle some things. But . . . maybe not."

"Do you even know where she is?"

"No. But it wouldn't surprise me if she was in jail. Or dead. You can't live like that and hope to grow old."

They drove down out of the foothills into the valley.

Eventually Chyna said, "I can still see her standing in the steamy darkness on the banks of that canal, greasy with sweat, her hair hanging damp and all tangled, covered with mosquito bites, eyes bleary from vodka. Laura, even then she was *still* the most beautiful woman you've ever seen. She was always so beautiful, so perfect on the outside, like someone out of a dream, like an angel . . . but she was never half as beautiful as when she was excited, when there'd been violence. I can see her standing there, only visible because of the greenish glow from the headlights of the Mercedes rising through the murky canal water, so ravishing in that green light, glorious, the most beautiful person you've ever seen, like a goddess from another world."

Gradually Chyna's trembling subsided. The heat of shame faded from her face, but slowly.

She was immeasurably grateful for Laura's concern and support. A friend. Until Laura, Chyna had lived secretly with her past, unable to speak of it to anyone. Now, having unburdened herself of another hateful corrupting memory, she couldn't begin to put her gratitude into words.

"It's okay," Laura said, as if reading Chyna's mind.

They rode in silence.

They were late for dinner.

To Chyna, the Templeton house looked inviting at first glimpse: Victorian, gabled, roomy, with deep porches front and rear. It stood a half mile off the county road, at the end of a gravel driveway, surrounded by one hundred twenty acres of vineyards.

For three generations, the Templetons had grown grapes, but they had never made wine. They were under contract to one of the finest vintners in the valley, and because they owned fertile land with the highest-quality vines, they received an excellent price for their crop.

Sarah Templeton appeared on the front porch when she heard the Mustang in the driveway, and she came quickly down the steps to the stone walkway to greet Laura and Chyna. She was a lovely, girlishly slim woman in her early or mid forties, with stylishly short blond hair, wearing tan jeans and a long-sleeved emerald-green blouse with green embroidery on the collar, simultaneously chic and motherly. When Sarah hugged Laura and kissed her and held her with such evident and fierce love, Chyna was struck by a pang of envy and by a shiver of misery at never having known a mother's love.

She was surprised again when Sarah turned to her, embraced her, kissed her on the cheek, and, still holding her close, said, "Laura tells me you're the sister she never had, so I want you to feel at home here, sweetheart. When you're here with us, this is your place as much as ours."

Chyna stood stiffly at first, so unfamiliar with the rituals of family affection that she didn't know quite how to respond. Then she returned the embrace awkwardly and murmured an inadequate thank-you. Her throat was suddenly so tight that she was amazed to be able to speak at all.

Putting her arms around both Laura and Chyna, guiding them to the broad flight of porch steps, Sarah said, "We'll get your luggage later. Dinner's ready now. Come along. Laura's told me so much about you, Chyna."

"Well, Mom," said Laura, "I didn't tell you about Chyna being into voodoo. I sort of hid that part. She'll need to sacrifice a live chicken every night at midnight while she's staying with us."

"We only grow grapes. We don't have any chickens, dear," Sarah said. "But after dinner we can drive to one of the farms in the area and buy a few."

Chyna laughed and looked at Laura as if to say, *Where's the infamous Look?*

Laura understood. "In your honor, Chyna, all wire coat hangers and equivalent devices have been put away."

"Whatever are you talking about?" Sarah asked.

"You know me, Mom—a babbling ditz. Sometimes not even I know what I'm talking about."

Paul Templeton, Laura's father, was in the big kitchen, taking a potato-and-cheese casserole out of the oven. He was a neat, compact man, five feet ten, with thick dark hair and a ruddy complexion. He set the steaming dish aside, stripped off a pair of oven mitts, and greeted Laura as warmly as Sarah had done. After being introduced to Chyna, he took one of her hands in both of his, which were rough and work worn, and with feigned solemnity he said, "We prayed you'd make the trip in one piece. Does my little girl still handle that Mustang as if she thinks it's the Batmobile?"

"Hey, Dad," Laura said, "I guess you've forgotten who taught me to drive."

"I was instructing you in the basic techniques," Paul said. "I didn't expect you to acquire my *style.*"

Sarah said, "I refuse to think about Laura's driving. I'd just be worried sick all the time."

"Face it, Mom, there's an Indianapolis 500 gene on Dad's side of the family, and he passed it to me."

"She's an excellent driver," Chyna said. "I always feel safe with Laura."

Laura grinned at her and gave a thumbs-up sign.

Dinner was a long, leisurely affair because the Templetons liked to talk to one another, *thrived* on talking to one another. They were careful to include Chyna and seemed genuinely interested in what she had to say, but even when the conversation wandered to family matters of which Chyna had little knowledge, she somehow felt a part of it, as though she was, by a magical osmosis, actually being absorbed into the Templeton clan.

Laura's thirtyish brother, Jack, and his wife, Nina, lived in the care-taker's bungalow elsewhere in the vineyard, but a previous obligation had prevented them from joining the family for dinner. Chyna was as-sured that she would see them in the morning, and she felt no trepi-dation about meeting them, as she'd felt before she'd met Sarah and Paul. Throughout her troubled life, there had been no place where she had truly felt at home; while she might never feel entirely at home in this place either, at least she felt welcome here.

After dinner, Chyna and Laura went for a walk in the moonlit vine-yards, between the rows of low pruned vines that had not yet begun to sprout either leafy trailers or fruit. The cool air was redolent with the pleasant fecund smell of freshly plowed earth, and there was a sense of mystery in the dark fields that she found intriguing, enchanting—but at times disconcerting, as if they were among unseen presences, an-cient spirits that were not all benign.

When they had strolled deep into the vines and then turned back toward the house, Chyna said, "You're the best friend I've ever had."

"Me too," Laura said.

"More than that . . ." Chyna's voice trailed away. She had been about to say, *You're the only friend I've ever had,* but that made her seem so lame and, besides, was still an inadequate expression of what she felt for this girl. They were, indeed, in one sense sisters.

Laura linked arms with her and merely said, "I know."

"When you have babies, I want them to call me Aunt Chyna."

"Listen, Shepherd, don't you think I should find a guy and get married before I start pumping out the babies?"

"Whoever he is, he better be the best husband in the world to you, or I promise I'll cut his *cojones* off."

"Do me a favor, okay?" Laura said. "Don't tell him about this promise until after the wedding. Some guys might be put off by it."

From elsewhere in the vineyards came a disquieting sound that stopped Chyna. A protracted creaking.

"It's just the breeze working at a loose barn door, rusty hinges," Laura said.

It sounded as if someone were opening a giant door in the wall of night itself and stepping in from another world.

Chyna Shepherd could not sleep comfortably in strange houses. Throughout her childhood and adolescence, her mother had dragged her from one end of the country to the other, staying nowhere longer than a month or two. So many terrible things had happened to them in so many places that Chyna eventually learned to view each new house not as a new beginning, not with hope for stability and happiness, but with suspicion and quiet dread.

Now she was long rid of her troubled mother and free to stay only where she wished. These days, her life was almost as stable as that of a cloistered nun, as meticulously planned as any bomb squad's procedures for disarming an explosive device, and without any of the turmoil on which her mother had thrived.

Nevertheless, this first night in the Templetons' house, Chyna was reluctant to undress and go to bed. She sat in the darkness in a medallion-back armchair at one of the two windows in the guest room, gazing out at the moonlit vineyards, fields, and hills of the Napa Valley.

Laura was in another room, at the far end of the second-floor hall, no doubt sound asleep, at peace because this house was not at all strange to her.

From the guest-room window, the early-spring vineyards were barely visible. Vague geometric patterns.

Beyond the cultivated rows were gentle hills mantled in long dry grass, silver in the moonlight. An inconstant breeze stirred through the valley, and sometimes the wild grass seemed to roll like ocean waves across the slopes, softly aglimmer with lambent lunar light.

Above the hills was the Coast Range, and above those peaks were cascades of stars and a full white moon. Storm clouds coming across the mountains from the northwest would soon darken the night, turning the silver hills first to pewter and then to blackest iron.

When she heard the first scream, Chyna was gazing at the stars, drawn by their cold light as she had been since childhood, fascinated by the thought of distant worlds that might be barren and clean, free of pestilence. At first the muffled cry seemed to be only a memory, a fragment of a shrill argument from another strange house in the past, echoing across time. Often, as a child, eager to hide from her mother and her mother's friends when they were drunk or high, she climbed onto porch roofs or into backyard trees, slipped through windows onto fire escapes, away to secret places far from the fray, where she could study the stars and where voices raised in argument or sexual excitement or shrill drug-induced giddiness came to her as though from out of a radio, from faraway places and people who had no connection whatsoever with her life.

The second cry, though also brief and only slightly louder than the first, was indisputably of the moment, not a memory, and Chyna sat forward on her chair. Tense. Head cocked. Listening.

She wanted to believe that the voice had come from outside, so she continued to stare into the night, surveying the vineyards and the hills beyond. Breeze-driven waves swelled through the dry grass on the moon-washed slopes: a water mirage like the ghost tides of an ancient sea.

From elsewhere in the large house came a soft thump, as though a heavy object had fallen to a carpeted floor.

Chyna immediately rose from the chair and stood utterly still, expectant.

Trouble often followed voices raised in one kind of passion or another. Sometimes, however, the worst offenses were preceded by calculated silences and stealth.

She had difficulty reconciling the idea of domestic violence with Paul and Sarah Templeton, who had seemed kind and loving toward each other as toward their daughter. Nevertheless, appearances and realities were seldom the same, and the human talent for deception was far greater than that of the chameleon, the mockingbird, or the praying mantis, which masked its ferocious cannibalism with a serene and devout posture.

Following the stifled cries and the soft thump, silence sifted down like a snowfall. The hush was eerily deep, as unnatural as that in which the deaf lived. This was the stillness before the pounce, the quietude of the coiled snake.

In another part of the house, someone was standing as motionless as she herself was standing, as alert as she was, intently listening. Someone dangerous. She could sense the predatory presence, a subtle new pressure in the air, not dissimilar to that preceding a violent thunderstorm.

On one level, six years of psychology classes caused her to question her immediate fearful interpretation of those night sounds, which conceivably could be insignificant, after all. Any well-trained psychoanalyst would have a wealth of labels to pin on someone who leaped first to a negative conclusion, who lived in expectation of sudden violence.

But she had to trust her instinct. It had been honed by many years of hard experience.

Intuitively certain that safety lay in movement, she stepped quietly away from the chair at the window, toward the hall door. In spite of the moonglow, her eyes had adjusted to darkness during the two hours that she had sat in the lightless room, and now she eased through the gloom with no fear of blundering into furniture.

She was only halfway to the door when she heard approaching footsteps in the second-floor hall. The heavy, urgent tread was alien to this house.

Unhampered by the interminable second-guessing that accompanied an education in psychology, reverting to the intuition and defenses of childhood, Chyna quickly retreated to the bed. She dropped to her knees.

Farther along the hall, the footsteps stopped. A door opened.

She was aware of the absurdity of attributing rage to the mere opening of a door. The rattle of the knob being turned, the rasp of the unsecured latch, the spike-sharp squeak of an unoiled hinge—they were only sounds, neither meek nor furious, guilty nor innocent, and could have been made as easily by a priest as by a burglar. Yet she *knew* that rage was at work in the night.

Flat on her stomach, she wriggled under the bed, feet toward the headboard. It was a graceful piece of furniture with sturdy galbe legs, and fortunately it didn't sit as close to the floor as did most beds. One inch less of clearance would have prevented her from hiding under it.

Footsteps sounded in the hall again.

Another door opened. The guest-room door. Directly opposite the foot of the bed.

Someone switched on the lights.

Chyna lay with her head turned to one side, her right ear pressed to the carpet. Staring out from under the footboard, she could see a man's black boots and the legs of his blue jeans below mid-calf.

He stood just inside the threshold, evidently surveying the room. He would see a bed still neatly made at one o'clock in the morning, with four decorative needlepoint pillows arranged against the head-board.

She had left nothing on the nightstands. No clothes tossed on chairs. The paperback novel that she had brought with her for bed-time reading was in a bureau drawer.

She preferred spaces that were clean and uncluttered to the point of monastic sterility. Her preference might now save her life.

Again a faint doubt, the acquired propensity for self-analysis that plagued all psychology students, flickered through her. If the man in the doorway was someone with a right to be in the house—Paul Templeton or Laura's brother, Jack, who lived with his wife in the vineyard manager's bungalow elsewhere on the property—and if some crisis was unfolding that explained why he would burst into her room with-out knocking, she was going to appear to be a prime fool, if not a hys-teric, when she crawled out from under the bed.

Then, directly in front of the black boots, a fat red droplet—another, and a third—fell to the wheat-gold carpet. *Plop-plop-plop.* Blood. The first two soaked into the thick nylon pile. The third held its surface tension, shimmering like a ruby.

Chyna knew the blood wasn't that of the intruder. She tried not to think about the sharp instrument from which it might have fallen.

He moved off to her right, deeper into the room, and she rolled her eyes to follow him.

The bed had carved side rails into which the spread was tightly tucked. No overhanging fabric obstructed her view of his boots.

Obversely, without a spread draped to the floor, the space under the bed was more visible to him. From certain angles, he might even be able to look down and see a swatch of *her* blue jeans, the toe of one of her Rockports, the cranberry-red sleeve of her cotton sweater where it stretched over her bent elbow.

She was thankful that the bed was queen-size, offering more cover than a single or double.

If he was breathing hard, either with excitement or with the rage that she had sensed in his approach, Chyna couldn't hear him. With one ear pressed tightly to the plush carpet, she was half deaf. Wood slats and box springs weighed on her back, and her chest barely had room to expand to accommodate her own shallow, cautious, open-mouth inhalations. The hammering of her compressed heart against her breastbone echoed tympanically within her, and it seemed to fill the claustrophobic confines of her hiding place to such an extent that the intruder was certain to hear.

He went to the bathroom, pushed open the door, and flicked on the lights.

She had put away all her toiletries in the medicine cabinet. Even her toothbrush. Nothing lay out that might alert him to her presence.

But was the sink dry?

On retiring to her room at eleven o'clock, she had used the toilet and then had washed her hands. That was two hours ago. Any residual water in the bowl surely would have drained away or evaporated.

Lemon-scented liquid soap in a pump dispenser was provided at the sink. Fortunately, there was no damp bar of soap to betray her.

She worried about the hand towel. She doubted that it could still be damp two hours after the little use she had made of it. Nonetheless, in spite of a propensity for neatness and order, she might have left it hanging ever so slightly askew or with one telltale wrinkle.

He seemed to stand on the bathroom threshold for an eternity. Then he switched off the fluorescent light and returned to the bedroom.

Occasionally, as a little girl—and then not so little—Chyna had taken refuge under beds. Sometimes they looked for her there; sometimes, though it was the most obvious of all hidey-holes, they never thought to look. Of those who found her, a few had checked under the bed first—but most had left it for last.

Another red droplet fell to the carpet, as though the beast might be shedding slow tears of blood.

He moved toward the closet door.

Chyna had to turn her head slightly, straining her neck, to keep track of him.

The closet was deep, a walk-in with a chain-pull light in the center. She heard the distinctive snap of the tugged switch, then the clinking of the metal beads in the chain as they rattled against the light bulb.

The Templetons stored their own luggage at the back of that closet. Stacked with the other suitcases, Chyna's single bag and train case were not obviously those of a guest in residence.

She had brought several changes of clothes: two dresses, two skirts, another pair of jeans, a pair of chinos, a leather jacket. Because Chyna was the same size as Laura, the intruder might conclude that the few garments on the rod were just spillovers from the packed closet in Laura's room rather than evidence of a houseguest.

If he had been in Laura's bedroom, however, and had seen the condition of her closet—then what had happened to Laura?

She must not think about that. Not now. Not yet. For the moment, she needed to focus all her thoughts, all her wits, on staying alive.

Eighteen years ago, on the night of her eighth birthday, in a seaside cottage on Key West, Chyna had squirmed under her bed to hide from Jim Woltz, her mother's friend. A storm had been raging from the Gulf of Mexico, and the sky-blistering lightning had made her fearful of escaping to the sanctuary of the beach where she'd retreated on other nights. After committing herself to the cramped space under that iron bed, which had been lower slung than this one, she had discovered that she was sharing it with a palmetto beetle. Palmettos were not as exotic or as pretty as their name. In fact, they were nothing more than enormous tropical cockroaches. This one had been as large as her little-girl hand. Ordinarily the hateful bug would have scurried away from her. But it had seemed less alarmed by her than by the thundering Woltz, who had crashed around her small room in a drunken fury, rebounding tirelessly from the furniture and the walls, like an enraged animal throwing itself against the bars of its cage. Chyna had been barefoot, dressed in blue shorts and a white tube top, and the palmetto beetle had raced in a frenzy over all that exposed skin, between her toes, up and down her legs and up again, across her back, along her neck, into her hair, over her shoulder, the length of her slender arm. She hadn't dared to squeal in revulsion, afraid of drawing Woltz's attention. He had been wild that night, like a monster from a dream, and she had been convinced that, like all monsters, he possessed supernaturally keen sight and hearing, the better to hunt children. She hadn't even found the courage to strike out at the beetle or knock it away, for fear that Woltz would hear the smallest sound even over the shriek of the storm and the incessant crashing of thunder. She had endured the palmetto's attentions in order to avoid those of Woltz, clenching her teeth to bite off a scream, praying desperately for God to save her, then praying harder for God to take her, praying for an end to the torment even if by a bolt of lightning, an end to the torment, an end, dear God, an end.

Now, although she wasn't sharing the space under this galbe-leg bed with any cockroach, Chyna could feel one crawling over her toes as if she were that barefoot girl again, scurrying up her legs as if she were wearing not jeans but cotton shorts. She had never again worn her hair long since the night of her eighth birthday, when the bug had burrowed through her tresses, but now she felt the ghost of that palmetto in her closely cropped hair.

The man in the closet, perhaps capable of atrocities infinitely worse than the wickedest dreams of Woltz, tugged on the chain-pull. The light went out with a click followed by a tinkle of metal beads.

The booted feet reappeared and approached the bed. A fresh tear of blood glistened on the curve of black leather.

He was going to drop to one knee beside the bed.

*Dear God, he'll find me cowering like a child, choking on my own stifled scream, in a cold sweat, all dignity lost in the desperate struggle to stay alive, untouched and alive, untouched and alive.*

She had the crazy feeling that when he peered under the side rail, face-to-face with her, he would be not a man but an enormous palmetto with multifaceted black eyes.

She had been reduced to the helplessness of childhood, to the primal fear that she had hoped never to know again. He had stolen from her the self-respect that she had earned from years of endurance— that she had *earned*, God damn him—and the injustice of it filled her eyes with bitter tears.

But then his blurred boots turned away from her and kept moving. He walked past the bed to the open door.

Whatever he'd thought about the clothes hanging in the closet, apparently he had not inferred from them that the guest room was occupied.

She blinked furiously, clearing her tear-blurred vision.

He stopped and turned, evidently studying the bedroom one last time.

Lest he hear her child-shallow exhalations, Chyna held her breath.

She was glad that she wore no perfume. She was certain that he would have smelled her.

He switched off the light, stepped into the hall, and pulled the door shut as he went.

His footsteps moved off the way he had come, for her room was the last on the second floor. His tread swiftly faded, cloaked by the fierce pounding of her heart.

Her first inclination was to remain in that narrow haven between the carpet and the box springs, wait until daybreak or even longer, wait until there came a long silence that ceased to seem like the stillness of a crouched predator.

But she didn't know what had happened to Laura, Paul, or Sarah. Any of them—all of them—might be alive, grievously wounded but drawing breath. The intruder might even be keeping them alive to torture them at his leisure. Any newspaper regularly reported stories of cruelty no worse than the possible scenarios that now unreeled vividly in her mind. And if any of the Templetons still lived, Chyna might be their only hope of survival.

She had crawled out of all the many hideaways of her childhood with less fear than she felt when she hesitantly slid out from under this bed. Of course she had more to lose now than before she had walked out on her mother, ten years ago: a decent life built on a decade of ceaseless struggle and hard-won self-respect. It seemed madness to take this risk when safety was assured simply by her staying put. But personal safety at the expense of others was cowardice, and cowardice was a right only of small children who lacked the strength and experience to defend themselves.

She couldn't simply retreat into the defensive detachment of her childhood. Doing so would mean the end of all self-respect. Slow-motion suicide. It's not possible to retreat into a bottomless pit—one can only plunge.

In the open once more, she rose into a crouch beside the bed. For a while that was as far as she got. She was frozen by the expectation that the door would crash open and that the intruder would burst in again.

The house was as echo-free as any airless moon.

Chyna rose to her feet and silently crossed the dark guest room. Unable to see the trio of blood drops, she tried to step around the place where they had fallen earlier.

She pressed her left ear to the crack between the door and the jamb, listening for movement or breathing in the hall. She heard nothing, yet she remained suspicious.

He could be on the other side of the door. Smiling. Deeply amused to think that she was listening. Biding his time. Patient because he knew that eventually she would open the door and step into his arms.

*Screw it.*

She put her hand on the knob, turned it cautiously, and winced as the spring latch scraped softly out of its notch. At least the hinges were lubricated and silent.

Even in the inkiness to which her vision had not totally readapted, she could see that no one was waiting for her. She stepped out of her room and soundlessly pulled the door shut.

The guest quarters were off the shorter arm of the L-shaped upstairs hall. To her right were the back stairs, which led down to the kitchen. To her left lay the turn into the longer arm of the L.

She ruled out the back stairs. She had descended them earlier in the evening, when she and Laura went out to walk the vineyards. They were wooden and worn. They creaked and popped. The stairwell acted as an amplifier, as hollow and efficient as a steel drum. With the house so preternaturally silent, it would be impossible to creep down the back stairs undetected.

The second-floor hall and the front stairs, on the other hand, were plushly carpeted.

From around the corner, somewhere along the main hallway, came a soft amber glow. In the wallpaper, the delicate pattern of faded roses appeared to absorb the light rather than reflect it, acquiring an enigmatic depth that it had not previously possessed.

If the intruder had been standing anywhere between the junction of the hallways and the source of the light, he would have cast a distorted shadow across that luminous paper garden or on the wheat-gold carpet. There was no shadow.

Keeping her back close to the wall, Chyna edged to the corner, hesitated, and leaned out to scout the way ahead. The main hallway was deserted.

Two sources of faint amber light relieved the gloom. The first came from a half-open door on the right: Paul and Sarah's suite. The second was much farther down the hallway, past the front stairs, on the left: Laura's room.

The other doors all seemed to be closed. She didn't know what lay beyond them. Perhaps other bedrooms, a bath, an upstairs study, closets. Although Chyna was most drawn to—and most afraid of—the lighted rooms, every closed door was also a danger.

The unplumbable silence tempted her to believe that the intruder had gone. This was a temptation best resisted.

Forward, then, through the paper arbor of printed roses to the half-open door of the master suite. Hesitating there. On the brink.

When she found whatever waited to be found, all her illusions of order and stability might dissolve. The truth of life might then reassert itself, after ten years during which she had diligently denied it: chaos, like the flow of a stream of mercury, its course unpredictable.

The man in the blue jeans and black boots might have returned to the master suite after leaving the guest room, but more likely not. Other amusements in the house would no doubt be more appealing to him.

Fearful of lingering too long in the hall, she sidled across the threshold, without pushing the door open wider.

Paul and Sarah's room was spacious. A sitting area included a pair of armchairs and footstools facing a fireplace. Bookshelves crammed with hardcovers flanked the mantel, their titles lost in shadows.

The nightstand lamps were colorfully patterned ginger jars with pleated shades. One of them was aglow; crimson streaks and blots stained its shade.

Chyna stopped well short of the foot of the bed, already close enough to see too much. Neither Paul nor Sarah was there, but the sheets and blankets were in tangled disarray, trailing onto the floor on the right side of the bed. On the left, the linens were soaked with blood, and a wet spray glistened on the headboard and in an arc across the wall.

She closed her eyes. Heard something. Spun around, crouching in expectation of an assault. She was alone.

The noise had always been there, a background hiss-patter-splash of falling water. She hadn't heard it on entering the room, because she had been deafened by bloodstains as loud as the angry shouting of a maddened mob.

*Synesthesia.* The word had stuck with her from a psychology text, more because she thought it was a beautiful arrangement of syllables than because she expected ever to experience it herself. Synesthesia: a confusion of the senses in which a scent might register as a flash of color, a sound actually might be perceived as a scent, and the texture of a surface under the hand might seem to be a trilling laugh or a scream.

Closing her eyes had blocked out the roar of the bloodstains, whereupon she had heard the falling water. Now she recognized it as the sound of the shower in the adjoining bathroom.

That door was ajar half an inch. For the first time since she had entered from the hallway, Chyna noticed the thin band of fluorescent light along the bathroom jamb.

When she looked away from that door, reluctant to confront what might wait beyond it, she spotted the telephone on the right-hand nightstand. That was the side of the bed without blood, which made it more approachable for her.

She lifted the handset from the cradle. No dial tone. She had not expected to hear one. Nothing was ever that easy.

She opened the single drawer on the nightstand, hoping to find a handgun. No luck.

Still certain that her only hope of safety lay in movement, that crawling into a hole and hiding should always be the strategy of last resort, Chyna had gone around to the other side of the king-size bed before she quite realized that she had taken a first step. In front of the bathroom door, the carpet was badly stained.

Grimacing, she went to the second nightstand and eased open the drawer. In the mortal fall of light, she discovered a pair of reading glasses with yellow reflections in the half-moon lenses, a paperback men's adventure novel, a box of Kleenex, a tube of lip balm, but no weapon.

As she closed the drawer, she smelled burned gunpowder underlying the hot-copper stench of fresh blood.

She was familiar with that odor. Over the years, more than a few of her mother's friends either had used guns to get what they wanted or had been at least fascinated by them.

Chyna had heard no shots. The intruder evidently had a weapon with a sound suppressor.

Water continued to cascade into the shower beyond the door. That susurrous splash, though soft and soothing under other circumstances, now abraded her nerves as effectively as the whine of a dentist's drill.

She was sure that the intruder wasn't in the bathroom. His work here was done. He was busy elsewhere in the house.

Right this minute she was not as frightened of the man himself as she was of discovering exactly what he had done. But the choice before her was the essence of the entire human agony: not knowing was ultimately worse than knowing.

At last she pushed open the door. Squinting, she entered the fluorescent glare.

The roomy bath featured yellow and white ceramic tile. On the walls at chair-rail height and around the edges of the vanity and lavatory counters ran a decorative tile band of daffodils and green leaves. She had expected more blood.

Paul Templeton was propped on the toilet in his blue pajamas. Lengths of wide strapping tape across his lap fixed him to the bowl. More tape encircled both his chest and the toilet tank, holding him upright.

Through the semitransparent bands of tape, three separate bullet wounds were visible in his chest. There might have been more than three. She didn't care to look for them and had no need to know. He appeared to have died instantly, most likely in his sleep, and to have been dead before he was brought into the bathroom.

Grief welled in her, black and cold. Survival meant repressing it at all costs, and surviving was the thing that she did best.

A collar of strapping tape around Paul's neck became a leash that tethered him to a hand-towel rack on the wall behind the toilet. The purpose was to prevent his head from falling forward onto his chest— and to direct his dead gaze toward the shower. His eyelids were taped open, and in his right eye was a starburst hemorrhage.

Shuddering, Chyna looked away from him.

Although the intruder had needed to kill Paul in his sleep to establish control of the house quickly, here he had been fantasizing that the husband was being forced to watch the atrocities committed against the wife.

This was a classic tableau, a favorite of those sociopaths who took delight in performing for their victims. They actually seemed to believe that for a while the recently dead could still see, still hear, and were thus capable of admiring the bold antics and posing of a tormentor who feared neither man nor God. Textbooks described the delusion. In one of her aberrant-psychology classes at UCSF, a speaker from the FBI's Behavioral Science Section had given them more graphic descriptions of such scenes than any textbooks could provide.

Firsthand, however, the impact of this brutality was worse than words could convey. Almost paralyzing. Chyna's legs felt heavy and stiff. The tingling in her hands was incipient numbness.

Sarah Templeton was in the stall shower, which was separate from the tub. Although the glass door was closed—and frosted—Chyna was able to see a faint, vaguely pinkish shape huddled on the shower floor.

On the face of the soffit above the glass door, the killer had printed two words. The black letters appeared to have been made with multiple strokes of an eyebrow pencil: DIRTY BITCH.

Chyna had never wanted anything as much as she wanted to be free of the obligation to look into this shower stall. Surely Sarah could not be alive.

Yet if she turned away without being certain that the woman was beyond all help, ineradicable guilt would ensure that her own survival would become a kind of walking death.

Besides, she had committed her life to trying to understand this very aspect of human cruelty, and no published case study would ever bring her closer to comprehension than might the things that she saw here. In this house, on this night, the bleak landscape of the socio-pathic mind had been externalized.

Echoing off the tile walls, the sizzle-splash of the falling water sounded like the hissing of serpents and the brittle laughter of strange children.

The water must be cold. Otherwise, steam would have been seething over the top of the shower enclosure.

Chyna held her breath, gripped the anodized aluminum handle, and opened the stall door.

Sarah Templeton had been wearing a pale-green teddy and match-ing panties. Her garments were in a sodden ball in one corner of the shower.

After her husband had been shot, the woman had evidently been hammered unconscious, perhaps with the butt of the gun. Then she had been gagged; her cheeks bulged with whatever rag had been forced into her mouth. Strips of strapping tape had sealed her lips, but in the relentless icy spray, the edges of the tape had begun to peel away from her skin.

With Sarah, the killer had used a knife. She was not alive.

Chyna quietly closed the stall door.

If there was such a thing as mercy, then Sarah Templeton had never regained any awareness after being knocked unconscious.

She remembered the hug that Sarah had given her on the front walk when she had first arrived with Laura. Repressing tears, she wished that she herself were dead instead of the precious woman in the shower stall. Indeed, she *was* half dead and less alive by the minute, because a piece of her heart died with each of these people.

Chyna returned to the bedroom. She moved away from the bed but didn't go immediately toward the hall door. Instead, she stood in the darkest corner, shaking uncontrollably.

Her stomach rolled. An acidic burning rose in her chest, and a bitter taste filled the back of her mouth. She suppressed an urge to vomit. The killer might hear her retching, and then he would come to get her.

Although she'd met Laura's parents only the previous afternoon, Chyna had known them also from her friend's numerous anecdotes and colorful stories of family adventures. She should have felt even more grief than she did, but she had only a limited capacity for it right now. Later it would hit her harder. Grief thrived in a quiet heart, and right now hers thundered with terror and revulsion.

She was shocked that the killer had done so much damage while she had sat, unknowing, at the guest-room window, brooding on the stars and thinking of other nights when she had gazed at them from rooftops, backyard trees, and beaches. From what she'd seen, he had taken at least ten or fifteen minutes with Paul and Sarah before searching the rest of the large house to locate and overpower the remaining occupants.

Sometimes a man like this got a special thrill from risking interruption, even apprehension. Perhaps a half-asleep, bewildered child would be drawn into the parents' room by some commotion and then would have to be pursued and dragged down before escaping the house. Such possibilities heightened the pleasure that the creep took from his activities in the bedroom and the bath.

This *was* a pleasure to him. A compulsion, but not one over which he despaired. Fun. His recreation. No guilt—therefore, no anguish. Savagery gladdened him.

Somewhere in the house, he was either at play or resting until he was ready to begin the game again.

As her shakes subsided to shivers, Chyna grew increasingly afraid for Laura. Those two muffled cries, minutes ago, had surely come after Sarah was already dead, so Laura must have been surprised in her sleep by a man smelling of her mother's blood. As soon as he had overpowered and secured her, he had hurried to search the rest of the second floor, concerned that another member of the family might have been alerted by her stifled screams.

He might not have returned immediately to Laura. Having found no one in any of the other rooms, confident that the house was firmly under his reign, he most likely had gone exploring. If the textbooks were correct, he would probably wish to violate every private space.

Pore through the contents of his host's and hostess's closets and desk drawers. Eat food from their refrigerator. Read their mail. Perhaps finger and smell the soiled clothing in the laundry-room hamper. If he could locate collections of family photographs, he might even sit in the den for an hour or longer, amusing himself with those albums.

Sooner or later, however, he would return to Laura.

Sarah Templeton had been an extremely attractive woman, but night visitors like this man were drawn toward youth; they fed on innocence. Laura was his meat of choice, as irresistible as birds' eggs to certain tree-climbing serpents.

When at last Chyna overcame her racking nausea and was certain that she wouldn't betray herself by being suddenly and violently sick, she crept out of the corner and silently crossed the room.

She wouldn't have been safe in the master suite anyway. Before the visitor left, he was likely to return here for one last look at poor Sarah in the shower with her slender arms crossed in a pathetic and ineffective posture of defense.

At the half-open door, Chyna paused to listen.

Directly across the hall, the faded roses on the wallpaper seemed more mysterious than ever. The pattern had such enigmatic depth that she was almost convinced she might be able to part the thorny vines and step out of that paper arbor into a sunny realm where, when she looked back, this house would not exist.

With the light from the nightstand lamp behind her, she could not ease cautiously into the doorway and take her time peeking left and right, because when she moved onto the threshold, she would cast a shadow on those faded roses across the hall. Dawdling behind that unavoidable announcement of herself would be dangerous.

Seduced by a long silence that seemed to promise safety, she finally sidled between the half-open door and the jamb, into the hallway—and he was *there*. Ten feet away. Near the head of the front stairs, which lay to the right. His back was to her.

She froze. Half in the hallway. Half on the threshold to the master suite. If he turned, she would not be able to slip away before he glimpsed her from the corner of his eye—yet she was unable to move now while there was still a chance to avoid him. She was afraid that if she made any sound whatsoever, he would hear it and spin toward her. Even the microwhispers of carpet fibers compressing under her shoe, if she moved, seemed certain to draw his attention.

The visitor was doing something so bizarre that Chyna was as transfixed by his activity as by her fear. His hands were raised in front of him, stretched as high as he could reach, and his spread fingers languorously combed the air. He seemed to be in a trance, as though trying to seine psychic impressions from the ether.

He was a big man. Six feet two, maybe even taller. Muscular. Narrow waist, enormous shoulders. His denim jacket stretched tautly across his broad back.

His hair was thick and brown, neatly barbered against the nape of his bull neck, but Chyna could not see his face. She hoped never to see it.

His seining fingers, stained with blood, looked crushingly strong. He would be able to choke the life out of her with a single-hand grip.

"Come to me," he murmured.

Even in a whisper, his rough voice had a timbre and a power that were magnetic.

"Come to me."

He seemed to be speaking not to a vision that only he could see but to *Chyna*, as if his senses were so acute that he had been able to detect her merely from the movement of the air that she had displaced when she'd stepped soundlessly through the doorway.

Then she saw the spider. It dangled from the ceiling on a gossamer filament a foot above the killer's reaching hands.

"Please."

As if responding to the man's supplications, the spider spun out its thread, descending.

The killer stopped reaching, turned his hand palm-up. "Little one," he breathed.

Fat and black, the obedient spider reeled itself down into the big open palm.

The killer brought his hand to his mouth and tipped his head back slightly. He either crushed the spider and ate it—or ate it alive.

He stood motionless, savoring.

Finally, without looking back, he went to the head of the stairs on the right, at the midpoint of the hallway, and descended spider-quick and almost spider-silent to the first floor.

Chyna shuddered, stunned to be alive.

2

The house held a drowning depth of stillness as a dam held water, with tremendous pent-up power and pressure on the breast.

When Chyna found the courage to move, she cautiously approached the head of the stairs. She feared that the visitor had not fully descended to the first floor, that he was toying with her, standing just out of sight, waiting, smiling. He would reach for her, palms up, and say, *Come to me*.

She held her breath, risked exposure, and looked down. The stairs curved through gradients of gloom to the foyer below. She could see just well enough to be sure that he wasn't there.

As far as Chyna could discern, no lamps were on downstairs. She wondered what he was doing in that darkness, guided only by the pale moonglow at the windows. Perhaps he was in a corner, crouched like a spider, sensitive to the faintest changes in the patterns of the air, dreaming of silent stalkings and the frenzied rending of prey.

She went quickly past the head of the stairs, into the last length of hallway, to the next open door and the second source of amber light, dreading what she might find. But she could cope with both the dread and the finding. It was always *not* knowing, turning away from truth, that caused night sweats and bad dreams.

This room was smaller than the master suite, with no sitting area. A corner desk. A double bed. One nightstand with a brass lamp, a dresser, a vanity with a padded bench.

On the wall above the bed was a poster-size portrait of Freud. Chyna loathed Freud. But Laura, dear of heart and idealistic, clung to a belief in many aspects of Freudian theory; she embraced the dream of a guiltless world, with everyone a victim of his troubled past and yearning for rehabilitation.

Laura was lying facedown on the bed, atop the sheets and the blankets. Her wrists were handcuffed behind her. A second pair of handcuffs secured her ankles. Linking both of those shiny steel restraints was a shackling chain.

She had been violated. The pants of her baggy blue pajamas had been cut off with a neatness worthy of a conscientious tailor; the blue panels of cloth had been smoothed across the blankets to both sides of her. The pajama shirt had been shoved up her back; now it was gathered in rumpled folds across her shoulders and the nape of her neck.

Chyna moved deeper into the room, her fear equaled now by a swelling sorrow that seemed to enlarge her heart yet leave it cold and empty. When she caught a faint odor of spilled semen, her fear and sorrow were matched by anger. As she stooped beside the bed, her hands curled into such hard fists that her fingernails pressed painfully into her palms.

Sweat-damp blond hair was pasted to the side of Laura's face. Her delicate features were salt-pale and clenched in anxiety, and her eyes were squeezed tightly shut.

She was not dead. Not dead. It seemed impossible.

The girl—terror had reduced her to the condition of a girl—was murmuring so softly that the words couldn't be heard even from a distance of inches, yet so urgently that the meaning was harrowingly clear. It was a prayer, one that Chyna had recited on numerous nights long ago, in far places: a prayer for mercy, a plea to be delivered from this horror untouched and alive, dear God, please, untouched and alive.

On those other nights, Chyna had been spared both violation and death. Already, half of Laura's petition had gone unanswered.

Chyna's throat tightened with anguish, and she could barely speak: "It's me."

Laura's eyelids sprang open, and her blue eyes rolled like those of a terrified horse, wide with disbelief. "All dead."

"Ssshhh," Chyna whispered.

"Blood. His hands."

"Ssshhh. I'll get you out of here."

"Stank like blood. Jack's dead. Nina. Everyone."

Jack, her brother, whom Chyna had not met. Nina, her sister-in-law. Evidently the killer had been to the vineyard manager's bungalow before coming to the main house. Four dead. There was no help to be found anywhere on the sprawling property.

Chyna glanced worriedly at the open door, then quickly rose to test the handcuffs on Laura's wrists. Securely locked.

With fettered hands and fettered ankles linked by a chain, Laura was thoroughly hobbled. She wouldn't be able to stand, let alone walk.

Chyna wasn't strong enough to carry her.

She saw her reflection in the vanity mirror across the room, and she realized with a shock how nakedly her terror was revealed in her wrenched face.

Trying to look more composed for Laura's sake, Chyna stopped beside the bed again and murmured almost as softly as her friend had been praying: "Is there a gun?"

"What?"

"A gun in the house?"

"No."

"Nowhere in the house?"

"No, no."

"Shit."

"Jack."

"What?"

"Has one."

"A gun? At the bungalow?" Chyna asked.

"Jack has a gun."

Chyna didn't have time to get to the bungalow and back before the killer returned to Laura's room. Anyway, more likely than not, he had already found the gun and confiscated it.

"Do you know who he is?"

"No." Laura's sky-blue eyes appeared to darken with despair. "Get out."

"I'll find a weapon."

"*Get out,*" Laura whispered more urgently, cold sweat glistening on her brow.

"A knife," Chyna said.

"Don't die for me." Then, *sotto voce,* tremulously but fiercely, fiercely she said: "Run, Chyna. Oh, God, please *run!*"

"I'll be back."

*"Run."*

From outside, a sound arose. A truck engine. Approaching.

Astonished, Chyna shot to her feet. "Someone's coming. Help's coming."

Laura's bedroom was toward the front of the house. Chyna stepped to the nearer of two windows, which provided a view of the half-mile driveway leading in from the two-lane county road.

A quarter of a mile away, bright headlights pierced the night. Judging by the height of the lights from the ground, Chyna concluded that the truck was big.

How miraculous that anyone would show up at this hour, in this lonely place.

As a thrill of hope swept through Chyna, she realized that the killer would have heard the engine too. The man or men in the truck wouldn't know what trouble they were getting into. When they stopped in front of the house, they would be dead men breathing.

"Hold on," she said, touched Laura's damp forehead to reassure her, and then crossed the room to the door, leaving her friend under the smug and somber gaze of Sigmund Freud.

The hallway was deserted.

Chyna hurried to the head of the curved stairs, hesitated to commit herself to the tenebrous lair below, but then realized that she had nowhere else to go. She went down as fast as she dared without the support of the handrail. Staying clear of the balustrade. Too exposed there. Close to the wall was better.

She quickly passed a series of large landscape paintings in ornate frames, which seemed almost to be windows on actual pastoral vistas. Earlier, they had been bright and cheerful scenes. Now they were ominous: goblin forests, black rivers, killing fields.

The foyer. An oval area rug on polished oak. Through a closed door to the right was Paul Templeton's study. Through the archway on the left was the dark living room.

The killer could be anywhere.

Outside, the roar of the truck grew louder. It was almost to the house. The driver would be shot through the windshield the moment that he braked to a stop. Or gunned down when he stepped out from behind the steering wheel.

Chyna had to warn him, not solely for his sake but for her own, for Laura's. He was their only hope.

Certain that the spider-eating intruder was nearby, she expected a savage attack and, abandoning caution, *flew* at the front door. The oval rug rucked beneath her feet, twisted, and nearly spun out from under her. She stumbled, reached out to break her fall, and slammed both palms flat against the front door.

Such a noise, hellacious noise, booming through the house, had surely drawn the killer's attention away from the approaching truck.

Chyna fumbled, found the knob, and twisted it. The door was unlocked. Gasping, she pulled it open.

A cool breeze out of the northwest, faintly scented by freshly turned vineyard earth and fungicide, whistled through the bare limbs of the maple trees that flanked the front walkway. Snuffling like a pack of hounds, it rushed past her into the foyer as she stepped out onto the front porch.

The truck had already passed the house and was heading away from her. It would come around for a second approach on the end-loop of the driveway, which was wide enough to accommodate produce haulers in the harvest season, and park facing out toward the county road. But it wasn't a truck after all. A motor home. An older model with rounded lines, well kept, forty feet long, either blue or green. Its chrome glimmered like quicksilver under the late-winter moon.

Amazed that she had not yet been stabbed or shot or struck from behind, glancing back at the open front door where the killer hadn't yet appeared, Chyna headed for the porch steps.

The motor home rounded the end of the loop, beginning to turn toward her. Its twin beams swept across the Templetons' barn and other outbuildings.

Larch and maple and evergreen shadows fled before the arcing headlights. They flickered darkly through the trellis at the end of the porch, along the white balustrade, across the lawn and the stone walkway, stretching impossibly, swooping into the night as if trying frantically to tear free of the trees that cast them.

The deep quiet in the house, the lack of lights downstairs, the killer's failure to attack her as she escaped, the timely arrival of the motor home—suddenly all of those things made chilling sense. The killer was driving the motor home.

"*No.*"

Chyna swiftly retreated from the porch steps and scrambled back into the foyer.

At her heels, the headlights came all the way around the end of the driveway loop. They pierced the trellis grid, projecting geometric patterns across the porch floor and the front wall of the house.

She closed the door and fumbled for the big lock above the knob. Found the thumb-turn. Engaged the heavy deadbolt.

Then she realized her mistake. The front door had been unlocked because the killer had gone out that way. If he found it locked now, he would know that Laura wasn't the only person alive in the house, and the hunt would begin.

Her sweaty fingers slipped on the brass thumb-turn, but the bolt snapped open with a hard *clack*.

Earlier, he must have parked the vehicle near the end of the half-mile-long driveway, out toward the county road, and must have walked to the house.

Now tires crunched through gravel. Air brakes issued a soft whoosh and a softer whine, and the motor home came to a full stop in front of the house.

Remembering the oval rug that had turned under her feet and had nearly sent her sprawling, Chyna dropped to her knees. She crawled across the wool, smoothing the rumples with her hands. If the killer tripped over the disarranged rug, he would know that it hadn't been in that condition when he'd left.

Footsteps arose outside: boot heels ringing off the flagstone walkway.

Chyna came to her feet and turned toward the study. No good. She couldn't know for sure where he would go when he reentered the house, and if he stepped into the study, she would be trapped in there with him.

His tread echoed hollowly from the wooden porch steps.

Chyna lunged across the foyer, through the archway, into the dark living room—and immediately came to a halt, afraid of stumbling into furniture and knocking it over. She edged forward, feeling her way with both hands, vision hampered by the muddy-red ghost images of the motor-home headlights, which still floated faintly across her retinas.

The front door opened.

Less than halfway across the living room, Chyna squatted beside an armchair. If the killer entered and switched on the lights, he would see her.

Without closing the door behind him, the man appeared in the foyer, beyond the arch. He was dimly limned by the glow from the second-floor hallway. He passed the living room and went directly to the stairs.

*Laura.*

Chyna still had no weapon.

She thought of the fireplace poker. Not good enough. Unless she caved in his skull on the first blow or broke his arm, he would wrest the poker away from her. She had the strength of terror, but maybe that wouldn't be enough.

Rather than rise to her feet and blunder blindly across the living room, she stayed down and crawled because it was safer and quicker. She reached the dining-room archway and angled toward where she thought she'd find the kitchen door.

She thumped into a chair. It rattled against a table leg. On the table, something shifted with a *clink-clink*, and she remembered seeing carefully arranged ceramic fruit in a copper bowl.

She didn't think that he could have heard these sounds all the way upstairs, so she kept going. There was nothing to do but keep going anyway, whether he had heard or not.

When she reached the swinging door sooner than she had expected, she got to her feet.

Though the infiltrating moonlight was already dim, it suddenly faded away, causing the flesh on the nape of her neck to crawl with a dire expectation. She turned, pressing her back against the doorframe, certain that the killer was close behind her, silhouetted in front of a window, blocking the lunar glow, but he wasn't there. The silver radiance no longer painted the glass. Evidently the storm clouds, rolling out of the northwest since before midnight, had finally shrouded the moon.

Pushing on the swinging door, she went into the kitchen.

She wouldn't need to switch on the overhead fluorescent panels. The upper of the double ovens featured a digital clock with green numerals that emitted a surprising amount of light, enough to allow her to find her way around the room.

She recalled having seen a section of butcher-block countertop to one side of the stainless-steel sinks. The sinks were in front of the wider of the two windows. She slid her hand along the cold granite counters until she located the remembered wooden surface.

The house above her seemed filled with a higher order of silence than ever before.

*What's the bastard doing up there in all that silence, up there in all that silence with Laura?*

Under the butcher block was a drawer where she expected to find knives. Found them. Neatly slotted in a holder.

She withdrew one. Too short. Another. This one was a bread knife with a blunt round end. The third that she selected proved to be a butcher knife. She carefully tested the cutting edge against the ball of her thumb and found it satisfyingly sharp.

Upstairs, Laura screamed.

Chyna started toward the dining-room door but sensed intuitively that she dared not go that way. She rushed instead to the back stairs, even though they couldn't be climbed without making noise.

She switched on the light in the stairwell. The killer could not see her here.

From the second floor, Laura cried out again—a terrible wail of despair, pain, horror, like a cry that might have been heard in the poison-gas chambers at Dachau or in the windowless interrogation rooms of Siberian prisons during the era of the gulags. It was not a scream for help or even a begging for mercy, but a plea for release at any cost, even death.

Chyna clambered up the stairs into that scream, which presented her with real resistance, as if she were a swimmer struggling toward the surface of a sea, against a great weight of water. As cold as an Arctic current, the cry chilled her, numbed her, throbbed icily in the hollows of her bones. She was overcome by a compulsion to scream *with* Laura as a dog wails in sympathy when it hears another dog suffering, a primal need to howl in misery at the sheer helplessness of human existence in a universe full of dead stars, and she had to fight that urge.

Laura's scream spiraled into a bawling for her mother, though she must know that her mother was dead. "Mommy, Mommy, *Mommeeeeee*." She was reduced to the dependency of an infant, too terrified of life itself to find solace anywhere but in the familiar succoring breast and in the sound of that same heartbeat remembered from the womb.

And then sudden quiet.

Bleak silence.

On the landing, halfway to the second floor, Chyna was surprised to realize that the thousand-fathom weight of the scream had brought her to a standstill. Her legs were weak; her calf and thigh muscles quivered as if she had run a marathon. She seemed on the brink of collapse.

Because it might signify the end of hope, the silence was now as oppressive as the scream. She bent her head under a hush as heavy as an iron crown, hunched her shoulders, and huddled miserably upon herself.

It would be so easy to lean against the wall, slide down to the floor, put the knife aside, and curl defensively. Just wait until he had gone away. Wait until a relative or a friend of the family arrived, discovered the bodies, went for the police, and took care of everything.

Instead, after pausing only a few seconds on the landing, Chyna forced herself to continue the climb, heart pounding so hard that it seemed as if each blow might knock her down.

Her arms shook uncontrollably. In her white-knuckle grip, the butcher knife carved wobbly patterns in the air in front of her, and she wondered if she would have the strength, in any confrontation, to thrust and slash effectively.

That was the thinking of a loser, and she hated herself for it. During the past ten years she had transformed herself into a winner, and she was determined not to backslide.

The old wooden stairs protested under her, but she moved fast, heedless of the noise. Whether Laura was alive or dead, the killer would be at play, distracted by his games, unlikely to hear anything other than the thunderous rush of his own blood in his ears and over whatever urgent inner voices spoke to him at that very moment when he held a life in his hands.

She stepped into the upstairs hall. Propelled by her fear for Laura and by a rage born from self-disgust at her moment of weakness on the landing, she hurried past the closed door of the guest room to the turn in the L-shaped corridor, around the corner, past the half-open door of the master suite and through the amber light that spilled from it. She dashed along the arbor of faded roses, rage swelling into fury as she went, shocked by her own boldness, seeming to glide along the carpet, as swift as if sliding down an icy slope, straight to the open door of Laura's room, without hesitation, knife raised high, her arm no longer shaking, steady and sure, crazy with terror and despair and righteousness, across the threshold and into the bedroom, where Freud was unshaken by what had happened under his gaze—and where the rumpled bed was empty.

Chyna whirled around in disbelief. Laura was gone. The room was deserted.

Over the rush of her breathing and the booming of her heart, she heard the rattle-clink of a shackle chain. Not in the room. Elsewhere.

Careless of danger, she returned to the hall, to the balustrade that overlooked the foyer.

Below, barely illuminated by the pale light from the upstairs hallway, the killer went through the open front door onto the porch. He was carrying Laura in his arms. She was wrapped in a bedsheet, one pale arm trailing limply, head lolling to the side, and face concealed by her golden hair: unconscious, offering no resistance.

He must have been descending the shadowy stairs when Chyna had passed them. She had been so focused on getting to Laura's room, so pumped for the attack, that she hadn't been aware of him, even though the chain and the cuffs must have been rattling then as well.

Evidently, he'd been making enough noise that he hadn't heard Chyna either.

Instinct had told her to take the back stairs, and she'd been wise to listen. If she'd been ascending the front stairs, she'd have met him as he'd been coming down. He would have thrown Laura at her, followed the two of them as they tumbled into the foyer, kicked the knife out of Chyna's hand if she hadn't lost it already, and savaged her where she'd fallen.

She couldn't let him take Laura away.

Afraid that thinking about the situation would paralyze her again, Chyna recklessly descended the stairs. If she could take him by surprise and plunge the knife into his back, Laura might yet have a chance.

She could do it too. She wasn't squeamish. She could slam the blade deep, try for his heart from the back, puncture a lung, yank the knife out of him and ram it in again, stab the son of a bitch and listen to him squealing for mercy and stab stab stab him until he was silent forever. Never had she done anything like that; never had she hurt anyone. But she could do it now, waste him, because she was terrified for Laura, because she was sick at the thought of failing her friend— and because she was a natural-born vengeance machine, a human being.

At the bottom of the stairs, the oval rug didn't spin out from under her as it had done before, and she went straight toward the open door.

She no longer held the knife high but held it low, at her side. If he heard her coming, he would turn, and then she could swing the knife up in an arc, under the girl that he held in his arms, and into his belly. That was better than trying to plunge it into his back, where the point might be deflected by a shoulder blade or rib, or might skid off his spine. Go for the softest part of him. She'd be face-to-face with him that way. Looking straight into his eyes. Would that make her hesitate? He had it coming. The bastard. She thought of Sarah on the floor of the shower stall, huddled naked in the cold drizzle. She could do it. She could do it.

Into the doorway, across the threshold, onto the porch, she was not only ready to kill but prepared to die in the attempt to get him. Yet as swift as she had been, she hadn't been swift enough, because he was not just that moment going down the porch steps, as she had hoped, but was *already* nearing the motor home. The burden of Laura hadn't slowed him at all. He was inhumanly quick.

She landed on only one stair tread from the front porch to the walkway, and the rubber soles of her shoes slapped the flagstones loud enough to carry even over the moaning of the wind. The moon was gone, and half the stars as well, displaced by towering palisades of clouds, but if the killer heard her and turned, he would be able to see her clearly.

Evidently, he didn't hear, for he didn't glance back, and Chyna angled off the walkway, onto the quieter grass, determinedly going after him.

Two doors were open on the motor home: one at the driver's side of the cockpit, the other on that same flank of the vehicle but two-thirds of the way toward the back. The killer chose the rear door.

With Laura in his arms, he was forced to turn sideways, pulling her tightly to him as he squeezed through the open door and crabbed up the two interior steps, but he was as agile as he was strong. He disappeared into the vehicle before Chyna could reach him.

She considered going inside after him. But all the windows were curtained, so she didn't know if he had turned left or right. And if he had put Laura down immediately upon entering, he would now be better able to defend himself against an attack. That was his turf, beyond the door, and she wasn't sufficiently reckless with vengeance to want to confront him there.

She pressed her back to the wall of the motor home, beside the open door, waiting for him. If he came outside again, she'd go at him even as his foot was reaching for the ground. The element of surprise was still working for her, maybe better than ever—because the killer was close to a clean getaway and feeling so good about himself that he might be careless.

Maybe he wouldn't come outside again, but at least he would have to reach out to pull the door shut. Standing on the step, leaning to grab at the handle, he would not be well balanced, and she would have the knife deep into him before he had a chance to jerk back.

Movement inside. A thump.

She tensed.

He didn't appear.

Silence again.

The scent of blood was suddenly heavy out of the northwest, as though a slaughterhouse lay upwind of her. Then it passed, and she realized that she hadn't actually smelled blood but had flashed back on the smell of the sodden sheets in the Templetons' master suite.

The aluminum wall of the motor home was cold against her spine, and she shivered because it seemed that some of the coldness of the man inside was seeping through to her.

Waiting, she began to lose her nerve. Resurgent fear tempered her rage, shifting the balance from vengeance to survival. But she could still do it. She could do it. She struggled to hold on to her crazy-hot anger.

Then the killer came out of the motor home, but he didn't use the exit beside her. He stepped from the open cab door at the front of the vehicle.

Chyna's breath caught in her throat, and the chill wind from the oncoming storm seemed bitter with the scent of failure.

He was too far away. No longer distracted by the weight of Laura in his arms and the rattling of her shackles, he would hear Chyna coming. She no longer had the element of surprise to even the odds.

He stood just outside the cab door, thirty feet from her, stretching almost lazily. He rolled his big shoulders as if to shake weariness from them, and he massaged the back of his neck.

If he turned his head to the left, he would see her at once. If she didn't remain absolutely still, he would surely spot her slightest movement even from the corner of his eye.

He was downwind of her, and she was half afraid that he would smell her fear. He seemed more animal than human, even in the fluid grace with which he moved, and she had no trouble believing that he was gifted with wild talents and preternatural senses.

Although he wasn't holding the silencer-fitted gun with which he had killed Paul Templeton, it might be tucked under his belt. If she tried to flee, he could draw the weapon and shoot her dead before she got far.

But he *wouldn't* shoot her dead. Nothing that easy. He'd pop her in the leg, bring her down, and take her captive. Load her into the motor home with Laura. He'd want to play with her later.

Finished stretching, he moved briskly toward the house. Up the walkway. Onto the porch. Inside.

He never looked back.

Chyna's pent-up breath stuttered from her in a tattoo of fear, and she inhaled with a shudder.

Before her courage faded further, she hurried forward to the cab door and climbed behind the steering wheel. Her best hope was to find keys in the ignition, in which case she would be able to start the engine and drive away with Laura, go into Napa to the police.

No keys.

She glanced at the house, wondering how long he would be gone. Maybe he was searching for valuables now that the killing was done. Or selecting souvenirs. That could take five minutes, ten minutes, even longer. Which might be enough time to get Laura out of the motor home and hide her somewhere. Somehow.

She still had the knife. And now that she was in the killer's domain without his knowledge, she had regained the precious element of surprise.

Nevertheless, her heart raced, and her dry mouth was filled with the slightly metallic taste of feverish anxiety.

The seat swiveled, clearing the console. She was able to step from behind the steering wheel into the lounge area, which featured built-in sofas upholstered in a hunter-plaid fabric.

The steel floor was carpeted, of course, but after long years of hard travel, it creaked softly under her feet.

She had expected the place to smell like a Grand Guignol theater where the sadistic plays involved no make-believe, but instead the air was redolent of recently brewed coffee and cinnamon rolls. How odd—and somehow profoundly disturbing—that a man like this should find any satisfaction at all in innocent pleasures.

"Laura," she whispered, as though the killer might hear her all the way from the house. Then more fiercely than ever, yet in a whisper: "*Laura!*"

Beyond the lounge and open to it were a kitchenette and a cozy dining alcove with a booth upholstered in red vinyl. Running off the battery, a lamp hung aglow over the dining-nook table.

Laura was not to be seen anywhere.

Moving swiftly out of the dining area, Chyna came to the rear door standing open on the right, through which the killer had entered with the unconscious girl in his arms.

"Laura."

Aft of the outer door, a short cramped hall led along the driver's side of the vehicle, illuminated by a low-voltage safety fixture. There was also a skylight, now black. On the left were two closed doors, and at the end a third stood ajar.

The first door opened into a tiny bath. The space was a marvel of efficient design: a toilet, a sink, a medicine cabinet, and a corner shower stall.

Behind the second door was a closet. A few changes of clothes hung from a chrome rod.

At the end of the hall was a small bedroom with imitation-wood paneling and a closet with an accordion-style vinyl door. The meager light from the hall didn't brighten the place much, but Chyna could see well enough to identify Laura; the girl was lying facedown on the narrow bed, swaddled in a sheet, with only her small bare feet and her golden hair revealed.

Urgently whispering her friend's name, Chyna stepped to the bed and dropped to her knees.

Laura didn't respond. Still unconscious.

Chyna couldn't lift the girl, couldn't carry her as the killer had done, so she had to try to rouse her instead. She pulled aside a flap of sheet and was eye-to-eye with her friend.

They were sapphire-blue eyes now, not pale-sky blue, perhaps because the light in the room was so poor or perhaps because they were occluded with death. Her mouth was open, and blood moistened her lips.

The crazy fucking hateful bastard had taken her with him even though she was dead, for God-knew-what purposes, maybe because she was something he could touch and look at and talk to for a few days to remind him of the glory. A souvenir.

Chyna's stomach cramped painfully, not with revulsion or disgust but with guilt, with failure and futility and sheer black despair.

"Oh, baby," she said to the dead girl. "Oh, baby, sweetie, I'm so sorry, I'm so sorry."

Not that she could have done anything more than she had tried to do. What could she have done? She couldn't have attacked the bastard bare-handed when she had stood behind him in the upstairs hall, when he had been cooing to the dangling spider. What could she have done? She couldn't have gotten to the kitchen any sooner, found the knife any faster, climbed the back stairs any quicker.

"I'm so sorry."

This beautiful girl, this dear heart, would never find the husband about whom she had fantasized, never have the children who would have been a betterment to the world by the simple virtue of having been *her* children. Twenty-three years of getting ready to make a contribution, to make a difference in the lives of others, so full of ideals and hope: But now her gift would never be given, and the world would be immeasurably poorer for it.

"I love you, Laura. We all love you."

Any words, any sentiment, any expression of grief was horribly inadequate; worse than inadequate—meaningless. Laura was gone, all that warmth and kindness gone forever, and even the most heartfelt words were only words.

Chyna's stomach cramped with a sense of loss, clenched tight and pulled her relentlessly into a black hole within herself.

At the same time she felt her breast swelling with a sob that, if voiced, would be explosive. A single tear would loose a flood. Even one soft sob would bring on an uncontrollable wail.

She couldn't risk grief. Not while she was in the motor home. The killer would be returning at any minute, and she couldn't mourn Laura until she was safely out of there and until he was gone. She no longer had any reason to stay, for Laura was indisputably dead and irretrievable.

Nearby a door slammed hard, shaking the thin metal walls around Chyna.

The killer was back.

Something rattled. Rattled.

With the butcher knife in hand, Chyna swiftly backed away from Laura to the wall next to the open door. Unexpressed grief was a high-octane fuel for rage, and in an instant she was burning with fury, afire with the need to hurt him, slash him, spill his guts, hear him scream, and bring the haunting awareness of mortality to his eyes as he had brought it to Laura's.

*He'll come into the room. I'll cut him. He'll come and I'll cut him.* It was a prayer, not a plan. *He'll come. I'll cut him. He'll come. I'll cut him.*

The shadowy room darkened. He was at the door, blocking the meager light from the hall.

Silently, the knife in her hand jittered furiously up and down like the needle on a sewing machine, stitching the pattern of her fear in the air.

He was at the threshold. Right there. Right *there.* He would come in for one more look at the pretty blond dead girl, for one more feel of her cool skin, and Chyna would get him when he crossed the threshold, cut him.

Instead, he closed the door and went away.

Aghast, she listened to his retreating footsteps, the creaking as the carpeted steel floor torqued under his boots, and she wondered what to do now.

The driver's door slammed. The engine started. The brakes released with a brief faint shriek.

They were on the move.

**3**

Dead girls lie as troubled in the dark as in the light. As the motor home sped along the runneled driveway, Laura's shackles clinked ceaselessly, only half muffled by the sheet in which she was loosely wrapped.

Blinded, still pressed to the fiberboard wall beside the bedroom door, Chyna Shepherd could almost believe that even in death Laura struggled against the injustice of her murder. *Clink-clink.*

Periodic sprays of gravel spurted from beneath the tires and rattled against the undercarriage. Shortly the motor home would reach the county road, smooth blacktop.

If Chyna tried to bail out now, the killer was sure to hear the back door bang open when the wind tore it out of her grasp, or spot it in his sideview mirror. In these winter-dormant grape fields, where the nearest houses were inhabited only by the dead, he would certainly risk stopping and giving chase, and she would not get far before he brought her down.

Better to wait. Give him a few miles on the county road, even until they reached a more major route, until they were likely to be passing through a town or traveling in at least sparse traffic. He wouldn't be as quick to come after her if people were nearby to respond to her cries for help.

She felt along the wall for a switch. The door was tightly shut; no light would spill into the hallway. She found the toggle, flicked it up, but nothing happened. The overhead bulb must have burned out.

She remembered seeing a pharmacy-style reading lamp bolted to the side of the built-in nightstand. By the time she felt her way across the small room, the motor home began to slow.

She hesitated with the lamp switch between thumb and forefinger, heart suddenly racing again because she was afraid that he was going to brake to a full stop, get out from behind the wheel, and come back to the little bedroom. Now that a confrontation could no longer save Laura, now that Chyna's molten rage had cooled to anger, she hoped only to avoid him, escape, and give the authorities the information that they would need to find him.

The vehicle didn't come to a full stop, after all, but hung a wide left turn onto a paved surface and picked up speed once more. The county road.

As far as Chyna could recall, the next intersection would be State Highway 29, which she and Laura had driven the previous afternoon. Between here and there, the only turnoffs were to other vineyards, small farms, and houses. He wasn't likely to pay a visit to any of those places or slaughter any more innocently sleeping families. The night was waning.

She clicked the lamp switch, and a circle of muddy light fell on the bed.

She tried not to look at the body, even though it was mostly concealed by the enwrapping linens. If she thought too much about Laura right now, she'd be sucked into a slough of black despondency. She needed to remain energized and clearheaded if she hoped to survive.

Although she wasn't likely to find any weapon better than the butcher knife, she had nothing to lose by searching for one. Since the killer was armed with a silencer-equipped pistol, he might keep other guns in the motor home.

The single nightstand had two drawers. The upper contained a package of gauze pads, a few green and yellow sponges of the size used to wash dishes, a small plastic squeeze bottle of some clear fluid, a roll of cloth tape, a comb, a hairbrush with a tortoiseshell handle, a half-empty tube of K-Y jelly, a full bottle of skin lotion with aloe vera, a pair of needle-nose pliers with yellow rubber-clad handles, and a pair of scissors.

She could imagine the uses to which he had put some of those items, and she didn't want to think about the others. Sometimes, no doubt, the women he brought into this room were alive when he put them on the bed.

She considered the scissors. But the butcher knife would be more effective if she needed to use it.

In the lower, deeper drawer was a hard-plastic container rather like a fishing-tackle box. When she opened it, she found a complete sewing kit, with numerous spools of thread in a variety of colors, a pincushion, packets of needles, a needle threader, an extensive selection of buttons, and other paraphernalia. None of that was helpful to her, and she put it away.

As she got up from her knees, she noticed that the window over the bed had been covered with a sheet of plywood that had been bolted to the wall. A couple of folded swatches of blue fabric were trapped between the plywood and the window frame: the edge of an underlying drapery panel.

From outside, the window would appear to be merely curtained. Anyone inside, even if clever and fortunate enough to struggle free of her bonds, would never be able to open the window and signal to passing motorists for help.

As there was no other furniture in the cramped bedroom, the closet was the only remaining place where Chyna could hope to find a gun or anything that might be used as a weapon. She circled the bed to the accordion-style vinyl door, which hung from an overhead track.

When she pulled the folding door aside, it compressed into pleats that stacked to the left, and in the closet was a dead man.

Shock threw Chyna back against the bed. The mattress caught her behind the knees. She almost fell backward atop Laura, kept her balance, but dropped the knife.

The rear of the closet appeared to have been retrofitted with welded steel plates fixed to the vehicle frame for added strength. Two ringbolts, widely separated and high-set, were welded to the steel. Wrists manacled to the ringbolts, the dead man hung with his arms spread in cruciform. His feet were together like the feet of Christ on the cross—not nailed, however, but shackled to another ringbolt in the closet floor.

He was young—seventeen, eighteen, surely not twenty. Clad in only a pair of white cotton briefs, his lean pale body was badly battered. His head didn't hang forward on his chest but was tipped to one side, and his left temple rested against the biceps of his raised left arm. He had thick curly black hair. His eyelids had been sewn tightly shut with green thread. With yellow thread, two buttons above his upper lip were secured to a pair of matching buttons just under his lower lip.

Chyna heard herself talking to God. An incoherent, beseeching babble. She clenched her teeth and choked on the words, though it was unlikely that her voice could have carried to the front of the motor home over the rumble of the engine and the droning of the big tires.

She pulled shut the pleated-vinyl panel. Though flimsy, it moved as ponderously as a vault door. The magnetic latch clicked into place with a sound like snapping bone.

In all the textbooks she had ever read, no case study of sociopathic violence had ever contained a description of a crime sufficiently vivid to make her want to retreat to a corner and sit on the floor and pull her knees against her chest and hug herself. That was precisely what she did now—choosing the corner farthest from the closet.

She had to get control of herself, quickly, starting with her manic breathing. She was gasping, sucking in great lungfuls, yet she couldn't seem to get enough air. The deeper and faster she inhaled, the dizzier she became. Her peripheral vision surrendered to an encroaching darkness until she seemed to be peering down a long black tunnel toward the dingy motor-home bedroom at the far end.

She told herself that the young man in the closet had been dead when the killer had gone to work with the sewing kit. And if he'd not been dead, at least he'd been mercifully unconscious. Then she told herself not to think about it at all, because thinking about it only made the tunnel longer and narrower, made the bedroom more distant and the lights dimmer than ever.

She put her face in her hands, and her hands were cold but her face seemed colder. For no reason that Chyna could understand, she thought of her mother's face, as clear as a photograph in her mind's eye. And then she *did* understand.

To Chyna's mother, the prospect of violence had been romantic, even glamorous. For a while they had lived in a commune in Oakland, where everyone talked of making a better world and where, more nights than not, the adults gathered around the kitchen table, drinking wine and smoking pot, discussing how best to tear down the hated system, sometimes also playing pinochle or Trivial Pursuit as they discussed the strategies that might bring utopia at last, sometimes far too enraptured by revolution to be interested in any lesser games. There were bridges and tunnels that could all be blown up with absurd ease, disrupting transportation; telephone-company installations could be targeted to throw communications into chaos; meat-packing plants must be burned to put an end to the brutal exploitation of animals. They planned intricate bank robberies and bold assaults on armored cars to finance their operations. The route they would have taken to peace, freedom, and justice was always cratered by explosions, littered with uncountable bodies. After Oakland, Chyna and her mother had hit the road for a few weeks and had wound up again in Key West with their old friend Jim Woltz, the enthusiastic nihilist who was deep in the drug trade, with a sideline in illegal weapons. Under his ocean-front cottage, he had carved out a bunker in which he stored a personal collection of two hundred firearms. Chyna's mother was a beautiful woman, even on bad days when depression plagued her, when her green eyes were gray and sad with miseries that she could not explain. But at that kitchen table in Oakland and in that cool bunker beneath the cottage in Key West—in fact, whenever she was at the side of a man like Woltz—her porcelain skin was even clearer than usual, almost translucent; excitement enlivened her exquisite features; she became magically more graceful, appeared more lithe and supple, was quicker to smile. The prospect of violence, playing at being Bonnie to any man's Clyde, filled her stunning face with a light as glorious as a Florida sunset, and her jewel-green eyes were, at those times, as compelling and mysterious as the Gulf of Mexico darkening toward twilight.

Although the prospect of violence might be romantic, the reality was blood, bone, decomposition, dust. The reality was Laura on the bed and the unknown young man sewn into silence behind the pleated vinyl door.

Chyna sat with her cold hands covering her colder face, aware that she would never be as strangely beautiful as her mother.

Eventually she regained control of her breathing.

The motor home rolled on, and she was reminded of nights when, as a child, she had dozed on trains, on buses, in the backseats of cars, lulled by the motion and the hum of wheels, unsure where her mother was taking her, dreaming of being part of a family like one of those on television—with befuddled but loving parents, an amusing next-door neighbor who might be frustrating but never malicious, and a dog that knew a few tricks. But good dreams never lasted, and she woke repeatedly from nightmares, gazing out windows at strange landscapes, wishing that she could travel forever without stopping. The road was a promise of peace, but destinations were always hell.

This time would be no different from all those others. Wherever they were bound, Chyna didn't want to go there. She intended to get off between destinations and hoped to find her way back to the better life that she had struggled so hard to build these past ten years.

She left the corner of the bedroom to retrieve the butcher knife, which she had dropped when she'd been rocked backward by the sight of the dead man in the closet. Then she went around the bed to the nightstand and switched off the pharmacy lamp.

Being in the dark with dead people didn't frighten her. Only the living were a danger.

The motor home slowed again and then turned left. Chyna leaned against the tilt of the vehicle to keep her balance.

They must be on State Highway 29. A right turn would have taken them down the Napa Valley, south into the town of Napa. She wasn't sure what communities lay to the north, other than St. Helena and Calistoga.

Even between the towns, however, there would be vineyards, farms, houses, and rural businesses. Wherever she got out of the motor home, she should be able to find help within a reasonable distance.

She sidled blindly to the door and stood with one hand on the knob, waiting for instinct to guide her once more. Much of her life had been lived like a balancing act on a spearpoint fence, and on a particularly difficult night when she was twelve, she had decided that instinct was, in fact, the quiet voice of God. Prayers *did* receive replies, but you had to listen closely and believe in the answer. At twelve, she wrote in her diary: "God doesn't shout; He whispers, and in the whisper is the way."

Waiting for the whisper, she thought about the battered body in the closet, which appeared to have been dead for less than a day, and about Laura, still warm on the sagging bed. Sarah, Paul, Laura's brother Jack, Jack's wife, Nina: six people murdered in twenty-four hours. The eater of spiders was not an ordinary homicidal sociopath. In the language of the cops and the criminologists who specialized in searching for and stopping men like this, he was *hot*, going through a *hot phase*, burning up with desire, need. But Chyna, who intended to follow her master's in psychology with a doctorate in criminology, even if she had to work six years waiting tables to get there, sensed that this guy was not just hot. He was a singularity, conforming only in part to standard profiles in aberrant psychology, as purely alien as something from the stars, a runaway killing machine, merciless and irresistible. She had no hope of eluding him if she didn't wait for the murmuring voice of instinct.

She remembered seeing a large rearview mirror when she'd briefly occupied the driver's seat earlier. The vehicle had no rear window, so the mirror was there to provide the driver with a view of the lounge and the dining area behind him. He would be able to see all the way into the end hall that served the bath and bedroom, and if the devil's luck was with him, he would glance up just when Chyna opened the door, stepped out, and was exposed.

When the moment felt right, Chyna opened the door.

A small blessing, a good omen: The ceiling light in the hall was out.

Standing in gloom, she quietly pulled shut the bedroom door.

The lamp above the dining table was on as before. At the front of the vehicle was the green glow of the instrument panel—and beyond the windshield, the headlights were silver swords.

After moving forward past the bathroom and out of the welcome shadows, she crouched behind the paneled side of the dining nook. She peered across the crescent booth to the back of the driver's head, about twenty feet away.

He seemed so close—and, for the first time, vulnerable.

Nevertheless, Chyna wasn't foolish enough to creep forward and attack him while he was driving. If he heard her coming or glanced at the rearview mirror and spotted her, he could wrench the steering wheel or slam on the brakes, sending her sprawling. Then he might be able to stop the vehicle and get to her before she could reach the rear door—or he might swivel in his chair and shoot her down.

The entrance through which he had carried Laura was immediately to Chyna's left. She sat on the floor with her feet in the step well, facing this door, concealed from the driver by the dining nook.

She put the butcher knife aside. When she leaped out, she would probably fall and roll—and she might easily stab herself with the knife if she tried to take it with her.

She didn't intend to jump until the driver either stopped at an intersection or entered a turn sharp enough to require him to cut his speed dramatically. She couldn't risk breaking a leg or being knocked unconscious in a fall, because then she wouldn't be able to get away from the road and safely into hiding.

She didn't doubt that he would be aware of her escape even as it began. He would hear the door open or the wind whistling at it, and he would see her either in his rearview or in his side-mounted mirror as she made her break for freedom. Even in the unlikely event that she was not seen, the wind would slam the door hard behind her the instant she was gone; the killer would suspect that he hadn't been alone with his collection of corpses, and he'd pull off the highway and come back along the pavement, panicky, to have a look.

Or perhaps not panicky. Not panicky at all. More likely, he would search with grim, methodical, machine efficiency. This guy was all about control and power, and Chyna found it difficult to imagine him *ever* succumbing to panic.

The motor home slowed, and Chyna's heart quickened. As the driver reduced speed further, Chyna rose into a crouch in the step well and put a hand on the lever-action door handle.

They came to a full stop, and she pressed down on the handle, but the door was locked. Quietly but insistently she pressed up, down, up—to no avail.

She couldn't find any latch button. Just a keyhole.

She remembered the rattling that she'd heard when she'd been in the bedroom and the spider eater had come back inside and closed this door. *Rattle, rattle.* The rattle of a key, perhaps.

Maybe this was a safety feature to prevent kids from tumbling out into traffic. Or maybe the crazy bastard had modified the door lock to enhance security, to make it more difficult for a burglar or casual intruder to stumble upon any lip-sewn or shackled cadavers that might just happen to be aboard. Can't be too careful when you have dead bodies stacked in the bedroom. Prudence requires certain security measures.

The motor home pulled forward through the intersection and began to pick up speed again.

She should have known that escape wouldn't be easy. *Nothing* was easy. Ever.

She sat down, leaning against the breakfast-nook paneling, still facing the door, thinking furiously.

Earlier, on her way back through the vehicle from the driver's seat, she'd seen a door on the other side, toward the front, behind the co-pilot's chair. Most motor homes had two doors, but this was a rare older model with three. She was reluctant to go forward to escape, however, and for the same reason that she didn't want to attack him: He might see her coming, rock her off her feet, and shoot her before she could get up.

All right, she had one advantage. He didn't know that she was aboard.

If she couldn't just open a door and jump out, if she was going to have to kill him, she could lie in wait here past the dining nook, surprise the bastard, gut him, step over him, and leave by the front. Just minutes ago she had been ready to kill him, and she could make herself be ready again.

The engine vibrations rose through the floor, half numbing her butt. Total numbing would have been welcome; the carpet soon proved to be inadequate padding, and her tailbone began to ache. She shifted her weight from cheek to cheek, leaned forward and then leaned back; nothing provided more than a few seconds of relief. The ache spread to the small of her back, and mild discomfort escalated into serious pain.

Twenty minutes, half an hour, forty minutes, an hour, longer, she endured the agony by striving to imagine all the ways that her escape might unfold once the motor home stopped and the killer got out from behind the wheel. Concentrating. Thinking it through. Planning for myriad eventualities. Finally, however, she couldn't think about anything but the pain.

The motor home was cool, and down in the step well, there was no heat at all. The engine and road vibrations penetrated her shoes, beating relentlessly on her heels and soles. She flexed her toes, afraid that her cold, achy feet and stiffening calf muscles would develop cramps and hobble her when the time came for action.

With a strange hilarity unnervingly close to despair, she thought, *Forget about grief. Forget about justice. Right now just give me a comfortable chair to pamper my ass, just let me sit for a while until my feet are warm again, and later you can have my life if you want it.*

The prolonged inactivity not only took a physical toll but soon began to depress her. Back at the house when she'd first heard the intruder, before he had even come to the guest room, Chyna had known that safety lay in movement. Now *emotional* safety lay in movement, distraction. But circumstances required her to be still and wait. She had too much time to think—and too many disturbing thoughts on which to dwell.

She worked herself into such a state of distress that tears welled—which was when she realized that she was not suffering unduly from butt ache or back pain or the cold throbbing in her feet. The real pain was in her heart, the anguish that she had been forced to repress since she'd found Paul and Sarah, since she'd detected the vague ammoniacal scent of semen in Laura's bedroom and had seen the dimly gleaming links of the shackling chain. Her physical pain was only a lame excuse for tears.

If she dared weep in self-pity, however, then a *flood* would come for Paul, for Sarah, for Laura, for the whole sorry damn screwed-up human race, and in useless resentment at the fact that hard-won hope so often spiraled into nightmare. She would bury her face in her hands, uselessly wailing the question that had been asked of God more often than any other: *Why, why, why, why, why?*

Surrendering to tears would be so easy, *satisfying*. These were selfish tears of defeat; they would not only purge the heart of grief but also wash out the need to care about anyone, anything. Blessed relief could be hers if she simply admitted that the long struggle to understand wasn't worth the pain of experience. Her sobbing would bring the motor home to a sudden halt, and the driver would come back to find her huddled at the step well. He would club her, drag her into the bedroom, rape her beside the body of her friend; there would be terror beyond anything that she had ever known before, but it would be brief. And this time it would be final. He would free her forever from the need to ask *why*, from the torment of repeatedly falling through the fragile floor of hope into this too familiar desolation.

For a long time, maybe even since the stormy night of her eighth birthday and the frenzied palmetto beetle, she'd known that being a victim was often a *choice* people made. As a child, she hadn't been able to put this insight into words, and she hadn't known why so many people chose suffering; when older, she had recognized their self-hatred, masochism, weakness.

Not all or even most suffering is at the hands of fate; it befalls us at our invitation.

She'd always chosen not to be victimized, to resist and fight back, to hold on to hope and dignity and faith in the future. But victimhood was seductive, a release from responsibility and caring: Fear would be transmuted into weary resignation; failure would no longer generate guilt but, instead, would spawn a comforting self-pity.

Now she trembled on an emotional high wire, not sure whether she would be able to keep her balance or would allow herself to fail and fall.

The motor home slowed again. They were angling to the right. Slowing. Maybe pulling off the highway and stopping.

She tried the door. She knew that it was locked, but she quietly worked the lever-action handle anyway, because she wasn't capable, after all, of simply giving up.

As they climbed a slight incline, their speed continued to drop.

Wincing at the pain in her calves and thighs as she moved, yet relieved to be off her butt, she rose just far enough to look across the dining nook.

The back of the killer's head was the most hateful thing that Chyna had ever seen, and it aroused fresh anger in her. The brain beneath that curve of bone hummed with vicious fantasies. It was infuriating that he should be alive and Laura dead. That he should be sitting here so smug, so content with all his memories of blood, recalling the pleas for mercy that must be like music to him. That he should ever see a sunset again and take pleasure from it, or taste a peach, or smell a flower. To Chyna, the back of this man's skull seemed like the smooth chitinous helmet of an insect, and she believed that if she ever touched him, he would be as cold as a squirming beetle under her hand.

Beyond the driver, beyond the windshield, at the top of the low rise toward which they were headed, a structure appeared, indistinct and unidentifiable. A few tall sodium-vapor arc lamps cast a sour, sulfurous light.

She squatted below the back of the dining nook again.

She picked up the knife.

They had reached the top of the rise. They were on level ground once more. Steadily slowing.

Turning around, facing away from the exit, she eased into the step well. Left foot on the lower step, right foot on the higher. Back pressed to the locked door, crouching in shadows beyond the reach of the nook lamp, she was ready to launch herself up and at him if he came back through the motor home and gave her a chance.

With a final sigh of air brakes, the vehicle stopped.

Wherever they were, people might be nearby. People who could help her.

But if she screamed, would those outside be near enough to hear?

Even if they heard, they would never reach her in time. The killer would get to her first, gun in hand.

Besides, maybe this was a roadside rest area: nothing more than a parking lot, some picnic tables, a poster warning about the dangers of campfires, and rest rooms. He might have taken a break to use the public facilities or the john in the trailer. At this dead hour, after three o'clock in the morning, they were likely to be the only vehicle on site, in which case she could scream until she was hoarse, and no one would come to her assistance.

The engine cut off.

Quiet. No vibrations in the floor.

Now that the motor home was still, Chyna was shaking. No longer depressed. Stomach muscles fluttering. Scared again. Because she wanted to live.

She would have preferred that he go outside and give her a chance to escape, but she expected him to use the trailer facilities instead of the public rest room. He would come right past her. If she couldn't escape, then she was hot to finish this.

Crazily, she wondered if what came out of him when he was cut would be blood—or the stuff that oozed from a fat beetle when it was crushed.

She expected to hear the bastard moving, heavy footfalls and the hollow *spong* when he stepped on a weak seam in the floor, but there was silence. Maybe he was taking a moment to stretch his arms, roll his achy shoulders, massage the back of his bull neck, and shrug off the weariness of travel.

Or perhaps he *had* glimpsed her in the rearview mirror, her face moon-bright in the light from the dining-table lamp. He could ease out of his seat and creep toward her, avoiding all the creaks in the floor because he knew where they were. Slide into the dining nook. Lean over the back of the booth. Shoot her point-blank where she crouched in the step well. Shoot her in the face.

Chyna looked up and to her left, across the back of the booth. Too low to see the lamp hanging over the center of the table, she saw only the glow of it. She wondered if the angle of his approach would give her a warning or if he would just be a sudden silhouette popping up from the booth as he opened fire on her.

**4**

Intensity.

He believes in living with intensity.

Sitting at the steering wheel, he closes his eyes and massages the back of his neck.

He isn't trying to get rid of the pain. It came on its own, and it will leave him naturally in time. He never takes Tylenol and other crap like that.

What he's trying to do is *enjoy* the pain as fully as possible. With his fingertips he finds an especially sore spot just to the left of the third cervical vertebra, and he presses on it until the pain causes faint sprays of twinkly white and gray lights in the blackness behind his eyelids, like distant fireworks in a world without color.

Very nice.

Pain is merely a part of life. By embracing it, one can find surprising satisfaction in suffering. More important, getting in touch with his own pain makes it easier for him to take pleasure in the pain of others.

Two vertebrae farther down, he locates an even more sensitive point of inflamed tendon or muscle, a wonderful little button buried in the flesh which, when pressed, causes pain to shoot all the way across his shoulder and down his trapezius. At first he works the spot with a lover's tender touch, groaning softly, then he attacks it vigorously until the sweet agony makes him suck air between his clenched teeth.

Intensity.

He does not expect to live forever. His time in this body is finite and precious—and therefore must not be wasted.

He does not believe in reincarnation or in any of the standard promises of an afterlife that are sold by the world's great religions— although at times he senses that he is approaching a revelation of tremendous importance. He *is* willing to contemplate the possibility that the immortal soul exists, and that his own spirit may one day be exalted. But if he is to undergo an apotheosis, it will be brought about by his own bold actions, not by divine grace; if he, in fact, becomes a god, the transformation will occur because he has already chosen to *live* like a god—without fear, without remorse, without limits, with all his senses fiercely sharpened.

Anyone can smell a rose and enjoy the scent. But he has long been training himself to *feel* the destruction of its beauty when he crushes the flower in his fist. If he were to have a rose now, and if he were to chew the petals, he would be able to *taste* not merely the rose itself but the redness of it; likewise, he could taste the yellowness of butter-cups, the blue of hyacinths. He could taste the bee that had crawled across the blossom on its eternal buzzing task of pollination, the soil out of which the flower had grown, and the wind that had caressed it through the summer of its growing.

He has never met anyone who can understand the intensity with which he experiences the world or the greater intensity for which he strives. With his help, perhaps Ariel will understand one day. Now, of course, she is too immature to achieve the insight.

One last squeeze of his neck. The pain. He sighs.

From the copilot's seat, he picks up a folded raincoat. No rain is yet falling, but he needs to cover his blood-spattered clothing before going inside.

He could have changed into clean clothes prior to leaving the Templeton house, but he enjoys wearing these. The patina excites him.

He gets out of the driver's seat, stands behind it, and pulls on the coat.

He washed his hands in the kitchen sink at the Templeton house, though he would have preferred to leave them stained too. While he can conceal his clothes under a raincoat, hiding his hands is not as easy.

He never wears gloves. To do so would be to concede that he fears apprehension, which he does not.

Although his fingerprints are on file with federal and state agencies, the prints he leaves at the scene will never match those that bear his name in the records. Like the rest of the world, police organizations are hell-bent on computerization; by now most fingerprint-image reference banks are in the form of digitized data, to facilitate high-speed scanning and processing. Even more easily than hard files, electronic files can be manipulated, because the work can be done at a great distance; there is no need to burglarize highly secure facilities, when instead he can be a ghost haunting their machines from across a continent. Because of his intelligence, talents, and connections, he has been able to meddle with the data.

Wearing gloves, even thin surgical latex gloves, would be an intolerable barrier to sensation. He likes to let his hand glide lightly over the fine golden hairs on a woman's thigh, take time to appreciate the texture of pebbled gooseflesh against his palm, to relish the fierce heat of skin and then, after, the warmth all fading, fading. When he kills, he finds it absolutely essential to feel the wetness.

The prints under his name in the various files are, in fact, those of a young marine named Bernard Petain, who died tragically during training maneuvers at Camp Pendleton many years ago. And the prints that he leaves at the scene, often etched in blood, cannot be matched to any on file with the military, the FBI, the Department of Motor Vehicles, or anywhere else.

He finishes buttoning the raincoat, turns up the collar, and looks at his hands. Stains under three fingernails. It might be grease or soil. No one will be suspicious of it.

He himself can smell the blood on his clothes even through the black nylon raincoat and insulated liner, but others are not sufficiently sensitive to detect it.

Staring at the residue under his nails, however, he can hear the screams again, that lovely music in the night, the Templeton house as reverberant as a concert hall, and no one to hear except him and the deaf vineyards.

If he is ever caught in the act, the authorities will print him again, discover his deception with the computers, and eventually link him to a long list of unsolved murders. But he isn't concerned about that. He'll never be taken alive, never be put on trial. Whatever they learn about his activities after his death will only add to the glory of his name.

He is Edgler Foreman Vess. From the letters of his name, one can extract a long list of power words: GOD, FEAR, DEMON, SAVE, RAGE, ANGER, DRAGON, FORGE, SEED, SEMEN, FREE, and others. Also words with a mystical quality: DREAM, VESSEL, LORE, FOREVER, MARVEL. Sometimes the last thing that he whispers to a victim is a sentence composed from this list of words. One that he especially likes and uses often is GOD FEARS ME.

Anyway, all questions of fingerprints and other evidence are moot, because he will never be caught. He is thirty-three years old. He has been enjoying himself in this fashion for a long time, and he has never had a close call.

Now he takes the pistol out of the open console between the pilot's and copilot's chairs. A Heckler & Koch P7.

Earlier, he had reloaded the thirteen-round magazine. Now he un-screws the sound suppressor, because he has no plans to visit other houses this night. Besides, the baffles are probably damaged from the shots that he has fired, diminishing both the effect of the silencer and the accuracy of the weapon.

Occasionally he daydreams about what it would be like if the im-possible happened, if he were interrupted at play and surrounded by a SWAT team. With his experience and knowledge, the ensuing show-down would be thrillingly *intense*.

If there is a single secret behind the success of Edgler Vess, it is his belief that no twist of fate is either good or bad, that no experience is qualitatively better than another. Winning twenty million dollars in the lottery is no more to be desired than being trapped by a SWAT team, and a shootout with the authorities is no more to be dreaded than winning all that money. The value of any experience isn't in its positive or negative effect on his life but in the sheer luminous power of it, the vividness, the ferocity, the amount and degree of pure sensa-tion that it provides. Intensity.

Vess puts the sound suppressor in the console between the seats.

He drops the pistol into the right-hand pocket of his raincoat.

He is not expecting trouble. Nevertheless, he goes nowhere un-armed. One can never be too careful. Besides, opportunities often arise unexpectedly.

In the driver's seat again, he takes the keys from the ignition and checks that the brake is firmly set. He opens the door and gets out of the motor home.

All eight gasoline pumps are self-service. He is parked at the outer of the two service islands. He needs to go to the cashier in the associ-ated convenience store to pay in advance and to identify the pump that he'll be using so it can be turned on.

The night breathes. At higher altitudes, a strong gale drives masses of clouds out of the northwest toward the southeast. Here at ground level, a lesser exhalation of cold wind huffs between the pumps, whistles alongside the motor home, and flaps the raincoat against Vess's legs. The convenience store—buff brick below, white aluminum siding above, big windows full of merchandise—stands in front of rising hills that are covered with huge evergreens; the wind soughs through their branches with a hollow, ancient, lonely voice.

Out on Highway 101, there is little traffic at this hour. When a truck passes, it cleaves the wind with a cry that seems strangely Jurassic.

A Pontiac with Washington State license plates is parked at the inner service island, under the yellow sodium-vapor lamps. Other than the motor home, it is the only vehicle in sight. A bumper sticker on the back announces that ELECTRICIANS KNOW HOW TO PLUG IT IN.

On the roof of the building, positioned for maximum visibility from 101, is a red neon sign that announces OPEN 24 HOURS. Red is the quality of the sound each passing truck makes out there on the highway. In the glow, his hands look as if he never washed them.

As Vess approaches the entrance, the glass door swings open, and a man comes out carrying a family-size bag of potato chips and a six-pack of Coke in cans. He is a chubby guy with long sideburns and a walrus mustache.

Gesturing at the sky, he says, "Storm's coming," as he hurries past Vess.

"Good," Vess says. He likes storms. He enjoys driving in them. The more torrential the rain, the better. With lightning flashing and trees cracking in the wind and pavement as slick as ice.

The guy with the walrus mustache goes to the Pontiac.

Vess enters the convenience store, wondering what an electrician from Washington is doing on the road in northern California at this ungodly hour of the night.

He's fascinated by the way in which lives connect briefly, with a potential for drama that is sometimes fulfilled and sometimes not. A man stops for gasoline, lingers to buy potato chips and Coke, makes a comment on the weather to a stranger—and continues on his journey. The stranger could as easily follow the man to the car and blow his brains out. There would be risks for the shooter, but not serious risks; it could be managed with surprising discretion. The man's survival is either full of mysterious meaning or utterly meaningless; Vess is unable to decide which.

If fate doesn't actually exist, it ought to.

The small store is warm, clean, and brightly lighted. Three narrow aisles extend to the left of the door, offering the usual roadside merchandise: every imaginable snack food, the basic patent medicines, magazines, paperback books, postcards, novelty items designed to hang from rearview mirrors, and selected canned goods that sell to campers and to people, like Vess, who travel in homes on wheels. Along the back wall are tall coolers full of beer and soft drinks, as well as a couple of freezers containing ice cream treats. To the right of the door is the service counter that separates the two cashiers' stations and the clerical area from the public part of the store.

Two employees are on duty, both men. These days, no one works alone in such places at night—and with good reason.

The guy at the cash register is a redhead in his thirties with freckles and a two-inch-diameter birthmark, as pink as uncooked salmon, on his pale forehead. The mark is uncannily like the image of a fetus curled in a womb, as if a gestating twin had died early in the mother's pregnancy and left its fossilized image on the surviving brother's brow.

The redheaded cashier is reading a paperback. He looks up at Vess, and his eyes are as gray as ashes but clear and piercing. "What can I do for you, sir?"

"I'm at pump seven," Vess says.

The radio is tuned to a country station. Alan Jackson sings about midnight in Montgomery, the wind, a whippoorwill, a lonesome chill, and the ghost of Hank Williams.

"How you want to pay?" asks the cashier.

"If I put any more on the credit cards, the Bank of America's going to send someone around to break my legs," says Vess, and he slaps down a hundred-dollar bill. "Figure I'll need about sixty bucks' worth."

The combination of the song, the birthmark, and the cashier's haunting gray eyes generates in Vess an eerie sense of expectancy. Something exceptional is about to happen.

"Paying off Christmas like the rest of us, huh?" says the cashier as he rings up the sale.

"Hell, I'll still be payin' off Christmas *next* Christmas."

The second clerk sits on a stool farther along the counter. He's not at a cash register but is laboring on the bookkeeping or checking inventory sheets—anyway, doing some kind of paperwork.

Vess has not previously looked directly at the second man, and now he discovers that this is the exceptional thing he felt looming.

"Storm coming," he says to the second clerk.

The man looks up from the papers spread on the counter. He is in his twenties, at least half Asian, and strikingly handsome. No. More than handsome. Jet-black hair, golden complexion, eyes as liquid as oil and as deep as wells. There is a gentle quality to his good looks that almost gives him an effeminate aspect—but not quite.

Ariel would love him. He is just her type.

"Might be cold enough for snow in some of the mountain passes," says the Asian, "if you're going that way."

He has a pleasant—almost musical—voice that would charm Ariel. He is really quite breathtaking.

To the cashier who is counting out change, Vess says, "Just hold on to that. I need a supply of munchies too. I'll be back as soon as I fill up the tank."

He leaves quickly, afraid that they might sense his excitement and become alarmed.

Although he's been in the store no more than a minute, the night seems markedly colder than it was when he went inside. Invigorating. He catches the fragrance of pine trees and spruce—even fir from far to the north—inhales the sweet *greenness* of the heavily timbered hills behind him, detects the crisp scent of oncoming rain, smells the ozone of lightning bolts not yet hurled, breathes in the pungent fear of small animals that already quake in the fields and forests in anticipation of the storm.

After she was certain that he had left the motor home, Chyna crept forward through the vehicle, holding the butcher knife in front of her.

The windows in the dining area and the lounge were curtained, so she was not able to see what lay outside. At the front, however, the windshield revealed that they had stopped at a service station.

She had no idea where the killer was. He had left no more than a minute earlier. He might be outside, within a few feet of the door.

She hadn't heard him removing the gas cap or jacking the pump nozzle into the tank. But from the way they were parked, fuel was evidently taken on board from the starboard side, so that was most likely where he would be.

Afraid to proceed without knowing his exact whereabouts, but even more afraid to remain in the motor home, she slipped into the driver's seat. The headlights were off, and the instrument panel was dark, but there was enough backglow from the dining-nook lamp to make her supremely visible from outside.

At the next island, a Pontiac pulled away from the pumps. Its red taillights swiftly dwindled.

As far as she could see, the motor home was now the only vehicle at the station.

The keys weren't in the ignition. She wouldn't have tried to drive off anyway. That had been an option back in the vineyard, when there had been no help nearby. Here, there must be employees—and whoever pulled off the highway next.

She cracked the door, wincing at the hard sound, jumped out, and stumbled when she hit the ground. The butcher knife popped from her hand as if greased, clattered against the pavement, and spun away.

Certain that she had drawn the killer's attention and that he was already bearing down on her, Chyna scrambled to her feet. She spun left, then right, with her hands out in front of her in pathetic defense. But the eater of spiders was nowhere to be seen on the brightly lighted blacktop.

She pressed the door shut, searched the surrounding pavement for the knife, couldn't immediately spot it—and froze when a man came out of the station about fifty or sixty feet away. He was wearing a long coat, so at first Chyna was sure that he couldn't be the killer, but then immediately she recalled the inexplicable rustling of fabric to which she had listened before he had left the motor home, and she *knew*.

The only place to hide was behind one of the pumps at the next service island, but that was thirty feet away, between her and the store, with a lot of bright exposed pavement to cross. Besides, he was approaching the same island from the other side, and he would reach it first, catching her in the open.

If she tried to get around the motor home, he would spot her and wonder where she had come from. His psychosis probably included a measure of paranoia, and he would assume that she had been in his vehicle. He would pursue her. Relentlessly.

Instead, even as she saw him leaving the store, Chyna dropped flat to the pavement. Counting on the obstructing pumps at the first island to mask any movement close to the ground, she crawled on her belly under the motor home.

The killer didn't cry out, didn't pick up his pace. He hadn't seen her.

From her hiding place, she watched him approach. As he drew close, the sulfurous light was so bright that she could recognize his black leather boots as the same pair that she had studied from beneath the guest-room bed a couple of hours before.

She turned her head to follow him as he went around the back of the motor home to the starboard side, where he stopped at one of the pumps.

The blacktop was cold against her thighs, belly, and breasts. It leached the body heat out of her through her jeans and cotton sweater, and she began to shiver.

She listened as the killer disengaged the hose spout from the nozzle boot, opened the fuel port on the side of the motor home, and removed the tank cap. She figured it would take a few minutes to fill the behemoth, so she began to ease out of her hiding place even as she heard the spout thunk into the tank.

Still flat at ground level, she suddenly saw the butcher knife. Out on the blacktop. Ten feet from the front bumper. The yellow light glimmered along the cutting edge.

Even as she was sliding into the open, however, before she could push to her feet, she heard boot heels on blacktop. She glanced back under the motor home and saw that the killer evidently had fixed the nozzle trigger in place with the regulator clip, because he was on the move again.

Frantically and as silently as possible, she retreated beneath the vehicle once more. She could hear gasoline sloshing into the fuel tank.

The killer walked forward along the starboard side, around the front, to the driver's door. But he didn't open the door. He paused. Very still. Then he walked to the butcher knife, stooped, and picked it up.

Chyna held her breath, though it seemed impossible that the killer could intuit the meaning of the knife. He'd never seen it before. He couldn't know that it had come from the Templeton house. Although it was indisputably odd to find a butcher knife lying on a service-station approach lane, it might have fallen out of any vehicle that had passed through.

With the knife, he returned to the motor home and climbed inside, leaving the driver's door open behind him.

Over Chyna's head, the footsteps on the steel floor were as hollow as voodoo drums. As best she could tell, he stopped in the dining area.

Vess isn't prone to see omens and portents everywhere he looks. A single hawk flying across the face of the full moon, glimpsed at midnight, will not fill him with expectations of either disaster or good fortune. A black cat crossing his path, a mirror shattering while his reflection is captured in it, a news story about the birth of a two-headed calf— none of these things will rattle him. He is convinced that he makes his own fate and that spiritual transcendence—if such a thing can happen—ensues merely from one's acting boldly and living with intensity.

Nevertheless, the large butcher knife makes him wonder. It has a totemic quality, an almost magical aura. He carefully places it on the counter in the kitchen, where the light lays a wet sheen along the weapon's cutting edge.

When he picked it off the blacktop, the blade had been cold but the handle had been vaguely warm, as if with the anticipatory heat of his grip.

Eventually he will experiment with this strangely discarded blade to determine if anything special happens when he cuts someone with it. At the moment, however, it doesn't provide him with the advantage that he needs for the work at hand.

He has the Heckler & Koch P7 snug in the right-hand pocket of his raincoat, but he doesn't feel that even it is adequate to the situation.

The two lads behind the cashiers' counter are not in the war zone of a big-city 7-Eleven market, but they are smart enough to take precautions. Not even Beverly Hills and Bel Air, peopled by wealthy actors and retired football stars, are any longer safe at night either for or *from* their citizens. These fellows will have a firearm for self-protection and will know how to use it. Dealing with them will require an intimidating weapon with formidable stopping power.

He opens a cabinet to the left of the oven. A Mossberg short-barreled, pistol-grip, pump-action, 12-gauge shotgun is mounted in a pair of spring clamps on the shelf. He pops it loose of the clamps and lays it on the countertop.

The magazine tube of the 12-gauge is already loaded. Although he doesn't belong to the American Automobile Association, Edgler Vess is otherwise always prepared for any eventuality when he travels.

In the cabinet is a box of shotgun shells, open for easy access. He takes a few and puts them on the counter next to the Mossberg, though he is not likely to need them.

He quickly unbuttons the raincoat but doesn't take it off. He transfers the pistol from his right-hand exterior pocket to an interior, right-hand breast pocket in the lining. This is also where he places the spare shells.

From a kitchen drawer, he withdraws a compact Polaroid camera. He tucks it into the pocket from which he just removed the Heckler & Koch P7. From his wallet, he removes a trimmed Polaroid snapshot of his special girl, Ariel, and he slips it into the same pocket that contains the camera.

With his seven-inch switchblade, which is tacky from all the work for which it was used at the Templeton house, he slashes the lining of the left coat pocket. Then he rips away these tattered fragments of fabric. Now, if he were to drop coins into this pocket, they would fall straight to the floor.

He puts the shotgun under his open coat and holds it with his left hand, through the ruined pocket. The concealment is effective. He does not believe that he looks at all suspicious.

He quickly paces back to the bedroom, then forward, practicing his walk. He is able to move freely without banging the shotgun against his legs.

After all, he can draw upon the nimbleness and the grace of the spider from the Templeton house.

Although he doesn't care what damage he does to the birthmarked cashier with the ashen eyes, he'll have to be careful not to destroy the face of the young Asian gentleman. He must have good photographs for Ariel.

Overhead, the killer seemed to be occupied in the dining area. The floor creaked under him as he shifted his weight.

Unless he had drawn open the curtains, he couldn't see outside from where he was. With luck, Chyna could make a break for freedom.

She considered remaining under the vehicle, letting him tank up and drive away, and only then going inside to call the police.

But he had found the butcher knife; he would be thinking about it. Though she could see no way that he could grasp the significance of the knife, by now she had an almost superstitious dread of him and was irrationally convinced that he would find her if she remained where she was.

She crawled out from under the motor home, rose into a crouch, glanced at the open door, and then looked back and up at the windows along the side. The curtains were closed.

Emboldened, she got to her feet, crossed to the inner service island, and stepped between the pumps. She glanced back, but the killer remained inside the vehicle.

She went out of the night into bright fluorescent light and the twang of country music. Two employees were behind the counter on the right, and she intended to say *Call the police*, but then she glanced through the glass door that had just closed behind her, and she saw the killer getting out of the motor home and coming toward the store, even though he hadn't finished filling the fuel tank.

He was looking down. He hadn't seen her.

She moved away from the door.

The two men stared at her expectantly.

If she told them to call the police, they would want to know why, and there was no time for a discussion, not even enough time for the telephone call. Instead, she said, "Please don't let him know I'm here," and before they could reply, she walked away from them, along an aisle with goods shelved six feet high on both sides, to the far end of the store.

As she stepped out of the aisle to hide at the end of a row of display cases, Chyna heard the door open and the killer enter. A growl of wind came with him, and then the door swung shut.

The redheaded cashier and the young Asian gentleman with the liquid-night eyes are staring at him strangely, as if they know something they shouldn't, and he almost pulls the shotgun from under his coat the moment that he walks through the door, almost blows them away without preamble. But he tells himself that he is misreading them, that they are merely intrigued by him, because he is, after all, a striking figure. Often people sense his exceptional power and are aware that he lives a larger life than they do. He is a popular man at parties, and women are frequently attracted to him. These men are merely drawn to him as are so many others. Besides, if he whacks them immediately, without a word, he will be denying himself the pleasure of foreplay.

Alan Jackson is no longer singing on the radio, and cocking one ear appreciatively, Vess says, "Man, I like that Emmylou Harris, don't you? Was there ever anyone could sing this stuff so it got to you that way?"

"She's good," says the redhead. Previously he was outgoing. Now he seems reserved.

The Asian says nothing, inscrutable in this Zen temple of Twinkies, Hershey bars, beer nuts, snack crackers, and Doritos.

"I love a song about home fires and family," Vess says.

"You on vacation?" asks the redhead.

"Hell, friend, I'm always on vacation."

"Too young to be retired."

"I mean," says Vess, "life itself is a vacation if you look at it the right way. Been doing some hunting."

"Around these parts? What game's in season?" the redhead asks.

The Asian remains silent but attentive. He takes a Slim Jim sausage off a display rack and skins open the plastic wrapper without letting his gaze flicker from Vess.

They don't suspect for a second that they're both going to be dead in a minute, and their cow-stupid lack of awareness delights Vess. It is quite funny, really. How dramatically their eyes will widen in the instant that the shotgun roars.

Instead of answering the cashier's question, Vess says, "Are you a hunter?"

"Fishing's my sport," the redhead says.

"Never cared for it," says Vess.

"Great way to get in touch with nature—little boat on the lake, peaceful water."

Vess shakes his head. "You can't see anything in their eyes."

The redhead blinks, confused. "In whose eyes?"

"I mean, they're just *fish*. They just have these flat, glassy eyes. Jesus."

"Well, I never said they're pretty. But nothing tastes better than your own-caught salmon or a mess of trout."

Edgler Vess listens to the music for a moment, letting the two men watch him. The song genuinely affects him. He feels the piercing loneliness of the road, the longing of a lover far from home. He is a sensitive man.

The Asian bites off a piece of the Slim Jim. He chews daintily, his jaw muscles hardly moving.

Vess decides that he will take the unfinished sausage back to Ariel. She can put her mouth where the Asian had his. This intimacy with the beautiful young man will be Vess's gift to the girl.

He says, "Sure will be glad to get home to my Ariel. Isn't that a pretty name?"

"Sure is," says the redhead.

"Fits her too."

"She the missus?" asks the redhead. His friendliness is not as natural as when Vess spoke with him about turning on pump number seven. He is definitely uncomfortable and trying not to show it.

Time to startle them, see how they react. Will either of them begin to realize just how much trouble is coming?

"Nope," Vess says. "No ball and chain for me. Maybe one day. Anyway, Ariel's only sixteen, not ready yet."

They are not sure what to say. Sixteen is half his age. Sixteen is still a child. Jailbait.

The risk he's taking is enormous and titillating. Another customer might pull off the highway at any moment, raising the stakes.

"Prettiest thing you'll ever see this side of paradise," says Vess, and he licks his lips. "Ariel, I mean."

He takes the Polaroid snapshot from his coat pocket and drops it onto the counter. The clerks stare at it.

"She's pure angel," says Vess. "Porcelain skin. Breathtaking. Makes your scrotum twang like a bass fiddle."

With barely disguised distaste, the cashier looks at the pump-monitor board to the left of the cash register and says, "Your sixty bucks just finished going in the tank."

Vess says, "Don't get me wrong. I never touched her—that way. She's been locked in the basement the past year, where I can look at her anytime I want to. Waiting for my little doll to ripen, get just a little sweeter."

As glassy-eyed as fish, they gaze at him. He relishes their expressions.

Then he smiles, laughs, and says, "Hey, had you going there, didn't I?"

Neither man smiles back at him, and the redhead says tightly, "You still going to make some other purchases, or do you just want your change?"

Vess puts on his most sincere face. He can almost manage a blush. "Listen, sorry if I offended. I'm a joker. Can't help puttin' people on."

"Well," says the redhead, "I have a sixteen-year-old daughter, so I don't see what's funny."

Speaking to the Asian, Vess says, "When I go hunting, I take trophies. You know—like a matador gets the bull's tail and ears? Sometimes it's just a picture. Gifts for Ariel. She'll really like you."

As he speaks, he raises the Mossberg, draped with the raincoat as if with black funeral bunting, seizes it in both hands, blows the redheaded cashier off his stool, and pumps another shell into the breech.

The Asian. Oh, how his eyes widen. The expression in them is like nothing ever to be seen in the eyes of fish.

Even as the redhead crashes to the floor, this young Asian gentleman with the fabulous eyes has one hand under the counter, going for a weapon.

Vess says, "Don't, or I'll shove the bullets up your ass."

But the Asian brings up the revolver anyway, a Smith & Wesson .38 Chief's Special, so Vess thrusts the shotgun across the counter and fires point-blank at his chest, loath to mess up that perfect face. The young man is airborne off the stool, the revolver spinning from his hand even before he has a chance to squeeze off one round.

The redhead is screaming.

Vess walks to the gate in the counter and passes through to the work area.

The redheaded cashier with the sixteen-year-old daughter waiting at home is curled as if imitating the fetus-like pink birthmark on his forehead, hugging himself, holding himself together. On the radio, Garth Brooks sings "Thunder Rolls." Now the cashier is screaming and crying at the same time. The screams reverberate in the plate-glass windows, and the echo of the shotgun still roars in Vess's ears, and a new customer could walk into the store at any second. The moment is achingly intense.

One more round finishes the cashier.

The Asian is unconscious and going fast. Happily, his face is unmarked.

Like a pilgrim genuflecting before a shrine, Vess drops onto one knee as a final gasp rattles from the dying young man. A sound like the brittle flutter of insect wings. He leans close to inhale the other's exhalation, breathes deeply. Now small measures of the Asian's grace and beauty are a part of him, conveyed on the scent of the Slim Jim.

The Brooks song is followed by that old Johnny Cash number "A Boy Named Sue," which is silly enough to spoil the mood. Vess turns off the radio.

As he reloads, he surveys the area behind the counter and spots a row of wall switches. They are labeled with the locations of the lights that they control. He shuts down all the exterior lighting, including the OPEN 24 HOURS of red neon on the roof.

When he also switches off the fluorescent ceiling panels, the store is not plunged into total darkness. The display lights in the long row of coolers glow eerily behind the insulated glass doors. A lighted clock advertising Coors beer hangs on one wall, and at the counter, a gooseneck lamp illuminates the papers on which the Asian gentleman was working.

Nevertheless, the shadows are deep, and the place appears to be closed. It's unlikely that a customer will pull in from the highway.

Of course a county sheriff's deputy or highway patrol officer, curious about why this establishment that never closes is, in fact, suddenly closed, might investigate. Consequently, Vess doesn't dawdle over the tasks that remain.

Huddled with her back against the end panel of the shelves, as far as she could get from the cashiers' counter, Chyna felt exposed by the display-case light to her right and threatened by the shadows to her left. In the silence following the gunfire and the cessation of the music, she became convinced that the killer could hear her ragged, shuddery breathing. But she couldn't quiet herself, and she couldn't stop shaking any more than a rabbit could cease shivering in the shadow of a wolf.

Maybe the rumble of the compressors for the coolers and freezers would provide enough covering sound to save her. She wanted to lean out to one side and then the other to check the flanking aisles, but she could not summon the courage to look. She was crazily certain that, leaning out, she'd come face-to-face with the eater of spiders.

She had thought that nothing could be more devastating than finding the bodies of Paul and Sarah—and later Laura—but this had been worse. This time she had been in the same room when murder happened, close enough not merely to hear the screams but to feel them like punches in the chest.

She supposed the killer was robbing the place, but he didn't need to kill the clerks just to get the money. Necessity, of course, was not a deciding factor with him. He had killed them simply because he enjoyed doing so. He was on a roll. He was *hot*.

She seemed trapped in an endless night. A breakdown in the cosmic machinery, gears jammed. Stars locked in place. No sunrise ever rising. And coming down through the frozen sky, a terrible coldness.

A light flashed, and Chyna brought her hands up defensively in front of her face. Then she realized that the flash had come from the other end of the store. And again.

Edgler Vess is not a hunter, as he had told the redheaded cashier, but a connoisseur who collects exquisite images, recording most of them with the camera of his mind's eye but once in a while with the Polaroid camera. Memories of great beauty enliven his thoughts every day and form the basis of his gratifying dreams.

Each camera flash seems to linger in the huge eyes of the Asian clerk, glimmering as if it were his spirit trapped behind his corneas and seeking egress from the cooling mortal coil.

Once, in Nevada, Vess had killed an incomparable twenty-year-old brunette, whose face had made Claudia Schiffer and Kate Moss look like hags. Before meticulously destroying her, he had taken six photographs. With threats, he had even managed to make her smile in three of the shots; she had a radiant smile. Once every thirty days during the three months following that memorable episode, he had cut up and eaten one of the photos in which she'd been smiling, and with the consumption of each, he had been fiercely aroused by the destruction of her beauty. He had felt her smile in his belly, a warming radiance, and knew that he himself was more beautiful because he contained it.

He can't remember the brunette's name. Names are never of any importance to him.

Knowing the name of the young Asian gentleman, however, will be helpful when he describes this episode to Ariel. He puts aside the Polaroid, rolls the dead man over, and takes his wallet from his hip pocket.

Holding the driver's license in the light from the gooseneck lamp, he sees that the name is Thomas Fujimoto.

Vess decides to call him Fuji. Like the mountain.

He returns the license to the wallet and tucks the wallet in the pocket. He takes none of the dead man's money. He won't touch the cash in the register either—except to extract the forty dollars in change that is due him. He isn't a thief.

With three photographs taken, he needs only to keep his promise to Fuji and prove that he is a man of his word. It is an awkward bit of business, but he finds it amusing.

Now he must deal with the security system, which has recorded everything that he's done. A video camera is mounted over the front door and focused on the cashiers' counter.

Edgler Foreman Vess has no desire to see himself on television news. Living with intensity is virtually impossible when one is in prison.

Chyna was in control of her breathing again, but her heart knocked so hard that her vision pulsed, and the carotid arteries thumped in her throat as though jolts of electricity were slamming through them.

Again convinced that safety lay in movement, she leaned into the light and looked around the corner into the aisle in front of the coolers. The killer was not in sight, although she could hear him moving at the other end of the store: crisp furtive rustlings like a rat in a drift of autumn leaves.

On her hands and knees, stomach clenched in terror, she crawled into the spill of cooler light far enough to look along the narrow aisle, seeking something on the shelves to the right that might serve as a weapon. Without the butcher knife, she felt helpless.

No knives were conveniently for sale. Nearest to her were hanging displays of novelty key chains, fingernail clippers, pocket combs, styptic pencils, packets of moistened towelettes, eyeglass-cleaning papers, decks of playing cards, and disposable cigarette lighters.

She reached up and took one of the lighters off the rack. She wasn't sure how she could use it to defend herself, but in the absence of a satisfyingly sharp length of steel, fire was the only weapon available to her.

The overhead fluorescent panels blinked on. The brightness froze her.

She looked toward the far end of the store. The killer wasn't in sight, but across one wall his slouched shadow swelled huge and then shrank and then glided away like that of a moth swooping past a floodlamp.

Vess switches the lights on only to look at the video camera mounted above the front door.

Of course the incriminating tape is not contained in the camera. If access were that easy, even some of the dimwit thugs who make a living sticking up service stations and convenience stores would be smart enough to climb on a stool and eject the cassette to take it with them or otherwise destroy the evidence. The camera is sending the image to a video recorder elsewhere in the building.

The system is an add-on, so the transmission cable isn't buried in the wall. This is fortunate for Vess, because if the cable were hidden, the search would be more time-consuming. The line isn't even tucked up above the suspended acoustic-tile ceiling. Bracketed to the Sheetrock, it leads openly to the back partition behind the cashiers' counter and through a half-inch-diameter hole in that wall to another room.

There's a door to that room as well. He finds an office with one desk, gray metal filing cabinets, a small safe with a combination lock, and wood-pattern Formica storage cabinets.

Fortunately, the recorder isn't in the safe. The transmission cable comes through the wall from the store, continues through two more brackets for a distance of about seven feet, then drops down through the top of one of the storage cabinets. No attempt at concealment whatsoever.

He opens the upper doors to the cabinet, doesn't find what he seeks, and checks below. Three machines are stacked atop one another.

Tape whispers through the bottom machine, and the indicator light shines above the word RECORD. He presses the STOP button, then EJECT, and he drops the cassette into his raincoat pocket.

He might play it for Ariel. The quality will not be first-rate, because this is an old system, outdated technology. But the precious girl will be impressed by his bold performance even in too brightly lit scenes on black-and-white tape that has been re-recorded too often.

A telephone stands on the desk. He uncouples it from the cord that leads to the wall jack and uses the butt of the shotgun to smash the keypad.

A new shift of clerks will come on duty, probably at eight or nine o'clock, in four or five hours. By then Vess will be long gone. But there's no point in making it easy for them to call the police. Something might go wrong with his plans, delaying him here or on the highway, and then he will be glad that he bought himself an extra half hour by destroying the telephones.

Beside the door is a pegboard on which hang eight keys, each with its own tag. With the exception of the current regrettable interruption in service, this establishment is open twenty-four hours a day—yet there's a key to lock the front door. He slips it off its peg.

In the work area behind the cashiers' counter once more, after closing the office door behind him, Vess snaps down a switch, and the overhead fluorescents wink out.

He stands in the dim light that remains, breathing through his mouth, licking his lips, rolling his tongue over his gums, tasting the lingering acrid scent of gunfire. The gloom feels good against his face and the backs of his hands; the shadows are as erotic as slender, trembling hands.

Stepping around the bodies, he goes to the counter and takes only his forty dollars from the cash register drawer.

The young Asian's Smith & Wesson .38 Chief's Special lies on the counter, in the cone of light from the gooseneck lamp, where Vess carefully placed it minutes ago. He is no more capable of stealing the gun than he is of taking money that doesn't belong to him.

The Slim Jim, from which the Asian took a large bite, is also on the counter. Unfortunately, the wrapper was *peeled* off; therefore, it is useless.

Vess plucks another sausage from the display rack, neatly chews off the end of the plastic wrapper, and slides the tube of meat out of the package. He inserts the shorter sausage (missing the Asian's bite) into the wrapper and twists the end shut. He puts this in his pocket with the videotape—for Ariel.

He pays for the sausage that he threw away, making change from the open register drawer.

On the counter is a telephone. He unplugs it from the jack and smashes the keypad with the butt of the shotgun.

Now he goes shopping.

Chyna was relieved when the lights went off, frightened by the hammering, and then alert in the subsequent silence.

She had crept out of the cooler-lighted aisle and returned to her shelter at the end of the shelf row, where she had quietly peeled open the cardboard-and-plastic package that contained the disposable cigarette lighter. While the overhead fluorescents had been on and the flickering flame couldn't betray her, she had tested the lighter, and it had worked.

Now she clutched this pathetic weapon and prayed that the killer would finish whatever he was doing—maybe looting the cash register—and just, for God's sake, get out of here. She didn't want to have to go up against him with a Bic butane. If he stumbled onto her, she might be able to take advantage of his surprise, thrust the lighter in his face, and give him a nasty little burn—or even set his hair on fire—before he recoiled. More likely, his reflexes would be uncannily quick; he'd knock the lighter out of her hand before she could do any damage.

Even if she burned him, she would gain only precious seconds to turn and flee. Hurting, he would come after her, and with his long legs, he would be swift. Then the outcome of the race would depend on whether her terror or his insane rage was the greater motivating force.

She heard movement, the creak of the counter gate, footsteps. Half nauseated from protracted fear, she was gloriously heartened when it seemed that he was leaving.

Then she realized that the footsteps were not crossing toward the door at the front of the store. They were approaching her.

She was squatting on her haunches, back pressed to the end panel of the shelf row, not immediately sure where he was. In the first of the three aisles, toward the front of the store? In the center aisle immediately to her left?

No.

The third aisle.

To her right.

He was coming past the coolers. Not fast. Not as if he knew that she was here and intended to whack her.

Rising into a crouch but staying low, Chyna eased to the left, into the middle of the three passages. Here the glow from the coolers, one row removed, bounced off the acoustic-tile ceiling but provided little illumination. All the merchandise was shelved with shadows.

She started forward toward the cashiers' counter, thankful for her soft-soled shoes—and then she remembered the packaging from which she had extracted the Bic lighter. She'd left it on the floor where she'd been squatting at the end of the shelf row.

He would see it, probably even step on it. Maybe he would think that earlier in the night some shoplifter had slipped the lighter out of the packaging to conceal it more easily in a pocket. Or maybe he would *know*.

Intuition might serve him as well as it sometimes served Chyna. If intuition was the whisper of God, then perhaps another and less benevolent god spoke with equal subtleness to a man like this.

She turned back, leaned around the corner, and snatched up the empty package. The stiff plastic crinkled in her shaky grip, but the sound was faint and, luckily, masked by his footsteps.

He was at least halfway down the third aisle by the time she started forward along the second. But he was taking his time while she was scuttling as fast as she could, and she reached the head of her aisle before he arrived at the end of his.

At the terminus of the shelf row, instead of a flat panel like the one at the far end, there was a freestanding wire carousel rack holding paperback books, and Chyna nearly collided with it when she turned the corner. She caught herself just in time, slipped around the rack, and sheltered against it, between aisles once more.

On the floor lay a Polaroid photograph: a close-up of a strikingly beautiful girl of about sixteen, with long platinum-blond hair. The teenager's features were composed but not relaxed, frozen in a studied blandness, as though her true feelings were so explosive that she would self-destruct if she acknowledged them. Her eyes subtly belied her calm demeanor; they were slightly wide, watchful, achingly expressive, windows on a soul in torment, full of anger and fear and desperation.

This must be the photograph that he had shown to the clerks. Ariel. The girl in the cellar.

Although she and Ariel bore no resemblance to each other, Chyna felt as though she were staring into a mirror rather than looking at a picture. In Ariel, she recognized a terror akin to the fear that had suffused her own childhood, a familiar desperation, loneliness as deep as a cold polar ocean.

The killer's footsteps brought her back to the moment. Judging by the sound of them, he was no longer in the third aisle. He had turned the corner at the back of the store and was now in the middle passage.

He was coming forward, leisurely covering the same territory over which Chyna had just scuttled.

*What the hell is he doing?*

She wanted to take the photograph but didn't dare. She put it on the floor where she had found it.

She went around the paperback carousel into the third aisle, which the killer had just left, and she headed toward the end of the shelf row again. She stayed close to the merchandise on the left, away from the glass doors of the lighted coolers on the right, to avoid throwing a shadow on the ceiling tiles, which he might see.

When she was moving, she could still hear his heavy footsteps, but unless she stopped to listen, she couldn't tell in which direction he was headed. Yet she didn't dare stop to take a bearing on him, lest he circle again into this aisle and catch her in the open. When she reached the end of the row and turned the corner, she half expected to discover that he had changed directions, to collide with him, and to be caught.

But he wasn't there.

Sitting on her haunches, Chyna leaned back against the end panel of the shelf row, the very spot from which she'd started. Gingerly she put the empty Bic lighter package on the floor between her feet, in the same place from which she had retrieved it less than a minute before.

She listened. No footsteps. Other than the noise made by the coolers, only silence.

Thumb poised, she clutched the lighter in her fist, prepared to strike the flame.

Vess stuffs two snack packages of cheese-and-peanut-butter crackers, one Planters peanut bar, and two Hershey bars with almonds into his raincoat pockets, in which he's already carrying the pistol, the Polaroid, and the videotape.

He totals the cost in his head. Because he doesn't want to waste time going behind the register to make change, he rounds the figure to the nearest dollar and leaves the payment on the counter.

After picking up the fallen photograph of Ariel, he hesitates, soaking up the atmosphere of aftermath. There is a special quality to a room in which people have recently perished: like the hush in a theater during that instant between when the final curtain falls on a perfect performance and when the wild applause begins; a sense of triumph but also a solemn awareness of eternity suspended like a cold droplet at the point of a melting icicle. With the screaming done and the blood pooled in stillness, Edgler Vess is better able to appreciate the effects of his bold actions and to relish the quiet intensity of death.

Finally he leaves the store. Using the tagged key that he took from the pegboard, he locks the door.

At the corner of the building is one public telephone. With its armored cord, the handset isn't easily torn loose, so he hammers it against the phone box five, ten, twenty times, until the plastic cracks, revealing the microphone. He tears the mike out of the broken mouthpiece, drops it on the pavement, and methodically crushes it under his boot heel. Then he hangs the useless handset on the switch hook again.

His work here is done. Although satisfying, this interlude was unexpected; it has put him behind schedule.

He has much driving to do. He is not tired. He had slept all the previous afternoon and well into the evening, before visiting the Templetons. Nevertheless, he is loath to waste more time. He longs to be home.

Far to the north, sheets of lightning flutter softly between dense layers of clouds, pulses rather than bolts. Vess is pleased by the prospect of a big storm. Here at ground level, where life is lived, tumult and turmoil are fundamental elements of the human climate, and for reasons that he cannot understand, he is unfailingly reassured by the sight of violence in higher realms as well. Though he fears noth-ing, he is sometimes inexplicably disturbed by the sight of *serene* skies—whether blue or overcast—and often on a clear night when the sky is deep with stars, he prefers not to gaze into that immensity.

Now no stars are visible. Above lie only sullen masses of clouds harried by a cold wind, briefly veined with lightning, pregnant with a deluge.

Vess hurries across the blacktop toward the motor home, eager to resume his journey northward, to meet the promised storm, to find that best place in the night where the lightning will come in great shattering bolts, where a harder wind will crack trees, where rain will fall in destructive floods.

Crouching at the end of the shelf row, Chyna had listened to the door open and close, not daring to believe that the killer had left at last and that her ordeal might be over. Breath held, she'd waited for the sound of the door opening again and for his footsteps as he reentered.

When she had heard, instead, the key scraping-clicking in the lock and the deadbolt snapping into place, she had gone forward along the middle of the three aisles, staying low, cat-quiet because she expected, superstitiously, that he might hear the slightest sound even from outside.

A violent hammering, reverberating through the building walls, had brought her to a sudden halt at the head of the aisle. He was pounding furiously on something, but she couldn't imagine what it might be.

When the hammering stopped, Chyna hesitated, then rose from her crouch and leaned around the end of the shelves. She looked to the right, past the first aisle, toward the glass door and the windows at the front of the store.

With the outside lights off, the service islands lay in murk as deep as that on any river bottom.

She could not at first see the killer, who was at one with the night in his black raincoat. But then he moved, wading through the dark-ness toward the motor home.

Even if he glanced back, he wouldn't be able to see her in the dimly lighted store. Her heart thundered anyway as she stepped into the open area between the heads of the three aisles and the cashiers' counter.

The photograph of Ariel was no longer on the floor. She wished that she could believe it had never existed.

At the moment, the two employees who had kept the secret of her presence were more important than Ariel or the killer. The roar of the shotgun and the sudden cessation of the soul-shriveling screams had convinced her that they were dead. But she must be sure. If one of them clung miraculously to life, and if she could get help for him—police and paramedics—she would partially redeem herself.

She had been unable to do anything to stop the blood-loving bastard; she had only cowered out of his sight, praying frantically for invisibility. Now nausea rolled like a slop of chilled oysters in her stomach—and at the same time she was lifted by a sickening exhilaration that she had lived when so many others had died. Understandable though it was, the exhilaration shamed her, and for herself as well as for the two clerks, she hoped that she could still save them.

She pushed through the gate in the counter, and the piercing creak of a hinge scraped the hollows of her bones.

A gooseneck lamp provided some light.

The two men were on the floor.

"Ah," she said. And then: "God."

They were beyond her help, and immediately she turned away from them, her vision blurring.

On the counter, directly under the lamp, lay a revolver. She stared at it in disbelief, blinking back tears.

Evidently it had belonged to one of the clerks. She'd overheard the conversation between the killer and the two men; and she vaguely recalled a harsh admonition that might have been a warning to drop a gun. This gun.

She grabbed it, held it in both hands—a weight that buoyed her.

If the killer returned, she was ready, no longer helpless, for she knew how to use guns. Some of her mother's craziest friends had been expert with weaponry, hate-filled people with a queer brightness in the eyes that was a sign of drug use in some cases but that was visible in others only when they spoke passionately about their deep commitment to truth and justice. On an isolated farm in Montana, when Chyna was only twelve, a woman named Doreen and a man named Kirk had instructed her in the use of a pistol, although her slender arms had jumped wildly with the recoil. Patiently teaching her control, they had said that someday she would be a true soldier and a credit to the movement.

Chyna had wanted to learn about firearms not to use them in one noble cause or another but to protect herself from those people in her mother's strange circles who succumbed to drug-enhanced rages—or who stared at her with a sick desire. She had been too young to want their attention, too self-respecting to encourage them—but thanks to her mother, she had not been too innocent to understand what some of them wanted to do with her.

Now, with the dead clerk's revolver in hand, she turned and saw the shattered telephone.

"Shit."

She hurried back through the gate, into the public part of the store, directly to the front door.

The motor home was still parked on this side of the farther of the two service islands. The headlights were off.

The killer was not in sight at first—but then he walked into view around the back of the motor home, his unbuttoned coat flaring like a cape in the wind.

Although the man was about sixty feet away, surely he couldn't see her at the door. He wasn't even looking in her direction, but Chyna took a step backward.

Apparently he had been racking the hose at the gasoline pump and capping the fuel tank. He walked alongside the vehicle toward the driver's door.

She had planned to telephone the police and tell them that the killer was headed north on Highway 101. Now, by the time she got to a phone, called the cops, and made them understand the situation, he might have as much as an hour's lead. Within an hour, he would have several choices of other routes that branched off 101. He might continue north toward Oregon, turn east toward Nevada—or even angle west to the coast, thereafter turning south again along the Pacific and into San Francisco, vanishing in the urban maze. The more miles he traveled before an all-points bulletin went out for him, the harder he would be to find. He would soon be in another police agency's jurisdiction, first a different county and perhaps eventually a different state, complicating the search for him.

And now that she thought about it, Chyna realized that she had precious little information that would be helpful to the cops. The motor home might be blue or green; she wasn't sure which—or even if it was either—because she'd seen it only in the darkness and then in the color-distorting yellow glow of the service station's sodium-vapor lights. She didn't know the make of it either, and she hadn't seen the license plate.

He was getting away.

Unhurried, clearly confident that he was in no imminent danger of discovery, he climbed into the motor home and pulled shut the driver's door.

*He's going to get away. Jesus. No, intolerable, unthinkable. He can't be allowed to get away, never pay for what he did to Laura, to all of them—even worse, have a chance to do it again. No, God, please, let me drop the hateful rotten fucking bastard with a shot in the head.*

She stepped close to the door again. It could be unlocked only with a key. She didn't have a key.

She heard the motor-home engine turn over.

If she shot out the glass, he would hear. Even over the roar of the engine and from a distance, he would hear.

Once through the door, she would be too far away to shoot him. Fifty or sixty feet, at night, with a handgun, the gasoline pumps intervening. No way. She had to get close, right up against the motor home, put the muzzle to the window.

But if he heard her shoot her way through the locked door and saw her coming out of the store, she wouldn't have a chance to get close to him, not in a million years, and then *he* would be stalking *her* again, across the service-station property, wherever she went, and his shotgun was better armament than her revolver.

Out at the motor home, he switched on the headlights.

"No."

She ran to the gate in the counter, shoved through it, stepped around the dead men, and went to the door in the back wall.

There had to be a rear entrance. Both practical function and fire codes would require it.

The door opened onto blackness. As far as she could tell, there were no windows ahead of her. Maybe it was only a supply closet or a bathroom. She stepped across the threshold, closed the door behind her to prevent light from leaking into the store, felt along the wall to her left, found a switch, and risked turning on the lights.

She was in a cramped office. On the desk was another shattered telephone.

Directly across the room from the door that she had just used was another door. No obvious lock. That *would* be a bathroom.

To her left, in the back wall of the building, a metal door featured a pair of over-and-under deadbolts with thumb-turns. She disengaged the locks and opened the door, and a flood tide of cold wind washed into the office.

Behind the store spread a twenty-foot-wide paved area, and then a steep hillside rose with serried trees that were black in the night and restless in the wind. A security light in a wire cage revealed two parked cars, which probably belonged to the clerks.

Cursing the killer, Chyna turned to the right and sprinted along the shorter length of the building, around the corner, past public rest rooms. She had never caused anyone physical harm, not once in her life, but she was ready to kill now, and she knew that she could do it without hesitation, with no thought of mercy, with a vengeance, because *he* had empowered her to do it. This was what he had reduced her to—this blind, animal fury—and the worst thing was that it felt *good*, this rage, so good in comparison to the fear and helplessness she had endured, a sweet singing of rushing blood in the veins and an exhilarating sense of savage strength. She should have been appalled at the lust for blood that seized her, but she *liked* it, and she knew that she would like it even more when she caught up with the motor home and shot him through the driver's-side window, pulled open the door and shot him again where he sat bleeding, dragged him out and let him sprawl on the pavement and emptied the revolver into him until he could never again go hunting.

She rounded the second corner and reached the front of the building.

The motor home was pulling away from the pumps.

She raced after it, faster than she had ever run in her life, cleaving a resistant wind that stung new tears from her eyes, shoes pounding noisily on the blacktop.

Now it was *Dear Lord, let me catch him* instead of *Dear Lord, let me get away from him*, and now it was *Dear Lord, let me kill him* instead of *Dear Lord, don't let him kill me*.

The motor home picked up speed. It was already out of the service area, entering the eighth-of-a-mile lane that would take it back onto the highway.

She would never be able to catch it.

He was getting away.

She halted and planted her feet wide apart. The revolver was in her right hand. She raised it, gripped it with both hands, arms extended, elbows locked. Shooter's stance. Every good girl should know it, come the revolution.

Her heart didn't merely beat, it crashed, and every explosive pump shook her arms, so she couldn't hold the revolver on target. The motor home was too distant anyway. She'd miss it by yards. And even if she got lucky and put one round in the back wall, it would be nowhere near the driver. He was out of her reach, beyond harm, cruising away.

It was over. She could go for help, find the nearest working phone, call the local police, and try to cut his lead time as short as possible— but for now and here, it was over.

Except that it wasn't over, and she knew it wasn't, no matter how much she wanted to be finished with it, because she said aloud, "Ariel."

*Sixteen. Prettiest thing this side of paradise. Pure angel. Porcelain skin. Breathtaking. Locked in the basement for a year. Never touched her—that way. Waiting for her to ripen, get just a little sweeter.*

In Chyna's mind's eye, the Polaroid photograph of Ariel was as clear and detailed as it had been when she'd held it in her hand. That bland expression, maintained with obvious effort. Those eyes, brimming with anguish.

Earlier, listening to the conversation between the killer and the two clerks, Chyna had *known* that he was not merely playing games with them, that he was telling the truth. The creep was letting them in on his secrets, admitting his perverse crimes, getting a kick out of revealing his guilt because he knew that they were going to die and that they would never have a chance to repeat his admissions to anyone. Even if she'd never seen the photograph, she would have *known*.

Ariel. Those eyes. The anguish.

While she had been concentrating on her own survival, Chyna had blocked all thoughts of the captive girl from her mind. And when she had found the revolver, she had at once convinced herself that all she wanted was to kill this son of a bitch, blow his brains out, because the truth was something that she hadn't quite been able to face.

The truth had been that she didn't dare kill him, because when he was dead, they might never find Ariel—or find her days too late, after she had died of starvation or thirst in her basement cell. He might have the girl locked under his house, which they would probably be able to locate from whatever identification he was carrying, but he might have stashed her elsewhere, in a place remote, to which he and only he could lead them. Chyna had pursued the killer to disable him, so the cops would be able to wrench from him the location at which Ariel was being held. If she could have caught up with the motor home, she would have tried to yank open the driver's door, shoot the vicious bastard in the leg as she ran alongside, wound him badly enough that he would have to stop the vehicle. But she'd had to hide that truth from herself because trying to wound him was a lot riskier than going for a head shot through the window, and she might not have had the courage to run so fast and try so hard if she had admitted to herself what, in fact, had needed to be done.

With its burden of corpses, with its driver whose name might well be Legion, the big motor home dwindled down the service road toward Highway 101, quite literally Hell on wheels.

Somewhere he had a house, and under the house was a basement, and in the basement was a sixteen-year-old girl named Ariel, held prisoner for a year, untouched but soon to be violated, alive but not for long.

"She's real," Chyna whispered to the wind.

The taillights receded into the night.

She frantically surveyed the lonely stretch of countryside. She was unable to see help in any direction. No house lights in the immediate vicinity. Just trees and darkness. Something glowed faintly to the north, beyond a hill or two, but she didn't know the source, and anyway she couldn't get that far quickly on foot.

On the highway, a truck appeared from the south behind a blaze of headlights, but it didn't pull off to tank up at the shuttered service station. It shrieked past, the driver oblivious of Chyna.

The lumbering motor home was almost to the far end of the connecting road.

Sobbing with frustration, with anger, with fear for the girl whom she had never met, and with despair for her own culpability if that girl died, Chyna turned away from the motor home. Hurried past the gasoline pumps. Around the building, back the way she had come.

Throughout her own childhood, no one had ever held out a hand to her. No one had ever cared that she was trapped, frightened, and helpless.

Now, when she thought of the Polaroid snapshot, the image was like one of those holograms that changed depending on the angle at which it was viewed. Sometimes it was Ariel's face, but sometimes it was Chyna's own.

As she ran, she prayed that she wouldn't have to go inside again. And search the bodies.

Distant lightning flickered, and faraway thunder clattered like boot heels on hollow basement stairs. On the steep hills behind the building, black trees thrashed in the escalating wind.

The first car was a white Chevrolet. Ten years old. Unlocked.

When she scrambled in behind the steering wheel, the worn-out seat springs creaked, and a candy-bar wrapper or something crackled underfoot. The interior stank of stale cigarette smoke.

The keys were not in the ignition. She checked behind the sun visor. Under the driver's seat. Nothing.

The second car was a Honda, newer than the Chevy. It smelled of a lemon-scented air freshener, and the keys were in a coin tray on the console.

She placed the revolver on the passenger seat, within easy reach, reluctant to let it out of her hand. As an adult, she had always relied on prudence and caution to stay out of harm's way. She hadn't held a gun since she'd walked out on her mother at the age of sixteen. Now she could not imagine living without a weapon at her side, and she doubted that she ever would do so again—which was a development that dismayed her.

The engine turned over at once. The tires shrieked, and she peeled rubber getting started. Smoke bloomed from the spinning wheels, but then she shot out from behind the building and rocketed past the service islands.

The connecting road to the freeway was deserted. The motor home was out of sight.

At this point, 101 was a four-lane divided highway, so the motor home couldn't have gotten across the median to turn south. The killer had to have gone north, and he couldn't have traveled far in the little lead time that he had.

Chyna went after him.

At four o'clock in the morning, oncoming traffic is sparse, but each set of headlights purls through the fine hairs in Edgler Vess's ears. This is a pleasant sound, separate from the passing roar of engines and the Doppler-shift whine of other vehicles' tires on the pavement.

As he drives, he eats one of the Hershey bars. The silkiness of melting chocolate on his tongue reminds him of the music of Angelo Badalamenti, and the music of Badalamenti brings to mind the waxy surface of a scarlet anthurium, and the anthurium sparks an intensely sensual recollection of the cool taste and crispness of cornichons, which for several seconds completely overwhelms the actual taste of the chocolate.

Listening to the murmur of oncoming headlights, engaged in this free association of sensory input and memory, Vess is a happy man. He experiences life far more intensely than do other people; he is a singularity. Because his mind is not cluttered with foolishness and false emotions, he is able to perceive what others cannot. He understands the nature of the world, the purpose of existence, and the truth behind the Big Lie; because of these insights, he is free, and because he is free, he is always happy.

The nature of the world is sensation. We drift in an ocean of sensory stimuli: motion, color, texture, shape, heat, cold, natural symphonies of sound, an infinite number of scents, tastes beyond the human ability to catalogue. Nothing but sensation endures. Living things all die. Great cities do not last. Metal corrodes and stone crumbles. Over eons, continents are reshaped, whole mountain ranges vanish, and seas run dry. The planet itself will be vaporized when the sun self-destructs. But even in the void of deep space, between solar systems, in that profound vacuum that will not transmit sound, there is nevertheless light and darkness, cold, motion, shape, and the awful panorama of eternity.

The sole purpose of existence is to open oneself to sensation and to satisfy all appetites as they arise. Edgler Vess knows that there is no such thing as a good or bad sensation—only raw sensation itself—and that every sensory experience is worthwhile. Negative and positive values are merely human interpretations of value-neutral stimuli and, therefore, are only as enduring—which is to say, as meaningless—as human beings themselves. He enjoys the most bitter taste as much as he relishes the sweetness of a ripe peach; in fact, he occasionally chews a few aspirin not to relieve a headache but to savor the incomparable flavor of the medication. When he accidentally cuts himself, he is never afraid, because he finds pain fascinating and welcomes it as merely another form of pleasure; even the taste of his own blood intrigues him.

Mr. Vess is not sure if there is such a thing as the immortal soul, but he is unshakably certain that if souls exist, we are not born with them in the same way that we are born with eyes and ears. He believes that the soul, if real, *accretes* in the same manner as a coral reef grows from the deposit of countless millions of calcareous skeletons secreted by marine polyps. We build the reef of the soul, however, not from dead polyps but from steadily accreted sensations through the course of a lifetime. In Vess's considered opinion, if one wishes to have a formidable soul—or any soul at all—one must open oneself to every possible sensation, plunge into the bottomless ocean of sensory stimuli that is our world, and *experience* with no consideration of good or bad, right or wrong, with no fear but only fortitude. If his belief is correct, then he himself is building what may be the most intricate, elaborated —if not to say baroque—and *important* soul that has ever transcended this level of existence.

The Big Lie is that such concepts as love, guilt, and hate are real. Put Mr. Vess into a room with any priest, show them a pencil, and they will agree on its color, size, and shape. Blindfold them, hold cinnamon under their noses, and they will both identify it from the smell. But bring before them a mother cuddling her baby, and the priest will see love where Mr. Vess will see only a woman who enjoys the sensations provided by the infant—the scrubbed smell of it, the softness of its pink skin, the undeniably pleasing roundness of its simply-formed face, the musicality of its giggle; its apparent helplessness and dependence deeply satisfy her. The greatest curse of humanity's high intelligence is that, in most members of the species, it leads to a yearning to be more than they are. All men and women, in Vess's view, are fundamentally nothing other than animals—smart animals, indeed, but animals nonetheless; reptiles, in fact, evolved from whatever fish with legs first crawled out of the primordial sea. They are, he knows, motivated and formed solely by sensory stimuli, yet unable to admit to the primacy of physical sensation over intellect and emotion. They are even frightened of the reptile consciousness within, its needs and hungers, and they attempt to restrict its sensation seeking by using lies such as love, guilt, hate, courage, loyalty, and honor.

This is the philosophy of Mr. Edgler Vess. He embraces his reptilian nature. The glory of him is to be found in his unmatched accretion of sensations. This is a functional philosophy, requiring its adherent to endorse neither the black-and-white values that so hamper religious persons nor the embarrassing contradictions of the situational ethics that characterize both the modern atheist and those whose religion is politics.

Life *is*. Vess lives. That is the sum of it.

Driving north on Highway 101, finishing the second of his two Hershey bars, Vess considers, not for the first time, that there is a similarity between the texture of melting chocolate and that of thickening blood.

He recalls the restful silence of the blood pooled around Mrs. Templeton in the shower stall before he disturbed it by turning on the cold water.

The memory of the hollow drumming in that shower makes him aware of the coldness of all the rain as yet unleashed by the pending storm toward which he is driving.

He sees a quick blush of lightning along the face of the clouds, and he knows that it tastes like ozone.

Above the monotonous rumble of the motor-home engine, he hears a peal of thunder, and that sound is also a vivid image in his mind: the young Asian's eyes opening wide, wide, wide with the first crash of the shotgun.

Even in the airless void between galaxies: the light and the darkness, color, texture, motion, shape, and pain.

The highway rose, and the forests crowded close. On a wide curve, the headlights of the Honda swept across the flanking hills, revealing that some of the looming trees were immense spruces and pines. Soon, perhaps, redwoods.

Chyna kept her foot down hard on the accelerator. To the best of her recollection, this was the first time she had ever broken a speed limit. She'd never been fined for a traffic violation; but she would be grateful now if a cop pulled her over.

Her unblemished driving record resulted from her preference for moderation in all things, including the pace at which she ordinarily drove. Judging by the catastrophes that she had seen befall others, survival was closely related to moderation, and her whole life was about survival, as any nun's life might be defined by the word *faith* or any politician's by *power*. She seldom drank more than one glass of wine, never used drugs, engaged in no dangerous sports, ate a diet low in fat and salt and sugar, stayed out of neighborhoods reputed to be dangerous, never expressed strong opinions, and in general was safely inconspicuous—all in the interest of getting by, hanging on, surviving.

Against the odds, she had already survived the events of the past few hours. *The killer didn't even know that she existed.* She had made it. She was free. It was over. The smart thing, the wise thing, the sane thing—the *Chyna* thing—to do was to let him go, just let him get away, pull off to the side of the road, stop, surrender to the shakes that she was strenuously repressing, and thank God that she was untouched and alive.

As she drove, Chyna argued against her previous conviction, insisting that the teenage girl in the cellar, Ariel of the angelic face, wasn't real. The photo might be of a girl whom he had already killed. The story of her incarceration might be only a sick fantasy, a psychotic's version of a Brothers Grimm tale, Rapunzel underground, merely a mind game that he'd been playing with the two clerks.

"Liar," she called herself.

The girl in the photo was alive somewhere, imprisoned. Ariel was no fantasy. Indeed, she was Chyna; they were one and the same, because all lost girls are the same girl, united by their suffering.

She kept her foot pressed firmly on the accelerator, and the Honda crested a hill, and the aged motor home was on the long gradual downslope ahead, five hundred feet away. Her breath caught in her throat, and then she exhaled with a whispered, "*Oh, Jesus.*"

She was approaching him at too great a speed. She eased off the accelerator.

By the time she was two hundred feet from the motor home, she had matched speeds with it. She fell back farther, hoping that he hadn't noticed her initial haste.

He was driving between fifty and fifty-five miles per hour, a prudent pace on that highway, especially as they were now traveling on a stretch without a median strip and with somewhat narrower lanes than previously. He wouldn't necessarily expect her to pass him, and he shouldn't be suspicious when she remained behind; after all, at this sleepy hour, not every driver in California was in a blistering hurry or suicidally reckless.

At this more reasonable speed, she didn't have to concentrate as intently as before on the road ahead, and she quickly searched the immediate interior of the car in hopes of finding a cellular telephone. She was pessimistic about the chances that a night clerk at a service station would have a portable phone, but on the other hand, half the world seemed to have them now, not just salesmen and Realtors and lawyers. She checked the console box. Then the glove box. Under the driver's seat. Unfortunately, her pessimism proved well founded.

Southbound traffic passed in the oncoming lanes: a big rig with a lead-footed driver, a Mercedes close in its wake—then, following a long gap, a Ford. Chyna paid special attention to the cars, hoping that one of them would be a police cruiser.

If she spotted a cop, she intended to get his attention with the car horn and by making a weaving spectacle of herself in his rearview mirror. If she was too late with the horn and if the cop didn't look back and catch a glimpse of her reckless slalom, she would turn and pursue him, reluctantly letting the motor home out of her sight.

She wasn't hopeful about finding a cop anytime soon.

All the luck seemed to be with the killer. He conducted himself with a confidence that unnerved Chyna. Perhaps that confidence was the only guarantor of his good luck—although even for one as rooted in reality as Chyna, it was easy to let superstition overwhelm her, attributing to him powers dark and supernatural.

No. He was only a man.

And now she had a revolver. She was no longer helpless.

The worst was past.

Lightning traveled the northern sky again, but this time it was not pale or diffused through cloud layers. The bolts were as bright as though the naked sun were breaking through from the other side of the night.

In those stroboscopic flashes, the motor home seemed to vibrate, as if divine wrath would shatter it and its driver.

In this world, however, retribution was left to mortal men and women. God was content to wait for the next life to mete out punishment; in Chyna's view, this was His only cruel aspect, but in this was cruelty enough.

Explosions of thunder followed the lightning. Although something above should have broken, nothing did, and the rain remained bottled higher in the night.

She hoped to spot a sign for a highway patrol depot, where she could seek help, but none appeared. The nearest town of appreciable size, where she might be fortunate enough to find a police station or a cruising squad car, was Eureka, which was hardly a metropolis. And even Eureka was at least an hour away.

As a child, flat under beds and curled in the backs of closets, perched on rooftops and balanced in the upper reaches of trees, in winter barns and on warm night beaches, she had hidden and waited out the passions and the rages of adults, always with dread but also with patience and with a Zen-like disconnection from the realities of time. Now impatience plagued her as never before. She wanted to see this man caught, manacled, harried to justice, *hurt*. Desperately she wanted this and without a single additional minute of delay, *before he could kill again*. Her own survival wasn't currently at stake but that of a teenage girl whom she had never met, and she was surprised—and made uneasy—to discover that she could care so ferociously about a stranger.

Perhaps she had always possessed that capacity and simply had never been in a situation that required recognition of it. But no. That was self-deception. Ten years ago, she would never have followed the motor home. Nor five years ago. Nor last year. Perhaps not even yesterday.

Something had profoundly changed her, and it hadn't been the brutality that she'd seen a few hours earlier at the Templeton house. Viscerally she was aware that this unsettling metamorphosis had been a long time coming, like the slow alteration in a river's course—by imperceptible fractions of a degree, day after day. Then suddenly mere survival was not enough for her any longer; the final palisade of soil crumbled, the last stone shifted, and the destination of the river changed.

She frightened herself. This reckless caring.

More lightning, more ferocious than before, revealed redwood trees so massive that they reminded her of cathedral spires. The steeple-shattering light was followed by quakes of thunder as violent as any shift in the San Andreas. The sky fissured, and rain fell.

In the first instant, the drops were fat and milky white in the head-lights, as if the night were an extinguished chandelier in which were suspended an infinite number of rock-crystal pendants. They shat-tered into the windshield, against the hood, across the blacktop.

On the highway ahead, the motor home began to disappear into the downpour.

In seconds the drops dwindled drastically in size even as they in-creased in number. They became silver gray in the headlamps, and fell not straight down as before but at an angle in the punishing wind.

Chyna switched the windshield wipers to their highest setting, but the motor home continued to slip rapidly away into the storm as visi-bility declined. The killer was not lowering his speed in respect of the worsening weather; he was accelerating.

Afraid to let him out of her sight for as much as a second, Chyna closed the gap between them to about two hundred feet. She was wor-ried that he would attach the correct significance to her maneuver and realize that somehow she was onto him.

Southbound traffic had been sparse to begin with, but now it de-clined in direct proportion to the power of the escalating storm, as though most motorists had been washed off the highway.

No headlights appeared in the rearview mirror either. The psy-chotic in the motor home had set a pace that no one but Chyna was likely to match.

She felt almost as alone with him here in the open as she had been inside his abattoir on wheels.

Then, as enough time passed to make the lonely lanes of blacktop and the dreary cataracts of rain less threatening than monotonous, the killer suddenly surprised her. With a quick touch of his brakes, with-out bothering to use a turn signal, he angled to the right onto an exit lane.

Chyna fell back somewhat, again concerned that he would become suspicious, seeing her take the same exit. Because theirs were the only two vehicles in sight, she could not be inconspicuous. But she had no choice other than to follow him.

By the time she reached the end of the ramp, the motor home had vanished into the rain and thin mist, but from the ramp entrance, she had seen it turn left. In fact, the two-lane road led only west, and a sign indicated that she was already within the boundaries of Humboldt Redwood State Park.

In addition, three communities lay ahead: Honeydew, Petrolia, and Capetown. She'd never heard of any of them, and she was sure that they were little more than wide places in the road, where she would find no police.

Leaning forward over the steering wheel, squinting through the rain-smeared windshield, she drove into the park, eager to catch up with the killer again, because he might live in or near one of those three small towns. She was wise to let him out of sight for a minute, so he wouldn't think that she was too eager to stay on his tail. But soon she would need to reestablish visual contact before he reached the far side of the park and, perhaps thereafter, turned off the county road onto a driveway or a private lane.

The deeper the road wound among the heaven-reaching trees, the less forcefully the rain beat against the Honda. The storm was not diminishing at all, but the huge ramparts of redwoods sheltered the pavement from the worst of the deluge.

On this narrower, twisting route, it wasn't possible to maintain the pace they had kept on Highway 101. Furthermore, the killer apparently had decided that he no longer needed to make good time, perhaps because he'd put what seemed a safe distance between himself and the dead men at the service station, and when Chyna caught up with him in hardly more than a minute, he was driving under the posted speed limit.

Now, closer than she'd been before, she noticed that the motor home didn't have license plates. California—and some other states, for all she knew—didn't issue temporary plates for a newly purchased vehicle, and it was legal to drive without the tags until they came in the mail from the Department of Motor Vehicles. Or perhaps before going to the Templetons' house, the killer had removed his plates rather than risk a witness with a good memory.

Easing off the accelerator, Chyna glanced at the speedometer—and spotted a red warning light. The fuel-gauge needle was below the EMPTY mark.

She had no idea how long the warning light had been burning, because she'd been concentrating intently on the motor home and the dangers of the slick pavement. The car might have a gallon or two in the tank—or even now be running on its last pint.

Trailing the killer to his home base was no longer an option.

The meaning of redwoods is not grandeur, beauty, peace, or the timelessness of nature. The meaning of redwoods is power.

As he drives, Edgler Vess rolls down the window beside him and draws deep breaths of the cold air, which is rich with the fragrance of redwoods, which is a scent of power. This power flows into him with the fragrance, and his own power is thus enhanced.

Redwoods are power because their great size is unmatched by any other trees, because they are ancient—many of these very specimens dating back centuries before the birth of Jesus Christ—because their extraordinary bark, as thick as armor and high in tannin, makes them all but impervious to insects, disease, and fire. They are power because they endure while all around them dies; men and animals pass among them and pass forever away; birds alight in their high branches and seem freer than anything rooted in rock and soil, but eventually, in a sudden quietness of the heart, the birds swoon off the sturdy limbs and thump to the ground or plummet from the sky, and the trees still soar; on the shadowed floors of these groves, sun-shy ferns and rhododendrons flourish season after season, but their immortality is illusory, for they too die, and new generations of their species rise in the decomposing remains of the old. Christ expired on a cross of dogwood, the prince of peace and prophet of love, but in the span of His life, not one of these trees had been brought down by any storm; though they cared not about peace and knew nothing of love, they had endured. Busily engaged on his endless harvests, Death casts frenetic shadows among the indifferent redwoods, a ceaseless flickering that dances across their massive trunks with no effect, like the dark equivalent of leaping firelight on hearthstones.

Power is living while others inevitably perish. Power is cool indifference to their suffering. Power is taking nourishment from the deaths of others, just as the mighty redwoods draw sustenance from the perpetual decomposition of what once lived, but lived only briefly, around them. This is also part of the philosophy of Edgler Foreman Vess.

Through the open window, he breathes in the scent of redwoods, and the molecules of their fragrance adhere to the surface cells of his lungs, and the power of millennia is conveyed therefrom into his freshly oxygenated blood, pumps through his heart, reaches to every extremity of him, filling him with strength and energy.

Power is God, God is nature, nature is power, and the power is in him.

His power is ever increasing.

If he worshiped, he would be an ardent pantheist, committed to the belief that all things are sacred, every tree and every flower and every blade of grass, every bird and every beetle. The world is full of pantheists these days; he would be at home among them if he were to join their ranks. When everything is sacred, *nothing* is. For him, that is the beauty of pantheism. If the life of a child is equal to the life of a bluegill or a barn owl, then Vess may kill attractive little girls as casually as he might crush a scorpion underfoot, with no greater moral offense though with considerably more pleasure.

But he worships nothing.

As he rounds a curve into a straightaway flanked by redwoods of even greater girth than any he has previously seen, stark white bones of lightning crack through the black skin of the sky. A roar of thunder like a bellow of rage shudders the air.

Rain washes the smell of lightning down through the night. Two scents of power, lightning and redwoods—electricity and time, fierce heat and stolid endurance—are offered to him now, and he inhales deeply with pleasure.

Taking this county road through the redwoods, along the coast, and reconnecting with Highway 101 south of Eureka will add between half an hour and an hour to his travel time, depending on the pace he sets and the strength of the storm. But as eager as he is to get home to Ariel, he could not have resisted the power of the redwoods.

Headlights appear behind him, visible in the angled side mirror. A car. For nearly an hour, one followed him on the freeway, hanging at a distance. This must be a different vehicle, because this driver is more aggressive than the one on the freeway, closing the distance between them at high speed.

Recklessly, the car—a Honda—pulls around the motor home, into the lane reserved for oncoming traffic, though this is not a passing zone. There is no other traffic, and they are on a straightaway, but the Honda has insufficient distance to complete the maneuver before the next blind turn in the road, especially on the treacherous rain-slick blacktop.

Vess reduces speed.

The racing Honda pulls alongside him.

Looking down through the windshield of the car, Vess has barely a glimpse of the person behind the steering wheel, because the rain and the high-speed windshield wipers inhibit his view. Nothing more than a suggestion of a deep-red shirt or sweater. A pale hand on the wheel. The wrist is slender enough to indicate that the driver is most likely a woman. She appears to be alone. Then the car moves far enough forward so that Vess is looking down on the roof, and the windshield is out of sight.

They are rapidly approaching the curve.

Vess further reduces his speed.

Through his open window, he listens to the shriek of the Honda as the driver accelerates. All the formidable power of that engine seems pathetically weak in these majestic groves, like the angry buzz of a gnat among a herd of elephants.

With so little effort that he would not increase his heartbeat, Vess could pull the wheel to the left, slam the motor home into the Honda, and force the car off the road. It would either roll and then explode— or shatter head-on into one of the twenty-foot-diameter redwood trunks.

He is tempted.

The spectacle would be gratifying.

He spares the woman in the Honda only because he's in a mood for subtle—rather than explosive—sensation. This gratifying expedition has brought him not merely the Napa Valley family that he originally set out to destroy, but the hitchhiker now hanging in the bedroom closet like Poe's lover of Amontillado in the stone wall of a wine cellar, as well as the two clerks at the service station. This is already a satiating richness. The reef of the soul is built from varied experience, not from repetitive sensation. Right now he doesn't need the somber music of blood and the spurting warmth of screams; instead, he needs to smell the wetness of the rain, feel the towering mass of the trees, and listen to the cool pendulousness of the night-hidden ferns.

He applies the brakes, cutting his speed.

The Honda streaks past him, kicking up a high spray of dirty water. It enters the curve ahead with a flash of brake lights: red in the black storm, red glimmering off the damp gray bark of the big conifers, apocalyptic tracers of red rippling across the pavement. Then gone.

Edgler Vess is alone again, behind the wheel of his ark, in a color-less world of gray rain, black shadows, and sparkling white headlight beams, at peace to commune with the redwoods and draw from them a measure of their power.

He thinks of Christ on the vertical bed of dogwood, and the idea of the meek inheriting the earth makes him smile. He doesn't wish to inherit anything. He is a raging fire, powerful and hot; he will burn all the color out of this world, consume every scintilla of sensation that it has to offer, and he will leave behind a realm of ashes. Let the meek inherit ashes.

Passing the motor home, going too fast to prevent the Honda from straddling the double yellow line all the way around the curve, Chyna had been afraid that the parched engine would cough and choke and fail. Now that she had seen the red warning light, she was aware of it—a peripheral radiance—even when she wasn't looking at the in-strument panel. But the Honda ran confidently on dregs, on fumes, on some strange grace.

She needed to put distance between herself and the killer, and gain time to set her plan in motion. She pushed the car as hard as she dared on the storm-greased pavement.

The narrow road rounded another bend, straightened out, entered a gradual descent, took another curve, rose on a gentle slope, but de-scended again, and in spite of the intermittent interruptions of these extremely low inclines, the land was generally monotonous in its con-tours, making its way steadily down toward the Pacific, not many miles to the west. Now low ramparts of soft earth flanked the black-top just beyond both shoulders, and this wasn't suitable for her pur-poses. But then the road returned to the same level as the surrounding forest, and she entered another almost imperceptibly declining straightaway and found the ideal circumstances she required.

She figured that she had gained a full minute on him, maybe a minute and a half, depending on whether he had appreciably in-creased his speed after she passed him. Anyway, a minute should be long enough.

She slowed to thirty miles an hour and nonetheless seemed to be *hurtling* through the woods. She let the speed decrease to twenty-five, wondering again about her headlong rush to heroism but still unable to fully understand it. Then she drove off the roadway, flew across the right shoulder, thumped through a shallow drainage swale, and rammed into the fortress base of one of the biggest of the redwoods. The left headlight burst, the impact-absorbing bumper cracked and crumpled and collapsed as it had been designed to do, and metal shrieked briefly.

Because she was wearing a safety harness, she wasn't thrown into the steering wheel or through the windshield. But the diagonal strap tightened so hard across her breasts that she grunted with shock and pain.

The engine was still running.

With no time to get out and inspect the front of the car, Chyna was afraid that the damage wasn't sufficiently impressive to convince the killer that someone could have been injured in the crash. When he came upon this scene a few seconds from now, he must take everything at face value without hesitation. Otherwise, if he was suspicious, nothing would work as she had planned.

Immediately she shifted the Honda into reverse and backed away from the tree, which stood inviolate. The ground was carpeted with wet redwood needles on which the tires spun before gripping, but not enough rain had fallen to churn the earth into mud. Rattling and clinking, the car bounced across the shallow drainage swale, which ran with only an inch or two of muddy water, and backed onto the pavement again.

Chyna glanced toward the top of the gently ascending slope down which she had just driven. As yet there was not even a faint glow of approaching headlights from beyond the curve.

He was coming. No doubt about that.

Soon.

She didn't have time to reverse even part of the way up the slope. But she needed to build a little speed.

With her left foot, she tramped the brake pedal as far toward the floorboards as it would go, and with her right foot she eased down on the accelerator. The engine whined, then shrieked. The car strained like a spurred horse pressing against the gate of a rodeo chute. She could feel it wanting to surge forward, as if it were a living thing, and she wondered how much acceleration would be too much, enough to kill her or trap her in wreckage. Then she gave it a little more juice, smelled something burning, and raised her left foot from the brake pedal.

The tires spun furiously on the glistering blacktop, and then with a shudder the Honda shot forward, rattled and splashed across the ditch, and slammed into the trunk of the redwood. The right headlight burst, metal squealed, the hood crumpled and tweaked and popped open with a sound oddly like a hard strum on a banjo, but the windshield didn't shatter.

The engine stuttered. Either the fuel had been exhausted at last or the crash had done severe mechanical damage.

Gasping for breath after the cinching punishment of the shoulder harness, praying that the engine wouldn't fail just yet, Chyna popped the car into reverse again.

Ideally, the Honda would be blocking the road when the killer came around the bend. She had to force him to stop—and to get out of his motor home.

The battered car wheezed, almost stalled, then unexpectedly revved, and Chyna said gratefully, "Jesus," as it rolled backward onto the pavement.

She pulled across both lanes but swung around a little, angling the car uphill so the killer would be able to see the damaged front end as soon as he negotiated the curve.

The engine clunked twice and died, but that was all right. She was in position.

Without the engine noise for competition, the rain seemed to be falling more forcefully than before, rattling on the roof and snapping against the glass.

At the upper curve, darkness still held.

She put the Honda in park, so it would not coast backward when she took her foot off the brake.

The headlights were both broken out, but the windshield wipers continued to thump back and forth, operating on battery power. She didn't switch them off.

She opened the driver's door and, feeling horribly exposed in the dome light, started to get out. She needed to be away from the car and in hiding by the time the motor home appeared—which would be in maybe twenty seconds, maybe ten, hard to say because she had lost track of how much time had passed since she herself had driven around the bend.

The gun.

Before she fully escaped the car, Chyna remembered the revolver. She swung back inside, reached for the weapon—but it was no longer on the seat.

In the first or second crash, the gun must have been thrown onto the floor. Leaning across the console between the front seats, she felt frantically in the darkness, found cold steel, the barrel, her finger actually slipping into the smooth muzzle. With a wordless murmur of relief, she fished the gun from the foot space and reversed her grip on it.

With the weapon firmly in hand, she scrambled out of the Honda. She left the driver's door standing open.

Rain chilled her, and wind.

In the direction from which she had come, the night brightened faintly, and the redwood trunks near the shoulder of the curve began to glow as if in the radiance of a sudden moon.

Chyna sprinted off the slippery blacktop and splashed through another shallow drainage ditch, shuddering as the icy water poured over the tops of her shoes. On this side of the pavement, the trees were set back twenty or thirty feet from the shoulder. She headed for the colossal woods at a point directly across the highway from the behemoth into which she had driven the Honda.

Long before she reached the nearest tree, she skidded on the spongy mat of wet needles, fell, and landed on a cluster of redwood cones. The cones crumbled slightly—a hard crunching sound against the small of her back—although judging by the flash of pain, it almost seemed as though her spine was the source of the cracking.

She would have preferred to crawl on her hands and knees to concealment, but she had to hold on to the revolver, and she was concerned that, crawling, she would inadvertently plug the barrel with dirt or wet needles. She was up and moving at once, therefore, as the highway behind her flared with light and an engine quarreled noisily with the storm.

The motor home had turned the bend.

She was only fifteen feet or so from the highway, which wasn't far enough, because there was little underbrush to provide cover beneath the giant redwoods—largely ferns, and more of them in the gloom ahead than in the area immediately around her. He must not see her. All was lost if he glimpsed her as she dashed for cover.

Fortunately, her blue jeans were dark, not stone-washed and highly reflective, and her sweater was cranberry red, which was not as bad as if it had been white or yellow, and her hair was not blond but dark. Yet she could have felt no more visible if she had been trying to run to cover in a wedding dress.

He would be focused on the Honda, surprised to see it angled across both lanes. He wouldn't immediately glance to either side of the highway, and when his attention did flicker away from the car, he was likely to look to the right, where the Honda had run off the road and struck the tree, not to the left, where Chyna was seeking shelter.

Telling herself that she was safe and had not been seen, but not actually believing herself, she reached the first phalanx of massive redwoods. They grew astonishingly close to one another, considering their daunting size. She slipped around the deeply corrugated trunk of a fifteen-foot-diameter giant that thrived in such intimacy with an even larger specimen that the passageway between the towering pair was less than two feet.

The lowest branches above her were a hundred fifty to a hundred eighty feet off the ground, visible only when lightning backlit them. Standing between these trunks was rather like standing between the nave columns of a cathedral too large ever to be built this side of Heaven; the bristled boughs formed majestic vaults fifteen stories overhead.

From her damp and cloistered retreat, she peered out warily at the highway.

Beyond the lacy screen of low ferns, silver plating the rain and growing brighter by the second, came the headlights of the motor home. They were accompanied by the soft pule of air brakes.

Mr. Vess stops on the pavement, as the shoulder is neither wide enough nor firm enough to accommodate his motor home. Although this scenic highway is obviously little used in these hours before dawn and in such foul weather as this, he is loath to block traffic any longer than is absolutely necessary. He well knows the California Vehicle Code.

He pushes the gearshift into park, engages the emergency brake, but leaves the engine running and the headlights on. He doesn't bother to slip into his raincoat, and when he gets out of the motor home, he leaves the door standing open.

The rain on the pavement is a drumming, and on the metal of the vehicles a singing, and on the foliage of the trees a chorus chanting wordlessly. The rain sounds please him, as does the chill, as does the fecund smell of ferns and loamy soil.

This is the same Honda that passed him a few minutes earlier. He is not surprised to see it in this sorry condition, considering the reckless speed at which it had been traveling.

Evidently, the car had skidded off the road and into the tree. Then the driver had backed it onto the pavement again before the engine failed.

But where is the driver?

Another motorist might have come along from the west and taken any injured person to get medical treatment. But that seems too fortuitous and too timely. After all, the accident can't have happened more than a minute or two ago.

The driver's door is open, and when Vess leans inside, he sees that the keys are in the ignition. The windshield wipers sweep the glass. The taillights, the interior ceiling light, and the gauges in the instrument panel are all aglow.

He steps away from the car and looks at the tree toward which the tire tracks lead. The bark is scarred from the impact but only superficially.

Intrigued, he surveys the rest of the grove on that side of the highway.

Quite possibly, the driver climbed out of the wrecked car, dazed from a blow to the head, and wandered into the redwoods. Even now she might be traveling farther into the primeval grove, lost and confused—or maybe, having collapsed from injuries, she lies unconscious in a fern glade.

The closely grown trees form a maze of narrow corridors, more wood than open space. Even at high noon on a cloudless day, sunshine would penetrate to the forest floor only in a few thin bright blades, and stubborn darkness would impose itself in most of these deep reaches, as though each of the many hundreds of thousands of nights since the grove's beginning had left its residue of shadows. Now, still on the witching side of dawn, that blackness is so pure that it seems almost like a thing alive, crouching and predatory and yet welcoming.

This special darkness stirs Mr. Vess and makes him yearn for experiences that he senses are available to him but that he cannot imagine, experiences that are mysterious and transforming, yet which he cannot even dimly envision. Far into the redwoods, down corridors of fissured bark, in some secret citadel of bestial passion, where shadows dwell that are older than human history, a mystical adventure awaits.

If the woman, in fact, is wandering in the woods, he could park the motor home and search for her. Perhaps the knife that he found at the service station is an omen, after all, and hers may be the blood that he is meant to draw with that blade.

He imagines what it would be like to take off his clothes and enter the grove naked with the knife, relying solely on his primitive instincts to stalk her and bring her down, the rain and mist cold on his skin, the air steaming once he has breathed it, unchilled by the rain but imparting his heat to the night, tearing ferociously at the woman's clothes as he drags her to the forest floor. He is already erect with the dream of it, but he wonders if he would attack her first with knife or phallus—or perhaps with his teeth. That decision would be made in the moment of capture, and much would depend on how attractive she was; but he is convinced that whatever might happen between them would be unprecedented and mysterious—and inexpressibly *intense*.

Dawn is coming in an hour or so, however, and he would be wise to be on his way. He must put more distance between himself and the places where he took his entertainment during the night.

Being good at being Edgler Vess requires, among other qualities, the ability to repress his most ardent passions when indulgence in them is dangerous. If he instantly gratified every desire, he would be less a man than an animal—and either long dead or imprisoned. Being Edgler Vess means being free but not reckless, being quick but not impulsive. He must have a sense of proportion. And good timing. Hell, he needs the timing of a tap-dance master. And a nice smile. A truly nice smile combined with self-control can take a person a long way.

He smiles at the forest.

The motor home stood on the pavement, approximately twenty feet from the battered Honda, shrunken in appearance because the redwoods dwarfed it.

As the killer had walked down the roadway to the abandoned car through the headlight beams from the motor home, Chyna had crept upslope through the dark forest, moving parallel to him but in the opposite direction. She had circled behind the tree to the right of her, gripping the revolver in her right hand, with her left hand flat against the trunk for balance in case she stumbled over a root or other obstruction. Under her palm, she had felt the deep pattern of repetitive Gothic arches formed by the fissures in the thick bark. With each uncertain step that she had taken around this great easy curve, she had felt that the tree was less like a tree than like a building, a windowless fortress erected against all the rage of the world.

After navigating a hemisphere of the trunk to the shoulder-wide gap between this tree and the next, she peered out once more. The killer stood near the open door of the Honda, gazing into the forest on the far side of the highway.

She was worried that another motorist would come along before she could carry out her plan.

She moved on, circling the next tree. It was even larger than the previous behemoth. The bark featured the familiar Gothic patterns.

In spite of the shrill wind keening high above and collected drizzles of rain spattering down from the lofty branches, the grove impressed her as a good safe place, dark but not in spirit, cold but not forbidding. She was still alone in her troubles—but curiously, for the first time all night, she didn't *feel* alone.

At the next trunk-framed gap in the forest wall, Chyna looked out again and saw the killer getting into the Honda. He would have to move the disabled car out of the way, because there wasn't room to drive around it.

She glanced at the motor home. Perhaps because she knew what lay within it—a dead man closeted in chains, a dead woman swaddled in a white shroud—the vehicle seemed as ominous as any war machine.

She could just wait in the grove. Forget about her plan. He would leave, and life would go on.

So easy to wait. Survive.

The police would find the girl. Ariel. Somehow. In time. Without the need for heroics.

Chyna leaned against the tree, suddenly weak. Weak and shaking. Shaking and almost physically ill with despair, with fear.

The taillights and interior lights of the Honda dimmed with the grinding of the starter, as the killer tried to get the engine to turn over.

Then another noise came to Chyna. Much closer than the car. Behind her. A rustle, a snap, a soft snort like a startled horse exhaling.

Frightened, she turned.

In the backwash of light from the motor home out on the highway, Chyna saw angels in the redwood grove. Or so it seemed for a moment. Regarding her were gentle faces, pale in the darkness, eyes luminous and inquisitive and kind.

But even in that meager moonlike glow, she was unable to sustain a hope of angels. After a brief initial confusion, she realized that these creatures were a breed of coastal elk without antlers.

Six stood together in a fifteen-foot-wide space between this outer row of trees and the deeper growth, so close that Chyna could have been among them in three steps. Their noble heads were lifted, ears pricked, gazes fixed intently on her.

The elk were curious, but although timid by nature, they seemed oddly unafraid of her.

Once, for two months, she and her mother had stayed on a ranch in Mendocino County, where a group of well-armed survivalists waited for the race wars that they believed would soon destroy the nation, and in that doomsday atmosphere, Chyna had spent as much time as possible exploring the surrounding countryside, hills and vales of singular beauty, groves of pines, golden fields where scattered oaks stood—each alone and huge and black-limbed against the sky—and where small herds of coastal elk appeared from time to time, always keeping at a distance from human beings and their works. She had stalked them not as a hunter but with awkward girlish guile, as shy as the elk themselves but irresistibly attracted to the tranquillity and the peace that they radiated in a world otherwise saturated with violence.

In those two months, she had never managed to get closer than eighty or ninety feet to the elk herds before they had reacted to her nonchalant approach, whidding to farther fields and ridges.

Now *they* had approached *her*, vigilant but not frightened, as if they were the same elk of her childhood, at long last willing to believe in her peaceable intentions.

Coastal elk should have been somewhat closer to the sea, in the open meadows beyond the redwoods, where the grass was lush and green from the winter rains, where the grazing was good. Although they were not strangers to the forest, their presence here, in the rainy predawn darkness, was remarkable.

Then she saw others in addition to the herd of six—one here, one there, and there a third, and still more—between trees, at a greater distance than the initial group. Some were barely visible in the bosky grove, at the extreme reach of the backwash from the motor-home headlights, but she thought that there were as many as a dozen altogether, all standing at attention, as though transfixed by woodland music beyond human hearing.

Lightning spread branches across the sky, put down jagged roots toward the earth, and briefly brightened the grove sufficiently for Chyna to see all the elk more clearly than before. More of them than she had thought. In mist and ferns, among flowering red rhododendron, revealed by fluttering leaves of light. Heads lifted, their breath steaming from black nostrils. Their eyes fixed on her.

She looked out at the highway.

The killer had given up trying to start the engine. He put the Honda in gear, and it began to roll backward on the slightly sloped pavement.

After one last glance at the elk, Chyna stepped out from between the two redwoods.

The killer pulled the steering wheel hard to the right, letting the momentum of the car carry it backward in an arc until it was facing downhill.

Through sparse ferns and scattered clumps of bunch grass, Chyna approached the highway. The weakness in her legs was gone, and her spasm of irresolution had passed.

Under the killer's guidance, the Honda coasted downhill and onto the right shoulder.

She could go after him, shoot him in the car or as he got out of the car. But he was fifty yards away now, sixty, and he would surely see her coming. She would have no hope of keeping the advantage of surprise, so she would have to shoot to kill, which would do Ariel no good at all, because with this bastard dead they would still have to search for the girl wherever she was hidden. And they might never find her. Besides, the creep probably had a gun on him, and if this turned into a shooting match, he would win, because he was far more practiced than she was—and bolder.

She had no one to whom she could turn. As in childhood.

So now get out of sight quickly. Don't be rash. Wait for the ideal situation. Pick the moment of the confrontation and control the showdown when it comes.

Fierce lightning again, and a long hard crash of thunder like vast structures collapsing high in the night.

She reached the motor home.

*Oh, God.*

The driver's door stood open.

*Oh, Jesus. Oh, God.*

She couldn't do it.

She *had* to do it.

Downhill, on the shoulder, with a rattle of twisted steel, the Honda was coasting to a stop.

She had the revolver. That made all the difference. She was safe with the gun.

*Who will save this girl hidden in a cellar, this girl ripening for this son-ofabitch bastard freak, this girl like me? Who is ever there for frightened girls hiding in the backs of closets or under beds, who is ever there but twitching palmetto beetles? Who will be there if not me, where will I be if not there, why is this the only choice—and when the answer is so obvious, why even ask why?*

Downslope, the Honda came to a full stop.

With the revolver heavy in her hand, Chyna climbed into the cockpit and behind the steering wheel. She swung around in the driver's seat, got up, and hurried back through the motor home, murmuring, "Jesus, Jesus," telling herself that it was all right, this crazy thing she was doing, all right because this time she had the revolver.

But she wondered if even the gun would give her enough of an edge when the time arrived to go face-to-face with this man.

Of course a direct confrontation might never have to take place. Chyna intended to hide until they arrived at his house and then find out where the girl was being held. With that information, she would be able to go to the police, and they could nail this creep and free Ariel and—

And what?

And in saving the girl, she would save herself. From what, she was not sure. From a life of merely surviving? From the endless and fruitless struggle to understand?

Crazy, crazy, but there was no turning back now. And in her heart she knew that risking all was less crazy than living a life that had no higher goal than survival.

As if thrown forward by the hard knocking of her heart, Chyna reached the rear of the motor home. The closed door to the only bedroom.

*Jesus.*

She didn't want to go in there. With Laura dead. The man in the closet. The sewing kit waiting to be used again.

*Jesus.*

But it was the best place to hide, so she opened the door and went in and closed the door behind her and eased to the left through the palpable darkness and put her back against the wall.

Maybe he wouldn't drive straight home. He might stop at some point between here and there to come to the back of the motor home and have a look at his trophies.

Then she would kill him the instant that he stepped through the door. Empty the revolver into him. Take no chances.

With him dead, they might never find Ariel. Or they might find her only after she had perished of starvation, an excruciatingly painful way to die.

Nevertheless, if the killer entered this bedroom, Chyna wouldn't rely on half measures. She would not attempt to wound him and keep him alive for police interrogation, not in this tight space with him looming over her and with so many ways that things could go wrong.

Lights off, windshield wipers off, Edgler Vess sits in the dead car by the side of the road. Thinking.

There are numerous ways that he can proceed from here. Life is always a laden buffet of treats, a vast smorgasbord groaning with infinite choices of sensations and experiences to thrill the heart—but never more so than now. He wishes to exploit the opportunity to the fullest possible extent, to extract from it the greatest possible excitement and the most poignant sensations, and he must, therefore, not act precipitously.

Luck had given him a glimpse of her in the rearview mirror: as fleet as a deer across the blacktop, hesitating at the open door of the motor home, and then up and inside and out of sight.

She must be the woman from the Honda. When she passed him earlier, he had looked down through the windshield of her car and had seen her red sweater.

In the accident, she might have received a hard blow to the head. Now perhaps she is dazed, confused, frightened. This would explain why she doesn't approach him directly and ask for help or for a ride to the nearest service station. If her thoughts are addled, the irrational decision to become a stowaway aboard the motor home might seem perfectly reasonable to her.

She did not appear to be suffering from a head injury, however, or any injury at all. She hadn't staggered or stumbled across the highway but had been swift and surefooted. At this distance and in the rearview mirror, Vess wouldn't have been able to see blood even if she had been bleeding; but he knows intuitively that there was no blood.

The longer he considers the situation, the more it seems to him that the accident was staged.

But *why?*

If the motive had been robbery, she would have accosted him the moment that he stepped onto the highway.

Besides, he isn't driving one of those elaborate three-hundred-thousand-dollar land yachts that, by their very flashiness, advertise their contents to thieves. His vehicle is seventeen years old and, though well maintained, worth considerably less than fifty thousand bucks. It seems pointless to wreck a relatively new Honda for the purpose of looting the contents of an aging vehicle that promises no treasures.

He has left his keys in the ignition, the engine running. She already could have driven away in the motor home if that had been her intention.

And a woman alone on a lonely highway at night is not likely to be planning a robbery. Such behavior doesn't fit any criminal profile.

He is baffled.

Deeply.

Mr. Vess's simple life is not often touched by mystery. There are things that can be killed and things that can't. Some things are harder to kill than others, and some are more fun to kill than others. Some scream, some weep, some do both, some only tremble silently and wait for the end as if having spent their whole lives in anticipation of this awful pain. Thus the days go by—pleasantly straightforward, a river of raw sensation upon which enigma seldom sets sail.

But this woman in a red sweater is an enigma, all right, as mysterious and intriguing as anyone Mr. Vess has ever known. What experiences he will have with her are difficult to imagine, and he is excited by the prospect of such novelty.

He gets out of the Honda and closes the door.

For a moment he stands staring at the forest in the cold rain, hoping to appear unsuspecting if the woman should be watching him from inside the motor home. Maybe he is wondering what happened to the driver of the Honda. Maybe he is a good citizen, concerned about her and considering a search of the woods.

Multiple bolts of lightning chase across the sky, as white and jagged as running skeletons. The subsequent blasts of thunder are so powerful that they rattle through Mr. Vess's bones, a vibration that he finds most agreeable.

Unfazed by the storm, several elk suddenly appear from out of the forest, drifting between the trees and into the bordering sward of ferns. They move with stately grace, in a silence that is ethereal behind the fading echo of thunder, eyes shining in the backwash of the headlight beams. They seem almost to be apparitions rather than real animals.

Two, five, seven, and yet more of them appear. Some stop as though posing, and others move farther but then stop as well, until now a dozen or more are revealed and standing still, and every one of them is staring at Mr. Vess.

Their beauty is unearthly, and killing them would be enormously satisfying. If he had one of his guns at hand, he would shoot as many of them as he could manage before they bolted beyond range.

As a young boy, he began his work with animals. Actually, he'd begun with insects, but soon he had moved on to turtles and lizards, and then to cats and larger species. As a teenager, as soon as he had gotten a driver's license, he had roamed back roads some nights and in the early mornings before school, shooting deer if he spotted any, stray dogs, cows in fields, and horses in corrals if he was certain that he could get away with it.

He is flushed with nostalgia at the thought of killing these elk. The sight of their blood would intensify the redness of his own and make his arteries sing.

Though usually reticent and easily spooked, the elk stare boldly at him. They do not seem to be watching with alarm, are not in the least skittish or poised to flee. Indeed, their directness strikes him as strange; uncharacteristically, he feels uneasy.

Anyway, the woman in the red sweater awaits him, and she is more interesting than any number of elk. He is a grown man now, no longer a boy, and his quest for intense experiences cannot be satisfactorily conducted along the byways of the past. Edgler Vess has long ago put aside childish things.

He returns to the motor home.

At the door, he sees that the woman is in neither the pilot's nor the copilot's position.

Swinging in behind the steering wheel, he glances back but can see no sign of her in the lounge or the dining area. The short and shadowy hall at the end appears deserted as well.

Facing forward but keeping his eyes on the rearview mirror, he opens the tambour-top console between the seats. His pistol is still there, where he left it, sans silencer.

Pistol in hand, he swivels in his chair, gets up, and moves back through the motor home to the kitchen and dining area. The butcher knife, found on the service-station blacktop, lies on the counter as before. He opens the cabinet to the left of the oven and discovers that the 12-gauge Mossberg is securely in its spring clamps, to which he returned it after killing the two clerks.

He doesn't know if she is armed with a weapon of her own. From the distance at which he'd seen her, he hadn't been able to discern whether she was empty-handed or, equally important, whether she was attractive enough to be a fun kill.

Farther back, then, through his narrow domain, with special caution at the end of the dining nook, behind which lies the step well. She's not crouched here either.

Into the hall.

The sound of the rain. The idling engine.

He opens the bathroom door, quickly and noisily, aware that stealth isn't possible in this reverberant tin can on wheels. The cramped bathroom is as it should be, no stowaway on the pot or in the shower stall.

Next the shallow wardrobe with its sliding door. But she isn't in there either.

The only place remaining to be searched is the bedroom.

Vess stands before this last closed door, positively enchanted by the thought of the woman huddled in there, unaware of those with whom she shares her hiding place.

No thread of light is visible along the threshold or the jamb, so she no doubt entered in darkness. Evidently she has not yet sat upon the bed and found the sleeping beauty.

Perhaps she has edged warily around the small room and, by blind exploration, has discovered the folding door to the closet. Perhaps if Vess opens this bedroom door, she will simultaneously pull aside those vinyl panels and attempt to slip swiftly and quietly into the closet, only to feel a strange cold form hanging there instead of sport shirts.

Mr. Vess is amused.

The temptation to throw open the door is almost irresistible, to see her carom off the body in the closet, then to the bed, then away from the dead girl, screaming first at the sewn-shut face of the boy and then at the manacled girl and then at Vess himself, in a comic pinball spin of terror.

Following that spectacle, however, they will have to get down to issues at once. He will quickly learn who she is and what she thinks she is doing here.

Mr. Vess realizes that he doesn't want this rare experience with mystery to end. He finds it more pleasing to prolong the suspense and chew on the puzzle for a while.

He was beginning to feel weary from his recent activities. Now he is energized by these unexpected developments.

Certain risks are involved, of course, in playing it this way. But it is impossible to live with intensity and avoid risk. Risk is at the heart of an intense existence.

He backs quietly away from the bedroom door.

Noisily, he steps into the bathroom, takes a piss, and flushes the toilet, so the woman will think that he came to the back of the motor home not in search of her but to answer the call of nature. If she continues to believe that her presence is unknown, she will proceed on whatever course of action brought her here in the first place, and it will be interesting to see what she does.

He goes forward again, pausing in the kitchen to pump a cup of hot coffee from the two-quart thermos on the counter by the cooktop. He also switches on a couple of lights so he will be able to see the interior clearly in the rearview mirror.

Behind the steering wheel once more, he sips the coffee. It is hot, black, and bitter, just the way he likes it. He secures the cup in a holder bracketed to the dashboard.

He tucks the pistol in the open console box between the seats, with the safeties off and the butt up. He can put his hand on it in a second, turn in his seat, shoot the woman before she can get near him, and still maintain control of the motor home.

But he doesn't think that she will try to harm him, at least not soon. If harming him was her primary intention, she would have gone after him already.

Strange.

"Why? What now?" he says aloud, enjoying the drama of his peculiar situation. "What now? What next? What ho? Surprise, surprise."

He drinks more coffee. The aroma reminds him of the crisp texture of burned toast.

Outside, the elk are gone.

A night of mysteries.

The mounting wind lashes the long fronds of the ferns. Like evidence of violence, bright wet rhododendron blossoms spray through the night.

The forest stands untouched. The power of time is stored in those massive, dark, vertical forms.

Mr. Vess shifts the motor home out of park and releases the emergency brake. Onward.

After he cruises past the damaged Honda, he glances at the rearview mirror. The bedroom door remains closed. The woman is in hiding.

With the motor home rolling again, perhaps the stowaway will risk turning on a light and will take this opportunity to meet her roommates.

Mr. Vess smiles.

Of all the expeditions that he has conducted, this is the most interesting and exciting. And it isn't over yet.

Chyna sat on the floor in the darkness. Her back was against the wall. The revolver lay at her side.

She was untouched and alive.

"Chyna Shepherd, untouched and alive," she whispered, and this was both a prayer and a joke.

Throughout her childhood, she frequently prayed earnestly for that double blessing—her virtue and her life—and her prayers were often as rambling and incoherent as they were frantic. Eventually she had worried that God was growing weary of her endless desperate pleas for deliverance, that He was sick of her inability to take care of herself and stay out of trouble, and that He might decide that she had used up all of the divine mercy allotted to her. God was busy, after all, running the entire universe, watching over so many drunks and fools, with the devil working mischief everywhere, volcanoes erupting, sailors lost in storms, sparrows falling. By the time Chyna was ten or eleven, in consideration of God's hectic schedule, she had condensed her rambling pleas, in times of terror, to this: "God, this is Chyna Shepherd, here in"—fill the blank with the name of the current place—"and I'm begging you, please, please, please, just let me get through this untouched and alive." Soon, realizing that God, being God, would know precisely where she was, she reduced her entreaty further to: "God, this is Chyna Shepherd. Please get me through this untouched and alive." Finally, certain that God was exasperatedly familiar with her panicky presumptions on His time and grace, she had shortened her plea to a telegraphic minimum: "Chyna Shepherd, untouched and alive." In crises—under beds or lost in closets behind concealing clothes or in cobwebbed attics smelling of dust and raw wood or, once, flattened against the ground in a mire of rat shit in the crawl space under a moldering old house—she had whispered those five words or chanted them silently, over and over, indefatigably, *Chyna-Shepherd-untouched-and-alive*, ceaselessly reciting them not because she was afraid that God might be distracted by other business and fail to hear her but to remind herself that He was out there, had received her message, and would take care of her if she was patient. And when each crisis passed, when the black flood of terror receded, when her stuttering heart finally began to speak each beat clearly and calmly again, she had repeated the five words once more but with a different inflection than she had used previously, not as a plea for deliverance this time but as a dutiful report, *Chyna-Shepherd-untouched-and-alive*, much as a sailor in wartime might report to his captain after the ship had survived a vigorous strafing by enemy planes—"All present and accounted for, sir." She was present; she was accounted for; and she let God know of her gratitude with the same five words, figuring that He would hear the difference in her inflection and would understand. It had become a little joke with young Chyna, and some-times she had even accompanied the report with a salute, which seemed all right because she had figured that God, being God, must have a sense of humor.

"Chyna Shepherd, untouched and alive."

This time, from the motor-home bedroom, it was simultaneously a report on her survival and a fervent prayer to be spared from what-ever brutality might be coming next.

"Chyna Shepherd, untouched and alive."

As a little girl, she had loathed her name—except when she had been praying to survive. It was frivolous, a stupid misspelling of a real word, and when other kids teased her about it, she wasn't able to mount a defense. Considering that her mother was called Anne, such a simple name, the choice of *Chyna* seemed not merely frivolous but thoughtless and even mean. During most of the time that Anne was pregnant, she had lived in a commune of radical environmentalists— a cell of the infamous Earth Army—who believed that any degree of violence was justifiable in defense of nature. They had spiked trees with the hope that loggers would lose hands in accidents with power saws. They had burned down two meat-packing plants and the hap-less night watchmen in them, sabotaged the construction equipment at new housing tracts that encroached upon the wilds, and killed a sci-entist at Stanford because they disapproved of his use of animals in his laboratory experiments. Influenced by these friends, Anne Shepherd had considered many names for her daughter: Hyacinth, Meadow, Ocean, Sky, Snow, Rain, Leaf, Butterfly. . . . By the time she had given birth, however, she had moved on from the Earth Army, and she had named Chyna after China because, as she had once explained, "Honey, I just suddenly realized one day that China is the only just so-ciety on earth, and it seemed like a beautiful name." She had never been able to recall why she had changed the *i* to *y*, though by then she had been a working partner in a methamphetamine lab, packaging speed in affordable five-dollar hits and sampling the merchandise often enough to have been left with a few blank days in her memory. Only when praying for deliverance had young Chyna *liked* her name, because she had figured that God would remember her more easily for it, would not get her confused with the millions of Marys and Car-olines and Lindas and Heathers and Tracys and Janes.

Now her name no longer dismayed or pleased her. It was just a name like any other.

She had learned that who she was—the true *person* she was—had nothing whatsoever to do with her name, and little to do with the life that she'd led with her mother for sixteen years. She couldn't be blamed for the dreadful hates and lusts she had seen, for the obscenities heard, for the crimes witnessed, or for the things that some of her mother's male friends had wanted from her. She was not defined either by a name or by shameful experience; instead, she was formed by dreams and hopes, by aspirations, by self-respect and perseverance. She wasn't clay in the hands of others; she was rock, and with her own determined hands, she could sculpt the person that she wanted to be.

She hadn't reached this realization until a year ago, when she was twenty-five. The wisdom had come to her not in a dazzling flash but slowly, in the way that a plot of bare earth is covered gradually by creeping ajuga until one day, as if miraculously, the brown dirt is gone and everywhere are emerald-green leaves and tiny blue flowers. Worthwhile knowledge always seemed hard-won while the winning was in progress—but seemed easily acquired in retrospect.

The old motor home lumbered through the night, creaking like a long-sealed door, ticking like a rusted clock too corroded to register every second faithfully, toward dawn.

Crazy. Crazy to be taking this trip.

But nowhere else to go.

This was where her entire life had been leading. Reckless courage wasn't restricted to the battlefield—or to men.

She was wet and cold and frightened—and strangely, for the first time in her entire life, she was at peace with herself.

"Ariel," Chyna said softly, one girl in the darkness speaking reassuringly to another.

**6**

Mr. Vess drives out of the redwoods into a drizzling dawn, first iron gray and then somewhat paler, through coastal meadows the same drear shades of metal as the sky, back onto Highway 101, into forests again, but of pine and spruce this time, out of Humboldt County into Del Norte County, ever more isolated terrain, eventually leaving 101 for a route that leads north-northeast.

For the first part of the journey, he glances frequently at the rearview mirror, but the bedroom door remains closed, and the woman seems comfortable with the cadavers or, perhaps, with her ignorance of them. In her retreat, the window is sealed off with plywood, and the light of dawn doesn't penetrate.

Vess is a superb driver, and he makes excellent time, even in bad weather. We do best those things that we enjoy doing, which is why Mr. Vess is such a success at killing and why he combines that enthusiasm with his love of driving rather than restrict himself to prey within a reasonable radius of his home.

Being on the open road with landscapes ever changing, Edgler Vess is the recipient of a constant influx of fresh visual sensation. And of course, to one with his exquisitely refined senses and his ability to use them in a hologrammatic manner, a beautiful sight can also be a musical sound. A scent caught through the open window can be not solely an olfactory experience but tactile too, the sweet fragrance of lilac like a woman's warm breath against his skin. Ensconced in the driver's seat of his motor home, he travels through a rich sea of sensation that washes him the way water ceaselessly washes the hull of a deeply submerged submarine.

Now he crosses into Oregon. The mountains come to him and pull him up into their fastnesses.

The thickening stands of trees on the steep slopes are more gray than green in the stubborn rain, and the sight of them is like biting on a piece of ice, hard between his teeth, a slight but pleasant metallic taste, and a shattering coldness against his lips.

He seldom glances at the rearview mirror any more. The woman is a mystery, and mysteries of this nature can't be resolved by the sheer desire to resolve them. Ultimately she will reveal herself, and the intensity of the experience will depend upon whatever purpose she has and what secrets she possesses.

The waiting is delicious.

Throughout the last few hours of the journey, Vess leaves the radio off, although not because he is afraid that music will mask the sounds of the woman stalking forward through the motor home. In fact, he rarely listens to the radio while driving. In his memory is a vast library of recordings of the music that he likes best: the cries and squeals, the prayerful whispers, the shrieks as thin as paper cuts, the pulsatory sobbings for mercy, and the erotic inducements of final desperations.

As he leaves the state highway for the county route, he recalls specifically Sarah Templeton in her shower stall, her screams and her frantic gagging muffled by the green dishwashing sponge that he'd stuffed into her mouth and by the two strips of strapping tape that sealed her lips. Nothing on the radio, from Elton John to Garth Brooks to Pearl Jam to Sheryl Crow—to Mozart or Beethoven, for that matter—can compare to this interior entertainment.

He follows the rain-swept, two-lane county route to his private driveway. The entrance is securely gated and flanked by thickets of pines and brambly underbrush.

The gate is made of tubular steel and barbed wire, set between stainless-steel posts in concrete footings. It features an electric motor with remote operation, and when Mr. Vess pushes a button on the hand-held control that he fishes from the console box, the barrier swings inward to the left, in a satisfying stately manner.

After driving the motor home onto his property, he brakes to a stop once more, rolls down his window, holds out the control unit, with the signal-transmission window reversed in his grip. In his side-view mirror, he watches as the gate closes.

The driveway is nearly as long as that at the Templeton family's vineyards, as his property encompasses fifty-four acres that back up to a government-owned wilderness, which measures many miles on a side. He is not as well-to-do as the Templetons; land here is far cheaper than in the Napa Valley.

In spite of the lack of paving, there is little mud and no real danger of the motor home bogging down. The topsoil is shallow; the lane was graded down to the underlying shale. The way is a bit rough, but this is not, after all, New York City, New York.

Vess drives up a modest incline, between looming ranks of tall pines, spruces, scattered firs, and then the trees recede a little, and he crosses the bald hilltop. The road descends easily, in a graceful curve, into a small vale, with the house at the end and the hills rising behind in the sheeting rain and morning fog.

His heart swells at the sight of home. Home is where his Ariel patiently awaits.

The two-story house is small but solidly built of logs mortared with cement. The old logs are nearly black with layers of pitch; and time has darkened the cement to a tobacco brown, except for the tan and gray mottling of recent repairs.

The house was constructed in the late 1920s by the owner of a family logging business, long before small operators were regulated out of such work and before the government declared the surrounding public lands off-limits to timber harvesters. Electricity was brought in sometime during the forties.

Edgler Vess has owned the house for six years. Upon purchasing the place, he rewired it, improved the plumbing, enlarged the second-floor bathroom. And, entirely on his own, of course, he undertook extensive and secret remodeling work in the basement.

To some, the property may seem isolated, inconveniently far from a 7-Eleven or a multiplex cinema. But for Mr. Vess, whose pleasures would never be understood by most neighbors, relative isolation is *the* fundamental requirement when he is shopping for real estate.

On a summer afternoon or evening, however, sitting in a bentwood rocker on the front porch, gazing out at the deep yard and the acres of wildflowers in the fields cleared by the logger and his sons, or staring at the great spread of stars, even the most meek and citified man would agree that isolation has its appeal.

In good weather, Mr. Vess likes to take his dinner and a couple of beers on the porch. When the mountain silences become boring, he allows himself to hear the voices of those who are buried in the field: their groveling and lamentations, the music that he prefers to any on the radio.

In addition to the house, there is a small barn, not because the original owner of the property farmed any of the land that he cleared of trees but because he kept horses. This second building is of traditional wood-frame construction on a concrete footing and fieldstone stem wall; wind, rain, and sun long ago laid down a silver patina on the durable cedar siding, which Vess finds lovely.

Since he owns no horses, he uses the barn as a garage.

Now, however, he pulls to a stop beside the house, rather than continuing to the barn. The woman is in the motor home, and he will soon need to deal with her. He prefers to park here, where he can watch her from the house and wait for developments.

He glances at the rearview mirror.

Still no sign of her.

Switching off the engine but not the windshield wipers, Vess waits for his guards to appear. The late-March morning is animate with slanting rain and wind-shaken things, but nothing moves of its own deliberation.

They have been trained not to charge willy-nilly at approaching vehicles and even to bide their time with intruders who are on foot, the better to lure them into a zone from which escape is impossible. These guards know that stealth is as important as savage fury, that the most successful assaults are preceded by calculated stillnesses to lull the quarry into a false confidence.

Finally the first black head appears, bullet sleek but for its pricked ears, low to the ground at the rear corner of the house. The dog hesitates to reveal more of himself, surveying the scene to make sure that he understands what is happening.

"Good fella," Vess whispers.

At the nearest corner of the barn, between the cedar siding and the trunk of a winter-bare maple, another dog appears. It is little more than a shadow of a shadow in the rain.

Vess wouldn't have noticed these sentries if he hadn't known to look for them. Their self-control is remarkable, a testament to his abilities as a trainer.

Two more dogs lurk somewhere, perhaps behind the motor home or belly crawling through shrubbery where he can't see them. They are all Dobermans, five and six years old, in their prime.

Vess has not cropped their ears or bobbed their tails, as is usually done with Dobermans, for he has an affinity for nature's predators. He is able to perceive the world to a degree as he believes that animals perceive it—the elemental nature of their view, their needs, the importance of raw sensation. They have a kinship.

The dog by the corner of the house slinks into the open, and the dog at the barn emerges from beneath the black-limbed maple. A third Doberman rises from behind the massive and half-petrified stump of a long-vanquished cedar in the side yard, around which has grown a tangled mass of holly.

The motor home is familiar to them. Their vision, while not their strongest suit, is probably sufficient to allow them to recognize him through the windshield. With a sense of smell twenty thousand times more acute than that of the average human being, they no doubt detect his scent even through the rain and even though he is inside the motor home. Yet they don't wag their tails or in any way exhibit pleasure, because they are still on duty.

The fourth dog remains hidden, but these three drift warily toward him through the rain and the mist. Their heads are lifted, pointy ears flicked up and forward.

In their disciplined silence and indifference to the storm, they remind him of the herd of elk in the redwood grove the previous night, eerily intent. The big difference, of course, is that these creatures, if confronted by anyone other than their beloved master, would not respond with the timidity of elk but would tear the throat out of that luckless person.

Although she would not have believed it possible, Chyna had been lulled into sleep by the hum of the tires and the motion of the motor home. Her dreams were of strange houses in which the geometry of the rooms was ever changing and bizarre; something eager and hungry lived within the walls, and at night it spoke to her through vent grilles and electrical outlets, whispering its needs.

The brakes woke her. Immediately she realized that the motor home had come to a full halt once before and then had started up again, only moments ago; she had dozed through that first stop, disturbed in her sleep but not fully awakened. Now, although they were on the move again and the killer was obviously still behind the steering wheel,

Chyna grabbed the revolver from the floor beside her, scrambled to her feet, and stood with her back to the wall, tense and alert.

From the tilt of the floor and the laboring sound of the engine, she knew that they were climbing a hill. Then they reached the top and headed downward. Soon they stopped again, and at last the engine cut out.

The rain was the only sound.

She waited for footsteps.

Although she knew that she was awake, she seemed to be in a dream, rigid in darkness, with the susurrant rain like whispering in the walls.

Mr. Vess takes the time to put on his raincoat and to slip his Heckler & Koch P7 into one pocket. He removes the Mossberg shotgun from the cabinet in the kitchenette, in case the woman searches the place after he leaves. He switches off the lights.

When he descends from the motor home, heedless of the cold rain, the three big dogs come to him, and then the fourth from behind the vehicle. All are quivering with excitement at his return but still holding themselves in check, not wanting to be thought derelict in their duty.

Just before departing on this expedition, Mr. Vess had placed the Dobermans on attack status by speaking the name *Nietzsche*. They will remain primed to kill anyone who walks onto the property until he speaks the name *Seuss*, whereupon they will be as affable as any other group of sociable mutts—except, of course, if anyone unwisely threatens their master.

After propping his shotgun against the side of the motor home, he holds his hands out to the dogs. They eagerly crowd around to sniff his fingers. Sniffing, panting, licking, licking, yes, yes, they have missed him so very much.

He squats on his haunches, coming down to their level, and now their delight is uncontainable. Their ears twitch, and shivers of pure pleasure pass visibly along their lean flanks, and they whine softly with sheer happiness, jealously pressing all at once at him, to be touched, patted, scratched.

They live in an enormous kennel against the back of the barn, which they can enter and leave at will. It is electrically heated during cold weather to ensure their comfort and their continued good health.

"Hi there, Muenster. How you doing, Liederkranz? Tilsiter, boy, you look like one mean sonofabitch. Hey, Limburger, are you a good boy, are you my good boy?"

Each, at the mention of his name, is filled with such joy that he would roll on his back and bare his belly and paw the air and grin at death—if he weren't still on duty. Part of the fun for Vess is watching the struggle between training and nature in each animal, a sweet agony that makes two of them pee in nervous frustration.

Mr. Vess has rigged electrically operated dispensers inside the kennel, which in his absence automatically pay out measured portions of food for each Doberman. The system clock has a backup battery to continue timing meals even during a power failure of short duration. In the event of a long-term loss of power, the dogs can always resort to hunting for their sustenance; the surrounding meadows are full of field mice and rabbits and squirrels, and the Dobermans are fierce predators. Their communal water trough is fed by a drip line, but if it should ever cease to function, they can find their way to a nearby spring that runs through the property.

Most of Mr. Vess's expeditions are three-day weekends, rarely as long as five days, and the dogs have a ten-day food supply without counting rabbits, mice, and squirrels. They constitute an efficient and reliable security system: never a short in any circuit, never a failed motion detector, never a corroded magnetic contact—and never a false alarm.

Oh, and how these dogs love him, how unreservedly and loyally, as no memory chips and wires and cameras and infrared heat sensors ever could. They smell the bloodstains on his jeans and denim jacket, and they push their sleek heads under his open raincoat, ears laid back, sniffing eagerly now, detecting not merely the blood but the lingering stench of terror that his victims exuded when in his hands, their pain, their helplessness, the sex that he had with the one named Laura. This mélange of pungent odors not only excites the dogs but increases their respect for Vess. They have been taught to kill not merely in self-defense, not just for food; with a degree of iron self-control, they have been taught to kill for the sheer savage pleasure of it, to please their master. They are acutely aware that their master can match their savagery. And unlike them, he has never needed to be taught. Their high regard for Edgler Vess soars higher, and they mewl softly and quiver and roll their soulful eyes at him in worshipful awe.

Mr. Vess gets to his feet. He picks up the shotgun and slams the door of the motor home.

The dogs spring to his side, jostling one another to be close to him, alertly surveying the rain-shrouded day for any threat to their master.

Quietly, so the woman inside cannot possibly hear the word, he says, "Seuss."

The dogs freeze, looking up at him, heads cocked.

"Seuss," he repeats.

The four Dobermans are no longer on attack status and will not automatically tear to pieces anyone who enters the property. They shake themselves, as if casting off tension, then pad around in a vaguely bewildered fashion, sniffing at the grass and at the front tires of the motor home.

They are like Mafia hit men who, following their own executions, have now regained a baffled self-awareness after being reincarnated, only to discover that they are accountants in this new life.

If any visitor were to attempt to harm their master, of course, they would leap to his defense, whether or not he had time to shout the word *Nietzsche*. The result wouldn't be pretty.

They are trained first to tear out the throat. Then they will bite the face to effect maximum terror and pain—go for the eyes, the nose, the lips. Then the crotch. Then the belly. They won't kill and turn at once away; they will be busy for a while with their quarry, after they have brought it down, until no doubt exists that they have done their job.

Even a man with a shotgun could not take out all of them before at least one managed to sink its teeth into his throat. Gunfire will not drive them away or even make them flinch. Nothing can frighten them. Most likely, the hypothetical man with the shotgun would be able to wipe out only two before the remaining pair over-whelmed him.

"Crib," says Mr. Vess.

This single word instructs the dogs to go to their kennel, and they take off as one, sprinting toward the barn. Still, they do not bark, for he has schooled them in silence.

Ordinarily he would allow them to stay with him and enjoy his company and spend the day in his house with him and even pile up like a black and tan quilt with him as he sleeps away the afternoon. He would cuddle them and coo to them; for they have been, after all, such good dogs. They deserve their reward.

The woman in the red sweater, however, prevents Mr. Vess from dealing with the dogs as he usually would. If they are a visible presence, they will inhibit her, and she may cower inside the motor home, afraid to exit.

The woman must be given enough freedom to act. Or at least the illusion of freedom.

He is curious to see what she will do.

She must have a purpose, some motivation for the strange things that she has done thus far. Everyone has a purpose.

Mr. Vess's purpose is to satisfy all appetites as they arise, to seek ever more outrageous experience, to immerse himself deeply in sensation.

Whatever the woman *believes* her purpose to be, Vess knows that in the end, her true purpose will be to serve his. She is a glorious variety of powerful and exquisite sensations in human skin, packaged solely for his enjoyment—rather like a Hershey bar in its brown and silver wrapper or a Slim Jim sausage snug in its plastic tube.

The last of the racing Dobermans vanishes behind the barn, to the kennel.

Mr. Vess walks through the soggy grass to the old log house and climbs a set of fieldstone steps to the front porch. Although he carries the pistol-grip 12-gauge Mossberg, he makes an effort to appear otherwise nonchalant, in case the woman has come forward from the bedroom at the rear of the motor home to watch him through a window.

The bentwood rocker has been stored away until spring.

Trailing silvery slime across the wet floorboards of the porch, several early-spring snails test the air with their semitransparent, gelatinous feelers, hauling their spiral shells on strange quests. Mr. Vess is careful to step around them.

A mobile hangs at one corner of the porch, from the fascia board at the edge of the shake-shingle roof. It is made of twenty-eight white seashells, all quite small, some with lovely pink interiors; most are spiral in form, and all are relatively exotic.

The mobile does not make a good wind chime, because most of the notes that it strikes are flat. It greets him with a flurry of atonal clinking, but he smiles because it has . . . well, not sentimental but at least nostalgic value to him.

This fine piece of folk craft once belonged to a young woman who lived in a suburb of Seattle, Washington. She had been an attorney, about thirty-two, sufficiently successful to live alone in her own house in an upscale neighborhood. For a person tough enough to thrive in the combative legal profession, this woman had kept a surprisingly frilly—in fact, downright girlish—bedroom: a four-poster bed with a pink canopy trimmed with lace and fringe, rose-patterned bedspread, and starched dust ruffles; a big collection of teddy bears; paintings of English cottages hung with morning-glory vines and surrounded by lush primrose gardens; and several seashell mobiles.

He had done exciting things to her in that bedroom. Then he had taken her away in the motor home to places remote enough to allow him to perform other acts even more exciting. She had asked *why?*— and he had answered, *Because this is what I do.* That was all the truth and all the reason of him.

Mr. Vess can't recall her name, though he fondly remembers many things about her. Parts of her were as pink and smooth and lovely as the insides of some of these dangling seashells. He has an especially vivid mental image of her small hands, almost as slender and delicate as those of a child.

He had been fascinated by her hands. Enchanted. He had never sensed anyone's vulnerability so intensely as he'd sensed hers when he held her small, trembling, but strong hands in his. Oh, he had been like a swooning schoolboy with her hands.

When he had hung the mobile on the porch, as a memento of the attorney, he had added one item. It dangles, now, on a piece of green string: her slender index finger, reduced to bare bones but still undeniably elegant, the three phalanges from tip to the base knuckle, clinking against the little conch shells and miniature bivalve fans and trumpet shells and tiny spirals similar to the whorled homes of snails.

*Clink-clink.*

*Clink-clink.*

He unlocks the front door and enters the house. He closes but does not lock the door behind him, allowing the woman to have access if she chooses to take it.

Who knows what she will choose to do?

Already her behavior is as astonishing as it is mysterious.

She excites him.

Vess turns from the shadowy front room to the narrow enclosed stairs immediately to his left. He quickly climbs the steps two at a time, one hand on the oak banister, to the second floor. A short hallway serves two bedrooms and a bath. His room is to the left.

In his private chamber, he drops the Mossberg on the bed and crosses to the south-facing window, which is covered by a blue drape with blackout lining. He doesn't need to draw the drape aside to see the motor home on the driveway below. The two pleated panels of fabric don't quite meet, and when he puts his eye to the two-inch gap, he has a clear view of the entire vehicle.

Unless she slipped out of the motor home immediately behind him, which is highly doubtful, the woman is still inside. He can see down through the windshield at an angle into the pilot's and copilot's seats, and she has not advanced to either.

He takes the pistol from his pocket and puts it on the dresser. He shrugs out of the raincoat and tosses it atop the chenille spread on the neatly made bed.

When he checks at the window again, there is as yet no sign of the mystery woman at the motor home below.

He hurries into the hallway to the bathroom. White tile, white paint, white tub, white sink, white toilet, polished brass fixtures with white ceramic knobs. Everything gleams. Not a single smudge mars the mirror.

Mr. Vess likes a bright, clean bathroom. For a while, lifetimes ago, he lived with his grandmother in Chicago, and she was incapable of keeping a bathroom clean enough to meet his standards. Finally, exasperated beyond endurance, he had killed the old bitch. He'd been eleven when he put the knife in her.

Now he reaches behind the shower curtain and cranks the COLD faucet all the way open. He isn't actually going to take a shower, so there's no point in wasting hot water.

He quickly adjusts the shower head until the spray is as heavy as it gets. The water pounds down into the fiberglass tub, filling the bathroom with thunder. He knows from experience that the sound carries throughout the small house; even with rain on the roof, this is much louder than the sound of the shower in Sarah Templeton's bedroom, and it will be heard downstairs.

On a wall shelf above the toilet is a clock radio. He switches it on and adjusts the volume.

The radio is set to a Portland station featuring twenty-four-hour-a-day news. Ordinarily, when bathing and attending to his toilet, Mr. Vess likes to listen to the news, not because he has any interest in the latest political or cultural developments but because these days the news is largely about people maiming and killing one another—war, terrorism, rape, assault, murder. And when people can't kill one another in sufficient numbers to keep the reporters busy, nature always saves the day with a tornado, a hurricane, a big earthquake, or an outbreak of flesh-eating bacteria.

Sometimes, listening to the news and letting the various reports spark fond memories of his own homicidal exploits, he realizes that he himself is also a force of nature: a hurricane, a lightning storm, a planet-smashing asteroid hurtling through the void, the distillate of all human ferocity in a single body. Elemental power. The thought pleases him.

Now, however, news will not set the stage properly. Hastily he turns the tuning knob until he finds a station playing music. "Take the A Train" by Duke Ellington.

Perfect.

The big-band sound brings to his mind's eye an image of light flaring off cut crystal and luminous bubbles rising in a champagne glass, and it reminds him of the smell of fresh-cut limes, lemons. He can *feel* the notes in the air, some shimmering-bursting like bubbles and others bouncing off him like hundreds of little rubber balls and some like windblown leaves crisp with autumn: a very *tactile* music, exuberant and exhilarating.

The woman will be subtly lulled by the swing beat. It will be difficult for her to believe, really believe, that anything bad can happen to her with such music as background.

Perfect.

He hurries back to his bedroom, to the window, having been away from it no more than a minute.

Rain snaps against the glass, streams.

On the driveway below, the motor home stands as before.

The woman still must be inside. She probably won't just burst out of the vehicle and run pell-mell; she's likely to exit warily, hesitant on both sides of the door. Although there might have been time for her to get out of the motor home while Mr. Vess was in the bathroom, she would almost certainly be huddling against it, getting her bearings, assessing the situation. From this high vantage point, he can see around most of the vehicle, with the exception of blind spots toward the rear on the port side and at the very back, and the woman is not in sight.

"Ready when you are, Miss Desmond," he says, referring to the Gloria Swanson character in *Sunset Boulevard*.

That movie had had a great effect on him when he'd first seen it on television. He'd been thirteen, a year out of counseling for the murder of his grandmother. On one level, he had known that Norma Desmond was supposed to be the tragic villain of the piece, that the writer and director *intended* for her to fulfill that role—but he had admired her, *loved* her. Her selfishness was thrilling, her self-absorption heroic. She was the truest character he had ever seen in a movie. *This* was what people were actually like, under the pretense and hypocrisy, under all the crap about love, compassion, altruism; they were all like Norma Desmond but couldn't admit it to themselves. Norma didn't give a *shit* about the rest of the world, and she bent everyone to her iron will even when she was no longer young or beautiful or famous, and when she couldn't bend William Holden's character as far as she wanted, she just boldly picked up a gun and *shot* him, which was *so* powerful, *so* audacious, that young Edgler had been too excited to sleep that night. He had lain awake wondering what it would be like to encounter a woman as superior and genuine as Norma Desmond—and then to break her, kill her, take all the strength of her selfishness and make it his own.

Maybe this mystery woman is a little bit like Norma Desmond. She's bold, sure enough. He can't figure what the hell she's doing, what she's after; and when he understands her motivation, maybe she won't be anything like Norma Desmond. But at least she is already something new and interesting in his experience.

The rain.

The wind.

The motor home.

"Take the A Train" has given way to "String of Pearls."

Murmuring softly against the blue drapes, Mr. Vess says, "Ready when you are."

After the killer had gotten out of the motor home and slammed the door, Chyna had waited in the dark bedroom for a long while in the one-note lullaby of rain.

She had told herself that she was being prudent. Listen. Wait. Be sure. Absolutely sure.

But then she'd been forced to admit that she had lost her nerve. Although she had mostly dried out during the ride north from Humboldt County, she was still cold, and the source of her chills was the ice of doubt in her guts.

The eater of spiders was gone, and to Chyna, even remaining in blackness with two dead bodies was far preferable to going outside where she might encounter him again. She knew that he would be back, that this bedroom was not, in fact, a safe place, but for a while, what she *knew* was overruled by what she *felt*.

When at last she broke her paralysis, she moved with reckless abandon, as though any hesitation would result in another and worse paralysis, which she would be unable to overcome. She yanked open the bedroom door, plunged into the hall, with the revolver held in front of her because maybe the murderous bastard hadn't gotten out after all, and she went all the way forward past the bathroom and through the dining area and into the lounge, where she stopped a few feet back from the driver's seat.

The only light was a bleak gray haze that came through the skylight in the hall behind her and through the windshield ahead, but she could see that the killer wasn't here. She was alone.

Outside, directly ahead of the motor home, lay a sodden yard, a few dripping trees, and a rough driveway leading to a weathered barn.

Chyna moved to a starboard window, cautiously peeled back one corner of the greasy drape, and saw a log house about twenty feet away. Mottled with time and many coats of creosote, streaming with rain, the walls glistened like dark snakeskin.

Although she had no way of being certain, she assumed that it was the killer's house. He had told the men in the service station that he was going home after his "hunting" trip, and everything he had told them had sounded to her like the truth, including—and especially—the taunts about young Ariel.

The killer must be inside.

Chyna went forward again and leaned over the driver's seat to look at the ignition. The keys weren't there. They weren't in the console box either.

She slipped into the copilot's seat, feeling frightfully exposed in spite of the blurring rain that washed down the windows. She could find nothing in the console box, in the shallow glove box, in either door pouch, or under either front seat that revealed the name of the owner or anything else about him.

He would be returning soon. For some demented reason, he had gone to a lot of trouble and taken risks to bring the cadavers, and most likely he would not leave them in the motor home for long.

The obscuring rain made it difficult for her to be sure, but she thought that the drapes were drawn at the first-floor windows on this side of the house. Consequently, the killer would not casually glance out and spot her when she stepped from the motor home. She couldn't see the pair of second-floor windows half as well as those lower down, but they also might be draped.

She cracked open the door, and a cold knife of wind thrust at her through the gap. She got out and closed the door behind her as quietly as possible.

The sky was low and turbulent.

Forested hills rose rank after rank behind the house, vanishing into the pearly mist. Chyna sensed mountains looming above the hills in the overcast; they would still be capped with snow this early in the spring.

She hurried to the flagstone steps and went up onto the porch, out of the rain, but it was coming down so hard that already she was soaked again. She stood with her back to the rough wall.

Windows flanked the front door, and the drapes were drawn behind the nearer of the two.

Music inside.

Swing music.

She stared out at the meadows, along the lane that led from the house to the top of a low hill and thence out of sight. Perhaps, beyond the hill, other houses stood along that unpaved track, where she would find people who could help her.

But who had ever helped her before, all these long years?

She remembered the two brief stops that had awakened her, and she suspected that the motor home had passed through a gate. Nevertheless, even if this was a private driveway, it would lead sooner or later to a public road, where she would find assistance from residents or passing motorists.

The top of the hill was approximately a quarter of a mile from the house. This was a lot of open ground to cover before she would be out of sight. If he saw her, he would probably be able to chase her down before she got away.

And she still didn't know that this was his house. Even if it *was* his house, she couldn't be sure that this was where he kept Ariel. If Chyna brought back the authorities and Ariel wasn't here, then the killer might never tell them where to find the girl.

She had to be sure that Ariel was in the basement.

But if the girl *was* here, then when Chyna came back with the cops, the killer might barricade himself in the house. It would take a SWAT team to pry him out of the place—and before they got to him, he might kill Ariel and commit suicide.

In fact, that was almost certainly how it would play out as soon as any cops showed up. He would know that his freedom was at an end, that his games were over, that he would have no more *fun*, and all he would see available to him was one last, apocalyptic celebration of madness.

Chyna couldn't bear to lose this imperiled girl so soon after losing Laura, failing Laura. Intolerable. She couldn't keep failing people as, all her life, others had failed her. Meaning wasn't to be found in psychology classes and textbooks but in caring, in hard sacrifice, in faith, in *action*. She didn't want to take these risks. She wanted to live—but for someone other than herself.

At least now she had a gun.

And the advantage of surprise.

Earlier, at the Templeton house and in the motor home and then at the service station, she'd also had the advantage of surprise, but she hadn't been in possession of the revolver.

She realized that she was arguing herself into taking the most dangerous course of action open to her, making excuses for going into the house. Going into the house was obviously crazy, Jesus, a totally crazy move, Jesus, but she was striving hard to rationalize it, because she had already made up her mind that this was what she was going to do.

Coming out of the motor home, the woman has a gun in her right hand. It looks as if it might be a .38—perhaps a Chief's Special.

This is a popular weapon with some cops. But this woman doesn't move like a cop, doesn't handle the weapon as a cop would—although clearly she is somewhat comfortable with a gun.

No, she's definitely not an officer of the law. Something else. Something weird.

Mr. Vess has never been so intrigued by anyone as he is by this spunky little lady, this mysterious adventurer. She's a real treat.

The moment she sprints from the motor home to the house and out of sight, Vess moves from the window on the south wall of his bedroom to the window on the east wall. It is also covered by a blue drape, which he parts.

No sign of her.

He waits, holding his breath, but she doesn't head east along the lane. After half a minute or so, he knows that she isn't going to run.

If she had taken off, she would have sorely disappointed him. He doesn't think of her as a person who would run. She is bold. He wants her to be bold.

Had she run, he would have sent the dogs after her, not with instructions to kill but merely to detain. Then he would have retrieved her to question her at his leisure.

But *she* is coming to *him*. For whatever unimaginable reason, she will follow him into the house. With her revolver.

He will need to be cautious. But oh, what fun he is having. Her gun only makes the game more intense.

The front porch is immediately below this window, but he isn't able to see it because of the overhanging roof. The mystery woman is somewhere on the porch. He can *feel* her close, perhaps directly under him.

He retrieves his pistol from the nightstand and glides quietly across the wall-to-wall carpet into the open doorway. He steps into the hall and quickly to the head of the enclosed stairs, where he stops. He can see only the landing below, not the living room, but he listens.

If she opens the front door, he will know, because one of the hinges makes a dry ratcheting sound. It's not a loud noise, but it is distinctive. Because he's listening specifically for that corroded hinge, not even the drumming of the rain on the roof, the pounding of the shower into the bathtub, and "In the Mood" on the radio can entirely mask the sound.

Crazy. But she was going to do it. For Ariel. For Laura. But also for herself. Maybe most of all for herself.

After all these years under beds, in closets, in attic shadows—no more hiding. After all these years of getting by, keeping her head down, drawing no attention to herself—suddenly she had to *do* something or explode. She'd been living in a prison since the day she'd been born, even after leaving her mother, a prison of fear and shame and

lowered expectations, and she'd been so accustomed to her circumscribed life that she had not recognized the bars. Now righteous rage
released her, and she was crazy with freedom.

The chilly wind kicked up, and shatters of rain blasted under the
porch roof.

Seashell wind chimes clattered, an irritation of flat notes.

Chyna eased past the window, trying to avoid several snails on the
porch floor. The drapes remained tightly shut.

The front door was closed but unlocked. She slowly pushed it inward. One hinge rasped.

The big-band tune finished with a flourish, and at once two voices
arose from deeper in the house. Chyna froze on the threshold, but
then she realized that she was listening to an advertisement. The
music had been coming from a radio.

It was possible that the killer shared the house with someone other
than Ariel, and other than the procession of victims or dead bodies
brought back from his road trips. Chyna couldn't conceive of his having a family, a wife and children, a psychotic Brady Bunch waiting for
him; but there were rare cases on record of homicidal sociopaths
working together, like the two men who proved to be the Hillside
Strangler in Los Angeles a couple of decades ago.

Voices on a radio, however, were no threat.

With the revolver held in front of her, she went inside. The incoming wind whistled into the house, rattling a wobbly lampshade
and threatening to betray her, so she closed the door.

The radio voices came down an enclosed stairwell to her left. She
kept one eye on the doorless opening at the foot of those steps, in case
more than voices descended.

The front room on the ground floor ran the entire width of the
small house, and although it was illuminated only by the gray light
from the windows, it was nothing like what she had expected to find.
There were hunter-green leather armchairs with footstools, a tartan-
plaid sofa on large ball feet, rustic oak end tables, and a section of
bookshelves that held perhaps three hundred volumes. On the hearth
of the big river-rock fireplace were gleaming brass andirons, and on
the mantel was an old clock with two bronze stags rearing up on their
hind legs. The decor was thoroughly but not aggressively masculine—
no glassily staring deer or bear heads on the walls, no hunting prints,
no rifles on display, just cozy and comfortable. Where she had been

expecting pervasive clutter as evidence of his seriously disordered mind, there was neatness. Instead of filth, cleanliness; even in the shadows, Chyna could see that the room was well dusted and swept. Rather than being burdened with the stench of death, the house was redolent of lemon-oil furniture polish and a subtle pine-scented air freshener, as well as the faint and pleasant smell of char from the fireplace.

Selling H & R Block tax services and then doughnuts, the radio voices bounced with enthusiasm down the stairs. The killer had it cranked up too loud; the volume level seemed wrong to Chyna, as if he was trying to mask other sounds.

There *was* another sound, similar to but different from the rain, and after a moment she recognized it. A shower.

That was why he had set the radio so loud. He was listening to the music while taking a shower.

She was in luck. As long as the killer was in the shower, she could search for Ariel without the risk of being discovered.

Chyna hurriedly crossed the front room to a half-open door, went through, and found a kitchen. Canary-yellow ceramic tile with knotty-pine cabinets. On the floor, gray vinyl tile speckled with yellow and green and red. Well scrubbed. Everything in its place.

She was soaked, rain dripping off her hair and still seeping from her jeans onto the clean floor.

Taped to the side of the refrigerator was a calendar already turned forward to April, with a color photograph that showed one white and one black kitten—both with dazzling green eyes—peering out from a huge spray of lilies.

The normality of the house terrified her: the gleaming surfaces, the tidiness, the homey touches, the sense that a person lived here who might walk in daylight on any street and pass for human in spite of the atrocities that he had committed.

Don't think about it.

Keep moving. Safety in movement.

She went past the rear door. Through the four glass panes in the upper half, she saw a back porch, a green yard, a couple of big trees, and the barn.

Without any architectural division, the kitchen opened into the dining area, and the combined space was probably two-thirds the width of the house. The round dinette table was dark pine, supported by a thick central drum rather than legs; the four heavy pine captain's chairs featured tie-on back and seat cushions.

Upstairs, the music started again, but it was softer in the kitchen than in the front room. If she had been an aficionado of big-band music, however, she would have been able to recognize the tune from here.

The noise of the running shower was more apparent in the kitchen than in the living room, because the pipes were channeled through the rear wall of the old house. Water being drawn upward to the bathroom made an urgent, hollow rushing sound through copper. Furthermore, the pipe wasn't tied down and insulated as well as it ought to have been, and at some point along its course, it vibrated against a wall stud: rapid knocking behind plasterboard, *tatta-tatta-tatta-tatta-tatta*.

If that noise abruptly stopped, she would know that her safe time in the house was limited. In the subsequent silence, she could count on no more than a minute or two of grace while he toweled off. Thereafter he might show up anywhere.

Chyna looked around for a telephone but saw only a wall jack into which one could be plugged. If there had been a phone, she might have paused to call 911, supposing there *was* 911 service out here in . . . well, wherever the hell they were—these boondocks. Knowing that help was on the way would have made the remainder of the search less nerve-racking.

At the north end of the dining area was another door. Although the killer was in the shower upstairs, she turned the knob as quietly as she could and crossed the threshold with caution.

Beyond lay a combination laundry and storage room. A washer. An electric dryer. Boxes and bottles of laundry supplies were stored in an orderly fashion on two open shelves, and the air smelled like detergent and bleach.

The rush of water and the knocking pipe were even louder here than they had been in the kitchen.

To the left, past the washer and dryer, was another door—rough pine, painted lime green. She opened it and saw stairs leading down to a black cellar, and her heart began to beat faster.

"Ariel," she said softly, but there was no answer, because she had spoken more to herself than to the girl.

No windows at all below. Not even a turbid leak of gray storm light seeping through narrow casements or screened ventilation cutouts. Dungeon dark.

But if the bastard was keeping a girl down there, how odd that he wouldn't have added a lock to this upper door. It offered only the spring latch that retracted with a twist of the knob, not a real lock of any kind.

The captive might be sealed in a windowless room deep below, of course, or even manacled. Ariel might have no hope of reaching these stairs and this upper door, even if left alone for days to worry at her restraints, which would explain why the killer was confident that one more barrier to her flight wasn't necessary even when he was away from home.

Nevertheless, it seemed peculiar that he wouldn't be concerned about a thief breaking into the house when he was gone, descending to the cellar, and inadvertently discovering the imprisoned girl. Considering the obvious age of the structure, its rusticity, and the lack of any apparent alarm keypads, Chyna doubted that the house had a security system. The killer, with all his secrets, ought to have installed a steel door to the cellar, with locks as impregnable as those on a bank vault.

The lack of special security might mean that the girl, Ariel, was not here.

Chyna didn't want to dwell on that possibility. She *had* to find Ariel.

Leaning through the doorway, she felt along the stairwell wall for the switch, and snapped it up. Lights came on both at the upper landing and in the basement.

The bare concrete steps—a single flight—were steep. They appeared to be much newer than the house itself, perhaps even a relatively recent addition.

The high-velocity surge of water through plumbing and the hard rapping of the loose pipe in the wall told her that the killer was still busy in the bathroom above, scrubbing away all traces of his crimes. *Tatta-tatta-tatta* . . .

Louder than before but still in a whisper, she said: "Ariel."

Out of the still air below, no response.

Louder. "Ariel."

Nothing.

Chyna didn't want to go down into this windowless pit, with no way out except the stairs, even with a lockless door above. But she couldn't think of any way to avoid the descent, not if she was to learn for sure whether Ariel was here.

*Tatta-tatta-tatta-tatta-tatta . . .*

It always came to this, even with childhood long past and being grown up and everything supposedly in control, everything supposedly all right; even then it *still* came to this: alone, dizzy with fear, alone, down into a bleak-dark-cramped place, no exits, sustained only by mad hope, with the world indifferent, no one to wonder about her or care where she might have gone.

Listening intently for the slightest change in the sound of the rushing water and the vibrating pipe, Chyna went down one step at a time, her left hand on the iron railing. The gun was extended in her right hand; she was clenching it so fiercely that her knuckles ached.

"Chyna Shepherd, untouched and alive," she said shakily. "Chyna Shepherd, untouched and alive."

Halfway down the stairs, she glanced back and up. At the end of a trail of her wet shoeprints, the landing seemed a quarter of a mile above her, as far away as the top of the knoll had seemed from the front porch of the house.

*Alice down the rabbit hole into a madness without tea parties.*

At the open doorway between the in-kitchen dining area and the laundry room, Mr. Edgler Vess hears the mystery woman call to Ariel. She is only a few feet away from him, around the corner, past the washer and the dryer, so there can be no mistake about what name she speaks.

*Ariel.*

Stupefied, he stands blinking and open-mouthed in the fragrance of laundry detergent and in the wall-muffled rattle of copper pipes, with her voice echoing in memory.

There is no way for her to know about Ariel.

Yet she calls to the girl again, louder than before.

Mr. Vess suddenly feels terribly violated, oppressed, observed. He glances back at the windows in the dining area and the kitchen, expecting to discover the radiant faces of accusing strangers pressed to those panes. He sees only the rain and the drowned gray light, but he is still anguished.

This is not fun any longer. Not fun at all.

The mystery is *too* deep. And alarming.

It is as if this woman didn't come to him out of that Honda but came through an invisible barrier between dimensions, out of some world beyond this one, from which she has been secretly watching him. The flavor is distinctly supernatural, the texture otherworldly, and now the laundry detergent smells like burning incense, and the cloying air seems thick with unseen presences.

Fearful and plagued by doubt, unaccustomed to both of those emotions, Mr. Vess steps into the laundry room, raising the Heckler & Koch P7. His finger wraps the trigger, already beginning to squeeze off a shot.

The cellar door stands open. The stairwell light is on.

The woman is not in sight.

He eases off the trigger without firing.

On those infrequent occasions when he has guests to the house to dinner or for a business meeting, he always leaves a Doberman in the laundry room. The dog lies in here, silent and dozing. But if anyone other than Vess were to enter, the dog would bark and snarl and drive him backward.

When the master is away, Dobermans vigilantly patrol the entire property, and no one has a hope of getting into the house itself, let alone into the cellar.

Mr. Vess has never put a lock on the door to the cellar steps because he is concerned that it might accidentally trip, imprisoning him down there when he is at play and unawares. With a key-operated deadbolt, of course, this catastrophe could never happen. He himself is incapable of imagining how any such mechanism could malfunction and trap him; nevertheless, he's too concerned about the prospect to take the risk.

Over the years, he has seen coincidence at work in the world, and people perishing because of it. One late-June afternoon near dusk, as Mr. Vess was driving to Reno, Nevada, on Interstate 80, a young blonde in a Mustang convertible had passed his motor home. She was wearing white shorts and a white blouse, and her long hair streamed red-gold in the twilight wind. Filled with an instant and powerful need to smash her beautiful face, he had pressed the motor home to its limits to keep her swifter Mustang in sight, but his quest had seemed doomed. As the highway rose into the Sierras, the speed of the motor home had fallen, and the Mustang had pulled away. Even if he had been able to draw close to the woman, the traffic had been too heavy—too many witnesses—for him to try anything as bold as forcing her off the highway. Then one of the tires on the Mustang had blown. Traveling at such high speed, she nearly spun out, nearly rolled, swerved from lane to lane, blue smoke pouring off the tires, but then she got control and pulled the car off the road onto the shoulder. Mr. Vess had stopped to assist her. She had been grateful for his offer of help, smiling and pleasantly shy, a nice girl with a one-inch gold cross on a chain around her neck, and later she had wept so bitterly and struggled so excitingly to resist surrendering her beauty, to turn her face away from his various sharp instruments, just a high-spirited young woman full of life and on the way to Reno until coincidence gave her to him.

And if a blown tire, why not a malfunctioning lock?

If coincidence can give, it can take.

Mr. Vess lives with intensity but not without caution.

Now this woman, calling for Ariel, has come into his life, like a blown tire, and suddenly he's not sure if she is a gift to him or he to her.

Remembering her revolver and wishing for Dobermans, he glides across the laundry room to the cellar door.

The woman's voice rises from the stairs below: "China Shepherd untouched and alive."

The words are so strange—the meaning so mysterious—that they seem to be an incantation, encoded and cryptic.

Confirming that perception, the woman repeats herself, as though she is chanting: "China Shepherd untouched and alive."

Though Vess is not usually superstitious, he experiences a heightened sense of the supernatural, beyond anything he's felt thus far. His scalp prickles, and the flesh on the nape of his neck crawls, and his hand tightens on the pistol.

After a hesitation, he leans through the open door and looks down the cellar stairs.

The woman is only a few steps from the bottom. She's got one hand on the railing, the revolver held out in front of her in the other hand.

Not a cop. An amateur.

Nonetheless, she might be Mr. Vess's blown tire, and he's jumpy, twitchy, still extremely curious about her but prepared to put his safety ahead of his curiosity.

He eases through the doorway onto the upper landing.

As close as she is, she does not hear him because all is concrete, nothing to creak.

He aims his pistol at the center of her back. The first shot will catapult her off her feet, send her flying with her arms spread toward the basement below, and the second shot will take her as she is in flight. Then he'll race down the stairs behind her, firing the third and fourth rounds, hitting her in the legs if possible. He'll drop on top of her, press the muzzle into the back of her head, and then, then, then when he's totally in control of her, dominant, he can decide whether she's still a threat or not, whether he can risk questioning her or whether she's so dangerous that nothing will do but to put a couple of rounds in her brain.

As the woman passes under the light near the foot of the stairs, Mr. Vess gets a better look at her revolver. It is indeed a Smith & Wesson .38 Chief's Special, as he had thought earlier, when he had seen it from the second-floor bedroom window, but suddenly the make and model of the weapon have electrifying meaning for him.

He smells a Slim Jim sausage. He remembers liquid-night eyes widening in shock, terror, and despair.

He has seen two of these guns in the past several hours. The first belonged to the young Asian gentleman at the service station, who drew it from under the counter in self-defense but never had the opportunity to fire.

Although the Chief's Special is a popular revolver, it is not so universally admired that one sees it everywhere in use. Edgler Vess *knows*, with the certainty of a fox on the scent of a rabbit in the weeds, that this is the same gun.

Although there are still many mysteries about the woman on the stairs below him, though her presence here is no less astonishing to him than it was before, there is nothing supernatural about her. She knows the name *Ariel* not because she has been watching from some world beyond this one, not because she is in the dutiful service of some higher force, but simply because she must have been *there*, in the service station, when Vess was chatting up the two clerks and when, moments later, he killed them.

Where she could have been hiding, how he could have overlooked her, why she would feel the need to pursue him, where she got all the courage for this reckless adventure—these are things he can't discern through intuition alone. But now he will have the opportunity to put these questions to her.

Lowering his pistol, he steps back into the laundry room, lest she glance up the stairs and see him.

His uncharacteristic fear, his eerie perception of oppressive super-natural forces, lifts like a fog from him, and he is amazed by his own brief spasm of gullibility. He, who has no illusions about the nature of existence. He, who is so clear-seeing. He, who knows the primacy of pure sensation. Even he, the most rational of all men, has spooked.

He almost laughs at his foolishness—and at once puts it out of his mind.

The woman must be to the bottom of the stairs by now.

He will allow her to explore. After all, for whatever bizarre rea-sons, this is what she has come here to do, and Vess is curious about her reactions to the things that she discovers.

He is having fun again.

Once more, the game is on.

Chyna reached the bottom of the stairs.

The outer wall of mortared stone was to her right. There was nowhere to go in that direction.

To her left was a chamber about ten feet from front to back, and as wide as the house. She moved away from the foot of the stairs, into this new space.

At one end stood an oil-fired furnace and a large electric water heater. At the other end were tall metal storage cabinets with vent slits in the doors, a workbench, and a tool chest on wheels.

Directly ahead, in a concrete-block wall, a strange door waited.

*Click-whoosh.*

Chyna swung to the right and almost squeezed off a shot before she realized that the sound had come from the furnace: the electric pilot light clicking on, fuel taking flame.

Over the sound of the furnace, she was still able to hear the vi-brating pipe. *Tatta-tatta-tatta.* It was fainter here than on the stairs, but still audible.

She could barely make out the music from the second-floor bath-room, an inconstant thread of melody, primarily the passages in brass or wailing clarinet.

Evidently for soundproofing, the door in the back wall was padded like a theater door, in leather-grain maroon vinyl divided into quilt-like squares by eight upholstery nails with large round heads covered in matching vinyl. The frame was upholstered in the same material.

No lock, not even a spring latch, prevented her from proceeding.

Putting her hand on the vinyl, Chyna discovered that the padding was even more plush than it appeared to be. As much as two inches of foam covered the underlying wood.

She gripped the long stainless-steel, U-shaped handle. When she pulled, the vinyl-encased door softly scraped and squeaked across the upholstery on the jamb. The fit was snug: When the door swung all the way free of the jamb and the seal was broken, there was a faint sound similar to that made when one opened a jar of vacuum-packed peanuts.

The door was upholstered on the inside as well. The overall thickness was in excess of five inches.

Beyond this new threshold lay a six-foot-square chamber with a low ceiling, which reminded her of an elevator, except that every surface other than the floor was upholstered. The floor was covered with a rubber mat of the kind used in many restaurant kitchens for the comfort of cooks who worked on their feet for hours at a time. In the dim light from the recessed overhead bulb, she saw that the fabric here wasn't vinyl but gray cotton with a nubbly texture.

The strangeness of the place sharpened her fear, yet at the same time she was so sure she understood the purpose of the padded vestibule that her stomach rolled with faint nausea.

Directly opposite the door that Chyna held open was one more door. It was also padded and set in an upholstered frame.

Finally, here were locks. The gray upholstery plumped around two heavy-duty brass lock cylinders. She couldn't proceed without keys.

Then she noticed a small padded panel overlying the door itself—at eye level, perhaps six by ten inches with a knob attached. It was like the sliding panel over the view port in the solid door of a maximum-security prison cell.

*Tatta-tatta-tatta . . .*

The killer seemed to be taking an unusually long shower. On the other hand, Chyna hadn't been in the house more than three minutes; it just seemed longer. If he was having a leisurely scrub, he might not be half done.

*Tatta-tatta . . .*

She would have preferred to hold open the outer door while she stepped into the vestibule and slid aside the panel on the inner view port, but the distance was too great. She had to let the door fall shut behind her.

The moment that the upholstered door met the upholstered jamb with a whisper-squeak of softly abraded vinyl, Chyna could no longer hear the vibrating water pipe. The quiet was so profound that even her ragged breathing was barely audible. Under the padding, the walls must have been covered with layers of sound-attenuating insulation.

Or perhaps the killer had shut off the shower just as the door had fallen shut. And was now toweling dry. Or pulling on a robe without bothering to towel off. On his way downstairs.

Fearful, unable to breathe, she opened the door again.

*Tatta-tatta-tatta* and the rush of water moving at high velocity, under pressure.

She exhaled explosively with relief.

She was still safe.

*All right, okay, be cool, keep moving, find out if the girl is here and then do what has to be done.*

Reluctantly she allowed the door to fall shut. The rattling of the pipe was again sealed out.

She felt as though she was suffocating. Perhaps ventilation in the vestibule was inadequate, but it was the sound-deadening effect of the padded walls, at least as much as poor airflow, that made the atmosphere seem as thick as smoke and unbreathable.

Chyna slid aside the padded panel on the inner door.

Beyond was rose-colored light.

The port was fitted with a sturdy screen to protect the viewer from assault by whoever or whatever was within.

Chyna put her face to the port and saw a large chamber nearly the size of the living room under which it was situated. In portions of the space, shadows were pooled deep, and the only light came from three lamps with fringed fabric shades and pink bulbs that were each putting out about forty watts.

At two places along the back wall were panels of red and gold brocade that hung from brass rods as if covering windows, but there could be no windows underground; the brocade was just set dressing to make the room more comfortable. On the wall to the left, barely touched by light, was a large tattered tapestry: a scene of women in long dresses and cloche hats riding horses sidesaddle through spring grass and flowers, past a verdant forest.

The furnishings included a plump armchair with antimacassars, a double bed with a white headboard painted with a scene not quite discernible in the rose light, bookcases with acanthus-leaf molding, cabinets with mullioned doors, a small dining table with a heavily carved apron, two Directoire chairs with flower-pattern upholstery flanking the table, and a refrigerator. An immense dark-stained armoire, featuring crackle-glazed flower appliqués on all the door panels, was old but probably not a genuine antique, battered but handsome. A padded vanity bench sat before a makeup table with a triptych mirror in a gilded, fluted frame. In a far corner was a toilet and a sink.

As weird as this subterranean room was, like a storage vault for the stage furniture from a production of *Arsenic and Old Lace*, the collection of dolls was by far the strangest thing about it. Kewpie dolls, Cabbage Patch Kids, Raggedy Ann, and numerous other varieties, both old and new, some more than three feet tall, some smaller than a milk carton, were dressed in diapers, snowsuits, elaborate bridal dresses, checkered rompers, cowboy outfits, tennis togs, pajamas, hula skirts, kimonos, clown suits, overalls, nighties, and sailor suits. They filled the bookshelves, peered out through the glass doors of some of the cabinets, perched on the armoire, sat atop the refrigerator, stood and sat on the floor along the walls. Others were piled atop one another in a corner and at the foot of the bed, legs and arms jutting at odd stiff angles, heads cocked as on broken necks, like stacks of gaily attired corpses awaiting transport to a crematorium. Two hundred, or three hundred, or more small faces either glowed in the gentle light or were ghost-pale in the shadows, some of bisque and some of china and some of cloth, some wood and some plastic. Their glass, tin, button, cloth, and painted-ceramic eyes reflected the light, shone brightly where the dolls were placed near any of the three lamps, glowed as moodily as banked coals where they were consigned to the darker corners.

For a moment, Chyna was half convinced that these dolls could actually see, except for a few individuals who appeared to be blind behind cataracts of rose light, and that *awareness* glimmered in their terrible eyes. Although none of them moved—or even shifted their gaze—they had an aura of life about them. Their power was uncanny, as though the killer were also a warlock who stole the souls of those he murdered and imprisoned them in these figures.

Then quiet movement in the room, a shadow coming out of gloom, proved to be the captive, and when she stepped into sight, the dolls lost their eerie magic. She was the most beautiful child that Chyna had ever seen, more beautiful even than in the Polaroid snapshot, with straight lustrous hair that was an enchanting shade of auburn in the peculiar light though platinum blond in reality. Fine-boned, slender, graceful, she possessed a beauty that was ethereal, angelic, and she seemed to be not a real girl but an apparition bearing a message about redemption, a manger, hope, and a guiding star.

She was dressed in black penny loafers, white knee socks, a blue or black skirt, and a short-sleeved white blouse with dark piping on the collar and across the pocket flap, as though she was in the uniform of a parochial school.

No doubt the killer provided the girl with the clothes that he wished her to wear, and Chyna saw at once why he would favor outfits like this. Though physically she was undoubtedly sixteen, she seemed younger when dressed in this fashion; with her slender arms, with her delicate wrists and hands, in this blushing light, the demure uniform made her seem like a child of eleven, shy of her confirmation Sunday, naive and innocent.

Sociopaths like this man were drawn to beauty and to innocence, because they were compelled to defile it. When innocence was stripped away, when beauty was cut and crushed, the malformed beast could at last feel superior to this person he had coveted. After the innocent and the beautiful were left dead and rotting, the world was to some degree made to more closely resemble the killer's interior landscape.

The girl sat in the armchair.

She was holding a book. She opened it, turned a few pages, and appeared to read.

Although she had surely heard the panel sliding back from the view port in the door, she did not look up. Apparently she assumed that her visitor was, as always, the eater of spiders.

With a rush of emotion that pinched her heart and surprised her with its intensity, Chyna said, "Ariel."

The name fell through the port as into an airless void, having carried no distance whatsoever, creating no echo.

The girl's cell obviously had been lined with numerous layers of soundproofing, perhaps with even more layers than the vestibule, and all this attention to the containment of her shouts and screams seemed to indicate that from time to time the killer invited people into his home. Perhaps to dinner. Or to have a few beers and watch a football game. That he would dare such a thing was only one more proof of his outrageous boldness.

But that he would have friends at all chilled Chyna, friends not demented like him, who would be horrified to discover the girl in his cellar and to know that their host slaughtered whole families for his entertainment. He passed for human in the workaday world. People laughed at his jokes. Sought his advice. Shared their joys and sorrows with him. Perhaps he attended church. On some Saturday nights, did he go dancing, smoothly two-stepping around the floor with a smiling woman in his arms, keeping time to the same music everyone else heard?

Chyna raised her voice: "Ariel."

The girl failed to look up.

Louder still, all but shouting it through the screened port in the padded door: "*Ariel!*"

In the chair, knees primly together, the book in her lap, head bowed to the page, wings of hair hiding most of her face, Ariel sat as if deaf—or as if she were a girl in the back of a closet, tuning out the shouted arguments of drunk and drug-sodden adults, tuning out further and further until she was in a great deep silent place of her own, untouchable.

Chyna recalled times, as a young girl, when simply hiding from her mother and her mother's more dangerous friends had not provided her with a sufficient sense of security. Sometimes the arguments or the celebrations became too violent or too boisterous; the chaos of noise and crazy laughter and cursing spun like a tornado around her even where she had concealed herself, and her fear spiraled out of control, until she thought that her heart would burst or her head explode. Then she went away to more welcoming places in her mind, through the back of the old wardrobe into the land of Narnia, which she had read about in the wonderful books of Mr. C. S. Lewis, or to visit Toad Hall and the Wild Wood from *The Wind in the Willows*, or into realms that she herself invented.

She had always been able to come back from those escapements. But on occasion, she had thought about how wonderful it would be to stay in that faraway place, where neither her mother nor her mother's kind would ever be able to find her again, no matter how hard they looked. In those exotic kingdoms, there was often danger, but there were also true and faithful friends like none found on *this* side of magical wardrobes.

Now, peering through the screened port at the girl in the chair, Chyna was sure that Ariel had sought refuge in just such a far place and was detached from this sorry world in every way that counted. After a year in this dismal hole, from time to time suffering the attentions of the sociopath upstairs, perhaps she had wandered so far along the road of inner adventure that she could not easily—or ever—return.

In fact, the girl raised her gaze from the book and sat staring neither at Chyna's face in the door port nor apparently at anything in the room, but at something in a world twice removed from this one. Even in the inadequate rose light, Chyna could see that Ariel's eyes were out of focus and as strange as the eyes of any of the dolls that surrounded her.

The killer had told the men at the service station that he had not yet touched Ariel in "that way," and Chyna believed him. Because once he had taken her innocence, he would need to smash her beauty; and when that was done, he would kill her. The fact that she was alive argued that she was still untouched.

Yet day after day, month after dreadful month, she had lived in exhausting suspense, waiting for the hateful son of a bitch to decide that she was "ripe," waiting for his brutal assault, his sour breath on her face, his hot and insistent hands, the terrible irresistible weight of him, every indignity and humiliation. In her single room, there had been nowhere to hide; she could not escape to the rooftop, to the beach, to the attic, to the crawlspace, to the upper limbs of the tree in the backyard.

"Ariel."

The refuge to which she had escaped might be in the pages of the book that she now held. She functioned in this world, grooming and feeding and bathing and dressing herself, but she *lived* in some other dimension.

Chyna's heart rolled in a sea of sorrow in a storm of rage, and through the port in the upholstered door, she said, "I'm here, Ariel. I'm here. You aren't alone any more."

Ariel's gaze didn't shift out of dreams, and she was as still as any of the dolls.

"I am your guardian, Ariel. I'll keep you safe."

As the girl followed a long and winding road farther into her private Elsewhere, her hands relaxed, and the book slipped out of them. It slid off the edge of the chair and thumped to the floor, and all except a whisper of the sound was absorbed by the special walls and ceiling. She was not aware of having dropped the volume, and she sat unmoving.

"I'm your guardian," Chyna repeated, and wondered vaguely at her choice of words.

She was more afraid for Ariel than for herself, and her heart was racing faster than ever before.

"Your guardian."

Hot tears blurred Chyna's vision, disabling tears, an indulgence she could not afford. She blinked furiously until her eyes were dry and her vision was clear.

She turned from the locked inner door and angrily pushed open the outer one.

*Tatta-tatta-tatta-tatta-tatta . . .*

As she stepped out of the heavy sound-baffling of the vestibule and into the first room in the basement, the rattling pipe seemed louder than she remembered.

*Tatta-tatta-tatta . . .*

Perhaps a minute had passed since she'd slid aside the padded panel on the view port.

The son of a bitch bastard freak was still in his shower, naked and defenseless. And now that Chyna knew where Ariel was, she didn't have to worry that the cops would need him to lead them to the girl.

The gun felt good in her hand.

It felt wonderful in her hand.

If she could have freed Ariel and gotten her out of there, she would have done that rather than take the violent option. But she didn't possess a key, and that inner door was not going to be easy to break down.

*Tatta-tatta-tatta . . .*

She had only one choice. She went to the cellar stairs.

Blue steel gleaming in her hand.

Even if he finished showering and shut off the water before Chyna was able to reach him, he'd still be naked and defenseless, toweling off, so she would go in there, into the bathroom, and open fire on him point-blank, shoot him down, empty the revolver into him, the first shot right through his fucking heart, then put at least one round in his face, to be sure that he was really done for. Take no chances. No chances at all. Use every round, squeeze the trigger until the hammer click-click-clicked on the expended cartridges in a totally empty cylinder. She could do it. Kill the crazy freak, kill him over and over again, kill him until he stayed killed. She could do it, *would* do it.

She climbed the steep stairs, treading on wet footprints that she'd left in her descent: Chyna Shepherd no longer hiding, up and out of that hole, untouched, alive, coming out of Narnia forever.

*Tatta-tatta-tatta* . . .

Thinking ahead as she moved, Chyna wondered if she should shoot him through the shower curtain—if it was, in fact, a curtain instead of a glass door—because if she *didn't* shoot him through it, then she would have to hold the revolver in just one hand while she yanked the curtain or the door aside. That would be risky, because a strange and dismaying weakness was creeping into her fingers and into her wrists. Her arms were shaking so badly that already she had to grip the weapon with both hands to prevent herself from dropping it.

Her heart rattling like the copper pipe, scared about the coming confrontation even if the crazy geek *was* naked and defenseless, Chyna reached the upper landing and entered the laundry room.

She couldn't shoot him through the curtain, because she wouldn't know whether she'd hit him or not. She'd be shooting blind, unable to aim for his chest or head.

Past the dryer and the washer, through the fragrance of laundry detergent, she reached the open door to the kitchen. Crossing the threshold, she belatedly registered the important thing that she had seen on the landing at the head of the cellar stairs: wet shoeprints larger than her own, among her prints, overlapping her prints, where he had stood only a short while ago.

She was already rushing into the kitchen, with too much momentum to halt, and the killer came at her from the right, past the dinette set. He was big, strong, a juggernaut, neither naked nor defenseless, the shower having been a ruse all along.

He was fast, but she was marginally faster. He tried to drive her backward and slam her against the cabinets, but she slid out of the way, raising the revolver, with the muzzle three feet from his face, and she pulled the trigger, and the hammer made a dry, stick-breaking sound as it fell on an empty chamber.

She backed hard into the side of the refrigerator, dislodging the kittens-and-lilies calendar, which clattered to the floor at her feet.

The killer was still rushing at her.

She squeezed the trigger, and the revolver clicked again, which made no sense—*shit*—because the clerk in the service station never had a chance to fire it before he had been blown away by the shotgun. No cartridges should be missing.

This was the first time that she had seen the killer's face. Always before, she'd glimpsed just the back of his head, the top of his skull, the side of his face but from a distance. He was not what she had expected, not moon-faced and pale-lipped and heavy-jawed. He was handsome, with blue eyes that were a beautiful contrast with his dark hair—nothing crazy in his clear eyes—broad clean features, and a nice smile.

Smiling, he continued to come straight at her as she squeezed the trigger a third time, and the hammer fell yet again on an empty chamber. Smiling, he tore the revolver out of her hand with such force that she thought her finger broke before it slipped through the trigger guard, and she squealed in pain.

The killer backed away from her, holding the weapon, his eyes sparkling with excitement. "What a kick *that* was."

Chyna huddled against the side of the refrigerator, tramping on kitten faces.

"I knew it was the same gun," he said, "but what if I'd been wrong? I'd have one big hole in my face right now, wouldn't I, little lady?"

Weak and dizzy with terror, she looked around desperately for anything that could be used as a weapon, but there was nothing close at hand.

"One big hole in my face," he repeated, as if he found that prospect amusing.

One of the cabinets might contain knives, but she had no way of knowing which drawer to check.

"Intense," he said, smiling at the revolver in his hand.

A pistol lay on the counter across the kitchen, beside the sink, well out of her reach. Chyna couldn't believe this: He had brought a gun of his own, but he hadn't used it, had set it aside, and had gone for her bare-handed instead.

"You're an attractive woman."

She looked away from the pistol, hoping he hadn't noticed that she'd seen it. But she was fooling herself, and she knew it, because he saw everything, everything.

He pointed the revolver at her. "You were back there in the service station last night."

She was gasping for breath, but she didn't seem to be drawing any air. She was breathing too fast and too shallowly, in danger of hyperventilating, and she was furious with herself, *furious*, because he was so calm.

He said, "I know you were there, somehow, somewhere, and I know you found this Chief's Special after I left, but for the life of me, I can't figure why you're *here*."

Maybe she would be able to get to the pistol before he could stop her. It was a million-to-one chance. Two million, three. Hell, face it, impossible.

From five feet away, aiming the revolver at the bridge of her nose, his voice bubbly with exhilaration, the killer said, "But even though it was the Asian's piece, I was walking into the mouth of the dragon here. I was lucky just now. Are you?"

Although reaching the pistol was probably impossible, she didn't have any alternatives. Nothing to lose.

With a note of impatience, he said, "Honey, listen to me, please, I'm talking to you. Do you feel lucky right now? As lucky as I've been?"

Trying not to stare at the pistol, reluctant to look into his too-normal eyes, she gazed down the bore of the revolver and managed to say, "No," and she half believed that she heard that single word echoing back to her out of the barrel, *No*.

"Let's see if you are."

"No."

"Oh, be adventurous, sweetheart. Let's see if you're lucky," he said, and he pulled the trigger.

Although the weapon had failed to fire three times, she expected it to explode in her face, because that seemed to be the way luck was running for her, and she flinched.

*Click.*

"You *are* lucky, even more so than I am."

Chyna didn't know what he was talking about. She couldn't focus her thoughts on anything but the pistol by the sink, this last miraculous chance.

"When Fuji started to pull this piece on me," the killer said, "didn't you hear what I promised him?"

All this talking and the bastard's calm demeanor unnerved Chyna even further. She expected him to shoot her, cut her, beat her, and probably rape her, torture answers from her before or after, but she didn't expect to have to *chat* with him, for God's sake, as if what they had been through was only a pleasant little road trip, a shared vacation that had taken a couple of interesting twists.

Still pointing the revolver at her, he said, "What I told Fuji was, 'Don't, or I'll shove the bullets up your ass.' I always keep my promises. Don't you?"

His patter finally captured her undivided attention.

"In such poor light, and with all that blood everywhere, not wanting to look, squeamish, you probably didn't see that Fuji's pants were pulled down."

He was right. After a glance showed her that the clerks were both dead, she had averted her eyes and stepped around their bodies.

He said, "I managed to insert four rounds in him."

Now she closed her eyes. Opened them at once. She didn't want to see him, looming and handsome with his nice smile, dry bloodstains on his clothes and nothing disturbing in his eyes. But she didn't dare look away.

*Chyna Shepherd, untouched and alive.*

"I put four bullets in," he said, "but then they started popping back out. A little postmortem gas release. It was ridiculous, quite funny, really, but I was pressed for time, as you might understand, and finally it was just too much trouble to do the fifth."

Maybe this was best. Maybe one more round of Russian roulette, and then peace at long last, no more trying to understand why there was so much cruelty in the world when kindness was the easier choice.

He said, "This is a five-shot weapon."

The empty socket of the muzzle stared blindly at her, and she wondered if she would see the flash and hear the roar or whether the blackness in the barrel would become her own blackness, without any awareness of the exchange.

Then the killer turned the revolver away from her and pulled the trigger. The blast rattled windows, and the slug tore through a cabinet door along the nearest wall, spraying splinters of pine and shattering dishes inside.

Bits of wood were still flying when Chyna grabbed a drawer and yanked it out of the cabinet. It was so heavy that it almost pulled out of her hand, but she was suddenly strong with desperation, and she slung it upward at the killer's head, the contents spilling from it as it arced high toward his brow.

Spoons, forks, butter knives dueling in the air, flashing with cold fluorescent reflections, ringing down on him and across the tile floor, startled him backward into the dinette table.

Even as the killer stumbled away in surprise, Chyna was moving toward the sink. An instant after she heard the empty drawer crash against something, she put her hand on the grip of the pistol. She saw a red dot on the steel frame, which was probably exposed when the safety was off, as on other pistols with which she was familiar, and she didn't have to worry about empty chambers, as with the revolver, because if there was even one bullet in the magazine, just one, it would be in the breech, *please*, and at this close range one round might be all that she needed.

But her trigger finger was already stiffening and swelling, and when she tried to hook it through the guard, the flare of pain rocked her. She bobbled on a black tide of nausea, swayed, fumbling at the trigger guard with her middle finger.

Skating across the littered floor with an ice-brittle clatter-clink of scattering tableware, the killer reached Chyna before she could bring the gun up and turn. He slammed his arm down on hers and trapped her hand against the countertop.

Reflexively her finger pulled the trigger. A bullet smashed the backsplash. Chips of yellow ceramic tile sprayed in her face, and she might have been blinded if she hadn't squeezed her eyes shut in time.

He slammed the heel of his hand against the side of her head, sending a spray of darkness across the backs of her eyes, like shards of exploding black glass, and then he clubbed his fist against the nape of her neck.

With no memory of having fallen, Chyna was lying on the kitchen floor, with a bug's-eye view across the vinyl tile, gazing through a cataclysmic tumble of eating utensils. Interesting. Spoons were the size of shovels. Forks as big as pitchforks. Knives were lances.

The killer's boots. Black boots. Moving around.

For a moment she became confused, thinking that she was back in the Templeton house in the Napa Valley, hiding under the bed in the guest room. But there hadn't been flatware scattered across that bedroom floor, and when she focused on the stainless-steel utensils again, her thoughts cleared.

"Now I'm going to have to wash all these," the killer said, "before I put them away."

He was circling through the kitchen, picking up the flatware and being methodical about it, keeping spoons with spoons, knives with knives.

Chyna was surprised that she could move her arm, which was as heavy as a great tree limb, a petrified tree once wood but now stone. Nevertheless, she managed to point at the killer and even curl her throbbing trigger finger, swallowing her pain and the bitter taste that came with it.

The gun didn't fire.

She squeezed the trigger again, and still there was no boom, and then she realized that her hand was empty. She wasn't holding the pistol.

Strange.

One of the knives was near her hand. It was a table knife with a finely serrated edge, suitable for spreading butter or for slicing well-cooked chicken or for cutting green beans into bite-size pieces, but not ideal for stabbing someone to death. A knife was a knife, however, better than no weapon at all, and she quietly closed her hand around it.

Now all she had to do was find the strength to get off the floor. Curiously, she couldn't even lift her head. She had never before felt so *tired*.

She had been hit hard on the back of the neck. She wondered about spinal injury.

She refused to weep. She had the knife.

The killer came to her, stooped, and extracted the knife from her hand. She was amazed at how easily it *slipped* from her fingers, even though she clutched it ferociously, as if it hadn't been a knife at all but a sliver of melting ice.

"Bad girl," he said, and rapped the flat of the blade against the top of her skull.

He continued with the cleanup.

While trying not to think about spinal injuries, Chyna managed to get her hand around a fork.

He returned and took that away from her too. "No," he said, as though he were training a recalcitrant puppy. "No."

"Bastard," she said, dismayed to hear a slur in her voice.

"Sticks and stones."

"Fucking bastard."

"Oh, very pretty," he said scornfully.

"Shithead."

"I should wash your mouth out with soap."

"Asshole."

"Your mother never taught you words like that."

"You don't know my mother," she said thickly.

He hit her again, a hard chop to the side of the neck this time.

Then Chyna lay in darkness, listening worriedly to her mother's distant gay laughter and strange men's voices. Shattering glass. Cursing. Thunder and wind. Palm trees thrashing in the night over Key West. The quality of the laughter changed. Mocking now. Crashes that weren't thunder. And the skittery palmetto beetle over her bare legs and across her back. Other times. Other places. In the vapory realm of dreams, the iron fist of memory.

7

Shortly after nine o'clock in the morning, after dealing with the woman and washing the flatware, Mr. Vess sets loose the dogs.

At the back door, at the front door, and in his bedroom, there are call buttons that, when pushed, sound a soft buzzer in the kennel behind the barn. When the Dobermans have been sent there with the word *crib*, as they were sent earlier, the buzzer is a command that at once returns them to active patrol.

He uses the call button by the kitchen door and then steps to the large window by the dinette to watch the backyard.

The sky is low and gray, still shrouding the Siskiyou Mountains, but rain is no longer falling. The drooping boughs of the evergreens drip steadily. The bark on the deciduous trees is a sodden black; their limbs—some with the first fragile green buds of spring, others still barren—are so coaly that they appear to have been stripped by fire.

Some people might think that the scene is passive now, with the thunder spent and the lightning extinguished, but Mr. Vess knows that a storm is as powerful in its aftermath as in its raging. He is in harmony with this new kind of power, the quiescent power of growth that water bestows on the land.

From the back of the barn come the Dobermans. They pad side by side for a distance, but then split up and proceed each in his own direction.

They are not on attack status at this time. They will chase down and detain any intruder, but they will not kill him. To prime them for blood, Mr. Vess must speak the name *Nietzsche*.

One of the dogs—Liederkranz—comes onto the back porch, where he stares at the window, adoring his master. His tail wags once, and then once again, but he is on duty, and this brief and measured display of affection is all that he will allow himself.

Liederkranz returns to the backyard. He stands tall, vigilant. He gazes first to the south, then west, and then east. He lowers his head, smells the wet grass, and at last he moves off across the lawn, sniffing industriously. His ears flatten against his skull as he concentrates on a scent, tracking something that he imagines might be a threat to his master.

On a few occasions, as a reward to the Dobermans and to keep them sharp, Mr. Vess has turned loose a captive and has allowed the dogs to stalk her, forgoing the pleasure of the kill himself. It is an entertaining spectacle.

Secure behind the screen of his four-legged Praetorian Guard, Mr. Vess goes upstairs to the bathroom and adjusts the water in the shower until it is luxuriously hot. He lowers the volume of the radio but leaves it tuned to the swing-music program.

As he strips off his soiled clothing, clouds of steam pour over the top of the shower curtain. This humidity enhances the fragrance of the dark stains in his garments. Naked, he stands for a couple of minutes with his face buried in the blue jeans, the T-shirt, the denim jacket, breathing deeply at first but then delicately sniffing one exquisite nuance of odor after another, wishing that his sense of smell were twenty thousand times more intense than it is, like that of a Doberman.

Nevertheless, these aromas transport him into the night just past. He hears once more the soft popping of the sound suppressor on the pistol, the muffled cries of terror and the thin pleas for mercy in the night calm of the Templeton house. He smells Mrs. Templeton's lilac-scented body lotion, which she'd applied to her skin before retiring, the fragrance of the sachet in the daughter's underwear drawer. He tastes, in memory, the spider.

Regretfully, he puts the clothes aside for laundering, because by this evening he must pass for the ordinary man that he is not, and this reverse lycanthropy requires time if the transformation is to be convincing.

Therefore, as Benny Goodman plays "One O'clock Jump," Mr. Vess plunges into the stinging-hot water, being especially vigorous with the washcloth and lavish with a bar of Irish Spring, scrubbing away the too pungent scents of sex and death, which might alarm the sheep. They must never suspect the shepherd of having a snaggletoothed snout and a bushy tail inside his herdsman's disguise. Taking his time, bopping to song after song, he shampoos his thick hair twice and then treats it with a penetrating conditioner. He uses a small brush to scrub under his fingernails. He is a perfectly proportioned man, lean but muscular. As always, he takes great pleasure in soaping himself, enjoying the sculpted contours of his body under his slippery hands; he feels like the music sounds, like the soap smells, like the taste of sweetened whipping cream.

Life *is*. Vess lives.

Chyna came out of Key West darkness and tropical thunder into a fluorescent glare that stung her bleary eyes. At first she mistook the fear that drove her pounding heart for the fear of Jim Woltz, her mother's friend; she thought that her face was pressed to the floor under the bed in his seaside cottage. But then she remembered the killer and the captive girl.

She was sitting forward in a chair, slumped over the round table in the dining area off the knotty-pine kitchen. Her head was turned to her right, and she was looking through a window at the back porch, the backyard.

The killer had removed a seat cushion from one of the other chairs and had placed it under her head, so her face wouldn't press uncomfortably against the wood. She shuddered at his thoughtfulness.

As she tried to lift her head, pain shot up the back of her neck and throbbed in the right side of her face. She almost blacked out, and decided not to be in a rush about getting up.

When she shifted in the chair, the clink of chains indicated that getting up might not be a choice either now or later. Her hands were in her lap, and when she tried to lift one, she lifted both, for her wrists were cuffed.

She tried to pull her feet apart—and discovered that her ankles were shackled. Judging by the noisy rattling and clinking that her small movements generated, there were other encumbrances as well.

Outside, something as black as soot bounded across the green lawn, scampered up the steps, and crossed the porch. It came to the window, jumped up, put its paws on the window stool, and peered in at her. A Doberman pinscher.

Against her breasts, Ariel holds an open book as if it is a shield, hands splayed across the binding. She is in the enormous armchair, legs drawn up beneath her, the only perfect doll of all those in the room.

Mr. Vess sits on a footstool before her.

He cleans up well. Showered, shampooed, shaved, and combed, he is presentable in any company, and any mother, seeing him on the arm of her daughter, would think that he was a prize. He is wearing loafers without socks, beige cotton Dockers, a braided leather belt, and a pale-green chambray shirt.

In her schoolgirl uniform, Ariel looks good too. Vess is pleased to see that she has regularly groomed herself in his absence, as she was instructed. It is not easy for her, taking only sponge baths and shampooing her glorious hair in the sink.

He constructed this room for others, who came before her, none of whom was in residence longer than two months. Until he'd met his Ariel, and learned what an engagingly independent spirit she was, he'd never imagined that he would insist on anyone staying this long. Consequently, a shower had seemed unnecessary.

He had first seen the girl in a newspaper photograph. Though only a tenth-grader, she had been something of a prodigy and had led her Sacramento high school team to victory in a statewide California academic decathlon. She had looked so tender. The newspaper had trembled in his hands when he had seen her, and he had known at once that he must drive to Sacramento and meet her. He'd shot the father. The mother had owned an enormous collection of dolls and had made dolls of her own as a hobby. Vess had beaten her to death with a ventriloquist dummy that had a large, carved-maple head as effective as a baseball bat.

"You're more beautiful than ever," he tells Ariel, and his voice is muffled by the soundproofing, as if he were speaking from inside a coffin, buried alive.

She does not reply or even acknowledge his presence. She is in her silent mode, as she has been without interruption for more than six months.

"I missed you."

These days, she never looks at him but stares at a point above his head and off to one side. If he were to stand up from the footstool and move into her line of sight, she would *still* be looking over his head and to one side, though he would never quite be able to see her eyes shift in avoidance.

"I brought a few things to show you."

From a shoe box on the floor beside the footstool, he extracts two Polaroid photographs. She will not accept them or turn her eyes to them, but Vess knows that she will examine these mementos after he leaves.

She is not as lost to this world as she pretends to be. They are engaged in a complicated game with high stakes, and she is a good player.

"This first is a picture of a lady named Sarah Templeton, the way she looked before I had her. She was in her forties but very attractive. A lovely woman."

The armchair is so deep that the seat cushion provides a ledge in front of Ariel on which Vess can place the photograph.

"Lovely," he repeats.

Ariel doesn't blink. She is capable of staring fixedly without blinking for surprisingly long periods. Now and then Mr. Vess worries that she will damage her striking blue eyes; corneas require frequent lubrication. Of course, if she goes too long without blinking and her eyes become dangerously dry, the irritation will cause tears to spring up involuntarily.

"This is a second photograph of Sarah, after I was finished with her," Mr. Vess says, and he also places this picture on the chair. "As you can see if you choose to look, the word *lovely* doesn't apply any more. Beauty never lasts. Things change."

From the shoe box he takes two more photographs.

"This is Sarah's daughter, Laura. Before. And after. You can see she was beautiful. Like a butterfly. But there's a worm in every butterfly, you know."

He places these snapshots on the chair and reaches into the box again.

"This was Laura's father. Oh, and here's her brother . . . and the brother's wife. They were incidental."

Finally he brings out the three Polaroids of the young Asian gentleman and the Slim Jim with the bite missing.

"His name is Fuji. Like the mountain in Japan."

Vess puts two of the three photos on the chair.

"I'll keep one for myself. To eat. And then I'll be Fuji, with the power of the East and the power of the mountain, and when the time comes for me to do you, you'll feel both the boy and the mountain in me, and so many other people, all their power. It'll be very exciting for you, Ariel, so exciting that when it's over, you won't even care that you're dead."

This is a long speech for Mr. Vess. He is for the most part not a garrulous man. The girl's beauty, however, moves him now and then to speeches.

He holds up the Slim Jim.

"The missing bite was taken by Fuji just before I killed him. His saliva will have dried on the meat. You can taste a little of his quiet power, his inscrutable nature."

He puts the wrapped sausage on the chair.

"I'll be back after midnight," Mr. Vess promises. "We'll go out to the motor home, so you can see Laura, the real Laura, not just the picture of her. I brought her back so you could see what becomes of all pretty things. And there's a young man too, a hitchhiker that I picked up along the way. I showed him a photograph of you, and I just didn't like the way he looked at it. He wasn't respectful. He leered. I didn't like something he said about you, so I sewed his mouth shut, and I sewed his eyes shut because of the way he looked at your picture. You'll be excited to see what I did to him. You can touch him . . . and Laura."

Vess watches her closely for any tic, shudder, flinch, or subtle change in the eyes that will indicate that she hears him. He *knows* that she hears, but she is clever at maintaining a solemn face and a pretense of catatonic detachment.

If he can force one faint flinch from her, one tic, then he will soon shatter her completely and have her howling like a goggle-eyed patient in the deepest wards of Bedlam. That collapse into ranting insanity is always fascinating to watch.

But she is tough, this girl, with surprising inner resources. Good. The challenge thrills him.

"And from the motor home we'll go out to the meadow with the dogs, Ariel, and you can watch while I bury Laura and the hitchhiker. Maybe the sky will clear by that time, and maybe there'll be stars or even moonlight."

Ariel huddles on the chair with her book, eyes distant, lips slightly parted, a deeply still girl.

"Hey, you know, I bought another doll for you. An interesting little shop in Napa, California, a place that sells the work of local craftsmen. It's a clever rag doll. You'll like it. I'll give it to you later."

Mr. Vess gets up from the footstool and takes a casual inventory of the contents of the refrigerator and the cabinet that serves as the girl's pantry. She has enough supplies to carry her three more days, and he will restock her shelves tomorrow.

"You're not eating quite as much as you should," he admonishes. "That's ungrateful of you. I've given you a refrigerator, a microwave, hot and cold running water. You've got everything you need to take care of yourself. You should eat."

The dolls are no less responsive than the girl.

"You've lost two or three pounds. It hasn't affected your looks yet, but you can't lose any more."

She gazes into thin air, as if waiting for her voice-box string to be pulled before she recites recorded messages.

"Don't think you can starve yourself until you're haggard and unattractive. You can't escape me that way, Ariel. I'll strap you down and force-feed you if I have to. I'll make you swallow a rubber tube and pump baby food into your stomach. In fact, I'd enjoy it. Do you like pureed peas? Carrots? Applesauce? I guess it doesn't matter, since you won't taste them—unless you regurgitate."

He gazes at her silken hair, which is red blond in the filtered light. This sight translates through all five of Vess's extraordinary senses, and he is bathed in the sensory splendor of her hair, in all the sounds and smells and textures that the look of it conveys to him. One stimulus has so many associations for him that he could lose himself for hours in the contemplation of a single hair or one drop of rain, if he chose, because that item would become an entire world of sensation to him.

He moves to the armchair and stands over the girl.

She doesn't acknowledge him, and although he has entered her line of sight, her gaze has somehow shifted above and to one side of him without his being aware of the moment when it happened.

She is magically evasive.

"Maybe I could get a word or two out of you if I set you on fire. What do you think? Hmmm? A little lighter fluid on that golden hair—and *whoosh!*"

She does not blink.

"Or I'll give you to the dogs, see if that unties your tongue."

No flinch, no tic, no shudder. What a girl.

Mr. Vess stoops, lowering his face toward Ariel's, until they are nose-to-nose.

Her eyes are now directly aligned with his—yet she is still not looking at him. She seems to peer *through* him, as if he is not a man of flesh and blood but a haunting spirit that she can't quite detect. This isn't merely the old trick of letting her eyes swim out of focus; it's a ruse infinitely more clever than that, which he can't understand at all.

Nose-to-nose with her, Vess whispers, "We'll go to the meadow after midnight. I'll bury Laura and the hitchhiker. Maybe I'll put you into the ground with them and cover you up, three in one grave. Them dead and you alive. Would you speak then, Ariel? Would you say *please?*"

No answer.

He waits.

Her breathing is low and even. He is so close to her that her exhalations are warm and steady against his lips, like promises of kisses to come.

She must feel his breath too.

She may be frightened of him and even repulsed by him, but she also finds him alluring. He has no doubt about this. Everyone is fascinated by bad boys.

He says, "Maybe there'll be stars."

Such a blueness in her eyes, such sparkling depths.

"Or even moonlight," he whispers.

The steel cuffs on Chyna's ankles were linked by a sturdy chain. A second and far longer chain, connected by a carabiner to the first, wound around the thick legs of the chair and around the stretcher bars between the legs, returned between her feet, encircled the big barrel that supported the round table, and connected again to the carabiner. The chains didn't contain enough play to allow her to stand. Even if she'd been able to stand, she would have had to carry the chair on her back, and the restricting shape and the weight of it would have forced her to bend forward like a hunchbacked troll. And once standing, she could not have moved from the table to which she was tethered.

Her hands were cuffed in front of her. A chain was hooked into the shackle that encircled her right wrist. From there it led around her, wound between the back rails of the chair behind the tie-on pad, then to the shackle on her left wrist. This chain contained enough slack to allow her to rest her arms on the table if she wished.

She sat with her hands folded, leaning forward, staring at the red and swollen index finger on her right hand, waiting.

Her finger throbbed, and she had a headache, but her neck pain had subsided. She knew that it would return worse than ever in another twenty-four hours, like the delayed agony of severe whiplash.

Of course, if she was still alive in another twenty-four hours, neck pain would be the least of her worries.

The Doberman was no longer at the window. She had seen two at once on the lawn, padding back and forth, sniffing the grass and the air, pausing occasionally to prick their ears and listen intently, then padding away again, obviously on guard duty.

During the previous night, Chyna had used rage to overcome her terror before it had incapacitated her, but now she discovered that humiliation was even more effective at quelling fear. Having been unable to protect herself, having wound up in bondage—that was not the source of her humiliation; what mortified worse was her failure to fulfill her promise to the girl in the cellar.

*I am your guardian. I'll keep you safe.*

She kept returning, in memory, to the upholstered vestibule and the view port on the inner door. The girl among the dolls had given no indication that she had heard the promise. But Chyna was sick with the certainty that she had raised false hopes, that the girl would feel betrayed and more abandoned than ever, and that she would withdraw even further into her private Elsewhere.

*I am your guardian.*

In retrospect, Chyna found her arrogance not merely astonishing but perverse, delusional. In twenty-six years of living, she'd never saved anyone, in any sense whatsoever. She was no heroine, no mystery-novel-series character with just a colorful dash of angst and a soupçon of endearing character flaws and, otherwise, the competence of Sherlock Holmes and James Bond combined. Keeping herself alive, mentally stable, and emotionally intact had been enough of a struggle for her. She was still a lost girl herself, fumbling blindly through the years for some insight or resolution that probably wasn't even out there to be found, yet she'd stood at that view port and promised deliverance.

*I am your guardian.*

She opened her folded hands. She flattened her hands on the table and slid them across the wood as if smoothing away wrinkles in a tablecloth, and as she moved, her chains rattled.

She wasn't a fighter, after all, no one's paladin; she worked as a waitress. She was good at it, piling up tips, because sixteen years in her mother's bent world had taught her that one way to ensure survival was to be ingratiating. With her customers, she was indefatigably charming, relentlessly agreeable, and always eager to please. The relationship between a diner and a waitress was, to her way of thinking, the *ideal* relationship, because it was brief, formal, generally conducted with a high degree of politeness, and required no baring of the heart.

*I am your guardian.*

In her obsessive determination to protect herself at all costs, she was always friendly with the other waitresses where she worked, but she never made friends with any of them. Friendships involved commitment, risks. She had learned not to make herself vulnerable to the hurt and betrayal that ensued from commitments.

Over the years, she'd had affairs with only two men. She had liked both and had loved the second, but the first relationship had lasted eleven months and the second only thirteen. Lovers, if they were worthwhile, required more than simple commitment; they needed revelation, sharing, the bond of emotional intimacy. She found it difficult to reveal much about her childhood or her mother, in part because her utter helplessness during those years embarrassed her. More to the point, she had come to the hard realization that her mother had never really loved her, perhaps had never been capable of loving her or anyone. And how could she expect to be cherished by any man who knew that she'd been unloved even by her mother?

She was aware that this attitude was irrational, but awareness didn't free her. She understood that she was not responsible for what her mother had done to her, but regardless of what so many therapists claimed in their books and on their radio talk shows, understanding alone didn't lead to healing. Even after a decade beyond her mother's control, Chyna was at times convinced that all the dark events of all those troubled years could have been avoided if only she, Chyna, had been a better girl, more worthy.

*I am your guardian.*

She folded her hands on the table again. She leaned forward until her forehead was pressed to the backs of her thumbs, and she closed her eyes.

The only close friend she'd ever had was Laura Templeton. Their relationship was something that she had wanted badly but had never sought, desperately needed but did little to nurture; it was purely a testament to Laura's vivaciousness, perseverance, and selflessness in the face of Chyna's caution and reserve, a result of Laura's dear heart and her singular capacity to love. And now Laura was dead.

*I am your guardian.*

In Laura's room, under the dead gaze of Freud, Chyna had knelt beside the bed and whispered to her shackled friend, *I'll get you out of here.* God, how it hurt to think of it. *I'll get you out of here.* Her stomach knotted excruciatingly with self-disgust. *I'll find a weapon,* she had promised. Laura, selfless to the end, had urged her to run, to get out. *Don't die for me,* Laura had said. But Chyna had answered, *I'll be back.*

Now here came grief again, swooping like a great dark bird into her heart, and she almost let its wings enfold her, too eager for the strange solace of those battering pinions—until she realized that she was using grief to knock humiliation from its perch. Grieving, she would have no room for self-loathing.

*I am your guardian.*

Although the clerk had never fired the revolver, she should have checked it. She should have known. Somehow. Some way. Though she could not possibly have known what Vess had done with the bullets, she should have *known.*

Laura had always told her that she was too hard on herself, that she would never heal if she kept inflicting new bruises on the old in endless self-flagellation.

But Laura was dead.

*I am your guardian.*

Chyna's humiliation festered into shame.

And if humiliation was a good tool for repressing terror, shame was even better. Steeping in shame, she knew no fear at all, even though she was in shackles in the house of a sadistic murderer, with no one in the world looking for her. Justice seemed served by her being there.

Then she heard footsteps approaching.

She raised her head and opened her eyes.

The killer entered from the laundry room, evidently returning from the girl in the cellar.

Without speaking to Chyna, without glancing at her, as if she didn't exist, he went to the refrigerator, removed a carton of eggs, and put it on the counter beside the sink. He deftly broke eight eggs into a bowl and threw the shells in the trash. He set the bowl in the refrigerator and proceeded to peel and chop a Bermuda onion.

Chyna hadn't eaten in more than twelve hours; nonetheless, she was dismayed to discover that she was suddenly ravenous. The onion was the sweetest scent that she had ever known, and her mouth began to water. After so much blood, after losing the only close friend she'd ever had, it seemed heartless to have an appetite so soon.

The killer put the chopped onion into a Tupperware container, snapped the lid tight, and placed it in the refrigerator beside the bowl of eggs. Next he grated half a wedge of cheddar cheese into another Tupperware container.

He was brisk and efficient in the kitchen, and he seemed to be enjoying himself. He kept his work area neat. He also washed his hands thoroughly between each task and dried them on a hand towel, not on the dish towel.

Finally the killer came to the dinette table. He sat across from Chyna, relaxed and self-confident and college-boy casual in his Dockers, braided belt, and soft chambray shirt.

Shame, which had seemed on the verge of consuming her, instead had burned itself out for the time being. A strange combination of smoldering anger and bitter despondency had replaced it.

"Now," he said, "I'm sure you're hungry, and as soon as we have a little chat, I'll make cheese omelets with stacks of toast. But to earn your breakfast, you have to tell me who you are, where you were hiding at that service station, and why you're here."

She glared at him.

With a smile, he said, "Don't think you can hold out on me."

She would be damned rather than tell him anything.

"Here's how it is," he said. "I'll kill you anyway. I'm not sure how yet. Probably in front of Ariel. She's seen bodies before, but she's never been there at the moment itself, to hear that last scream, in the sudden wetness of it all."

Chyna tried to keep her eyes on him, show no weakness.

He said, "However I choose to do you, I'll make it a lot harder for you if you don't talk to me willingly. There are things I enjoy that can be done before or after you're dead. Cooperate, and I'll do them after."

Chyna tried unsuccessfully to see some sign of madness in his eyes. Such a merry shade of blue.

"Well?"

"You're a sick sonofabitch."

Smiling again, he said, "The last thing I expected you to be was tedious."

"I know why you sewed shut his eyes and mouth," she said.

"Ah, so you found him in the closet."

"You raped him before you killed him or while you killed him. You sewed his eyes shut because he'd seen, sewed his mouth shut because you're ashamed of what you did and you're afraid that, even dead, he might tell someone."

Unfazed, he said, "Actually, I didn't have sex with him."

"Liar."

"But if I had, I wouldn't have been embarrassed. You think I'm that unsophisticated? We're all bisexual, don't you think? I have the urge for a man, sometimes, and with some of them I've indulged it. It's all sensation. Just sensation."

"Maggot."

"I know what you're trying to do," he said amiably, clearly amused by her, "but it just won't work. You're hoping one insult or another will set me off. As if I'm some hair-trigger psychopath who'll just explode if you call me the right name, push the right button, maybe insult my mother or say nasty things about the Lord. Then you hope I'll kill you fast, in a wild rage, and get it over with."

Chyna realized that he was right, although she had not been consciously aware of her own intentions. Failure, shame, and the helplessness of being shackled had reduced her to a despair that she had preferred not to consider. Now she was sickened less by him than by herself, wondering if she was a quitter and a loser, after all, just like her mother.

"But I'm not a psychopath," he said.

"Then what are you?"

"Oh . . . call me a homicidal adventurer. Or perhaps the only clear-thinking person you've ever met."

" 'Maggot' works better for me."

He leaned forward in his chair. "Here's the thing—either you tell me all about yourself, everything I want to know, or I'll work on your face with a knife while you sit there. For every question you refuse to answer, I'll take off a piece—the lobe of an ear, the tip of your pretty nose. Carve you like scrimshaw."

He said this not threateningly but matter-of-factly, and she knew that he had the stomach for it.

"I'll take all day," he said, "and you'll be insane long before you're dead."

"All right."

"All right what—conversation or scrimshaw?"

"Conversation."

"Good girl."

She was prepared to die if it came to that, but she saw no point in suffering needlessly.

"What's your name?" he asked.

"Shepherd. Chyna Shepherd. C-h-y-n-a."

"Ah, not a cryptic chant, after all."

"What?"

"Odd name."

"Is it?"

"Don't spar with me, Chyna. Go on."

"All right. But first, may I have something to drink? I'm dehydrated."

At the sink, he drew a glass of water. He put three ice cubes in it. He started to bring it to her, then halted and said, "I could add a slice of lemon."

She knew he wasn't joking. Home from the hunt, he was working now to recast himself from the role of savage stalker into that of accountant or clerk or real estate agent or car mechanic or whatever it was that he did when he was passing for normal. Some sociopaths could put on a false persona that was more convincing than the best performances of the finest actors who had ever lived, and this man was probably one of those, although after immersion in wanton slaughter, he needed this period of adjustment to remind himself of the manners and courtesies of civilized society.

"No, thanks," she said to the offer of lemon.

"It's no trouble," he graciously assured her.

"Just the water."

When he put the glass down, he slipped a cork-lined ceramic coaster under it. Then he sat across the table from her again.

Chyna was repelled by the prospect of drinking from a glass that he had handled, but she really was dehydrated. Her mouth was dry, and her throat was vaguely sore.

Because of the cuffs, she picked up the glass in both hands.

She knew that he was watching her for signs of fear.

The water didn't slop around in the tumbler. The rim of the glass didn't chatter against her teeth.

She truly wasn't afraid of him any more, at least not for the moment, although maybe later. Certainly later. Now her interior landscape was a desert under sullen skies: numbing desolation, with the angry flicker of lightning toward a far horizon.

She drank half of the water before she put the glass down.

"When I entered the room a moment ago," the killer said, "you were sitting with your hands folded, your head bowed against your hands. Were you praying?"

She thought about it. "No."

"There's no point in lying to me."

"I'm not lying. I wasn't praying just then."

"But you do pray?"

"Sometimes."

"God fears me."

She waited.

He said, "*God fears me*—those are words that can be made from the letters of my name."

"I see."

"Dragon seed."

"From the letters of your name," she said.

"Yes. And . . . forge of rage."

"It's an interesting game."

"Names are interesting. Yours is passive. A place name for a first name. And Shepherd—bucolic, fuzzily Christian. When I think of your name, I see an Asian peasant on a hillside with sheep . . . or a slant-eyed Christ making converts among the heathens." He smiled, amused by his banter. "But clearly, your name doesn't define you well. You're not a passive person."

"I have been," she said, "most of my life."

"Really? Well, you weren't passive last night."

"Not last night," she agreed. "But until then."

"My name, on the other hand, is a power name. Edgler Foreman Vess." He spelled it for her. "Not Edgar. Edge-ler. Like 'on the edge.' And Vess . . . if you draw it out, it's like a serpent hissing."

"Demon."

"Yes, that's right. It's there in my name—*demon.*"

"Anger."

He seemed pleased by her willingness to play. "You're good at this, especially considering that you don't have pen and paper."

"Vessel," she said. "That's in your name too."

"An easy one. But also *semen.* Vessel and semen, female and male. Would you like to craft an insult out of that, Chyna?"

Instead of replying, she picked up the glass and drank half of the remaining water. The ice cubes were cold against her teeth.

"Now that you've wet your whistle," Vess said, "I want to know all about you. Remember—scrimshaw."

Chyna told him everything, beginning with the moment that she had heard a scream while sitting at the guest-bedroom window in the Templeton house. She delivered her account in a monotone, not by calculation but because suddenly she could speak no other way. She tried to vary her inflection, put life into her words—but failed.

The sound of her voice, droning through the events of the night, scared her as Edgler Vess no longer did. Her account came to her as if she were listening to someone else speak, and it was the voice of a lost and defeated person.

She told herself that she was not defeated, that she still had hope, that she would get the best of this murderous bastard one way or another. But her inner voice lacked all conviction.

In spite of Chyna's spiritless recitation of events, Vess was a rapt listener. He began in a relaxed slouch, lounging back in his chair, but by the time Chyna finished, he was leaning forward with his arms on the table, hunched toward her.

He interrupted her several times to ask questions. At the end, he sat for a while in contemplative silence.

She could not bear to look at him. She folded her hands on the table, closed her eyes, and put her forehead against the backs of her church-door thumbs, as she had been when Vess had come out of the laundry room.

She wasn't praying this time either. She lacked the hope needed for prayer.

After a few minutes, she heard Vess's chair slide back from the table. He got up. She heard him moving around, and then the familiar clatter of any cook being busy in any kitchen.

She smelled butter heating in a pan, then browning onions.

In the telling of her story, Chyna had lost her appetite, and it didn't return with the aroma of the onions.

Finally Vess said, "Funny that I didn't smell you right away at the Templetons'."

"You can do that?" she asked, without raising her head from her hands. "You can just smell people out, as if you were a damn dog?"

"Usually," he said, taking no offense, and with what seemed to be utmost seriousness. "And you must have made a sound more than once through the night. You surely can't be *that* stealthy. Even your breathing I should have heard."

Then came the sound of a wire whisk vigorously beating eggs in a bowl.

She smelled bread toasting.

"In a still house, with everyone dead, your movement should have made currents in the air, like a cool breath on the back of my neck, shivering the fine hairs on my hands. Your *every* movement should have been a different texture against my eyes. And when I walked through a space where you'd just been, I should have sensed the displacement of air caused by your passage."

He was stone crazy. So cute in his chambray shirt, with his beautiful blue eyes, his thick dark hair combed straight back from his forehead, and the dimple in his left cheek—but pustulant and canker-riddled inside.

"My senses, you see, are unusually acute."

He ran the water in the sink. Without looking, she knew that he was rinsing the whisk. He wouldn't put it aside dirty.

He said, "My senses are so sharp because I've given myself to sensation. Sensation is my religion, you might say."

A sizzling arose, much louder than the cooking sound of onions, and a new aroma.

"But you were invisible to me," he said. "Like a spirit. What makes you special?"

Bitter, she murmured against the tabletop, "If I was special, would I be here in chains?"

Although Chyna hadn't actually spoken to him and wouldn't have thought that he could hear her above the crisp sputtering of eggs and onions, Vess said, "I suppose you're right."

Later, when he put the plates on the table, she raised her head and moved her hands.

"Rather than make you eat with your hands, I'm going to give you a fork," he said, "because I assume you see the pointlessness of throwing it and trying to stick me in the eye."

She nodded.

"Good girl."

On her plate was a plump four-egg omelet oozing cheddar cheese and stippled with sautéed onions. On top were three slices of a firm tomato and a sprinkling of chopped parsley. Two pieces of buttered toast, each neatly sliced on the diagonal, were arranged to bracket the omelet.

He refilled her water glass and added two more cubes of ice.

Famished only a short while ago, Chyna now could hardly tolerate the sight of food. She knew that she must eat, so she picked at the eggs and nibbled the toast. But she would never be able to finish all that he had given her.

Vess ate with gusto but not noisily or sloppily. His table manners were beyond reproach, and he used his napkin frequently to blot his lips.

Chyna was deep in her private grayness, and the more Vess appeared to enjoy his breakfast, the more her own omelet began to taste like ashes.

"You'd be quite attractive if you weren't so rumpled and sweaty, your face smudged with dirt, your hair straggly from the rain. Very attractive, I think. A real charmer under that grime. Maybe later I'll bathe you."

*Chyna Shepherd, untouched and alive.*

Uncannily, after a further silence, Edgler Vess said, "Untouched and alive."

She *knew* that she had not spoken the prayer aloud.

"Untouched and alive," he repeated. "Is that what you said . . . on the stairs earlier, on your way down to Ariel?"

She stared at him, speechless.

"Is it?"

Finally: "Yes."

"I've been wondering about it. You said your name and then those three words, though none of it made sense when I didn't know that Chyna Shepherd was your name."

She looked away from him, at the window. A Doberman roamed the backyard.

"Was it a prayer?" he asked.

In her desolation, Chyna hadn't thought that he could scare her any more, but she had been wrong. His intuitiveness was frightening—and not entirely for reasons that she could understand.

She looked away from the Doberman and met Vess's eyes. For one brief moment, she saw the dog within, a dark and merciless aspect.

"Was it a prayer?" he asked again.

"Yes."

"In your heart, Chyna, deep in your heart, do you truly believe that God really exists? Be truthful now, not just with me but with yourself."

At one time—not long ago—she had been just barely sure enough of what she believed to answer *Yes*. Now she was silent.

"Even if God exists," Vess said, "does he know that *you* do?"

She took another bite of the omelet. It seemed greasier than before. The eggs and butter and cheese, too rich, cloyed in her mouth, and she could hardly swallow.

She put down her fork. She was finished. She'd eaten no more than a third of her meal.

Vess finished the food on his plate, washing it down with coffee that he didn't offer her—no doubt because he thought that she would try to throw the hot brew in his eyes.

"You look so glum," Vess said.

She didn't reply.

"You're feeling like such a failure, aren't you? You've failed poor Ariel, yourself, and God too, if He exists."

"What do you want with me?" she asked. She meant, *Why put me through this, why not kill me and get it over with?*

"I haven't figured that out yet," Vess said. "Whatever I do with you, it's got to be special. I feel you're special, whether you think you are or not, and whatever we do together should be . . . intense."

She closed her eyes and wondered if she could find Narnia again after all these years.

He said, "I can't answer your question as to what I want with you—but I have no doubts about what I want with Ariel. Would you like to hear what I intend to do with her?"

Most likely, she was too old to believe in anything, even just a magic wardrobe.

Vess's voice came out of her internal grayness, as if he lived there as well as in the real world: "I asked you a question, Chyna. Remember our bargain? You can either answer it—or I'll slice off a piece of your face. Would you like to hear what I intend to do with Ariel?"

"I'm sure I know."

"Yes, some of it. Sex, that's obvious. She's a luscious piece. I haven't touched her yet, but I will. And I believe she's a virgin. At least, in the days when she still talked, she said she was, and she didn't seem like the kind of girl who would lie."

Or there was the Wild Wood beyond the River, Ratty and Mole and Mr. Badger, green boughs hanging full in the summer sun and Pan piping in the cool shadows under the trees.

"And I want to hear her crying, lost and crying. I want to smell the purity of her tears. I want to feel the exquisite texture of her screams, know the clean smell of them, and the taste of her terror. There's always that. Always that."

Neither the languid river nor the Wild Wood materialized, though Chyna strained to see them. Ratty, Mole, Mr. Badger, and Mr. Toad were gone forever into the hateful death that claims all things. And the sadness of this, in its way, was as great as the sadness of what had happened to Laura and what would soon happen to Chyna herself.

Vess said, "Once in a while, I bring one of them back to the room in the cellar—and always for the same purpose."

She didn't want to hear this. The handcuffs made it difficult to cover her ears. And if she had tried, he would have shackled her wrists to her ankles. He would insist that she listen.

"The most intense experiences of my life have all taken place in that room, Chyna. Not the sex. Not the beating or the cutting. That all comes later, and it's a lagniappe. First, I break them down, and *that* is when it gets intense."

Her chest was tight. She could breathe only shallowly.

He said, "The first day or two, they all think they'll go out of their minds with fear, but they're wrong. It takes longer than a day or two to drive someone insane, truly and irrevocably insane. Ariel is my seventh captive, and the others all held on to their sanity for weeks. One of them cracked on the eighteenth day, but three of them lasted a full two months."

Chyna gave up on the elusive Wild Wood and met his gaze across the table.

"Psychological torture is so much more interesting and difficult to undertake than the physical variety, although the latter can be undeniably thrilling," Vess said. "The mind is so much tougher than the body, a greater challenge by far. And when the mind goes, I swear that I can hear the *crack*, a harder sound than bone splitting—and oh, how it reverberates."

She tried to see the animal consciousness in his eyes, which she had glimpsed unexpectedly before. She *needed* to see it.

"When they crack, some of them writhe on the floor, thrash, rend their clothes. They tear at their hair, Chyna, and claw their faces, and some of them bite themselves hard enough to draw blood. They maim themselves in so many inventive ways. They sob and sob, can't stop for hours, sometimes for days, sobbing in their sleep. They bark like dogs, Chyna, and screech and flail their arms as if they're convinced that they can fly. They hallucinate and see things more frightening than I am to them. Some speak in tongues. It's called *glossolalia*. Do you know the condition? Quite fascinating. Convincingly like a language yet meaningless, a ranting or pleading babble. Some lose control of their bodily functions and wallow in their filth. Messy but riveting to watch—the true base condition of humanity, to which most people can only admit in madness."

As hard as she tried, Chyna could see no beast in his eyes, only a placid blueness and the watchful darkness of the pupil, and she was no longer sure that she had ever seen it. He wasn't half man and half wolf, not a creature that fell to all fours in the light of the full moon. Worse, he was nothing but a man—living at one extreme end of the spectrum of human cruelty, but nonetheless only a man.

"Some take refuge in catatonic silences," Vess continued, "as Ariel has done. But I always break them out of that. Ariel is by far the most stubborn, but that only makes her interesting. I'll break her too, and when her *crack* comes, Chyna, it'll be like no other. Glorious. Intense."

"The most intense experience of all is showing mercy," Chyna said, and had no idea whatsoever where she had found those words. They sounded like a plea, and she didn't want him to think that she was begging for her life. Even in her despair, she would not be reduced to groveling.

A sudden smile made Vess look almost like a boy, one given to puns and pranks, collector of baseball cards, rider of bikes, builder of model airplanes, and altar boy on Sundays. She thought that he was smiling at what she'd said, amused by her naiveté, but this was not the case, as he made clear with his next words.

"Maybe . . . what I want from you," Vess said, "is to be with me when I finally make Ariel snap. Instead of killing you in front of her to drive her over the edge, I'll drive her some other way. And you can watch."

*Oh, God.*

"You're a psychology student, after all, almost a genuine *master* of psychology. Right? Sitting there in such stern judgment of me, so certain that my mind is 'aberrant' and that you know exactly how I think. Well, then, how interesting it would be to see if any of the modern theories of the working of the mind are undone by this little experiment. Don't you think so? After I break Ariel, you could write a paper about it, Chyna, for my eyes only. I'd enjoy reading your considered observations."

Dear God, it would never come to that. She'd never be a witness to such a thing. Though in shackles, she would find a way to commit suicide before she would let him take her down to that room to watch that lovely girl . . . to watch her dissolve. Chyna would bite open her own wrists, swallow her tongue, contrive to fall down the steps and break her neck, something. Something.

Evidently aware that he had jolted her out of gray despair into stark horror, Vess smiled again—and then turned his attention to her breakfast plate. "Do you intend to eat the rest of that?"

"No."

"Then I'll have it."

He slid his empty plate aside and pulled hers in front of him. Using her fork, he cut a bite-size piece of the cold omelet, put it in his mouth, and moaned softly in delight. Slowly, sensuously, Vess extracted the tines from his mouth, pressing his lips firmly around them as they slid loose, then reaching with his tongue for one last lick.

After he swallowed the bite of eggs, he said, "I could taste you on the fork. Your saliva has a lovely flavor—except for a faint bitterness. No doubt that's not a usual component, just the result of a sour stomach."

She could find no escape by closing her eyes, so she watched as he devoured the remains of her breakfast.

When he finished, she had a question of her own. "Last night . . . why did you eat the spider?"

"Why not?"

"That's no answer."

"It's the best answer to any question."

"Then give me second-best."

"You think it was disgusting?"

"I'm just curious."

"No doubt, you see it as a negative experience—eating an icky, squirmy spider."

"No doubt."

"But there are no negative experiences, Chyna. Only sensations. No values can be attached to pure sensation."

"Of course they can."

"If you think so, then you're in the wrong century. Anyway, the spider had an interesting flavor, and now I understand spiders better for having absorbed one. Do you know about flatworm learning?"

"Flatworm?"

"You should have encountered it in a basic biology course along the way to becoming such a highly educated woman. You see, certain flatworms can gradually learn to negotiate a maze—"

She did remember, and interrupted: "Then if you grind them up and feed them to another batch of flatworms, batch number two can run the same maze on the first try."

"Good. Yes." Vess nodded happily. "They absorb the knowledge with the flesh."

She didn't need to consider how to phrase her next question, for Vess could be neither insulted nor flattered. "Jesus, you don't actually believe you now know what it's like to be a spider, have all the knowledge of a spider, because you've eaten one?"

"Of course not, Chyna. If I were that literal-minded, I'd be crazy. Wouldn't I? In an institution somewhere, talking to a crowd of imaginary friends. But because of my sharp senses, I *did* absorb from the spider an ineffable quality of spiderness that you'll never be able to understand. I heightened my awareness of the spider as a marvelously engineered little hunter, a creature of power. *Spider* is a power word, you know, though it can't be formed from the letters of my name." He hesitated, pondering, and then continued: "It *can* be formed from the letters of your name."

She didn't bother to remind him about her mother's precious spelling. Only *spyder* could be found in *Chyna Shepherd*.

"And it was risky, eating a spider, which added considerably to the appeal," Vess continued. "Unless you're an entomologist, you can't be sure if any particular specimen is poisonous or not. Some, like the brown recluse, are extremely dangerous. A bite on the hand is one thing . . . but I had to be sure that I was quick and crushed it against the roof of my mouth before it could bite my tongue."

"You like taking risks."

He shrugged. "I'm just that kind of guy."

"On edge."

"Words in my name," he acknowledged.

"And if you'd been bitten on the tongue?"

"Pain is the same as pleasure, just different. Learn to enjoy it, and you're happier with life."

"Even pain is value neutral?"

"Sure. Just sensation. It helps grow the reef of the soul—if there is a soul."

She didn't know what the hell he was talking about—the reef of the soul—and she didn't ask. She was weary of him. Weary of fearing him, even weary of hating him. With her questions, she was striving to *understand*, as she had striven all her life, and she was tired to death of this search for meaning. She would never know why some people committed countless little cruelties—or bigger ones—and the struggle to understand had only exhausted her and left her empty, cold, and gray inside.

Pointing to her red and swollen index finger, Vess said, "That must hurt. And your neck."

"The headache's the worst of it. And none of it's anything like pleasure."

"Well, I can't easily show you the way to enlightenment and prove you're wrong. It takes time. But there's a smaller lesson, quick to learn. . . ."

He got up from his chair and went to a spice rack at the end of the kitchen cabinets. Among the small bottles and tins of thyme, cloves, dill, nutmeg, chili pepper, ginger, marjoram, and cinnamon was a bottle of aspirin.

"I don't take this for headaches, because I like to savor the pain. But I keep aspirin on hand because, once in a while, I like to chew on them for the taste."

"They're vile."

"Just bitter. Bitterness can be as pleasing as sweetness when you learn that every experience, every sensation, is worthwhile."

He returned to the table with the bottle of aspirin. He put it in front of her—and took away her glass of water.

"No, thanks," she said.

"Bitterness has its place."

She ignored the bottle.

"Suit yourself," Vess said, clearing the plates off the table.

Although Chyna needed relief from her various pains, she refused to touch the aspirin. Perhaps irrationally—but nonetheless strongly—she felt that by chewing a few of the tablets, even strictly for the medicinal effect, she would be stepping into the strange rooms of Edgler Vess's madness. This was a threshold that she didn't care to cross for any purpose, even with one foot solidly anchored in the real world.

He hand-washed the breakfast plates, bowls, pans, and utensils. He was efficient and fastidious, using steaming hot water and lots of lemon-scented dishwashing liquid.

Chyna had one more question that could not go unasked, and at last she said, "Why the Templetons? Why choose them of all people? It wasn't random, was it, not just the place you happened to stop in the night?"

"Not just random," he agreed, scrubbing the omelet pan with a plastic scouring pad. "A few weeks back, Paul Templeton was up this way on business, and when—"

"You *knew* him?"

"Not really. He was in town, the county seat, on business like I said, and as he was taking something from his wallet to show me, a set of those little hinged plastic windows fell out, you know, with little wallet-size photographs, and I picked them up for him. One of the pictures was his wife. Another was Laura. She looked so . . . fresh, unspoiled. I said something like 'That's a pretty girl,' and Paul was off and running about her, every inch the proud papa. Told me she was soon going to have her master's degree in psychology, three-point-eight grade average and everything. He told me how he really missed her away at school, even after six years of getting used to it, and how he couldn't wait for the end of the month, because Laura was coming home for a three-day weekend. He didn't mention she was bringing along a friend."

An accident. Photos dropped. A casual exchange, mere idle conversation.

The arbitrariness of it was breathtaking and almost more than Chyna could bear.

Then, as she watched Vess thoroughly wiping off the counters and rinsing the dishpan and scrubbing the sink, Chyna began to feel that what had happened to the Templeton family was worse than merely arbitrary. All this violent death began to seem fated, an inexorable spiral into lasting darkness, as if they had been born and had lived only for Edgler Vess.

It was as if she too had been born and had struggled this far only for the purpose of bringing one moment of sick satisfaction to this soulless predator.

The worst horror of his rampages was not the pain and fear that he inflicted, not the blood, not the mutilated cadavers. The pain and the fear were comparatively brief, considering all the routine pain and anxiety of life. The blood and bodies were merely aftermath. The worst horror was that he stole meaning from the unfinished lives of those people he killed, made *himself* the primary purpose of their existence, robbed them not of time but of fulfillment.

His base sins were envy—of beauty, of happiness—and pride, bending the whole world to his view of creation, and these were the greatest sins of all, the same transgressions over which the devil himself, once an archangel, had stumbled and fallen a long way out of Heaven.

Hand-drying the plates, pans, and flatware in the drainage rack, returning each piece to the proper shelf or drawer, Edgler Vess looked as pink-clean as a freshly bathed baby and as innocent as the stillborn. He smelled of soap, a good bracing aftershave, and lemon-scented dishwashing liquid. But in spite of all this, Chyna found herself superstitiously expecting to detect a whiff of brimstone.

Every life led to a series of quiet epiphanies—or at least to opportunities for epiphanies—and Chyna was washed by a poignant new grief when she thought about this grim aspect of the Templeton family's interrupted journeys. The kindnesses they might have done for others. The love they might have given. The things they might have come to understand in their hearts.

Vess finished the breakfast clean-up and returned to the table. "I have a few things to do upstairs, outside—and then I'll have to sleep four or five hours if I can. I've got to go to work this evening. I need my rest."

She wondered what work he did, but she didn't ask. He might be talking about a job—or about his dogged assault on Ariel's sanity. If the latter, Chyna didn't want to know what was coming.

"When you shift around in the chair, do it easy. Those chains will scrape the wood if you're not careful."

"I'd hate to mar the furniture," she said.

He stared at her for perhaps half a minute and then said, "If you're stupid enough to think you can get free, I'll hear the chains rattling, and I'll have to come back in here to quiet you. If that's necessary, you won't like what I'll do."

She said nothing. She was hopelessly hobbled and chained down. She couldn't possibly escape.

"Even if you somehow get free of the table and chairs, you can't move fast. And attack dogs patrol the grounds."

"I've seen them," she assured him.

"If you weren't chained, they'd still drag you down and kill you before you'd gone ten steps from the door."

She believed him—but she didn't understand why he felt the need to press the point so hard.

"I once turned a young man loose in the yard," Vess said. "He raced straight to the nearest tree and got up and out of harm's way with only one bad bite in his right calf and a nip on the left ankle. He braced himself in the branches and thought he would be safe for a little while, with the dogs circling below and watching him, but I got a twenty-two rifle and went out on the back porch and shot him in the leg from there. He fell out of the tree, and then it was all over in maybe a minute."

Chyna said nothing. There were moments when communicating with this hateful thing seemed no more possible than discussing the merits of Mozart with a shark. This was one of those moments.

"You were invisible to me last night," he said.

She waited.

His gaze traveled over her, and he seemed to be looking for a loose link in one of the chains or a handcuff left open and unnoticed until now. "Like a spirit."

She was not sure that it was ever possible to discern what this thing was thinking—but right now, by God, it seemed to be vaguely uneasy about leaving her alone. She couldn't for the life of her imagine *why*.

"Stay?" he said.

She nodded.

"Good girl."

He went to the door between the kitchen and the living room.

Realizing that they had one more issue to discuss, she said, "Before you go . . ."

He turned to look at her.

"Could you take me to a bathroom?" she asked.

"It's too much trouble to undo the chains just now," he said. "Piss in your pants if you have to. I'm going to clean you up later anyway. And I can buy new chair cushions."

He pushed through the door into the living room and was gone.

Chyna was determined not to endure the humiliation of sitting in her own waste. She had a faint urge to pee, but it wasn't insistent yet. Later she would be in trouble.

How odd—that she could still care about avoiding humiliation or think about the future.

Halfway across the living room, Mr. Vess stops to listen to the woman in the kitchen. He hears no clink of chains. He waits. And still no sound. The silence troubles him.

He's not sure what to make of her. He knows so much about her now—yet she still contains mysteries.

Shackled and in his complete control, surely she cannot be his blown tire. She smells of despair and defeat. In the beaten tone of her voice, he sees the gray of ashes and feels the texture of a coffin blanket. She is as good as dead, and she is resigned to it. Yet . . .

From the kitchen comes the clink of chains. Not loud, not a vigorous assault on her bonds. Just a quiet rattle as she shifts position—perhaps to clasp her thighs tightly together to repress the urge to urinate.

Mr. Vess smiles.

He goes upstairs to his room. From the top shelf at the back of his walk-in closet, he takes down a telephone. In the bedroom, he plugs it into a wall jack and makes two calls, letting people know that he has returned from his three-day vacation and will be back in harness by this evening.

Although he is confident that the Dobermans, in his absence, will never allow anyone to get into the house, Vess keeps only two phones and secretes them in closets when he is not at home. In the extremely unlikely event that an intruder should manage to sprint through the attacking dogs and get into the house alive, he will not be able to call for help.

The danger of cellular phones has been on Mr. Vess's mind in recent days. It's difficult to imagine a would-be burglar carrying a portable phone or using it to call the police for help from a house in which he's become trapped by guard dogs, but stranger things have happened. If Chyna Shepherd had found a cellular phone in the clerk's Honda the previous night, she would not be the one now languishing in shackles.

The technological revolution here at the end of the millennium offers numerous conveniences and great opportunities, but it also has dangerous aspects. Thanks to his expertise with computers, he has cleverly altered his fingerprint files with various agencies and can go without gloves at places like the Templeton house, enjoying the full sensuality of the experience without fear. But one cellular phone in the wrong hands at the wrong time could lead suddenly to the most intense experience of his life—and the final one. He sometimes longs for the simpler age of Jack the Ripper, or the splendid Ed Gein, who inspired *Psycho*, or Richard Speck; he dreams wistfully of the less complicated world of earlier decades and of killing fields that were less trampled, then, by such as he.

By feverishly pursuing high ratings, by hyping every story steeped in blood, by making celebrities out of killers, and by fawning over celebrity killers, the electronic news media happily may have inspired more of his clear-thinking kind. But they have also alarmed the sheep too much. Too many in the herd are walleyed with alertness and quick to run at the first perception of danger.

Still, he manages to have his fun.

After making his calls, Mr. Vess goes out to the motor home. The license plates, the blunt-end screws and the nuts to attach them to the vehicle, and a screwdriver are in a drawer in the kitchenette.

By various means, usually two or three weeks prior to one of his expeditions, Mr. Vess carefully selects his primary targets, like the Templeton family. And though he sometimes brings back a living prize for the cellar room, he nearly always travels well beyond the borders of Oregon to minimize the chances that his two lives—good citizen and homicidal adventurer—will cross at the most inconvenient moment. (Though he didn't employ this method to get Laura Templeton, he has found that clandestine browsing, via computer, through the huge Department of Motor Vehicles' records in neighboring California is an excellent method of locating attractive women. Their driver's license photographs—head shots only—are now on file with the DMV. Provided with each picture are the woman's age, height, and weight—statistics that assist Vess in identifying unacceptable candidates, so he can avoid grandmothers who photograph well and plump women with thin faces. And though some people list post office boxes only, most use their street addresses; thereafter, Mr. Vess needs only a series of good maps.) Upon nearing the end of his drive, when he gets within fifty miles of the target residence, he removes the license plates from the motor home. Later, because he makes a point of being far away from the scene of his games by the time anyone finds the aftermath, he could be tracked down only if someone in the victim's neighborhood happened to see the motor home and, though it looked perfectly innocent, happened to glance at the plates and—that damn blown tire again—happened to have a photographic memory. Therefore, he leaves the tags off his vehicle until he is safely back in Oregon.

If he were stopped by a police officer for speeding or for some other traffic violation, he would express surprise when asked about his missing license plates and would say that, for God knows what reason, they must have been stolen. He is a good actor; he could sell his bafflement. If the chance arose to do so without putting himself in serious jeopardy, he would kill the cop. And if no such opportunity presented itself, he would most likely be able to count on a swift resolution of the problem by calling upon professional courtesy.

Now he squats on his haunches and attaches one of the tags to the frame in the front license-plate niche.

One by one the dogs come to him, sniffing at his hands and his clothes, perhaps disappointed to find only the scents of aftershave and dishwashing soap. They are starved for attention, but they are on duty. None of them lingers long, each returning to its patrol after one pat on the head, a scratch behind the ears, and a word of affection.

"Good dog," Mr. Vess says to each. "Good dog."

When he finishes with the front plate, he stands, stretches, and yawns while surveying his domain.

At ground level, anyway, the wind has died. The air is still and moist. It smells of wet grass, earth, moldering dead leaves, and pine forests.

With the rain finished, the mist is lifting off the foothills and off the lower flanks of the mountains behind the house. He can't see the peaks of the western range yet or even the blanket of snow lingering on the higher slopes. But directly overhead and to the east, where the mist doesn't intervene, the clouds are more gray than thunderhead black, a soft moleskin gray, and they are moving rapidly southeast in front of a high-altitude wind. By midnight, as he promised Ariel, there might be stars and even a moon to light the tall grass in the meadow and to shine in the milky eyes of the dead Laura.

Mr. Vess goes to the back of the motor home to attach the second license plate—and discovers odd tracks on the driveway. As he stands staring at them, a frown pools and deepens on his face.

The driveway is shale, but during a heavy rain, mud washes out from the surrounding yard. Here and there it forms a thin skin atop the stone, not soupy but dark and dense.

In this skin of mud are hoof impressions, perhaps those of a deer. A sizable deer. It has crossed the driveway more than once.

He sees a place where it stood for a while, pawing the ground.

No tire tracks mar the mud, because they were erased by the rain that had been falling when he'd come home. Evidently the deer spoor date from after the storm.

He crouches beside the tracks and puts his fingers to the cold mud. He can feel the hardness and smoothness of the hooves that stamped the marks.

A variety of deer thrive in the nearby foothills and mountains. They rarely venture onto Mr. Vess's property, however, because they are frightened of the Dobermans.

This is the most peculiar thing about the deer tracks: that among them are no paw prints from the dogs.

The Dobermans have been trained to focus on human intruders and, as much as possible, to ignore wildlife. Otherwise, they might be distracted at a moment crucial to their master's safety. They will never attack rabbits or squirrels or possums—or deer—unless severe hunger eventually drives them to it. They won't even give playful chase.

Nevertheless, the dogs will take notice of other animals that cross their path. They indulge their curiosity within the limits of their training.

They would have approached this deer and circled ever closer as it stood here, either paralyzing it with fright or spooking it off. And after it had gone, they would have padded back and forth across the driveway, sniffing its spoor.

But not one paw print is visible among the hoof impressions.

Rubbing his muddy fingertips together, Mr. Vess rises to his full height and slowly turns in a circle, studying the surrounding land. The meadows to the north and the distant piney woods beyond. The driveway leading east to the bald knoll. The yard to the south, more meadows beyond, and woods again. Finally the backyard, past the barn, to the foothills. The deer—if it was a deer—is gone.

Edgler Vess stands motionless. Listening. Watchful. Breathing deeply, seeking scents. Then for a while he inhales through his open mouth, catching what he can upon his tongue. He feels the moist air like the clammy skin of a cadaver against his face. All his senses are open wide, irised to the max, and the freshly washed world drains into them.

Finally he can detect no harm in the morning.

As Vess is putting the license plate on the back of the motor home, Tilsiter pads to him. The dog nuzzles his master's neck.

Vess encourages the Doberman to stay. When he is finished with the plate, he points Tilsiter to the nearby deer spoor.

The dog seems not to see the tracks. Or, seeing them, he does not have any interest.

Vess leads him to the spoor, right in among the prints. Once more he points to them.

Because Tilsiter appears to be confused, Vess places his hand on the back of the dog's head and presses his muzzle into one of the tracks.

The Doberman catches a scent at last, sniffs eagerly, whimpers with excitement—then decides that he doesn't like what he smells. He squirms out from under his master's hand and backs off, looking sheepish.

"What?" says Vess.

The dog licks his chops. He looks away from Vess, surveys the meadows, the lane, the yard. He glances at Vess again, but then he trots off to the south, returning to patrol.

The trees still dripping. The mists rising. The spent clouds scudding fast toward the southeast.

Mr. Vess decides to kill Chyna Shepherd immediately.

He will haul her into the yard, make her lie facedown on the grass, and put a couple of bullets in the back of her skull. He has to go to work this evening, and before that he has to get some sleep, so he won't have time to enjoy a slow kill.

Later, when he gets home, he can bury her in the meadow with the four dogs watching, insects singing and feeding on one another in the tall grass, and Ariel forced to kiss each of the corpses before it goes forever into the ground—all this in moonlight if there is any.

Quickly now, finish her and sleep.

As he hurries toward the house, he realizes that the screwdriver is still in his hand, which might be more interesting than using the pistol, yet just as quick.

Up the flagstone steps, onto the front porch, where the finger of the Seattle attorney hangs silent among the seashells in the cool windless air.

He doesn't bother to wipe his feet, a rare breach of compulsive procedure.

The ratcheting hinge is matched by the sound of his own ragged breathing as he opens the door and steps into the house. When he closes the door, he is startled to hear his thudding heartbeats chasing one another.

He is never afraid, never. With this woman, however, he has been *unsettled* more than once.

A few steps into the room, he halts, getting a grip on himself. Now that he is inside again, he doesn't understand why killing her seemed to be such an urgent priority.

Intuition.

But never has his intuition delivered such a clamorous message that has left him this conflicted. The woman is special, and he so badly wants to use her in special ways. Merely pumping two shots into the back of her head or sticking the screwdriver into her a few times would be such a waste of her potential.

He is never afraid. Never.

Even being unsettled like this is a challenge to his dearest image of himself. The poet Sylvia Plath, whose work leaves Mr. Vess uncharacteristically ambivalent, once said that the world was ruled by panic, "panic with a dog-face, devil-face, hag-face, whore-face, panic in capital letters with no face at all—the same Johnny Panic, awake or asleep." But Johnny Panic does not rule Edgler Vess and never will, because Mr. Vess has no illusions about the nature of existence, no doubts about his purpose, and no moments of his life that ever require reinterpretation when he has the time for quiet reflection.

Sensation.

Intensity.

He cannot live with intensity if he is afraid, because Johnny Panic inhibits spontaneity and experimentation. Therefore, he will not allow this woman of mysteries to spook him.

As both his breathing and his heartbeat subside to normal rates, he turns the rubberized handle of the screwdriver around and around in his hand, staring at the short blunt blade at the end of the long steel shank.

The moment Vess entered the kitchen, before he spoke, Chyna sensed he had changed from the man that she had known thus far. He was in a different mood from any that had previously possessed him, although the precise difference was so subtle that she was not able to define it.

He approached the table as if to sit down, then stopped short of his chair. Frowning and silent, he stared at her.

In his right hand was a screwdriver. Ceaselessly he rolled the handle through his fingers, as if tightening an imaginary screw.

On the floor behind him were crumbling chunks of mud. He had come inside with dirty shoes.

She knew that she must not speak first. They were at a strange juncture where words might not mean what they had meant before, where the most innocent statement might be an incitement to violence.

A short while ago, she had half preferred to be killed quickly, and she had tried to trigger one of his homicidal impulses. She had also considered ways that, although shackled, she might be able to commit suicide. Now she held her tongue to avoid inadvertently enraging him.

Evidently, even in her desolation, she continued to harbor a small but stubborn hope that was camouflaged in the grayness where she could not see it. A stupid denial. A pathetic longing for one more chance. Hope, which had always seemed ennobling to her, now seemed as dehumanizing as feverish greed, as squalid as lust, just an animal hunger for more life at any cost.

She was in a deep, bleak place.

Finally Vess said, "Last night."

She waited.

"In the redwoods."

"Yes?"

"Did you see anything?" he asked.

"See what?"

"Anything odd?"

"No."

"You must have."

She shook her head.

"The elk," he said.

"Oh. Yes, the elk."

"A herd of them."

"Yes."

"You didn't think they were peculiar?"

"Coastal elk. They thrive in that area."

"These seemed almost tame."

"Maybe because tourists drive through there all the time."

Slowly turning and turning the screwdriver, he considered her explanation. "Maybe."

Chyna saw that the fingers of his right hand were covered with a film of dry mud.

He said, "I can smell the musk of them now, the texture of their eyes, hear the greenness of the ferns swaying around them, and it's a cold dark oil in my blood."

No reply was possible, and she didn't try to make one.

Vess lowered his gaze from Chyna's eyes to the turning point of the screwdriver—and then to his shoes. He looked over his shoulder and saw the mud on the floor.

"This won't do," he said.

He put the screwdriver on a nearby counter.

He took off his shoes and carried them into the laundry room, where he left them to be cleaned later.

He returned in his bare feet and, using paper towels and a bottle of Windex, cleaned every crumb of mud from the tiles. In the living room, he used a vacuum cleaner to sweep the mud out of the carpet.

These domestic chores occupied him for almost fifteen minutes, and by the time he finished, he was no longer in the mood that had possessed him when he'd entered the kitchen. Housework seemed to scrub away his blues.

"I'm going to go upstairs and sleep now," he said. "You'll be quiet and not rattle your chains much."

She said nothing.

"You'll be quiet, or I'll come down and shove five feet of the chain up your ass."

She nodded.

"Good girl."

He left the room.

The difference between Vess's usual demeanor and his recent mood no longer eluded Chyna. For a few minutes, he had lacked his usual self-confidence. Now he had it back.

Mr. Vess always sleeps in the nude to facilitate his dreams.

In slumberland, all the people whom he encounters are naked, whether they are being torn asunder beneath him in glorious wetness or are running in a pack with him through high shadowed places and down into moonlight. There is a heat in his dreams that not only makes clothes superfluous but burns from him the very concept of clothes, so going naked is more natural in the dreamworld than in the real one.

He never suffers from nightmares. This is because, in his daily life, he confronts the sources of his tensions and deals with them. He is never dragged down by guilt. He is not judgmental of others and is never affected by what they think of him. He knows that if something he wishes to do *feels* right, then it *is* right. He always looks out for number one, because to be a successful human being, he must first like himself. Consequently, he always goes to his bed with a clear mind and an untroubled heart.

Now, within seconds of resting his head on his pillow, Mr. Vess is asleep. From time to time his legs cycle beneath the covers, as if he is chasing something.

Once, in his sleep, he says, "Father," almost reverentially, and the word hangs like a bubble on the air—which is odd, because when Edgler Vess was nine years old, he burned his father to death.

Chains rattling, Chyna leaned down and picked up the spare cushion from the floor beside her chair. She put it on the table, slumped forward, and rested her head on it.

According to the kitchen clock, it was a quarter till twelve. She had been awake well over twenty-four hours, except when she had dozed in the motor home and when she had sat here unconscious after Vess clubbed her.

Although exhausted, and numb with despair, she did not expect to be able to sleep. But she hoped that by keeping her eyes closed and letting her thoughts drift to more pleasant times, she might be able to take her mind off her mild but gradually increasing urge to pee and off the pain in her neck and trigger finger.

She was walking in a wind full of torn red blossoms, curiously unafraid of the darkness and of the lightning that sometimes split it, when she was awakened not by thunder but by the sound of scissors clipping through paper.

She lifted her head from the pillow and sat up straight. The fluorescent light stung her eyes.

Edgler Vess was standing at the sink, cutting open a large bag of potato chips.

He said, "Ah, you're awake, you sleepyhead."

Chyna looked at the clock. Twenty minutes till five.

He said, "I thought it might take a brass band to bring you around."

She had been asleep almost five hours. Her eyes were grainy. Her mouth was sour. She could smell her body odor, and she felt greasy.

She had not wet herself in her sleep, and she was briefly lifted by an absurd sense of triumph that she had not yet been reduced to that lower level of humiliation. Then she realized how pathetic she was, priding herself on her continence, and her internal grayness darkened by a degree or two.

Vess was wearing black boots, khaki slacks, a black belt, and a white T-shirt.

His arms were muscular, enormous. She would never be able to struggle successfully against those arms.

He brought a plate to the table. He had made a sandwich for her. "Ham and cheese with mustard."

A ruffle of lettuce showed at the edges of the bread. He had placed two dill pickle spears beside the sandwich.

As Vess put the bag of potato chips on the table, Chyna said, "I don't want it."

"You have to eat," he said.

She looked out the window at the deep yard in late-afternoon light.

"If you don't eat," he said, "I'll eventually have to force-feed you." He picked up the bottle of aspirin and shook it to get her attention. "Tasty?"

"I didn't take any," she said.

"Ah, then you're learning to enjoy your pain."

He seemed to win either way.

He took away the aspirin and returned with a glass of water. Smiling, he said, "You've got to keep those kidneys functioning or they'll atrophy."

As Vess cleaned the counter where he'd made the sandwich, Chyna said, "Were you abused as a child?" and hated herself for asking the question, for *still* trying to understand.

Vess laughed and shook his head. "This isn't a textbook, Chyna. This is real life."

"Were you?"

"No. My father was a Chicago accountant. My mom sold women's wear at a department store. They loved me. Bought me too many toys, more than I could use, especially since I preferred playing with . . . other things."

"Animals," she said.

"That's right."

"And before animals—insects or very little things like goldfish or turtles."

"Is that in your textbooks?"

"It's the earliest and worst sign. Torturing animals."

He shrugged. "It was fun . . . watching the stupid thing crawl on fire inside its shell. Really, Chyna, you have to learn to get beyond these petty value judgments."

She closed her eyes, hoping he would go to work.

"Anyway, my folks loved me, all caught up in *that* delusion. When I was nine, I set a fire. Lighter fluid in their bed while they were sleeping, then a cigarette."

"My God."

"There you go again."

"Why?"

He mocked: "Why not?"

"Jesus."

"Want the second-best answer?"

"Yes," she said.

"Then look at me when I talk to you."

She opened her eyes.

His gaze cleaved her. "I set them on fire because I thought maybe they were beginning to catch on."

"To what?"

"To the fact that I was something special."

"They caught you with the turtle," she guessed.

"No. A neighbor's kitten. We lived in a nice suburb. There were so many pets in the neighborhood. Anyway, when they caught me, there was talk of doctors. Even at nine, I knew I couldn't allow that. Doctors might be harder to fool. So we had a little fire."

"And nothing was done to you?"

Finished with his cleaning, he sat down at the table. "No one suspected. Dad was smoking in bed, the firemen said. It happens all the time. The whole house went. I barely got out alive, and Mommy was screaming, and I couldn't get to her, couldn't help my mommy, and I was *so* scared." He winked at her. "After that, I went to live with my grandma. She was an annoying old biddy, full of rules, regulations, standards of conduct, manners, and courtesies I had to learn. But she couldn't keep a clean house. Her bathroom was just disgusting. She led me into my second and last mistake. I killed her while she was standing in the kitchen, just like this, preparing dinner. It was an impulsive thing, a knife twice in each kidney."

"How old?"

Slyly playing with her, he said, "Grandma or me?"

"You."

"Eleven. Too young to be put on trial. Too young for anyone to *really* believe that I knew what I was doing."

"They had to do *something* to you."

"Fourteen months in a caring facility. Lots of therapy, lots of counseling, lots and lots of attention and hugs. Because, you see, I must have offed poor grandma because of my unexpressed grief over the accidental deaths of my parents in that awful, awful fire. One day I realized what they were trying to tell me, and I just broke down and cried and cried. Oh, Chyna, how I cried, and wallowed in remorse for poor Grandma. The therapists and social workers were so appreciative of the wallowing."

"Where did you go from the facility?"

"I was adopted."

Speechless, she stared at him.

"I know what you're thinking," he said. "Not many twelve-year-old orphans get adopted. People are usually looking for infants to mold in their own image. But I was such a *beautiful* boy, Chyna, an almost ethereally beautiful boy. Can you believe that?"

"Yes."

"People want beautiful children. Beautiful children with nice smiles. I was sweet-tempered and charming. By then I'd learned to hide better among all you hypocrites. I'd never again be caught with a bloody kitten or a dead grandmother."

"But who . . . who would adopt you after what you did?"

"What I did was expunged from my record, of course. I was just the littlest boy, after all. Chyna, you wouldn't expect my whole life to be ruined just because of one mistake? Psychiatrists and social workers were the grease in my wheels, and I will always be beholden to them for their sweet, earnest desire to believe."

"Your adoptive parents didn't know?"

"They knew that I'd been traumatized by the death of my parents in a fire, that the trauma had led to counseling, and that I needed to be watched for signs of depression. They wanted so badly to make my life better, to prevent depression from ever touching me again."

"What happened to them?"

"We lived there in Chicago two years, and then we moved here to Oregon. I let them live for quite a while, and I let them pretend to love me. Why not? They enjoyed their delusions so much. But then, after I graduated from college, I was twenty years old and needed more money than I had, so there had to be another dreadful accident, another fire in the night. But it was eleven long years since the fire that took my real mom and dad, and half a continent away. No social workers had seen me in years, and there were no files about my horrible mistake with Grandma, so no connections were ever made."

They sat in silence.

After a while he tapped the plate in front of her. "Eat, eat," he cajoled. "I'll be eating at a diner myself. Sorry I can't keep you company."

"I believe you," she said.

"What?"

"That you were never abused."

"Though that runs against everything you've been taught. Good girl, Chyna. You know the truth when you hear it. Maybe there's hope for you yet."

"There's no understanding you," she said, though she was talking more to herself than to him.

"Of course there is. I'm just in touch with my reptilian nature, Chyna. It's in all of us. We all evolved from that slimy, legged fish that first crawled out of the sea. The reptile consciousness . . . it's still in all of us, but most of you struggle so hard to hide it from yourselves, to convince yourselves that you're something cleaner and better than what you really are. The irony is, if you'd just for once acknowledge your reptile nature, you'd find the freedom and the happiness that you're all so frantic to achieve and never do."

He tapped the plate again, and then the glass of water. He got up and tucked his chair under the table.

"That conversation wasn't quite as you expected, was it, Chyna?"

"No."

"You were expecting me to equivocate, to whine on about being a victim, to indulge in elaborately structured self-delusions, to spit up some tale of warping incest. You wanted to believe your clever probing might expose a secret religious fanaticism, bring revelations that I hear godly voices in my head. You didn't expect it to be this straightforward. This *honest*."

He went to the door between the kitchen and the living room, and then turned to look at her. "I'm not unique, Chyna. The world is filled with the likes of me—most are just less free. You know where I think a lot of my type wind up?"

In spite of herself, she asked, "Where?"

"In politics. Imagine having the power to start wars, Chyna. How gratifying that would be. Of course, in public life, one would generally have to forgo the pleasure of getting right down in the wet of it, hands dirty with all the wonderful fluids. One would have to be satisfied with the thrill of sending thousands to their deaths, remote destruction. But I believe I could adapt to that. And there would always be photos from the war zone, reports, all as graphic as one requested. *And never a danger of apprehension.* More amazing—they build monuments to you. You can bomb a small country into oblivion, and dinners are given in your honor. You can kill thirty-four children in a religious community, crush them with tanks, burn them alive, claim they were dangerous cultists—then sit back to the sound of applause. Such power. Intensity."

He glanced at the clock.

A few minutes past five.

He said, "I'll finish dressing and be gone. Back as soon after midnight as I can be." He shook his head as if saddened by the sight of her. "Untouched and alive. What kind of existence is that, Chyna? Not one worth having. Get in touch with your reptile consciousness. Embrace the cold and the dark. That's what we are."

He left her in chains as twilight entered the world and the light withdrew.

Mr. Vess steps onto the porch, locks the front door, and then whistles for the dogs.

The day is growing cooler as it wanes, and the air is bracing. He zips up his jacket.

From different points of the compass, the four Dobermans sprint out of the twilight and race to the porch. As they scamper to Vess and jostle one another to be the closest to him, their big paws thump on the boards in a fandango of canine delight.

He kneels among them, generously doling out affection once more.

Oddly like people, these Dobermans appear to be unable to detect the insincerity of Mr. Vess's love. They are only tools to him, not treasured pets, and the attention he gives them is like the 3-In-One oil with which he occasionally lubricates his power drill, hand-held belt sander, and chain saw. In the movies, it is always a dog that senses the werewolf potential in the moon-fearing man and greets him with a growl, always a dog that shies away from the character who is secretly harboring the alien parasite in his body. But movies are not life.

The dogs are no doubt deceiving him just as he deceives them. Their love is nothing but respect—or sublimated fear of him.

He stands, and the dogs look up expectantly. Earlier, they had been summoned from their kennel by the buzzer; therefore, they are now merely on an apprehend-and-detain status.

"Nietzsche," he says.

As one, the four Dobermans twitch and then become rigid. Their ears first prick at the command word but then flatten.

Their black eyes shine in the dusk.

Abruptly they depart the porch, scattering across the property, having been elevated to attack status.

Putting on his hat, Mr. Vess walks toward the barn, where he keeps his car.

He leaves the motor home parked beside the house. Later, to minimize the distance that the two bodies will have to be carried, he will back the vehicle along the lane, closer to the meadow of unmarked graves.

As he walks, Mr. Vess draws slow, deep breaths and clears his mind, preparing himself for reentry into the workaday world.

He enjoys the charade of his second life, passing for one of the repressed and deluded who, in uncountable multitudes, rule the earth with lies, who pass their lives in denial, anxiety, and hypocrisy. He is like a fox in a pen of mentally deficient chickens that are unable to distinguish between a predator and one of their own, and this is a fine game for a fox with a sense of humor.

Every day, all day long, Vess weighs other people with his eyes, furtively tests their firmness with a friendly touch, breathes the enticing scents of their flesh, selecting among them as if choosing packaged poultry at a market. He does not often kill those whom he meets in his public persona—only if he is absolutely certain that he can get away with it and if the particular chicken promises to be tasty.

If Chyna Shepherd hadn't disturbed his usual routine, Vess would have spent more time reacclimating himself to his role as an ordinary guy. He might have watched a game show on television, read a couple of chapters in a romance novel by Robert James Waller, and skimmed an issue of *People* to remind himself of those things that the desperate ruck of humanity uses to anesthetize itself against the awareness of its true animal nature and the inevitability of death. He might have stood before a mirror for a while, practicing his smile, studying his eyes.

Nevertheless, by the time he reaches the silvered-cedar barn, he is confident that he will slide back into his second life without a ripple and that all those who look into his pond will be comforted to see their own faces reflected. Most people have expended so much effort and time in the denial of their predatory nature that they cannot easily recognize it in others.

He opens the man-size door beside the larger roll-up, pauses, and glances toward the back of the house. He left the woman in the dark, so he can't even vaguely discern her form through the distant window.

The sunless, somber twilight is still bright enough, however, for Ms. Shepherd, the eminent psychologist, to have seen him as he walked to the barn. She could be watching now.

Mr. Vess wonders what she thinks of him in this surprising new guise. She must be shocked. More illusions shattered. Seeing him on his way to his second life, realizing that indeed he passes for a stand-up citizen, she must be plunged into a despair deeper than any she has yet known.

He has such a way with women.

After Vess turned off the lights and left the kitchen, Chyna leaned back in the pine captain's chair, away from the table, because the smell of the ham sandwich sickened her. It wasn't spoiled; it smelled like a ham sandwich ought to smell. But the very idea of food made her gag.

About twenty-one hours had passed since she'd finished her most recent full meal, dinner at the Templeton house. The few bites of cheese omelet that she'd had at breakfast weren't enough to sustain her, especially considering all of the physical activity of the previous night; she should have been famished.

Eating was an admission of hope, however, and she didn't want to hope any more. She had spent her life hoping, a fool intoxicated with optimistic expectations. But every hope proved to be as empty as a bubble. Every dream was glass waiting to be shattered.

Until last night, she had thought that she'd climbed far out of childhood misery, up a greased ladder toward phenomenal heights of understanding, and she had been quietly proud of herself and of her accomplishments. Now it seemed that she had not been climbing after all, that her ascent had been an illusion, and that for years her feet had been slipping over the same two well-lubricated rungs, as if she'd been on one of those exercise machines, a StairMaster, expending enormous energy—but not one inch higher when she stopped than she had been when she'd started. The long years of waitressing, the sore legs and the stubborn pain in the small of her back from being on her feet for hours, taking the toughest classes she could find at the University of California, studying late into the night after she returned home from work, the countless sacrifices, the loneliness, the ceaseless striving, striving—all of that had led *here*, to this dismal place, to these chains, into this deepening twilight.

She had hoped one day to understand her mother, to find good reason to forgive. She had even, God help her, secretly hoped that they might reach a truce. They could never have a healthy mother-daughter relationship, and they could never be friends; but it had seemed possible, at least, that she and Anne might one day have lunch together at any café with a view of the sea, alfresco on the patio under a huge umbrella, where they would never speak of the past but would make pleasant small talk about movies, the weather, the way the sea-gulls wheeled across the sapphire sky, perhaps with no healing affection but without any hatred between them. Now she knew that even if by some miracle she escaped untouched and alive from this imprisonment, she would never reach that dreamed-of degree of understanding; rapprochement between her and her mother could not be achieved.

Human cruelty and treachery surpassed all understanding. There were no answers. Only excuses.

Chyna felt lost. She was in a stranger place than Edgler Vess's kitchen and in a more forbidding darkness.

In all her years, she had never before felt lost, not truly lost. Frightened, yes. Sometimes confused and bleak. But always she had held a map in her mind, with a route marked if only vaguely, and she had believed that in her heart was a compass that couldn't fail her. She had been in the wrong place many times, but she'd always been sure that there was a way out—just as in any fun-house mirror maze there is always a safe path through the infinite images of oneself, through more fearful reflections, and through all of the enigmatic silver shadows.

No map this time.

No compass.

Life itself was the ultimate fun-house mirror maze, and she was lost in its nautilus chambers, with no one to turn to for comfort, no hand to hold.

Finally admitting that she had been essentially motherless since birth and always would be motherless, and with her only close friend lying dead in Edgler Vess's motor home, Chyna wished that she knew her father's name, that she had at least once seen his face. Her mother's maiden name was Shepherd; she had never been married. "Be glad you're illegitimate, baby," Anne had said, "because that means you're *free*. Little bastard children don't have as many relatives clinging like psychic leeches and sucking away their souls." Over the years, when Chyna had asked about her father, Anne had said only that he was dead, and she had been able to say it dry-eyed, even light-heartedly. She wouldn't provide details of his appearance, discuss what work he'd done, reveal where he'd lived, or acknowledge that he'd had a name. "By the time I was pregnant with you," Anne once said, "I wasn't seeing him any more. He was history. I never told him about you. He never knew."

Chyna liked to daydream about him sometimes: She imagined that her mother had lied about this, as about so many things, and that her dad was alive. He would be a lot like Gregory Peck in *To Kill a Mockingbird*, a big man with gentle eyes, soft-spoken, kind, quietly humorous, with a keen sense of justice, certain of who he was and of what he believed. He would be a man who was admired and respected by other people but who thought himself no more special than anyone else. He would love her.

If she had known his name, either first or last, she would have spoken it now, aloud. The mere sound of her father's name would have comforted her.

She was crying. Through the many hours since she had come under Vess's thrall, she had felt tears welling more than once, and she had repressed them. But she couldn't dam this hot flood. She despised herself for crying—but only briefly. These bitter tears were a welcome admission that there was no hope for her. They washed her free of hope, and that was what she wanted now, because hope led only to disappointment and pain. All her troubled life, since at least her eighth birthday, she had refused to weep freely, really let loose with tears. Being tough and dry-eyed was the only way to get respect from those people who, on seeing the smallest weakness in another, got a fearful muddy light in their eyes and closed in like jackals around a gazelle with a broken leg. But withholding tears wouldn't fend off the jackal who had promised to be back after midnight, and a lifetime of grief and hurt burst from her. Great wet sobs shook Chyna so hard that her chest began to ache worse than her neck or her sprained finger. Her throat soon felt hot and raw. She sagged in her clinking chains, in her imprisoning chair, face clenched and streaming and hot, stomach clenched and cold, the taste of salt in her mouth, gasping, groaning in despair, choking on the smothering awareness of her terrible solitude. She shuddered uncontrollably, and her hands spasmed into frail fists but then opened and grasped at the air around her head as if her anguish were a cowl that might be torn off and cast aside. Profoundly alone, unloved and lost, she spiraled down into a mental mirror maze without even her father's name for comfort.

After a while, an engine roared. She heard the brassy toot of a horn: two short blasts and then two more.

Chyna lifted her head, looked through the nearby window, and saw the headlights of a car leaving the barn. Her vision was blurred by tears. She couldn't see the car itself as it sped past the house in the gray dusk, but it must be driven by Vess, of course. Then it was gone.

The jaunty toot of the horn mocked her, but that mockery wasn't enough to rekindle her anger.

She stared out at the gloaming and didn't care that it might be the last twilight she ever saw. She cared only that she had spent too much of her twenty-six years alone, with no one at her side to share the sunsets, the starry skies, the turbulent beauty of storm clouds. She wished that she had reached out to people more, instead of retreating inward, wished that she had not made her heart into a sheltering closet. Now, when nothing mattered any more, when the insight couldn't do her any damn good at all, she realized that there was less hope of survival alone than with others. She'd been acutely aware that terror, betrayal, and cruelty had a human face, but she had not sufficiently appreciated that courage, kindness, and love had a human face as well. Hope wasn't a cottage industry; it was neither a product that she could manufacture like needlepoint samplers nor a substance she could secrete, in her cautious solitude, like a maple tree producing the essence of syrup. Hope was to be found in other people, by reaching out, by taking risks, by opening her fortress heart.

This insight seemed so obvious, the simplest of wisdom, yet she had not been able to arrive at it until *in extremis*.

And the chance had long ago passed to act upon it. She would die as she had lived—alone. This further realization might have wrung greater rivers of tears from her but, instead, drove her into a bleaker place than she'd been before, an interior garden of stone and ashes.

Then, as she was still gazing out the window, she saw something moving in the last of the dusk. Though it was blurred by her tears, she could see that it was too large to be a Doberman.

But if Vess had gone, how could it be a man?

Chyna blotted her eyes on the sleeve of her sweater, and she blinked until the mysterious shape resolved out of tears and twilight shadows. It was an elk. A female, without antlers.

It ambled across the backyard, from the forested foothills to the west, pausing twice to tear up a mouthful of the succulent grass. As Chyna knew from her months on the ranch in Mendocino County many years ago, these animals were highly sociable and always traveled in herds, but this one seemed to be alone.

The Dobermans should have been after this intruder, barking and snarling and excited by the prospect of blood. Surely the dogs would be able to smell it even from the farthest corners of the property. Yet no Dobermans were in sight.

Likewise, the elk should have caught the scent of the dogs and galloped at once for safety, wild-eyed and snorting. Nature had made its kind prey to mountain lions and wolves and packs of coyotes; as dinner-on-the-hoof to so many predators, elk were always watchful and cautious.

But this specimen seemed utterly unconcerned that dogs were in the immediate neighborhood. Except for the two brief pauses to graze on the lush grass, it came directly to the back porch, with no sign of skittishness.

Although Chyna was not a wildlife expert, this seemed to her to be a *coastal* elk, the same type she had encountered in the grove of redwoods. Its coat was gray-brown, and it had the familiar white and black markings on the body and face.

Yet she was sure that this place was too far from the sea to be a suitable home for coastal elk or to provide the ideal vegetation for their diet. When she'd gotten out of the motor home, she'd had an impression of mountains all around. Now the rain had stopped and the mist had lifted; in the west, where the dregs of daylight swiftly drained away, the black silhouettes of high peaks pressed against tattered clouds and electric-purple sky. With a mountain range of such formidable size between here and the Pacific Ocean, coastal elk could not have found their way so far inland, for they were basically a lowland breed partial to plains and gentle hills. This must be a different type of elk—although with coloration strikingly similar to that of the animals she had seen the previous night.

The imposing creature stood outside the wooden balustrade of the shallow porch, no more than eight feet away, staring directly at the window. At Chyna.

She found it difficult to believe that the elk could see her. With the lights off, the kitchen was currently darker than the dusk in which the animal stood. From its perspective, the interior of the house should have been unrelievedly black.

Yet she couldn't deny that its eyes met hers. Large dark eyes, shining softly.

She remembered Vess's sudden return to the kitchen this morning. He'd been inexplicably tense, ceaselessly turning the screwdriver in his hand, an odd light in his eyes. And he'd been full of questions about the elk in the redwood grove.

Chyna didn't know why the elk mattered to Vess any more than she could imagine why this one stood here, now, unchallenged by the dogs, studying her intently through the window. She didn't puzzle long over this mystery. She was in a mood to accept, to experience, to admit that understanding was not always achievable.

As the deep-purple sky turned to indigo and then to India ink, the eyes of the elk grew gradually more luminous. They were not red like the eyes of some animals at night, but golden.

Pale plumes of breath streamed rhythmically from its wet black nostrils.

Without breaking eye contact with the animal, Chyna pressed the insides of her wrists together as best she could with the handcuffs intervening. The steel chains rattled: all the lengths between her and the chair on which she sat, between her and the table, between her and the past.

She remembered her solemn pledge, earlier in the day, to kill herself rather than be a witness to the complete mental destruction of the young girl in the cellar. She had believed that she would be able to find the courage to bite open the veins in her wrists and bleed to death. The pain would be sharp but relatively brief . . . and then she would fade sleepily from this blackness into another, which would be eternal.

She had stopped crying. Her eyes were dry.

Her heartbeat was surprisingly slow, like that of a sleeper in the dreamless rest provided by a powerful sedative.

She raised her hands in front of her face, bending them backward as severely as possible and spreading her fingers wide so she could still gaze into the eyes of the elk.

She brought her mouth to the place on her left wrist where she would have to bite. Her breath was warm on her cool skin.

The light was entirely gone from the day. The mountains and the heavens were like one great black looming swell on a night sea, a drowning weight coming down.

The elk's heart-shaped face was barely visible from a distance of only eight feet. Its eyes, however, shone.

Chyna put her lips against her left wrist. In the kiss, she felt her dangerously steady pulse.

Through the gloom, she and the sentinel elk watched each other, and she didn't know whether this creature had mesmerized her or she had mesmerized it.

Then she pressed her lips to her right wrist. The same coolness of skin, the same ponderous pulse.

She parted her lips and used her teeth to pinch a thickness of flesh. There seemed to be enough tissue gathered between her incisors to make a mortal tear. Certainly she would be successful if she bit a second time, a third.

On the brink of the bite, she understood that it required no courage whatsoever. Precisely the opposite was true. *Not* biting was an act of valor.

But she didn't care about valor, didn't give a rat's ass about courage. Or about anything. All she cared about was putting an end to the loneliness, the pain, the achingly empty sense of futility.

And the girl. Ariel. Down in the hateful silent dark.

For a while she remained poised for the fatal nip.

Between its solemn measured beats, her heart was filled with the stillness of deep water.

Then, without being aware of releasing the pinch of flesh from between her teeth, Chyna realized that her lips were pressed to her unbitten wrist again. She could feel her slow pulse in this kiss of life.

The elk was gone.

Gone.

Chyna was surprised to see only darkness where the creature had stood. She didn't believe that she had closed her eyes or even blinked. Yet she must have been in a blinding trance, because the stately elk had vanished into the night as mysteriously as a stage magician's assistant dematerializes beneath an artfully draped black shroud.

Suddenly her heart began to pound hard and fast.

"No," she whispered in the dark kitchen, and the word was both a promise and a prayer.

Her heart like a wheel—spinning, racing—drove her out of that internal grayness in which she had been lost, out of that bleakness into a brighter landscape.

"No." There was defiance in her voice this time, and she did not whisper. "No."

She shook her chains as if she were a spirited horse trying to throw off its traces.

"No, no, no. Shit, no." Her protests were loud enough for her voice to echo off the hard surface of the refrigerator, the glass in the oven door, the ceramic-tile counters.

She tried to pull away from the table to stand up. But a loop of chain secured her chair to the barrel that supported the tabletop, limiting its movement.

If she dug her heels into the vinyl-tile floor and attempted to scoot backward, she would probably not be able to move at all. At best she would only drag the heavy table with her inch by inch. And in a lifetime of trying, she would not be able to put enough tension on the chain to snap it.

She was still adamant in her rejection of surrender—"No, damn it, no way, *no*"—pressing the words through clenched teeth.

She reached forward, pulling taut the chain that led around her back from the left handcuff to the right. It was wound between the spindles of the rail-back chair, behind the tie-on pad. She strained, hoping to hear the crack of dry wood, jerked hard, harder, and sharp pain sewed a hot seam in her neck; the agony of the clubbing was renewed in her neck and in the right side of her face, but she would not let pain stop her. She jerked harder than ever, scarring the nice furniture for damn sure, and again—*pull, pull*—firmly holding the chair down with her body while simultaneously half lifting it off the floor as she yanked furiously at the back rails, and yanked again, until her biceps quivered. *Pull.* As she grunted with effort and frustration, needles of pain stitched down the back of her neck, across both shoulders, and into her arms. *Pull!* Putting everything she had into the effort, straining longer than before, clenching her teeth so hard that tics developed in her jaw muscles, she pulled once more until she felt the arteries throbbing in her temples and saw red and silver pinwheels of light spinning behind her eyelids. But she wasn't rewarded with any breaking sounds. The chair was solid, the spindles were thick, and every joint was well made.

Her heart *boomed*, partly because of her struggles but largely because she was brimming with an exhilarating sense of liberation. Which was crazy, crazy, because she was still shackled, no closer to breaking her bonds than she had been at any moment since she'd awakened in this chair. Yet she felt as if she had already escaped and was only waiting for reality to catch up with the freedom that she had *willed* for herself.

She sat gasping, thinking.

Sweat beaded her brow.

Forget the chair for now. To get loose from it, she would have to be able to stand and move. She couldn't deal with the chair until she was free of the table.

She was unable to reach down far enough to unscrew the carabiner that joined the shorter chain between her ankles to the longer chain that entwined the chair and the table. Otherwise, she might easily have freed her legs from both pieces of furniture.

If she could overturn the table, the loop of chain that wrapped the supporting pedestal and connected with her leg irons would then slide free as the bottom of that barrel tipped up and off the floor. Wouldn't it? Sitting in the dark, she couldn't quite visualize the mechanics of what she was proposing, but she thought that turning the table on its side would work.

Unfortunately, the chair across from hers, the one in which Vess had sat, was an obstruction that would most likely prevent the table from tipping over. She had to get rid of it, clear the way. Shackled as she was, however, and with the barrel pedestal intervening, she couldn't extend her legs far enough to kick at the other chair and knock it aside. Hobbled and tethered, she was also unable to stand and reach across the big round table and simply push the obstruction out of the way.

Finally she tried scooting backward in her chair, hoping to drag the table with her, away from Vess's chair. The chain encircling the pedestal drew taut. As she strained backward, digging her heels into the floor, it seemed that the piece was too heavy to be dragged, and she wondered if the barrel was filled with a bag of sand to keep the table from wobbling. But then it creaked and stuttered a few inches across the vinyl tiles, rattling the sandwich plate and the glass of water that stood on it.

This was harder work than she had anticipated. She felt as though she were on one of those television shows devoted to stunts and stupid physical challenges, pulling a railroad car. A loaded railroad car. Nevertheless, the table moved grudgingly. In a couple of minutes, after pausing twice to get her breath, she stopped because she was concerned that she might back against the wall between the kitchen and the laundry room; she needed to leave herself some maneuvering space. Although it was difficult to estimate distance in the dark, she believed that she had dragged the table about three feet, far enough to be clear of Vess's chair.

Trying to favor her sprained finger, she placed her cuffed hands under the table and lifted. It weighed considerably more than she did—a two-inch pine top, the thick staves in the supporting barrel, the black iron hoops around the staves, perhaps that bag of sand—and she couldn't get much leverage while she was forced to remain seated. The bottom of the barrel tipped up an inch, then two inches. The water glass toppled, spilling its contents, rolled away from her, dropped off the table, and shattered on the floor. All the noise made it seem as if her plan was working—she hissed, "Yes!"—but then because she had underestimated the weight and the effort required to move it, she had to relent, and the barrel slammed down.

Chyna flexed her muscles, took a deep breath, and immediately returned to the task. This time she planted her feet as far apart as her shackles would allow. On the underside of the table, she flattened her upturned palms against the pine, thumbs hooked toward herself over the smooth bull-nose edge. She tensed her legs as well as her arms, and when she shoved up on the table, she pushed with her legs too, getting to her feet an inch at a time, one hard-won inch for each inch that the table tipped up and backward. She did not have enough slack in the various tethering chains to be able to get all the way—or halfway—erect, so she rose haltingly in a stiff and awkward crouch, cramped under the weight of the table. She put enormous strain on her knees and thighs, wheezing, shuddering with the effort, but she persevered because each precious inch that she was able to gain improved her leverage; she was using her entire body to lift, lift, lift.

The sandwich plate and the bag of potato chips slid off the table. China cracked and chips scattered across the floor with a sound unnervingly like scurrying rodents.

The pain in her neck was excruciating, and someone seemed to be twisting a corkscrew into her right clavicle. But pain couldn't stop her. It *motivated*. The greater her pain, the more she identified with Laura and the whole Templeton family, with the young man hanging in the motor-home closet, with the service-station clerks, and with all the people who might be buried down in the meadow; and the more she identified with them, the more she wanted Edgler Vess to suffer a world of hurt. She was in an Old Testament mood, unwilling to turn the other cheek just now. She wanted Vess screaming on a rack, stretched until his joints popped apart and his tendons tore. She didn't want to see him confined to a state hospital for the criminally insane, there to be analyzed and counseled and instructed as to how best to increase his self-esteem, treated with a panoply of antipsychotic drugs, given a private room and television, booked in card tournaments with his fellow patients, and treated to a turkey dinner on Christmas. Instead of having him consigned to the mercies of psychiatrists and social workers, Chyna wanted to condemn him to the skilled hands of an imaginative torturer, and then *see* how long the sonofabitch bastard freak remained faithful to his philosophy about all experiences being value neutral, all sensations equally worthwhile. This ardent desire, refined from her pain, was not noble in the least, but it was pure, a high-octane fuel that burned with an intense light, and it kept her motor running.

This side of the barrel pedestal was off the floor perhaps three inches—she could only guess—approximately as high as she had gotten it before, but she still had plenty of steam left. Bent in a backward Z, as hunched as a God-cursed troll, she muscled the table up, knees aching, thighs *quivering* with the strain, her butt clenched tighter than a politician's fist around a cash bribe. She encouraged herself aloud by talking to the table as if it possessed awareness: *"Come on, come on, come on, move, shit, shit, move, you sonofabitch, higher, come on, damn you, damn it, come on."*

A ludicrous mental image of herself flashed through her mind: She must resemble a character in one of those movie scenes where the deceived cowboy cottons to the truth and overturns the poker table on the dishonest itinerant cardshark, except that she was playing the drama in slow motion, as in a Western underwater.

Initially the chair remained exactly where it had been when her butt parted company with it, but as her arms lifted higher and stretched farther in front of her, the heavy chair was hoisted off the floor by the tightening chain that circled behind her from wrist to wrist and wound through the vertical spindles behind the tie-on pad. Now she was lifting the table in front and the chair at her back. The hard edge of the seat jammed against her thighs, and the curved pine headpiece of the railed back pressed cruelly below her shoulder blades, as the chair began to act like a V-clamp to prevent her from rising much further.

Nevertheless, Chyna squeezed against the table as she lifted it, separating herself from the confining chair enough to be able to rise out of her crouch just one more inch, then one more. At the extreme limits of strength and endurance, she grunted loudly, rhythmically: *"Uh, uh, uh, uh!"* Sweat glazed her face, stung her eyes, but there was no light in the kitchen anyway, no reason she had to see what she was doing in order to get it done. Her burning eyes didn't bother her; this was small-time pain; but she felt as though she was about to burst a blood vessel from the straining—or throw a clot off an artery wall and recapture it deep in her brain.

Fear was with her again, for the first time in hours, because even as she strained against the table, she couldn't help thinking about what Edgler Vess would do with her if he returned home to find her on the floor, dazed and incoherent from a stroke. With her mind reduced to hasty pudding, she would no longer be the sophisticated toy she had been; she'd be insufficiently responsive to provide him with the requisite thrills when he tortured her. Then perhaps Vess would revert to the crude turtle games of his youth. Maybe he would drag her into the backyard to set her on fire for the pleasure of watching her crawl jerkily in circles on crippled, blazing limbs.

The table crashed onto its side hard enough to jar the dishes in the kitchen cabinets and rattle a loose pane in a window.

Though she had been striving fiercely for precisely this result, she was so surprised by her abrupt success that she didn't cry out in triumph. She leaned against the curve of the tilted table and gasped for breath.

Half a minute later, when she tried to pull away, she discovered that the chain was still wrapped tightly around the barrel pedestal and that she remained encumbered.

She attempted to tug it loose. No luck.

Dropping to her hands and knees, carrying the chair on her back, she reached under the canted table, as though she were at the seashore and seeking shade beneath a giant beach umbrella. In the darkness she felt around the bottom of the barrel that served as the pedestal, and she discovered that this part of the job was not yet finished.

The table was tipped on its side—like a mushroom with a large cap, stem meeting the floor at an angle. Given the position from which she'd had to work, she had not been able to tip it completely over, with the pedestal straight up in the air. The bottom of the barrel, recessed inside a chime hoop, was fully exposed; however, the tethering chain was trapped in the angle between the floor and the *side* of the barrel.

Lifting the chair with her, Chyna struggled to her feet but rose only to a crouch. She reached down with both hands, hooked her fingers around the chime hoop, paused to gather her strength, and pulled upward.

Although she tried to hold her injured trigger finger out of the way, her sweaty hands slipped on the painted iron hoop. She stubbed the fingertips of her right hand hard against the rough bottom of the barrel, and such a brilliant pain flashed through her swollen index finger that she cried out in dazzled agony.

For a while she hunched over, protectively holding her injured hand against her breast, waiting for the pain to subside. Eventually it faded somewhat.

After blotting her hands on her jeans, she hooked her fingers around the chime hoop once more, hesitated, heaved, and the barrel pedestal came off the floor half an inch, an inch. With her left foot, she pawed at the loop of chain until she thought it was free, and then she let the pedestal drop to the floor again.

She scooted backward in her chair, and this time nothing impeded her. The loop of chain rattled across the floor, no longer anchoring her to the table.

Her chair bumped into the wall that separated the kitchen from the laundry room. She hitched sideways, out from behind the table, toward the window, which was but a faint gray rectangle between the blackness of the unlighted kitchen and the slightly less dark night.

Although Chyna was far from being free, farther still from being safe, she was exhilarated, because at least she had *done* something. A headache like an endless incoming tide throbbed in waves across her brow and along her right temple, and the pain in her neck was savage. Her swollen index finger was a world of misery in itself. In spite of her thick socks, her ankles felt as though they had been bruised and abraded by the shackles, and her left wrist stung where she had skinned it while trying to yank the spindles out of the back of the chair. Her joints ached and her muscles burned from the demands she had put on them, and she had a stitch in her left side that was pulling like a needle threaded with hot wire—yet she was grinning and exhilarated.

When she was beside the window, she let the legs of her chair touch the floor. She sat down.

As her heartbeat slowed from its frenzied hammering, Chyna leaned back against the cushion, still breathing hard, and surprised herself by laughing. Musical, unexpectedly girlish laughter burst from her, an astonishing giggle part delight, part nervous relief.

She blotted her sweat-stung eyes on one sleeve of her cotton sweater, and then on the other sleeve. With her cuffed hands, she awkwardly smoothed her short hair back from her brow, across which it had fallen in damp licks.

As a softer, more subdued trill of laughter bubbled from her, Chyna detected movement out of the corner of her right eye. She turned to the window, happily thinking, *The elk.*

A Doberman was staring at her.

Few stars and, as yet, no moon shone between the torn clouds, and the dog was oil black. Yet it was clearly visible, because its pointed face was only inches from hers, with nothing between them except the glass. Its inky eyes were cold and merciless, sharklike in their steadiness and glassy concentration. Inquisitively, it pressed its wet nose against the pane.

A thin whine escaped the Doberman, audible even through the glass: neither a whimper of fear nor a plea for attention, but a needful keening that perfectly expressed the killing passion in its eyes.

Chyna was no longer laughing.

The dog dropped from the window, out of sight.

She heard its paws thumping hollowly against the boards as it paced rapidly back and forth across the porch. Between urgent whines, it made a low quarrelsome sound.

Then the dog jumped into view, planting its broad forepaws on the window stool, eye-to-eye with her once more. Agitated, it bared its long teeth threateningly, but it didn't bark or snarl.

Perhaps the sound of the water glass shattering on the floor or the crash of the table tipping onto its side had carried into the backyard, and this Doberman had been close enough to hear. The dog might have been standing at this window for a while, listening to Chyna alternately cursing her bonds and encouraging herself as she had struggled to be free of the table; and certainly it had heard her laughter. Dogs had lousy eyesight, and this one would not be able to see more than her face, nothing of the wreckage. They had a phenomenal sense of smell, however, so maybe the beast was able to detect the scent of her sudden exuberance through the barrier of glass—and was alarmed by that.

The window was about five or six feet long and four feet high, divided into two sliding panels. Obviously not part of the original architecture, it appeared to have been installed during a relatively recent remodel. If there had been numerous smaller panes separated by wide sturdy mullions of wood, Chyna would have been a lot more confident. But either of the two sheets of glass was large enough to admit the agitated Doberman if it tried to smash through at her.

Surely that wouldn't happen. The dogs had been trained to patrol the grounds, not to assault the house.

The bared teeth were pearly, vaguely luminous, gray-white in the gloom: a wide but humorless smile.

Rather than make any sudden provocative movements, Chyna waited until the Doberman dropped from the window again before she reached to the floor and picked up the loop of excess chain to avoid tripping over it. Listening to the dog padding back and forth on the porch, she rose into the Rumpelstiltskin crouch that the burdening chair imposed. She edged around the kitchen, staying close to the walls and cabinets, feeling her way as best she could while cuffed and holding the loop of chain in one hand. She shuffled her feet more than her shackles required, hoping to shove the broken drinking glass and the fragments of the plate aside rather than step on them.

When she reached the doorway between the kitchen and the front room, she found the light switches but was reluctant to flip them up. Glancing back and seeing the Doberman at the window again, she wished that she could leave the kitchen dark.

She needed to search the drawers, however, so she snapped on the overhead lights. At the window, the Doberman twitched, flattened its ears to its skull, immediately pricked them again, found her with its eyes, and fixed her with its gaze.

Ignoring the Doberman, Chyna bent forward as far as her fetters would allow, hoisting the chair on her back. She strove to reach the carabiner that linked the shorter chain between her leg irons with the longer chain that had encircled the table pedestal and that still wrapped the stretcher bars of the chair. But even free of the table, she was trammeled in such a way that she could not put her fingers on this coupling.

She retraced her path along the cabinets. She opened one drawer after another and studied the contents.

When she passed the telephone jack in the wall, she paused to stare at it, frustrated. If Edgler Vess had a life other than that of a "homicidal adventurer," actually held a job and maintained any social life whatsoever as a cover for his true nature, he would have a telephone; the jack wasn't merely a dead plug left by the previous owners of the house. He must have hidden the phone.

For a psychotic killer, raging out of control on one level, Vess was surprisingly careful and methodical when it came to covering his ass. An agent of chaos, leaving behind rubble in the lives of others, he nevertheless kept his own affairs tidy and avoided mistakes.

She opened a few of the cupboard doors and peered into cabinets, but she found only pots, pans, dishes, and glasses. She soon gave up on the phone when she realized that Vess, having taken the trouble to unplug and conceal it, would have hidden it outside the kitchen and in a place where she was unlikely to find it even if she'd had hours to devote to the search.

She continued opening drawers. In the fourth, she discovered a compartmentalized plastic tray containing a collection of small culinary tools and gadgets.

She parked the chair beside the open drawer and sat down.

Outside, the Doberman was pacing again, paws thumping faster than before, all but *running* back and forth on the porch, back and forth, and whining louder as well. Chyna couldn't understand why it was still so agitated. She wasn't breaking dishes or overturning furniture any longer. She was quietly looking in drawers, minimizing the clatter of her chains, doing nothing to alarm the dog. It seemed to realize that she was escaping, but that was impossible; it was only an animal; it couldn't understand the complexities of her situation. Only an animal. Yet it raced worriedly from end to end of the porch, jumped to peer in the window again, fixed her with its fierce black eyes, and seemed to be saying, *Get away from the drawer, bitch!*

She plucked a wooden-handled corkscrew from the drawer, examined the spiraling point, and discarded it. A bottle opener. No. Potato peeler. Lemon-rind shaver. No. She found an eight-inch-long pair of heavy-duty tweezers, which Vess probably used to extract olives and pickles and similar items from tightly packed jars. The gripping blades of the tweezers proved too large to be inserted into the tight keyholes on her handcuffs, so she discarded them as well.

Then she located the ideal item: a five-inch-long steel pin, which she believed was called a poultry strut. A dozen were fixed together by a tightly wound rubber band, and she pulled one loose. The pin was rigid, about a sixteenth of an inch in diameter, with a point at the end of the shank and a half-inch-wide eye loop at the top. Smaller struts were made for pinning shut roasting chickens, but this one was for turkeys.

The thought of succulent roasted turkey brought the smell of it immediately to mind. Chyna's mouth watered, and her stomach growled, and she wished that she'd eaten some of the ham and cheese sandwich Vess had made for her.

She held the strut between the thumb and the middle digit of her right hand, sparing her swollen index finger, and slipped the point into the keyway on the left handcuff. Probing experimentally, she produced a lot of small ticking and scraping sounds, trying to feel the lock mechanism in the gateway of the cuff.

She remembered a movie in which the greatest psychotic killer and criminal genius of his age fashioned a handcuff key out of the metal ink tube from a ballpoint pen and an ordinary paper clip. He sprang one cuff and then the other in about fifteen seconds, maybe ten, after which he overpowered his two guards, killed them, and cut the face off one to wear as a disguise, although he used a penknife for the surgery, not the homemade handcuff key. Over the years, she had seen many other movies in which prisoners picked open cuffs and leg irons, and none of them had any more training for it than she did.

Ten minutes later, with her left cuff still securely locked, Chyna said, "Movies are full of shit."

She was so frustrated that her hand trembled and she couldn't control the strut. It jittered uselessly in the tight keyway.

On the porch, the dog wasn't pacing as fast as it had paced earlier, but it was still disturbed. Twice it clawed at the back door, once with considerable fervor, as if it thought it might be able to dig its way through the wood.

Chyna switched the strut to her left hand and worked on the right cuff for a while. Ticks, clicks, scrapes, and squeaks. She was concentrating so intently on picking the tiny lock that she was sweating as copiously as when she had been struggling to overturn the heavy table.

Finally she threw the turkey strut on the floor, and it bounced *ping-ping-ping* across the tiles, across a piece of the broken plate, and off a shard of the water glass.

Perhaps she could have freed herself in a wink if she had been the greatest psychotic killer and criminal genius of her age. But she was only a waitress and a psychology student.

Even as inconveniently sane and law-abiding as she was, she might be able to pop the handcuffs off her wrists and the larger shackles off her ankles with a more suitable tool than the turkey strut, but she would probably need hours to do it. She couldn't dedicate hours solely to the job of freeing herself from the chair and chains, because once she was unfettered, there were many other urgent tasks to be done before Vess returned.

She slammed the drawer shut. Holding the chain out of her way and hauling the chair with her, she got to her feet.

With a jangle worthy of the Ghost of Christmas Past, Chyna went to the door between the kitchen and the living room.

Behind her, at the window in the dining area, a weird screeching arose. She looked back and saw that the big Doberman was scratching frantically at the glass with both forepaws. Its claws squeaked down the pane with a sound as unsettling as fingernails dragged across a chalkboard.

She had intended to find her way into the dark living room by the light spilling through the open door, but the dog spooked her. While she'd picked at the cuff locks, the Doberman had grown slightly calmer, but now it was as disturbed as ever. Hoping to calm it before it decided to spring through the window, she turned off the overhead fluorescent panels.

*Squeak-squeak-squeak.*

Claws, glass.

*Squeak-squeak.*

She eased across the threshold, leaving the kitchen, and pushed the door shut behind her, blocking out the squeaking. Blocking out the damn dog as well, in case it proved to be crazed enough to burst through the glass.

She felt along the wall. Evidently the only switches were on the other side of the room, by the front door.

The living room seemed to be blacker than the kitchen. The drapes were drawn over one of the two expansive windows that faced onto the front porch. The other window was a barely defined gray rectangle that admitted no more light than had the double-pane slider in the kitchen.

Chyna stood motionless, taking time to orient herself, trying to recall the furnishings. She had been in the room only once before, briefly, and the space had been clotted with shadows. When she had entered from the front porch this morning, the kitchen door had been somewhat to her left in the back wall. The handsome sofa with ball feet, covered in a tartan-plaid fabric, had been to the right, which would put it, now, to her left as she faced toward the front of the house. Rustic oak end tables had flanked the large sofa—and on each end table had been a lamp.

Trying to hold this clear image of the room in her mind, she hobbled warily through the darkness, afraid of falling over a chair or a footstool or a magazine rack. Swaddled in chains and under the weight of the chair, she would be unable to check her fall in a natural manner and might be so twisted by her shackles that she would break an ankle or even a leg.

Whereupon, Edgler Vess would come home, dismayed by the mess and disappointed that she had damaged herself before he'd had a chance to play with her. Then either there would be turtle games or he would experiment with her fractured limb to teach her to enjoy pain.

The first thing she bumped into was the sofa, and she did not fall. Sliding her hand along the upholstered back, she sidled to the left until she came to the end table. She reached out and found the lamp shade, the wire ribs beneath the taut cloth.

She fumbled around the shell of the socket and then around the base of the lamp itself. As her fingers finally pinched the rotary switch, she was suddenly certain that a strong hand was going to come out of the darkness and cover hers, that Vess had crept back into the house, that he was sitting on the sofa only *inches* from her. With amusement, he had been listening to her struggles, sitting like a fat, patient spider in his tartan-plaid web, anticipating the pleasure of shattering her hopes when at last she hobbled this far. The light would blink on, and Vess would smile and wink at her and say, *Intense.*

The switch was a nub of ice between thumb and finger. Frozen to her skin.

Heart drumming like the wings of a frantic fettered bird, the beats so hard that they prevented her lungs from expanding, the pulse in her throat swelling so large that she was unable to swallow, Chyna broke her paralysis and clicked the switch. Soft light washed the room. Edgler Vess was not on the sofa. Not in an armchair. Not anywhere in the room. She exhaled explosively, with a shudder that rattled her chains, and leaned against the sofa, and gradually her fluttering heart grew calmer.

After those gray hours of depression during which she had been emotionally dead, she was energized by this siege of terror. If she ever suffered a killing bout of cardiac arrhythmia, the mere thought of Vess would be more effective at jump-starting her heart than the electrical paddles of a defibrillation machine. Fear proved that she had come back to life and that she had found hope again.

She shambled to the gray river-rock fireplace that extended from floor to ceiling across the entire north wall of the room. The deep hearth in the center wasn't raised, which would make her work easier.

She had considered going down to the cellar, where earlier she had seen a workbench, to examine the saws that were surely in Vess's tool collection. But she had quickly ruled out that solution.

Descending the steep cellar steps while hobbled, festooned with steel chains, and carrying the heavy pine chair on her back would be a stunt not quite equivalent to leaping the Snake River Gorge on a rocket-powered motorcycle, perhaps, but undeniably risky. She was moderately confident of making her way to the bottom without pitching forward and cracking her skull like an eggshell on the concrete or breaking a leg in thirty-six places—but far from *entirely* confident. Her strength wasn't what it ought to have been, because she hadn't eaten much in the past twenty-four hours and because she had already been through an exhausting physical ordeal. Furthermore, all her separate pains made her shaky. A trip to the cellar seemed simple enough, but under these circumstances, it would be equivalent to an acrobat slugging down four double martinis before walking the high wire.

Besides, even if she could find a sharp-toothed saw small enough to be easily handled, she wouldn't be able to use it at an angle that would allow her to bear down with effective force. To free the lower chain from the chair, she would have to cut through all three of the horizontal stretcher bars between the chair legs, each of which was an inch or an inch and a half in diameter, around which the links were wound. To accomplish this, she would have to sit, bend forward, and saw *backward* under the chair. Even if the upper chain had sufficient slack to allow her to reach down far enough for the task, which she doubted, she would only be able to scrape feebly at the wood. With luck, she'd whittle through the third stretcher sometime in the late spring. Then she would have to turn her attention to the five sturdy spindles in the back of the chair to free the upper chain, and not even a carnival contortionist born with rubber bones could get at them with a saw while pinioned as Chyna was.

Hacking through the steel chains was impossible. She would be able to get at them from an angle better than that from which she could approach the stretcher bars between the chair legs. But Vess wasn't likely to own saw blades that could carve through steel, and Chyna definitely didn't have the necessary strength.

She was resigned to more primitive measures than saws. And she was worried about the potential for injury and about how painful the process of liberation might be.

On the mantel, the bronze stags leaped perpetually, antlers to antlers, over the round white face of the clock.

Eight minutes past seven.

She had almost five hours until Vess returned.

Or maybe not.

He had said that he would be back as soon *after* midnight as possible, but Chyna had no reason to suppose that he'd been telling the truth. He might return at ten o'clock. Or eight o'clock. Or ten minutes from now.

She shuffled onto the floor-level flagstone hearth and then to the right, past the firebox and the brass andiron, past the deep mantel. The entire wall flanking the fireplace was smooth gray river rock— just the hard surface that she needed.

Chyna stood with her left side toward the rock, twisted her upper body to the left as far as possible without turning her feet, in the manner of an Olympic athlete preparing to toss a discus, and then swung sharply and forcefully to the right. This maneuver threw the chair— on her back—in the opposite direction from her body and slammed it into the wall. It clattered against the rock, rebounded with a ringing of chains, and thudded against her hard enough to hurt her shoulder, ribs, and hip. She tried the same trick again, putting even more energy into it, but after the second time, she was able to judge by the sound that she would, at best, scar the finish and chip a few slivers out of the pine. Hundreds of these lame blows might demolish the chair in time, turn it into kindling; but before she hammered it against the rock that often, suffering the recoil each time, she would be a bruised and bloodied mess, and her bones would splinter, and her joints would separate like the links in a pop-bead necklace.

By swinging the chair as though she were a dog wagging its tail, she couldn't get the requisite force behind it. She had been afraid of this. As far as she could determine, there was only one other approach that might work—but she didn't like it.

Chyna looked at the mantel clock. Only two minutes had passed since the last time she'd glanced at it.

Two minutes was nothing if she had until midnight, but it was a disastrous waste of time if Vess was on his way home right now. He might be turning off the public road, through the gate, into his long private driveway this very moment, the lying bastard, having set her up to believe that he would be gone until after midnight, then sneaking back early to—

She was baking a nourishing loaf of panic, plump and yeasty, and if she allowed herself to eat a single slice, then she'd gorge on it. This was an appetite she didn't dare indulge. Panic wasted time and energy.

She must remain calm.

To free herself from the chair, she needed to use her body as if it were a pneumatic ram, and she would have to endure serious pain. She was already in severe pain, but what was coming would be worse—devastating—and it scared her.

Surely there was another way.

She stood listening to her heart and to the hollow ticking of the mantel clock.

If she went upstairs first, maybe she would find a telephone and be able to call the police. They would know how to deal with the Dobermans. They would have the keys to get her out of the shackles and manacles. They would free Ariel too. With that one phone call, all burdens would be lifted from her.

But she knew in her heart—the old friend intuition—that she was not going to find any telephones upstairs either. Edgler Vess was unfailingly thorough. A phone would be in service in the house whenever he was home—but not when he was away. He might actually unplug the unit and take it with him each time he left.

Trammeled, unbalanced by the chair and therefore dangerously clumsy, Chyna would be risking a crippling fall if she climbed the stairs. She would face an even greater risk when, after finding no telephone, she had to come back down again. And in the process, she would have wasted precious time.

Turning her back to the river-rock wall, she shuffled six feet from it, stopped, closed her eyes, and gathered her courage.

Possibly one of the spindles in the rail-back chair would crack apart and be driven forward. The splintered end would puncture the tie-on cushion or slip past it and then skewer her, back to front, straight through her guts.

More likely, she'd sustain a spinal injury. With all the force of the impact directed against the lower half of the chair, the legs of it would be driven into *her* legs; the upper half would first pull away from her— then recoil and snap hard against her upper back or neck. The spindles were fixed between the seat and the wide slab of radius-cut pine that served as the headrail, and the headrail was so solid that it would do major damage if it cracked into her cervical vertebrae with sufficient force. She might wind up on the living-room floor, under the chair and chains, paralyzed from the neck down.

Sometimes she brooded about possibilities too much, dwelt beyond reason on all the myriad ways that any situation or any relationship could go terribly wrong. This was also a result of having spent her childhood hiding on the wrong side of bedsprings, waiting for either the fighting or the partying to stop.

For a while when Chyna was seven, she and her mother had stayed with a man named Zack and a woman named Memphis in a ramshackle old farmhouse not far from New Orleans, and one night two men had come to visit, carrying a Styrofoam cooler, and Memphis had killed them less than five minutes after they arrived. The visitors had been in the kitchen, sitting at the table. One of them had been talking to Chyna and the other had been twisting the cap off a bottle of beer— when Memphis withdrew a gun from the refrigerator and shot both men in the head, one after the other, so fast that the second one didn't even have time to dive for cover before she put a round in his face. As slippery and quick as a skink, Chyna fled, certain that Memphis had gone crazy and would kill them all. She hid in a drift of loose hay in the barn loft. During the hour that the adults took to find her, she so often visualized her own face dissolving with the impact of a bullet that every image in her mind's eye—even fleeting glimpses of the Wild Wood to which she could not quite escape—was entirely in shades of red, wet red.

But she had survived that night.

She had been surviving for a long time. Eternity.

And she would survive this too—or die trying.

Without opening her eyes, Chyna hurtled backward as fast as her leg irons would allow, and in spite of her fear, she figured that she must be at least a somewhat comic sight, because she had to shuffle frantically to build speed, had to throw herself toward spinal injury in quick little baby steps. But then she slammed into the rocks, and there was nothing whatsoever funny about *that*.

She'd been bent forward slightly to lift the legs of the chair behind her and to ensure that they, rather than another part of it, would strike first and take the hard initial blow. With her entire weight behind the assault, there was a satisfyingly splintery *thwack* on impact—and the pine legs were jammed painfully into the backs of her legs. Chyna stumbled forward, and the upper part of the chair whiplashed into her neck, as she had expected, and she was knocked off balance. She dropped to her knees on the flagstone hearth and fell forward with the chair still on her back, hurting in too many places to bother taking an inventory.

Hobbled, she couldn't get to her feet unless she was gripping something. She crawled to the nearest armchair and pulled herself up, grunting with effort and pain.

She didn't *like* pain the way Vess claimed to like it, but she wasn't going to bitch about it either. At least she could still crawl and stand. No spinal injury yet. Better to feel pain than nothing at all.

The legs of the chair and the stretcher bars between the legs seemed to be intact. But judging by the sound of the impact, she had weakened them.

Starting eight feet from the wall this time, Chyna shuffled backward as fast as she could, trying to ram the chair legs into the rock at the same angle as before. She was rewarded with a distinctive *crack*— the sound of splintering wood, though it felt like shattering bone.

A dam of pain burst inside her. Cold currents dragged her down, but she resisted the undertow with the desperate determination of a swimmer struggling against a drowning darkness.

She hadn't been knocked off her feet this time. She shuffled forward. Not pausing to catch her breath, still hunched to ensure that the chair legs would take the brunt of the impact, she charged backward into the rock wall.

Chyna woke facedown on the floor in front of the hearth, aware that she must have been unconscious for a minute or two.

The carpet was as cold and undulant as moving water. She wasn't floating in it but glimmering along the rippled surface, as though she were coppery spangles of sunlight or the dark reflection of a cloud.

The worst pain was in the back of her head. She must have struck it against something.

She felt so much better when she didn't think about her pain or her problems, when she simply accepted that she was nothing more than a cloud shadow riding on the mirrored surface of a rolling river, as insubstantial as the purling patterns on moving water, gliding away, liquid and cool, away, away.

Ariel. In the cellar. Among the watchful dolls.

*I am my sister's keeper.*

Somehow she got to her hands and knees.

She heard the hollow thump of paws on the front porch floor.

When she pulled herself to her feet against an armchair, she looked at the window that wasn't covered by drapes. Two Dobermans were standing with their forepaws on the windowsill, staring at her, their eyes radiant yellow with reflections of the soft amber light from the lamp on the end table.

At the base of the stone wall was one of the rear legs of the chair. That length of turned pine was all jagged splinters at the thicker end, where it had been fixed to the underside of the seat. Bristling from the side of it at a ninety-degree angle was the one-inch stretcher bar that had connected it to the other rear leg.

The lower chain was more than half free.

On the porch, one dog paced. The other still watched Chyna.

She worked the upper chain to the left through the spindles at her back, drawing her right hand behind her head, to provide as much slack as possible for her left hand. Then she reached down to her left, under the chair arm and then under the thick slab seat, feeling for the legs. The left rear leg was gone, obviously the one on the floor by the wall. The side stretcher still extended from the left front leg, but with the rear leg gone, it no longer connected to anything, and the chain had slipped off it.

When she worked the upper chain to the right, to be able to feel under the chair with that hand, she discovered that the other rear leg was slightly loose. She pulled, pushed, and twisted, trying to break it off. But she couldn't get adequate leverage, and the leg was still too firmly attached to succumb to her efforts.

No stretcher bar had ever linked the two front legs. Now the lower chain was prevented from slipping entirely free only by the stretcher bar between the legs on the right side.

Once more she charged backward hard, into the rock. Blazing pain exploded through her entire body, and she was almost blown away. But when the right rear leg didn't snap loose, she said, "Hell, no," refusing to surrender to hurt, to exhaustion, to anything, anything, and she hobbled forward and then launched herself backward once more. Wood split with a dry crackle, broken turnings of pine clattered off flagstones, and with a bright ringing, the lower chain fell free of the chair.

Bending forward, dizzy, filled with a whirling darkness, shaking violently, she leaned with both hands on the back of the big leather armchair. She was half sick with pain and with fear of what damage she might have done to her body, wondering about fractured vertebrae and internal bleeding.

*Squeak-squeak-squeak.*

One of the dogs clawed at the window glass.

*Squeak-squeak.*

Chyna wasn't free yet. She was still chained to the upper half of the chair.

The four spindles between the headrail and the seat were thinner than the stretcher bars between the legs, so they ought to break more easily than those bars had broken. She hadn't been able to keep the chair legs from mercilessly hammering the backs of her knees and her thighs, but for this part of the operation, the tie-on foam cushion between her and the spindles should provide her with some protection.

A pair of floor-to-ceiling rock pilasters flanked the firebox and supported the six-inch slab of laminated maple that served as the mantel. They were curved, and it seemed to Chyna that the radius would help focus the impact on one or two spindles at a time instead of spreading it across the four.

She moved the heavy andiron out of the way. She pushed aside a brass rack of fireplace tools. The lifting and shoving made her head spin and her stomach churn, and a hundred agonies assailed her.

She no longer dared to think about what she was doing. She just did it, past courage now, past consideration and calculation, driven by a blind animal determination to be free.

This time, she didn't hunch over; as far as she was able, she stood straight and rammed backward into the pilaster. The cushion did provide protection, but not enough. She was suffering so many contusions, wrenched muscles, and battered bones that the jarring blow would have been devastating even if it had been twice as well padded, like the tap of a dentist's rubber hammer on a rotten tooth in need of a root-canal job. Right now every joint in her body seemed to be a rotten tooth. She didn't pause, because she was afraid that all of those pains, pulsing at once, would soon shake her to the floor, shake her apart, so she would never be able to pull herself together and get up. She was rapidly running out of resources, and with a black tide lapping at the edges of her vision, she was also running out of time. Howling with misery in expectation of the pain, she rammed backward and screamed when the blow rattled her bones like dice in a cup. Agony. But immediately she threw herself into the pilaster again, chains jangling, and again, wood splintering, and again, screaming, *Jesus*, unable to stop screaming and frightened by her own cries, while the vigilant dogs made that needful keening at the window, and yet once more backward, *hammering* herself into the rock.

Then she was again facedown on the floor without remembering how she had gotten there, racked by dry heaves because there was nothing in her stomach to throw up, gagging on a vile taste in the back of her mouth, hands clenched against the very thought of defeat, feeling small and weak and pitiful, shuddering, shuddering.

The shudders gradually diminished, however, and the carpet began to undulate, pleasantly cool beneath her, and she was a cloud shadow on fast-moving waters. The sun-haloed shadow and the fathomless water moved in the same direction, always in the same direction, onward and forever, swift and silken, toward the edge of the world and then off into a void, flowing still, so dark.

Expecting dogs, Chyna woke from red dreams of refrigerator-chilled guns and exploding heads, but there were no dogs. She was alone in the living room, and all was quiet. The Dobermans were not padding back and forth on the porch, and when she was finally able to lift her head, she saw no dogs at the undraped window.

They were outside, calmer now because they realized that their time would come. Watching the door and windows. Waiting to see her face. Alert for the *snick* of a latch, the rasp of a hinge.

She was in so much pain that she was surprised to have regained consciousness. She was more surprised that her head was clear.

One pain was separate from and more urgent than all her other distresses. Unlike the agonies of tortured bones and muscles, this painful pressure could be relieved easily, and she wouldn't even have to put herself through the gruesome ordeal of moving from where she lay.

"Hell no," she mumbled, and slowly she sat up.

Getting to her feet, she disturbed deep hurts that had slept as long as she had been lying on the floor but woke as soon as she began to rise: grindings in her bones and hot flares in her muscles. Some were intense enough, at least initially, to make her freeze and gasp for breath, but by the time she was standing tall, she knew there was no single pain so terrible that it would cripple her; and while the burden of her combined agonies was daunting, she was going to be able to carry it.

She *didn't* have to carry the heavy chair any longer. It lay on the floor around her in fragments and splinters, and none of her chains was encumbered by it.

According to the mantel clock, the time was three minutes till eight, which unsettled her. The last she remembered, it had been ten minutes past seven. She wasn't sure how long she had taken to break free from the chair, but she suspected that she had lain unconscious for half an hour, perhaps longer. The sweat had dried on her body, and her hair was only slightly damp at the nape of her neck, so half an hour was probably correct. This realization made her feel weak and uncertain again.

If Vess could be believed, Chyna still had four hours until he returned. But there was much to be done, and four hours might not be time enough.

Chyna sat on the edge of the sofa. Freed from the pine dining chair, she was at last able to reach the carabiner on the short chain between her ankles. This steel coupling connected the shorter chain to the longer one that had wrapped the chair and the table pedestal. After screwing open the metal sleeve to reveal the gate in the carabiner, she disconnected herself from the longer chain.

Her ankles remained cuffed, and on her way to the stairs to the second floor, she still had to shuffle.

She switched on the stairwell light and laboriously climbed the narrow stairs, moving first her left foot and then her right onto each tread. Because of the hobbling chain, she was unable to ascend one foot per tread, step over step, as she normally would have done, and her progress was slow.

She kept a two-hand grip on the handrail. With the heavy chair gone from her back, she was no longer precariously balanced, but she remained wary of tripping in her fetters.

Past the landing, halfway up the second flight, all of her pains and the fear of falling and the hot pressure in her bladder combined to double her over with severe stomach cramps. She leaned against the wall of the stairwell, clutching the handrail, suddenly sheathed in sour sweat, moaning low and wordlessly in misery. She was certain that she was going to pass out, tumble backward, and break her neck.

But the cramps passed, and she continued climbing. Soon she reached the second floor.

She switched on the hall light and found three doors. Those to the left and right were closed, but the one at the end of the hallway stood open, revealing a bathroom.

In the bathroom, although her hands were manacled and trembling badly, she managed to unbuckle her belt, unbutton her jeans, unzip, and skin down jeans and panties. Sitting, she was hit by more waves of cramps, and these were markedly more vicious than those she had endured on the stairs. She had refused to wet herself at the kitchen table, as Vess had wanted her to do, refused to be reduced to that degree of helplessness. Now she couldn't make water, though she desperately wanted to do that—*needed* to do it to stop the cramps—and she wondered if she had held out so long that a bladder spasm was pinching off the flow. Such a thing was possible, and abruptly the cramps grew more severe, as if confirming her diagnosis. She felt as if her guts were being rolled through a wringer—but then the cramps passed and relief came.

With the sudden flood, she was surprised to hear herself say, "Chyna Shepherd, untouched and alive and able to pee." Then she was simultaneously laughing and sobbing, not with relief but with a weird sense of triumph.

Getting free of the table, shattering and shaking off the chair, and *not* wetting her pants seemed, together, to be an act of endurance and of courage equivalent to setting foot on the moon with the first astronauts to land there, slogging through blinding blizzards to the Pole with Admiral Peary, or storming the beaches of Normandy against the might of the German army. She laughed at herself, laughed until tears spilled down her face; nevertheless, she still felt *that* degree of triumph. She knew how small—even pathetic—her triumph was, but she felt that it was big.

"Rot in Hell," she said to Edgler Vess, and she hoped that someday she would have the chance to say it to his face just before she pulled a trigger and blew him out of this world.

She had so much pain in her back from the battering that she'd endured, especially low around her kidneys, that when she was done, she checked in the toilet bowl for blood. She was relieved to see that her urine was clear.

Glancing in the mirror above the sink, however, she was shocked by her reflection. Her short hair was tangled and lank with sweat. The right side of her face along the jaw seemed to be smeared with a purple ink, but when she touched it, she discovered that this was the trailing edge of a bruise that mottled that entire side of her neck. Where it wasn't bruised or smeared with dirt, her skin was gray and grainy, as if she had been suffering through a long and difficult illness. Her right eye was fiery, no white visible any more: just the dark iris and the darker pupil floating in an elliptical pool of blood. Both the bloodied eye and the clear left eye gazed back at her with a haunted expression so unnerving that she turned away from her own reflection in confusion and fear.

The face in the mirror was that of a woman who had already *lost* some battle. It wasn't the face of a winner.

Chyna tried to press that dispiriting thought out of her mind at once. What she had seen was the face of a fighter—no longer the face of a mere survivor, but a *fighter*. Every fighter sustained some punishment, both physical and emotional. Without anguish and agony, there was no hope of winning.

She shuffled from the bathroom to the door on the right side of the upstairs hall, which opened onto Vess's bedroom. Simple furniture and a minimum of it. A neatly made bed with a beige chenille spread. No paintings. No bibelots or decorative accessories. No books or magazines, or any newspapers folded open to crossword puzzles. This was nothing more than a place to sleep, not a room where he lingered or lived.

Where he truly lived was in the pain of others, in a storm of death, in the calm eye of the storm where all was orderly but where the wind howled on every side.

Chyna checked the nightstand drawers for a gun but didn't find one. She found no phone either.

The large walk-in closet was ten feet deep and as wide as the bedroom, essentially a room of its own. At a glance, the closet held nothing useful to her. She was sure to discover something worthwhile if she searched, maybe even a well-hidden gun. But there were built-in cabinets with laden shelves and packed drawers, and boxes were stacked on boxes; she would need hours to pore through everything. More urgent tasks awaited her.

She emptied the dresser drawers on the floor, but they contained only socks, underwear, sweaters, sweatshirts, and a few rolled belts. No guns.

Across the hall from Vess's bedroom was a Spartan study. Bare walls. Blackout blinds instead of drapes. On two long worktables stood two computers, each with its own laser printer. Of the numerous items of computer-related equipment, she could identify some but was mystified by others.

Between the long tables was an office chair. The floor was not carpeted; the bare wood was exposed, evidently to make it easier for Vess to roll between tables.

The drab, utilitarian room intrigued her. She sensed that it was an important place. Time was precious, but there was something here worth pausing to examine.

She sat in the chair and looked around, bewildered. She knew that the world was wired these days, even into the hinterlands, but it seemed odd to find all this high-tech equipment in such a remote and rustic house.

Chyna suspected that Vess was set up to enter the Internet, but there was no phone or modem in sight. She spotted two unused phone jacks in the baseboard. His meticulous security procedures had served him well again; she was stymied.

What did he do here?

On one of the tables were six or eight ring-bound notebooks with colorful covers, and she opened the nearest. The binder was divided into five sections, each with the name of an agency of the federal government. The first was the Social Security Administration. The pages were filled with what seemed to be notes from Vess to himself regarding the trial-and-error method by which he had hacked his way into the administration's data files and had learned to manipulate them. The second divider was labeled U.S. DEPT OF STATE (PASSPORT AGENCY), and judging by the following notes, Vess was engaged in an incomplete experiment to determine if, by a byzantine route, he might be able to enter and control the Passport Agency's computerized records without being detected.

Part of what he was doing, evidently, was preparing for the day when he slipped up in his "homicidal adventuring" and required new identities.

Chyna didn't believe, however, that Vess's only projects were the altering of his public records and the obtaining of fake ID. She was troubled by the feeling that this room contained information about Vess that could be of vital importance to her own survival if only she knew where to look for it.

She put down the notebook and swiveled in the chair to face the second computer. Under one end of this table stood a two-drawer file cabinet. She opened the top drawer and saw Pendaflex hanging files with blue tags; each tag featured a person's name, with the surname first.

Each folder contained a two-sheet dossier on a different law-enforcement officer, and after a couple of minutes of investigation, Chyna decided that they were deputies with the sheriff's department in the very county in which Vess's house was located. These dossiers provided all vital statistics on the officers plus information about their families and their personal lives. A Xerox of each deputy's official ID photo was also attached.

Did the freak see some advantage in collecting information on all the local cops as insurance against the day when he might find himself in a standoff with them? This effort seemed excessive even for one as meticulous as Edgler Vess; on the other hand, excess was his philosophy.

The lower drawer of the filing cabinet contained manila folders as well. The tabs of these also featured names, like those in the upper drawer, but only surnames.

In the first folder, labeled ALMES, Chyna found a full-page enlargement of the California driver's license of an attractive young blonde named Mia Lorinda Almes. Judging by the exceptional clarity, it wasn't a Xerox blow-up of the original license but a digitized data transmission received on a phone line, through a computer, and reproduced on a high-quality laser printer.

The only other items in the folder were six Polaroid photographs of Mia Lorinda Almes. The first two were close-ups from different angles. She was beautiful. And terrified.

This file drawer was Edgler Vess's equivalent of a scrapbook.

Four more Polaroids of Mia Almes.

*Don't look.*

The next two were full-body shots. The young woman was naked in both. Manacled.

Chyna closed her eyes. But opened them. She was compelled to look, perhaps because she was determined not to hide from anything any more.

In the fifth and sixth photos, the young woman was dead, and in the last her beautiful face was gone as if it had been blown off or sheared away.

The folder and the photographs fluttered from Chyna's hands to the floor, where they clicked against the wood and spun and were still. She hid her face in her hands.

She wasn't trying to block from her mind the gruesome image on the snapshot. Instead, she was striving to repress a nineteen-year-old memory of a farmhouse outside New Orleans, two visitors with a Styrofoam cooler, a gun taken from the refrigerator, and the cold accuracy with which a woman named Memphis had fired two rounds.

Memory, however, always has its way.

The visitors, who'd done business with Zack and Memphis before, had been there to make a drug purchase. The cooler had been filled with packets of hundred-dollar bills. Maybe Zack didn't have the promised shipment, or maybe he and Memphis just needed more money than they could get from a sale; whatever the reason, they had decided to rip off the two men.

After the gunfire, Chyna had hidden in the barn loft, certain that Memphis would kill them all. When Memphis and Anne found her, she fought them bitterly. But she was only seven years old and no match for them. With owls hooting in alarm and taking flight from the rafters, the women dragged Chyna out of the micc-infested hay and carried her to the house.

Zack had been gone by thcn, having taken the bodies elsewhere, and Memphis had cleaned up the blood in the kitchen while Anne had forced Chyna to drink a shot of whiskey. Chyna didn't want the whiskey, sealed her lips against it, but Anne said, "You're a wreck, for Christ's sake, you can't stop blubbering, and one shot isn't going to hurt you. This is what you need, kiddo, trust Mama, this is what you need. A shot of good whiskey will break a fever, you know, and what you've got now is a kind of fever. Come on, you little wuss, it's not poison. Jesus, you can be a whiny little shit sometimes. Either you drink it quick, or I'll hold you down and pinch your nose shut, and Memphis will pour it in when you open your mouth to breathe. That how you want it?" So Chyna drank the whiskey, and then took a second shot with a few ounces of milk when her mother decided that she needed it. The booze made her dizzy and strange but did not calm her.

She had appeared calmer to *them* because, good little fisher that she was, she'd caught her fear and reeled it inside, where they could not see it. Even by the age of seven, she had begun to understand that a show of fear was dangerous, because others interpreted it as weakness, and there was no place in this world for the weak.

Later that night, Zack had returned with whiskey on *his* breath too. He was exuberant, in a raucous and celebratory mood. He came straight to Chyna and hugged her, kissed her on the cheek, took her by the hands and tried to make her dance with him. "That bastard Bobby, the last time he was here, I *knew* by the way he couldn't take his eyes off Chyna that he was hot for little girls, a genuine sicko, so tonight he walks in and his tongue just about uncurls to his knees when he sees her! You could've shot the geek half a dozen times, Memphis, before he might've noticed!" Bobby had been the man sitting at the kitchen table, talking to Chyna, his beautiful gray eyes fixed intently on her, speaking *directly* to her in a way that few adults ever spoke to kids, asking whether she liked kittens or puppies best and did she want to grow up to be a famous movie star or a nurse or a doctor or what, when Memphis shot him in the head. "The way our Chyna girl was dressed," Zack said excitedly, "Bobby just about totally forgot anyone else was here." The night was hot and swamp-humid, and before the visitors arrived, Chyna's mother made her change out of her shorts and T-shirt into a brief yellow bikini swimsuit: "But only the bottoms because, child, you're going to get heatstroke in this weather." Although only seven, Chyna was old enough to feel peculiar about going bare-chested, even if she didn't quite know why she felt that way. She'd gone bare-chested when she was younger, even just the previous summer, when she was six; and it *was* an awfully hot, sticky night. When Zack said that the way she was dressed had something to do with Bobby's forgetting that anyone else was in the room, Chyna didn't understand what he meant. Years later, when she *did* understand, she had confronted her mother with it. Anne had laughed and said, "Oh, baby, don't get self-righteous on me. We get along by using what we've got, and one sure thing we girls have is our bodies. You were the perfect distraction. Anyway, poor dumb old Bobby never touched you, did he? He just got to gawk at you a little, that's all, while Memphis went for the gun. Don't forget, sweetie, we were cut in for a piece of that pie and lived well on it for a while." And Chyna had wanted to say, *But you used me, you put me right there in front of him where I'd see his head come apart, and I was only seven!*

All these years later, in Edgler Vess's study, she could still hear the crash of the shot and see Bobby's face explode; the memory was as vivid as ever it had been. She didn't know what gun Memphis used, but the ammunition must have been high-caliber hollow-point lead wadcutters that expanded on impact, because the damage they inflicted had been tremendous.

She lowered her hands from her face and looked at the open file cabinet. Vess had used three formats of folders, with staggered tab placement, so it was easy for Chyna to see all the names along the length of the drawer. Much farther back from the Almes file was one labeled TEMPLETON.

She pushed the drawer shut with her foot.

She'd found too much in this study—yet nothing helpful.

Before leaving the second floor, she turned off all the lights. If Vess came home early, before Chyna could get away with Ariel, the lights would warn him that something was amiss. He would be lulled by darkness, however, and as he crossed the threshold, she might have one last chance to kill him.

She hoped it wouldn't come to that. In spite of her fantasies of pulling the trigger on Vess, Chyna didn't want to have to confront him again, even if she found a shotgun and loaded it herself and had an opportunity to test fire it before he arrived. She was a survivor, and she was a fighter, but Vess was more than either: as unreachable as stars, something come down from a high darkness. She was no match for him, and she didn't want another chance to prove it.

One tread at a time, balanced against the handrail, as fast as she dared, Chyna went down to the living room. None of the Dobermans was at the undraped window.

The mantel clock put the time at twenty-two minutes past eight, and suddenly the night seemed to be a sled on a slope of ice, picking up speed.

She extinguished the lamp and shuffled through darkness to the kitchen. There she turned on the fluorescent lights, only to avoid tripping in the debris, falling, and cutting herself on broken glass.

No Dobermans were on the back porch either. At the window, only the night waited.

Entering the windowless laundry room, she shut off the kitchen lights behind her and pulled the door shut.

Down to the cellar, then, to the workbench and cabinets that she had seen earlier.

In the tall metal cabinets with the vent slits in the doors, she found cans of paint and lacquer, paintbrushes, and drop cloths folded as precisely as fine linen sheets. One entire cabinet was filled with thick pads from which dangled black leather straps with chrome-plated buckles; she didn't have any idea what they were, and she left them undisturbed. In the final cabinet, Vess stored several power tools, including an electric drill.

In one of the drawers on the big wheeled tool chest, she located an extensive collection of drill bits in three clear plastic boxes. She also found a pair of Plexiglas safety goggles.

A power strip with eight outlets was attached to the wall behind the workbench, but a duplex receptacle was also available low on the wall beside the bench. She needed the lower outlet, because it allowed her to sit on the floor.

Although the drill bits weren't labeled except as to size, Chyna figured that they were all meant for woodworking and would not bore easily—if at all—through steel. She didn't want to pierce the steel anyway; she wanted only to screw up the lock mechanisms on her leg irons enough to spring them open.

She chose a bit approximately the size of the leg-iron keyway, fitted it into the chuck, and tightened it. When she held the drill in both hands and squeezed the trigger, it issued a shrill whine. The spiral throat of the slender bit spun so fast that it blurred until it seemed as smooth and harmless as the shank.

Chyna released the trigger, set the silent drill aside on the floor, and put on the protective goggles. She was disconcerted by the thought that Vess had worn these goggles. Strangely, she expected that everything she saw through them would be distorted, as if the molecules of the lenses had been transformed by the magnetic power with which Vess drew all the sights of his world to his eyes.

But what she saw through the goggles was no different from what she saw without them, although her field of vision was circumscribed by the frames.

She picked up the drill with both hands again and inserted the tip of the bit into the keyway on the shackle that encircled her left ankle. When she pressed the trigger, steel spun against steel with a hellish shriek. The bit stuttered violently, jumped out of the keyway, and skipped across the two-inch-wide shackle, spitting tiny sparks. If her reflexes hadn't been good, the whirling auger would have bored through her foot, but she released the trigger and jerked up on the drill just in time to avoid disaster.

The lock might have been damaged. She couldn't be sure. But it was still engaged, and the shackle was secure.

She inserted the bit into the keyway again. She gripped the drill tighter than before and bore down with more effort to keep the bit from kicking out of the hole. Steel shrieked, shrieked, and blue wisps of foul-smelling smoke rose from the grinding point, and the vibrating shackle pressed painfully into her ankle in spite of the intervening sock. The drill shook in her hands, which were suddenly damp with cold sweat from the strain of controlling it. A spray of metal slivers swirled up from the keyway, spattered her face. The bit snapped, and the broken-off end *zinged* past her head, rang off the concrete-block wall hard enough to take a chip out of it, and clinked like a half-spent bullet across the cellar floor.

Her left cheek stung, and she found a splinter of steel embedded in her flesh. It was about a quarter of an inch long and as thin as a sliver of glass. She was able to grasp it between her fingernails and pluck it free. The tiny puncture was bleeding; she had blood on her fingertips and felt a thin warm trickle making its way down her face to the corner of her mouth.

She freed the shank of the broken bit from the drill and threw it aside. She selected a slightly larger bit and tightened it into the jaws of the chuck.

Again, she drilled the keyway. The shackle around her left ankle popped open. Not more than a minute later, the lock on the other shackle cracked too.

Chyna put the drill aside and rose shakily to her feet, every muscle in her legs trembling. She was shaky not because of her many pains, not because of her hunger and weakness, but because she had freed herself from the shackles after having been in despair only a couple of hours before. She had freed *herself.*

She was still handcuffed, however, and she could not hold the drill one-handed while she bored out the lock on each manacle. But she already had an idea about how she might extricate her hands.

Although other challenges faced her in addition to the manacles, although escape was by no means assured, jubilation swelled in Chyna as she climbed the cellar steps. She went tread over tread, not one step at a time as the shackles had required, *bounding* up the stairs in spite of her weakness and the tremors in her muscles, without even using the handrail, to the landing, into the laundry room, past the washer and dryer. And there she abruptly halted with her hands on the knob of the closed door, remembering how she had raced along this same route and into the kitchen this morning, reassured by the *tatta-tatta-tatta* of the vibrating water pipe in the wall, only to be blindsided by Vess.

She stood at the threshold until her breathing quieted, but she was unable to quiet her heart, which had been thundering with excitement and with the steepness of the stairs but now pounded with fear of Edgler Vess. She listened at the door for a while, heard nothing over the thudding in her breast, and turned the knob as stealthily as possible.

The hinges operated smoothly, soundlessly, and the door opened into the kitchen, which was as dark as she had left it. She found the light switch, hesitated, flipped it up—and Vess was not waiting for her.

As long as she lived, would she ever again be able to go through a doorway without flinching?

From a drawer where earlier Chyna had seen a set of cutlery, she extracted a butcher knife with a well-worn walnut handle. She put it on the counter near the sink.

She got a drinking glass from another cabinet, filled it from the cold-water tap, and drank the entire glassful in long swallows before lowering it from her lips. Nothing she had ever drunk had been half as delicious as those eight ounces.

In the refrigerator, she found an unopened coffeecake with white icing, cinnamon, walnuts. She ripped open the wrapper and tore off a chunk of the cake. She stood over the sink, eating voraciously, stuffing her mouth until her cheeks bulged, greedily licking icing from her lips, crumbs and chunks of walnuts dropping into the sink.

She was in an uncommon state of mind as she ate: now moaning with delight, now half choking with laughter, now gagging and on the verge of tears, now laughing again. In a storm of emotions. But that was okay. Storms always passed sooner or later, and they were cleansing.

She had come so far. Yet she had so far to go. That was the nature of the journey.

From the spice rack she removed the bottle of aspirin. She shook two tablets into the palm of her hand, but she didn't chew them. She drew another glass of water and took the aspirin, then took two more.

She sang, "I did it my way," from Sinatra's standard, and then added, "took the fucking aspirin my way." She laughed and ate more coffeecake, and for a moment she felt crazy with accomplishment.

*Dogs out there in the night,* she reminded herself, *Dobermans in the darkness, rotten bastard Nazi dogs with big teeth and eyes black like sharks' eyes.*

At a key organizer next to the spice rack, the keys to the motor home hung from one of the four pegs; the other pegs were empty. Vess would be careful with the keys to the soundproofed cell and would no doubt keep them on him at all times.

She picked up the butcher knife and the half-eaten coffee cake and went to the cellar, turning off the kitchen lights behind her.

Pintle and gudgeon.

Chyna knew these two exotic words, as she knew so many others, because, as a girl, she had encountered them in books written by C. S. Lewis and Madeleine L'Engle and Robert Louis Stevenson and Kenneth Grahame. And every time that she'd come across a word she had not known, she'd looked it up in a tattered paperback dictionary, a prized possession that she took with her wherever her restless mother chose to drag her, year after year, until it was held together with so much age-brittled Scotch tape that she could barely read some of the definitions through the strips of yellowing cellophane.

Pintle. That was the name of the pin in a hinge, which pivoted when a door opened or closed.

Gudgeon. That was the sleeve—or barrel—in which the pintle moved.

The thick inner door of the soundproofed vestibule was equipped with three hinges. The pintle in each hinge had a slightly rounded head that overhung the gudgeon by about a sixteenth of an inch all the way around.

From the tools in the wheeled cabinet, Chyna selected a hammer and a screwdriver.

With the workbench stool and a scrap of wood for a wedge, she propped open the outer padded door of the vestibule. Then she placed the butcher knife on the rubber mat on the vestibule floor, within easy reach.

She slid aside the cover on the view port in the inner door and saw the gathering of dolls in pinkish lamplight. Some had eyes as radiant as the eyes of lizards, and some had eyes as dark as those of certain Dobermans.

In the enormous armchair, Ariel sat with her legs drawn up on the seat cushion, head tipped forward, face obscured by a fall of hair. She might have been asleep—except that her hands were balled tightly in her lap. If her eyes were open, she would be staring at her fists.

"It's only me," Chyna said.

The girl didn't respond.

"Don't be afraid."

Ariel was so motionless that even her veil of hair did not stir.

"It's only me."

This time, deeply humbled, Chyna made no claim to being any-one's guardian or salvation.

She started with the lowest hinge. The length of chain between her manacles was barely long enough to allow her to use the tools. She held the screwdriver in her left hand, with the tip of the blade angled under the pintle cap. Without sufficient play in the manacle chain, she couldn't grasp the hammer by its handle, so she gripped it instead by the head and tapped the bottom of the screwdriver as forcefully as possible considering the limitations on movement. Fortunately, the hinge was well lubricated, and with each tap, the pintle rose farther out of the gudgeon. Five minutes later, in spite of some resistance from the third pin, she popped it out of the uppermost hinge.

The gudgeons were formed of interleaving knuckles that were part of the hinge leaf on the doorframe and that on the inner edge of the door itself. These knuckles separated slightly, because the pintles were no longer present to hold them together in a single barrel.

Now the door was kept in place only by the pair of locks on the right side, but one-inch deadbolts wouldn't swing like hinges. Chyna pulled the padded door by the knuckles of the gudgeons. At first only one inch of its five-inch width came out of the jamb on the left, vinyl squeaking against vinyl. She hooked her fingers around this ex-posed edge, yanked hard, and her vision clouded with a crimson tint as the pain in her swollen finger flared again. But she was rewarded with the shrill metallic *skreek* of the brass deadbolts working in the striker plates and then with a faint crack of wood as the whole lock assembly put heavy strain on the jamb. Redoubling her efforts, she pulled rhythmically, prying open the door in tiny increments, until she was gasping so hard that she was no longer able to curse with frustration.

The weight of the door and the position of the two deadbolts began to work to her advantage. The locks were close together, one set directly over the other, not evenly spaced like hinges, so the heavy slab tried to twist on them as if they were a single pivot point. Because a greater length of the door lay above the locks than below, the top tipped outward, induced by gravity. Chyna took advantage of these in-evitable forces, yanked harder, and grunted with satisfaction when wood splintered again. The entire five-inch width of the padded slab swung free of the jamb on the side that had been hinged. With the frame no longer in the way, she pulled the door to the left, and on the right side, the deadbolts slid out of the striker plates.

Suddenly the door came toward her, free of all restraint, and it was too heavy to be lowered slowly out of its frame. She backed rapidly into the cellar, letting the slab thud to the floor of the vestibule just as she vacated it.

Chyna waited, catching her breath, listening to the house for any indication that Vess had returned.

Finally she reentered the vestibule. She crossed the fallen door as if it were a bridge, and she went into the cell.

The dolls watched, unmoving and sly.

Ariel was sitting in the armchair, head lowered, hands fisted in her lap, exactly as she had been when Chyna had spoken to her through the port in the door. If she had heard the hammering and subsequent commotion, she had not been disturbed by it.

"Ariel?" Chyna said.

The girl didn't reply or raise her head.

Chyna sat on the footstool in front of the armchair. "Honey, it's time to go."

When she received no response, Chyna leaned forward, lowered her head, and looked up at the girl's shadowed face. Ariel's eyes were open, and her gaze was fixed on her white-knuckled fists. Her lips were moving, as though she were whispering confidences to someone, but no sound escaped her.

Chyna put her cuffed hands under Ariel's chin and lifted her head. The girl didn't try to pull away, didn't flinch, but was revealed when her veil of hair slid away from her face. Although they were eye-to-eye, Ariel stared through Chyna, as if all in this world were transparent, and in her eyes was a chilling bleakness, as if the landscape of her other world was lifeless, daunting.

"We have to go. Before he comes home."

Bright-eyed and attentive, perhaps the dolls listened. Ariel apparently did not.

With both hands, Chyna enfolded one of the girl's fists. The bones were sharp and the skin was cold, clenched as fiercely as if she had been suspended from rocks at a precipice.

Chyna tried to pry the fingers apart. The sculpted digits of a marble fist would have been hardly more resistant.

Finally Chyna lifted the hand and kissed it more tenderly than she had ever kissed anyone before, more tenderly than she had ever been kissed, and she said softly, "I want to help you. I *need* to help you, honey. If I can't leave here with you, there's no point in my leaving at all."

Ariel didn't respond.

"Please let me help you." Softer still: "*Please.*"

Chyna kissed the hand once more, and at last she felt the girl's fingers stir. They opened partway, cold and stiff, but would not relax entirely, as hooked and rigid as a skeleton's fingers in which the joints had calcified.

Ariel's desire to reach out for help, tempered by her paralyzing fear of commitment, was achingly familiar to Chyna. It struck in her a chord of sympathy and pity for this girl, for all lost girls, and her throat tightened so severely that for a moment she was unable to swallow or breathe.

Then she slipped one cuffed hand into Ariel's and the other over it, got up from the footstool, and said, "Come on, child. Come with me. Out of here."

Though Ariel's face remained as expressionless as an egg, though she continued to look through Chyna with the otherworldly detachment of a novitiate in the thrall of a holy visitation, her head spinning with visions, she got up from the armchair. After taking only two steps toward the door, however, she stopped and would not go farther in spite of Chyna's pleas. The girl might be able to envision an imaginary world in which she could find a fragile peace, a Wild Wood of her own, but perhaps she was no longer able to imagine that *this* world extended beyond the walls of her cell and, failing to visualize it, could not cross the threshold into it.

Chyna released Ariel's hand. She selected a doll—a bisque charmer with golden ringlets and painted green eyes, wearing a white eyelet pinafore over a blue dress. She pressed it against the girl's breast and encouraged her to embrace it. She wasn't sure why the collection was here, but perhaps Ariel liked the dolls, in which case she might come along more readily if given one for comfort.

Initially, Ariel was unresponsive, standing with one hand still fisted at her side and the other like a half-open crab claw. Then, without shifting her gaze from faraway things, she took the doll in both hands, gripping it by the legs. Like the shadow of a bird in flight, a fierce expression crossed her face and was gone before it could be clearly read. She turned, swung the doll as if it were a sledgehammer, and smashed its head into the top of the dinette table, shattering the unglazed-china face.

Startled, Chyna said, "Honey, no," and gripped the girl by the shoulder.

Ariel wrenched away from Chyna and slammed the doll into the table again, harder than before, and Chyna stepped backward, not in fear but in respect of the girl's fury. And fury it was, a righteous anger, not merely an autistic spasm, in spite of the fact that she remained expressionless.

She pounded the doll against the table repeatedly, until its smashed head broke and spun across the room and bounced off a wall, until both its arms cracked and fell away, until it was ruined beyond repair. Then she dropped it and stood trembling, arms hanging at her sides. She was still staring into the Elsewhere and was no more with Chyna than she had ever been.

From the bookcases, from atop the cabinets, from the shadowed corners of the room, the dolls watched intently, as if they were thrilled by her outburst and in some strange way feeding on it as Vess himself would have fed if he'd been there to see.

Chyna wanted to put her arms around the girl, but the handcuffs made it impossible to embrace her. Instead, she touched Ariel's face and kissed her on the forehead. "Ariel, untouched and alive."

Rigid, shaking, Ariel neither pulled away from Chyna nor leaned toward her. Gradually the girl's trembling subsided.

"I need your help," Chyna pleaded. "I need you."

This time, as if sleepwalking, Ariel allowed herself to be led from the cell.

They crossed the fallen door through the vestibule. In the cellar, Chyna picked up the drill from the floor, plugged it into the power strip on the wall, and put it on the workbench.

She had no timepiece for reference, but she was sure that nine o'clock had come and gone. In the night were dogs waiting and Edgler Vess somewhere at work, bemused by waking dreams of returning home to his pair of captives.

Trying unsuccessfully to get the girl's eyes to focus on her, Chyna explained what they needed to do. She might be able to drive the motor home while handcuffed, though not without some difficulty, as she would have to let go of the steering wheel to shift gears. Dealing with the dogs while cuffed would be a lot harder. Perhaps impossible. If they were to make the best use of the time remaining before Vess's return, and if they were to have the best chance of getting away, Ariel was going to have to drill out the locks on the manacles.

The girl gave no indication that she heard a word of what Chyna told her. Indeed, before Chyna finished, Ariel's lips were moving again in a silent conversation with some phantom; she didn't "speak" ceaselessly but paused from time to time as if receiving a response from an imaginary friend.

Nevertheless, Chyna showed her how to hold the drill and press the trigger. The girl didn't blink at the sudden shriek of the motor and the air-cutting whistle of the whirling bit.

"Now you hold it," Chyna said.

Oblivious, Ariel stood with her arms at her sides, hands half open and fingers hooked as they had been since she had dropped the ruined doll.

"We don't have much time, honey."

In her clockless Elsewhere, time meant nothing to Ariel.

Chyna put the drill on the workbench. She drew the girl in front of the tool and placed her hands on it.

Ariel didn't pull away or let her hands slide off the drill, but she didn't lift it either.

Chyna *knew* that the girl heard her, understood the situation, and, on some level, yearned to help.

"Our hopes are in your hands, honey. You can do it."

She retrieved the workbench stool from the outer vestibule door, which it had been propping open, and sat down. She put her hands on the workbench, wrists turned to expose the tiny keyhole on the left manacle.

Staring at the concrete-block wall, *through* the wall, speaking soundlessly to a psychic friend beyond all walls, Ariel seemed to be unaware of the drill. Or to her it might have been not a drill but another object altogether, one that filled her either with hope or with fear, the thing of which she spoke to her phantom friend.

Even if the girl picked up the drill and focused her eyes on the manacle, the chance that she would be able to perform this task seemed slim. The chance that she would avoid boring through Chyna's palm or wrist seemed slimmer still.

On the other hand, although the likelihood of salvation from any trouble or enemy in this life was always slim, Chyna had survived uncounted nights of blood rage and questing lust. Survival was far different from salvation, of course, but it was a prerequisite.

Anyway, she was ready to do now what she had never been able to do before, not even with Laura Templeton: *trust.* Trust without reservation. And if this girl tried and failed, let the drill slip and damaged flesh rather than steel, Chyna wasn't going to blame her for the failure. Sometimes, just *trying* was a triumph.

And she knew Ariel wanted to try.

She *knew*.

For a minute or so, Chyna encouraged the girl to begin, and when that didn't work, she tried waiting in silence. But silence led her thoughts to the bronze stags and the clock over which they leaped on the living room mantel, and in her mind's eye the clock acquired the face of the young man who hung in the motor home closet, eyelids tightly stitched and lips sewn shut in a silence even deeper than that in the cellar.

With no calculation, surprised to hear what she was doing but relying on instinct, Chyna began to tell Ariel what had happened on the long-ago night of her eighth birthday: the cottage in Key West, the storm, Jim Woltz, the frantic palmetto beetle under the low-slung iron bed . . .

Drunk on Dos Equis and high on a pair of small white pills that he had popped with the first bottle of beer, Woltz had teased Chyna because she had failed to blow out all the candles on her birthday cake in a single breath, leaving one aflame. "This is bad luck, kid. Oh, man, this brings a world of grief down on us. If you don't get all the candles out, you invite gremlins and trolls into your life, all sorts of bad characters after your stash and cash." Just then the night sky had convulsed with white light, and the shadows of palm fronds had leaped across the kitchen windows. The cottage rattled in the shock waves of thunderclaps as hard as bomb blasts, and the storm broke. "See?" Woltz said. "If we don't rectify this situation right away, then some bad guys will get the best of us and chop us up into bloody chunks and put us in bait buckets and go out on some deep-sea boat, trolling for sharks, using us as chum. Do you want to be shark chum, kid?" This speech frightened Chyna, but her mother found it amusing. Her mother had been drinking vodka with lemonade since late afternoon.

Woltz relit the candles and insisted that Chyna try once more. When she failed again to extinguish more than seven with one breath, Woltz seized her hand, licked her thumb and index finger, his tongue lingering in a way that disgusted her, and then forced her to snuff the remaining flame by pinching the candlewick. Although there was a brief hotness against her skin, she had not been burned; however, her fingers had been marked with black smudges from the smoking wick, and the sight of them had terrified her.

When Chyna began to cry, Woltz held her by one arm, keeping her in her chair, while Anne relit the eight, insisting that she try again. The third time, Chyna was able to extinguish only six candles with her first shuddery breath. When Woltz attempted to make her pinch both flames with her fingers, she pulled loose and ran out of the kitchen, intending to flee to the beach, but lightning had shattered like bright mirrors around the cottage, the night flashing with sharp silver fragments, and thunder as fierce as the cannonades of warships boomed out of the Gulf of Mexico, so she had fled instead to the small room in which she slept, crawled under the sagging bed, into those secret shadows where the palmetto beetle waited.

"Woltz, the stinking sonofabitch, came through the house after me," Chyna told Ariel, "shouting my name, knocking over furniture, slamming doors, saying he was going to chop me up for chum and then scatter me in the sea. Later I realized it was an act. He'd been trying to scare the crap out of me. He always liked to scare me, make me cry, 'cause I didn't cry easily . . . never easily. . . ."

Chyna stopped, unable to go on.

Ariel stared not toward the wall, as before, but down at the power drill on which her hands were placed. Whether she saw the drill was another matter; her eyes were still far away.

The girl might not be listening, yet Chyna felt compelled to tell the rest of what had happened that night in Key West.

This was the first time she had ever revealed to anyone, other than Laura, any of the things that had happened to her when she was a child. Shame had always silenced her, which was inexplicable because none of the degradation she endured had resulted from her own actions. She had been a victim, small and defenseless; yet she was burdened with the shame that all her tormentors, including her mother, were incapable of feeling.

She had hidden some of the worst details of her past even from Laura Templeton, her only good friend. Often, on the brink of a revelation to Laura, she would pull back from disclosure and speak not about the events that she had endured and not about the people who had tormented her but about places—Key West, Mendocino County, New Orleans, San Francisco, Wyoming—where she had lived. She was lyrical when the subject was the natural beauty of mountains, plains, bayous, or low moonlit breakers rolling in from the Gulf of Mexico, but she could feel anger tightening her face and shame coloring it when she told the harder truths about the friends of Anne who had populated her childhood.

Now her throat was tight. She was curiously aware of the weight of her heart, like a stone in her chest, heavy with the past.

Sick with shame and anger, she nevertheless sensed that she must finish telling Ariel what had happened during that Florida night of un-extinguished candles. Revelation might be a door out of darkness.

"Oh, God, how I hated him, the greasy bastard, stinking of beer and sweat, crashing around my room, drunk and screaming, going to cut me up for bait, Anne laughing out in the living room and then at the doorway, that drunken laugh of hers, hooting and shrill, thinking he was so funny, Jesus, and all the time it was my birthday, my special day, my *birthday*." Tears might have come now if she had not spent a lifetime learning to repress them. "And the palmetto all over me, frantic, scurrying, up my back and into my hair . . ."

In the sticky, suffocating Key West heat, thunder had rattled in the window and sung in the bedsprings, and cold blue reflections of lightning had fluttered like a dream fire across the painted wood floor. Chyna almost screamed when the tropical cockroach, as big as her little-girl hand, burrowed through her long hair, but fear of Woltz kept her silent. She endured, as well, when the beetle scuttled out of her hair, across her shoulder, down her slender arm, to the floor, hoping that it would flee into the room, not daring to fling it away for fear that any movement she made would be heard by Woltz in spite of the thunder, in spite of his shouted threats and curses, even over her mother's laughter. But the palmetto scurried along her side to one of her bare feet and began to explore that end of her again, foot and ankle, calf and thigh. Then it crawled under one leg of her shorts, into the cleft of her butt, antennae quivering. She had lain in a paralysis of terror, wanting only for the torment to end, for lightning to strike her, for God to take her away to somewhere better than this hateful world.

Laughing, her mother had entered the room: "Jimmy, you nut, she's not here. She's gone outside, along the beach somewhere, like always." And Woltz said, "Well, if she comes back, I'm going to cut her up for chum, I swear I am." Then he laughed and said, "Man, did you see her *eyes?* Christ! She was scared shitless." "Yeah," Anne said, "she's a gutless little wuss. She'll be hiding out there for hours. I don't know when the hell she'll ever grow up." Woltz said, "Sure doesn't take after her mother. You were *born* grown up, weren't you, baby?" "Listen, ass-hole," Anne said, "you pull any crap like that with me, I'm sure not going to run like she did. I'll kick your balls so hard you'll have to change your name to Nancy." Woltz roared with laughter, and from under the bed Chyna saw her mother's bare feet approach Woltz's feet, and then her mother was giggling.

Fat and obscene and agitated, the palmetto had crawled out from under the waistband of Chyna's shorts and into the small of her back, moving toward her neck, and she had been unable to bear the thought of it in her hair again. Regardless of the consequence, she reached back as the beetle crossed her tube top, and seized it. The thing twitched, squirmed in her hand, but she tightened her fist.

Head turned to the side, peering from under the bed, Chyna had still been gazing at her mother's bare feet. As flashes of lightning strobed the small room, a cloth swirled to the floor, a soft drift of yel-low linen around Anne's slender ankles. Her blouse. She giggled drunkenly as her shorts slid down her tanned legs, and she stepped out of them.

In Chyna's clenched hand, the angry beetle's legs had churned. An-tennae quivered, ceaselessly seeking. Woltz kicked off his sandals, and one of them clattered to the edge of the bed, in front of Chyna's face, and she heard a zipper. Hard and cool and oily, the palmetto's small head rolled between two of Chyna's fingers. Woltz's tattered jeans fell in a heap, with a soft *clink* of the belt buckle.

He and Anne had dropped onto the narrow bed, and the springs had twanged, and the weight had made the frame slats sag against Chyna's shoulders and back, pinning her to the floor. Sighs, murmurs, urgent encouragements, groans, breathless gasps, and coarse animal grunting—Chyna had heard it on other nights in Key West and else-where but always before through walls, from rooms next door. She didn't really know what it meant, and she didn't *want* to know, because she sensed that this knowledge would bring new dangers, with which she wasn't equipped to deal. Whatever her mother and Woltz were doing above her was both frightening and deeply sad, full of terrible meaning, no less strange or less powerful than the thunder breaking up the sky above the Gulf and the lightning thrown out of Heaven into the earth.

Chyna had closed her eyes against the lightning and the sight of the discarded clothes. She strove to shut out the smell of dust and mildew and beer and sweat and her mother's scented bath soap, and she imagined that her ears were packed full of wax that muffled the thunder and the drumming of the rain on the roof and the sounds of Anne with Woltz. As fiercely clenched as she was, she ought to have been able to squeeze herself into a safe state of insensate patience or even through a magical portal into the Wild Wood.

She had been less than half successful, however, because Woltz had rocked the narrow bed so forcefully that Chyna consciously had to time her breathing to the rhythm he established. When the frame slats swagged down with the full thrust of his weight, they pressed Chyna so hard against the bare wood floor that her chest ached and her lungs couldn't expand. She could inhale only when he lifted up, and when he bore down, he virtually forced her to exhale. It went on for what seemed to be a long time, and when at last it was over, Chyna lay shivering and sweat-soaked, numb with terror and desperate to forget what she had heard, surprised that the breath hadn't been crushed out of her forever and that her heart had not burst. In her hand was what remained of the large palmetto beetle, which she had unwittingly crushed; ichor oozed between her fingers, a disgusting slime that might have been vaguely warm when first it had gushed from the beetle but was now cool, and her stomach rolled with nausea at the alien texture of the stuff.

After a while, following a spate of murmurs and soft laughter, Anne had gotten off the bed, snatched up her clothes, and gone down the hall to the bathroom. As the bathroom door closed, Woltz switched on a small nightstand lamp, shifted his weight on the bed, and leaned over the side. His face appeared upside down in front of Chyna. The light was behind him and his face was shadowed but for a dark glitter in his eyes. He smiled at her and said, "How's the birthday girl?" Chyna was unable to speak or move, and she half believed that the wetness in her hand was a bloody hunk of chum. She knew that Woltz would chop her up for having heard him with her mother, chop her to pieces and put her in bait buckets and take her out to sea for the sharks. Instead, he'd gotten out of bed and—from her perspective once more just a pair of feet—he had squirmed into his jeans, put on his sandals, and left the room.

In Edgler Vess's cellar, thousands of miles and eighteen years from that night in Key West, Chyna saw that Ariel at last seemed to be star-ing *at* the power drill rather than through it.

"I don't know how long I stayed under the bed," she continued. "Maybe a few minutes, maybe an hour. I heard him and my mother in the kitchen again, getting another bottle of beer, fixing another vodka with lemonade for her, talking and laughing. And there was something in her laugh—a dirty little snicker . . . I'm not sure—but something that made me think she knew I'd been hiding under there, knew it but went along with Woltz when he unbuttoned her blouse."

She stared at her cuffed hands on the workbench.

She could feel the beetle's ichor as if it were even now oozing between her fingers. When she had crushed the insect, she had also crushed what remained of her own fragile innocence and all hope of being a daughter to her mother; though after that night, she had still needed years to understand as much.

"I've no memory at all of how I left the cottage, maybe through the front door, maybe through a window, but the next thing I knew, I was on the beach in the storm. I went to the edge of the water and washed my hands in the surf. The breakers weren't huge. They seldom are, there, except in a hurricane, and this was only a tropical storm, almost windless, the heavy rain coming straight down. Still, the waves were bigger than usual, and I thought about swimming out into the black water until I found an undertow. I tried to persuade myself that it would be all right, just swimming in the dark until I got tired, told myself I would just be going to God."

Ariel's hands appeared to tighten on the drill.

"But for the first time in my life, I was afraid of the sea—of how the breaking waves sounded like a giant heart, of how the nearby water was as shiny black as a beetle's shell and seemed to curve up, in the near distance, to meet a black sky that didn't shine at all. It was the endlessness and seamlessness of the dark that scared me—the *continuity*—although that wasn't a word I knew back then. So I stretched out on the beach, flat on my back in the sand, with the rain beating down on me so hard that I couldn't keep my eyes open. Even behind my eyelids, I could see the lightning, a bright ghost of it, and because I was too scared to swim out to God, I waited for God to come to me, blazing bright. But He didn't come, didn't come, and eventually I fell asleep. Shortly after dawn, when I woke, the storm had passed. The sky was red in the east, sapphire in the west, the ocean flat and green. I went inside, and Anne and Woltz were still asleep in his room. My birthday cake was on the kitchen table where it had been the night before. The pink and white icing was soft and beaded with yellowish oil in the heat, and the eight candles were all cockeyed. No one had cut a slice from it, and I didn't touch it either. . . . Two days later, my mother pulled up stakes and carted me off to Tupelo, Mississippi, or Santa Fe, or maybe Boston. I don't remember where, exactly, but I was relieved to be leaving—and afraid of who we would settle in with next. Happy only in the traveling, gone from one thing but not yet arrived at the next, the peace of the road or the rails. I could have traveled forever without a destination."

Above them, the house of Edgler Vess remained silent.

A spiky shadow moved across the cellar floor.

Looking up, Chyna saw a busy spider spinning a web between one of the ceiling joists and one of the lighting fixtures.

Maybe she'd have to deal with the Dobermans while handcuffed. Time was running out.

Ariel picked up the power drill.

Chyna opened her mouth to speak a few words of encouragement but then was afraid that she might say the wrong thing and send the girl deeper into her trance.

Instead, she spotted the safety goggles and, making no comment, got up and put them on the girl. Ariel submitted without objection.

Chyna returned to the stool and waited.

A frown surfaced in the placid pool of Ariel's face. It didn't subside again but floated there.

The girl pressed the trigger of the drill experimentally. The motor shrieked, and the bit whirled. She released the trigger and watched the bit spin to a stop.

Chyna realized that she was holding her breath. She let it out, inhaled deeply, and the air was sweeter than before. She adjusted the position of her hands on the workbench to present Ariel with the left cuff.

Behind the goggles, Ariel's eyes slowly shifted from the point of the drill bit to the keyhole. She was definitely looking *at* things now, but she still appeared detached.

Trust.

Chyna closed her eyes.

As she waited, the silence grew so deep that she began to hear distant imaginary noises, analogue to the phantom lights that play faintly behind closed eyelids: the soft solemn tick of the mantel clock upstairs, the restless movement of vigilant Dobermans in the night outside.

Something pressed against the left manacle.

Chyna opened her eyes.

The bit was in the keyway.

She didn't look up at the girl but closed her eyes again, more tightly this time than previously, to protect them from flying metal shavings. She turned her head to one side.

Ariel bore down on the drill to prevent it from popping out of the keyway, just as Chyna had instructed. The steel manacle pressed hard against Chyna's wrist.

Silence. Stillness. Gathering courage.

Suddenly the drill motor whined. Steel squealed against steel, and the sound was followed by the thin, acrid odor of hot metal. Vibrations in Chyna's wrist bones spread up her arm, exacerbating all the aches and pains in her muscles. A clatter, a hard *ping*, and the left manacle fell open.

She could have functioned reasonably well with the pair of cuffs dangling from her right hand. Perhaps it didn't make sense to risk injury for the relatively small additional advantage of being free of the manacles altogether. But this wasn't about logic. It wasn't about a rational comparison of risks and advantages. It was about faith.

The bit clicked against the keyway as it was inserted into the right manacle. The drill shrieked, and steel jittered-spun against steel. A spray of tiny shavings spattered across the side of Chyna's face, and the lock cracked.

Ariel released the trigger and lifted the drill away.

With a laugh of relief and delight, Chyna shook off the manacles and raised her hands, gazing at them in wonder. Both of her wrists were abraded—actually raw and seeping in places. But that pain was less severe than many others that afflicted her, and no pain could diminish the exhilaration of being free at last.

As if not sure what to do next, Ariel stood with the drill in both hands.

Chyna took the tool and set it aside on the workbench. "Thank you, honey. That was terrific. You did great, really great, you were perfect."

The girl's arms hung at her sides again, and her delicate pale hands were no longer hooked like claws but were as slack as those of a sleeper.

Chyna slipped the goggles off Ariel's head, and they made eye contact, *real* contact. Chyna saw the girl who lived behind the lovely face, the true girl inside the safe fortress of the skull, where Edgler Vess could get at her only with tremendous effort if ever.

Then, in an instant, Ariel's gaze traveled from this world to the sanctuary of her Elsewhere.

Chyna said, "Nooooo," because she didn't want to lose the girl whom she had so briefly glimpsed. She put her arms around Ariel and held her tight and said, "Come back, honey. It's okay. Come back to me, talk to me."

But Ariel did not come back. After pulling herself completely into the world of Edgler Vess long enough to drill out the locks on the manacles, she had exhausted her courage.

"Okay, I don't blame you. We're not out of here yet," Chyna said. "But now we only have the dogs to worry about."

Though still living in a far realm, Ariel allowed Chyna to take her hand and lead her to the stairs.

"We can handle a bunch of damn dogs, kid. Better believe it," Chyna said, though she was not sure if she believed it herself.

Free of manacles and shackles, no longer carrying a chair on her back, with a stomach full of coffeecake, and with a gloriously empty bladder, she had nothing to think about except the dogs. Halfway up the stairs toward the laundry room, she remembered something that she had seen earlier; it had been puzzling then, but it was clear now—and vitally important.

"Wait. Wait here," she told Ariel, and pressed the girl's limp hand around the railing.

She plunged back down the stairs, went to the metal cabinets, and pulled open the door behind which she had seen the strange pads trailing black leather straps with chrome-plated buckles. She pulled them out, scattering them on the floor around her, until the cabinet was empty.

They weren't pads. They were heavily padded garments. A jacket with a dense foam outer layer under a man-made fabric that appeared to be a lot tougher than leather. Especially thick padding around both arms. A pair of bulky chaps featured hard plastic under the padding, body-armor quality; the plastic was segmented and hinged at the knees to allow the wearer flexibility. Another pair of chaps protected the backs of the legs and came with a hard-plastic butt shield, a waist belt, and buckles that connected them to the front chaps.

Behind the garments were gloves and an odd padded helmet with a clear Plexiglas face shield. She also found a vest that was labeled

KEVLAR, which looked exactly like the bulletproof garments worn by members of police SWAT teams.

A few small tears marred the garments—and in many places other rips had been sewn shut with black thread as heavy as fishing line. She recognized the same neat stitches that she had seen in the young hitchhiker's lips and eyelids. Here and there in the padding were unrepaired punctures. Tooth marks.

This was the protective gear that Vess wore when he worked with the Dobermans.

Apparently he layered on enough padding and armor to walk safely through a pride of hungry lions. For a man who liked to take risks, who believed in living life on the edge, he seemed to take excessive precautions when putting his pack of Dobermans through their training sessions.

Vess's extraordinary safeguards told Chyna everything that she needed to know about the savagery of the dogs.

Less than twenty-two hours since the first cry in the Templeton house in Napa. A lifetime. And now toward another midnight and into whatever lay beyond.

Two lamps were aglow in the living room. Chyna no longer cared about keeping the house dark. As soon as she went out the front door and confronted the dogs, there would be no hope of lulling Vess into a false sense of security if he came home early.

According to the mantel clock, it was ten-thirty.

Ariel sat in one of the armchairs. She was hugging herself and rocking slowly back and forth, as if suffering from a stomachache, although she made no sound and remained expressionless.

Protective gear designed for Vess was huge on Chyna, and she vacillated between feeling ridiculous and worrying that she would be dangerously impeded by the bulky garb. She had rolled up the bottoms of the chaps and fixed them in place with large safety pins that she'd found in a sewing kit in the laundry room. The belts of the chaps featured loops and long Velcro closures, so she was able to cinch them tight enough to keep them from sliding down over her hips. The cuffs of the padded sleeves were folded back and pinned too, and the Kevlar vest helped to bulk her up, so she wasn't quite swimming in the jacket. She wore a segmented plastic-armor collar that encircled her neck and prevented the dogs from tearing out her throat. She couldn't have been more cumbersomely dressed if she'd been cleaning up nuclear waste in a post-meltdown reactor.

Nevertheless, she was vulnerable in places, especially at her feet and ankles. Vess's training togs included a pair of leather combat boots with steel toes, but they were much too big for her. As protection against attack dogs, her soft Rockports were hardly more effective than bedroom slippers. In order to get to the motor home without being severely bitten, she would have to be quick and aggressive.

She had considered carrying a club of some kind. But with her agility impaired by the layers of protective gear, she couldn't use it effectively enough to hurt any of the Dobermans or even dissuade them from attacking.

Instead, Chyna was equipped with two lever-action spray bottles that she'd found in a laundry-room cabinet. One had been filled with a liquid glass cleaner and the other with a spot remover for use on carpets and upholstery. She had emptied both bottles into the kitchen sink, rinsed them out, considered filling them with bleach, but chose pure ammonia, of which the fastidious Vess, the keeper of a spotless house, possessed two one-quart containers. Now the plastic spray bottles stood beside the front door. The nozzle on each could be adjusted to produce a spray or a stream, and both were set at STREAM.

In the armchair, Ariel continued to hug herself and to rock back and forth in silence, gazing down at the carpet.

Although it was unlikely that the catatonic girl would get up from the chair and go anywhere on her own, Chyna said, "Now, you stay right where you are, honey. Don't move, okay? I'll be back for you soon."

Ariel didn't reply.

"Don't move."

Chyna's layers of protective clothing were beginning to weigh painfully on her bruised muscles and sore joints. Minute by minute, the discomfort was going to make her slower mentally and physically. She had to act while she was still reasonably sharp.

She put on the visored helmet. She had lined the interior with a folded towel so it wouldn't sit loosely on her head, and the chin strap helped to keep it secure. The curved shield of Plexiglas came two inches below her chin, but the underside was open to allow air to flow in freely—and there were six small holes across the center of the pane for additional ventilation.

She stepped to one front window and then to the other, looking onto the porch, which was visible in the light that spilled out from the living-room lamps. There were no Dobermans in sight.

The yard beyond the porch was dark, and the meadow beyond the yard seemed as black as the far side of the moon. The dogs might be standing out there, watching her silhouette in the lighted windows.

In fact, they might be waiting just beyond the porch balustrade, crouched and ready to spring.

She glanced at the clock.

Ten thirty-eight.

"Oh, God, I don't want to do this," she murmured.

Curiously, she remembered a cocoon that she'd found when she and her mother had been staying with some people in Pennsylvania fourteen or fifteen years before. The chrysalis had been hanging from a twig on a birch tree, semitransparent and backlit by a beam of sunlight, so she had been able to see the insect within. It was a butterfly that had passed all the way through the pupa stage, a fully mature imago. Its metamorphosis complete, it had been quivering frantically within the cocoon, its wirelike legs twitching ceaselessly, as if it was eager to be free but frightened of the hostile world into which it would be born. Now, in her padding and hard-plastic armor, Chyna quivered like that butterfly, although she was not eager to burst free into the night world that awaited her but wanted to withdraw even deeper into her chrysalis.

She went to the front door.

She pulled on the stained leather gloves, which were heavy but surprisingly flexible. They were too large but had adjustable Velcro bands at the wrists to hold them in place.

She had sewn a brass key to the thumb of the right-hand glove, running the thread through the hole in the key bow. The entire blade, with all its tumbler-activating serrations, extended beyond the tip of the thumb, so it could be inserted easily into the keyway on the door of the motor home. She didn't want to have to fumble the key from a pocket with the dogs attacking from all sides—and she sure as hell didn't want to risk dropping it.

Of course, the vehicle might not be locked. But she wasn't taking any chances.

From the floor, she picked up the spray bottles. One in each hand. Again, she checked to be sure that they were set on STREAM.

She quietly disengaged the deadbolt lock, listened for the hollow thump of paws on the board floor, and finally cracked the door.

The porch looked clear.

Chyna crossed the threshold and quickly pulled the door shut behind her, fumbling at the knob because she was hampered by the plastic bottles in her hands.

She hooked her fingers around the levers on the bottles. The effectiveness of these weapons would depend on how fast the dogs came at her and whether she could aim well in the brief window of opportunity that they would give her.

In a night as windless as it was deep, the seashell mobile hung motionless. Not even a single leaf stirred on the tree at the north end of the porch.

The night seemed to be soundless. With her ears under the padded helmet, however, she wasn't able to hear small noises.

She had the weird feeling that the entire world was but a highly detailed diorama sealed inside a glass paperweight.

Without even the faintest breeze to carry her scent to the dogs, maybe they would not be aware that she had come outside.

*Yeah, and maybe pigs can fly but just don't want us to know.*

The fieldstone steps were at the south end of the porch. The motor home stood in the driveway, twenty feet from the bottom of the steps.

Keeping her back to the wall of the house, she edged to her right. As she moved, she glanced repeatedly to her left at the railed north side of the porch, and out past the balustrade into the front yard directly ahead of her. No dogs.

The night was so chilly that her breath formed a faint fog on the inside of her visor. Each flare of condensation faded quickly—but each seemed to fan out across the Plexiglas farther than the one before it. In spite of the ventilation from under her chin and through the six penny-size holes across the center of the pane, she began to worry that her own hot exhalations were gradually going to leave her effectively blind. She was breathing hard and fast, and she was hardly more able to slow her rate of respiration than quiet the rapid pounding of her heart.

If she *blew* each breath out, angling it toward the open bottom of the face shield, she would be able to minimize the problem. This resulted in a faint, hollow whistling characterized by a vibrato that revealed the depth of her fear.

Two small sliding steps, three, four: She eased sideways past the living-room window. She was uncomfortably aware of the light at her back. Silhouetted again.

She should have turned all the lights out, but she hadn't wanted Ariel to be alone in the dark. In her current condition, perhaps the girl would not have known if the lights were on or off, but it had felt wrong to leave her in blackness.

Having crossed half the distance from the door to the south end of the porch without incident, Chyna grew bolder. Instead of edging sideways, she turned directly toward the steps and shuffled forward as fast as the hampering gear would allow.

As black as the night out of which it came, as silent as the high patchy clouds sailing slowly across fields of stars, the first Doberman sprinted toward her from the front of the motor home. It didn't bark or growl.

She almost failed to see it in time. Because she forgot to exhale with calculation, a wave of condensation spread across the inside of the visor. At once, the pale film of moisture retreated like an ebbing surf, but the dog was already *there*, leaping toward the steps, ears flattened against its tapered skull, lips skinned back from its teeth.

She squeezed the lever of the spray bottle that she clutched in her right hand. Ammonia shot six or seven feet in the still air.

The dog wasn't within range when the first stream spattered onto the porch floor, but it was closing fast.

She felt stupid, like a kid with a water pistol. This wasn't going to work. Wasn't going to work. But oh, Jesus, it *had* to work or she was dog chow.

Immediately she pumped the lever again, and the dog was on the steps, where the stream fell short of it, and she wished that she had a sprayer with more pressure, one with at least a twenty-foot range, so she could stop the beast before it got near her, but she squeezed the trigger again even as the previous stream was still falling, and this one got the dog as it came up onto the porch. She was aiming for its eyes, but the ammonia splashed its muzzle, spattering its nose and its bared teeth.

The effect was instantaneous. The Doberman lost its footing and tumbled toward Chyna, squealing, and would have crashed into her if she hadn't jumped aside.

With caustic ammonia slathering its tongue and fumes filling its lungs, unable to draw a breath of clean air, the dog rolled onto its back, pawing frantically at its snout. It wheezed and hacked and made shrill sounds of distress.

Chyna turned from it. She kept moving.

She was surprised to hear herself speaking aloud: "Shit, shit, shit . . ."

Onward, then, to the head of the porch steps, where she glanced back warily and saw that the big dog was on its feet, wobbling in circles, shaking its head. Between sharp squeals of pain, it was sneezing violently.

The second dog virtually *flew* out of the darkness, attacking as Chyna descended the bottom step. From the corner of her eye, she detected movement to her left, turned her head, and saw an airborne Doberman—*oh, God*—like an incoming mortar round. Though she raised her left arm and started to swing toward the dog, she wasn't quick enough, and before she could loose a stream of ammonia, she was hit so hard that she was nearly bowled off her feet. She stumbled sideways but somehow maintained her balance.

The Doberman's teeth were sunk into the thick sleeve on her left arm. It wasn't merely holding her as a police dog would have done but was working at the padding as if chewing on meat, trying to rip off a chunk and severely disable her, tear open an artery so she would bleed to death, but fortunately its teeth hadn't penetrated to her flesh.

After coming at her in disciplined silence, the dog still wasn't snarling. But from low in its throat issued a sound halfway between a growl and a hungry keening, an eerie and needful cry that Chyna heard too clearly in spite of her padded helmet.

Point-blank, reaching across her body with her right hand, she squirted a stream of ammonia into the Doberman's fierce black eyes.

The dog's jaws flew open as if they were part of a mechanical device that had popped a tension spring, and it spun away from her, silvery strings of saliva trailing from its black lips, howling in agony.

She remembered the words of warning on the ammonia label: *Causes substantial but temporary eye injury.*

Squealing like an injured child, the dog rolled in the grass, pawing at its eyes as the first animal had pawed at its snout, but with even greater urgency.

The manufacturer recommended rinsing contaminated eyes with plenty of water for fifteen minutes. The dog had no water, unless it instinctively made its way to a stream or pond, so it would not be a problem to her for *at least* a quarter of an hour, most likely far longer.

The Doberman sprang to its feet and chased its tail, snapping its teeth. It stumbled and fell again, scrambled erect, and streaked away into the night, temporarily blinded, in considerable pain.

Incredibly, listening to the poor thing's screams as she hurried toward the motor home, Chyna winced with remorse. It would have torn her apart without hesitation if it could have gotten at her, but it was a mindless killer only by training, not by nature. In a way, the dogs were just other victims of Edgler Vess, their lives bent to his purpose. She would have spared them suffering if she had been able to rely solely on the protective clothing.

How many more dogs?

Vess had implied there was a pack. Hadn't he said *four?* Of course, he might be lying. There might be only two.

*Move, move, move.*

At the passenger-side cockpit door of the motor home, she tried the handle. Locked.

*No more dogs, just five seconds without dogs, please.*

She dropped the spray bottle from her right hand, so she could pinch the bow of the key between her thumb and finger. She was barely able to feel it through the thick gloves.

Her hand was shaking. The key missed the keyhole and chattered against the chrome face of the lock cylinder. She would have dropped it if it hadn't been sewn to the glove.

From behind this time, just as she was about to slip the key into the door on her second try, a Doberman hit her, leaping onto her back, biting at the nape of her neck.

She was slammed forward against the vehicle. The face shield on her helmet smacked hard against the door.

The dog's teeth were sunk into the thick rolled collar of the trainer's jacket, no doubt also into the padding on the segmented plastic collar that she wore under the jacket to protect her neck. It was holding on to her by its teeth, tearing at her ineffectively with its claws, like a demon lover in a nightmare.

As the dog's impact had pitched her forward against the motor home, now the weight of it and its furious squirming dragged her away from the vehicle. She almost toppled backward, but she knew that the advantage would go to the dog if it managed to drag her to the ground.

*Stay up. Stay tall.*

Lurching around a hundred eighty degrees as she struggled to keep her balance, she saw that the first Doberman was no longer on the porch. Astonishingly, the creature hanging from her neck must be the small one that she had squirted on the muzzle. Now it was able to get its breath again, back in service, undaunted by her chemical arsenal, giving its all for Edgler Vess.

On the plus side, maybe there *were* only two dogs.

She still had the spray bottle in her left hand. She squeezed the trigger, aiming several squirts over her shoulder. But the heavy padding in the jacket sleeves didn't allow her to bend her arms much, and she wasn't able to fire at an angle that could splash the ammonia in the dog's eyes.

She threw herself backward against the side of the motor home, much as she had hurtled into the fireplace earlier. The Doberman was trapped between her and the vehicle as the chair had been between her and the river-rock wall, and it took the brunt of the impact.

Letting go of her, falling away, the dog squealed, a pitiful sound that sickened her, but also a good sound—*oh, yes*—a good sound as sweet as any music.

Buckles jangling, padded chaps slapping together, Chyna scuttled sideways, trying to get out of the animal's reach, worried about her ankles, her vulnerable ankles.

But suddenly the Doberman no longer seemed to be in a fighting mood. It slunk away from her, tail tucked between its legs, rolling its eyes to keep a watch on her peripherally, shaking and wheezing as though it had damaged a lung, and favoring its hind leg on the right side.

She squeezed the trigger on the spray bottle. The creature was out of range, and the stream of ammonia arced into the grass.

Two dogs down.

*Move, move.*

Chyna turned to the motor home again—and cried out as a third dog, weighing more than she did, leaped at her throat, bit through the jacket, and staggered her backward.

Going down. *Shit.* And as she went, the dog was on top of her, chewing frenziedly at the collar of the jacket.

When Chyna hit the ground, her breath was knocked from her in spite of all the padding, and the spray bottle popped out of her left hand, spun into the air. She grabbed at it as it tumbled away, but she missed.

The dog ripped loose a strip of padding from around the jacket collar and shook its head, casting the scrap aside, spraying her face shield with gobs of foamy saliva. It bore in at her again, tearing more fiercely at the same spot, burrowing deeper, seeking meat, blood, triumph.

She pounded its sleek head with both fists, trying to smash its ears, hoping that they would be sensitive, vulnerable. "Get off, damn it, off! Off!"

The Doberman snapped at her right hand, missed, teeth clashing audibly, snapped again, and connected. Its incisors didn't instantly penetrate the tough leather glove, but it shook her hand viciously, as though it had hold of a rat and meant to snap its spine. Though her skin hadn't been broken, the grinding pressure of the bite was so painful that Chyna screamed.

In an instant, the dog released her hand and was at her throat again. Past the torn jacket. Teeth slashing at the Kevlar vest.

Howling in pain, Chyna stretched her throbbing right hand toward the spray bottle lying in the grass. The weapon was a foot beyond her reach.

When turning her head to look at the bottle, she inadvertently caused the bottom of her face shield to lift, giving the Doberman better access to her throat, and it thrust its muzzle under the curve of Plexiglas, above the Kevlar vest, biting into the thick padding on the exterior of the segmented hard-plastic collar, which was her last defense. Intent on tearing this band of body armor away, the dog jerked back so hard that Chyna's head was lifted off the ground, and pain flared across the nape of her neck.

She tried to heave the Doberman off her. It was heavy, bearing down stubbornly, paws digging frantically at her.

As the dog wrenched at Chyna's protective collar, she could feel its hot breath against the underside of her chin. If it could get its snout under the shield at a slightly better angle, it might be able to bite her chin, *would* be able to bite her chin, and at any moment it was going to realize this.

She heaved with all her strength, and the dog clung, but she was able to hitch a few inches closer to the spray bottle. She heaved again, and now the bottle was just six inches beyond her grasping fingertips.

She saw the other Doberman limping toward her, ready to rejoin the fray. She hadn't damaged its lungs, after all, when she slammed it between her and the motor home.

Two of them. She couldn't handle two of them at once, both on top of her.

She heaved, desperately hitching sideways on her back, dragging the clinging Doberman with her.

Its hot tongue licked the underside of her chin, licked, tasting her sweat. It was making that horrible, needful sound deep in its throat.

*Heave.*

Spotting her point of greatest vulnerability, the limping dog scuttled toward her right foot. She kicked at it, and the dog dodged back, but then it darted in again. She kicked, and the Doberman bit the heel of her Rockport.

Her frantic breathing fogged the inside of the visor. In fact, the breath of the clinging Doberman fogged it too, because its muzzle was under the Plexiglas. She was effectively blind.

Kicking with both feet to ward off the limping dog. Kicking, heaving sideways.

The other's hot tongue slathered her chin. Its sour breath. Teeth gnashing an inch short of her flesh. The tongue again.

Chyna touched the spray bottle. Closed her fingers around it.

Though the bite hadn't penetrated the glove, her hand was still throbbing with such crippling pain that she was afraid she wouldn't be able to hold on to the bottle or find the right grip, wouldn't be able to work the lever-action trigger, but then she blindly squeezed off a stream of ammonia. Unthinking, she had used her swollen trigger finger, and the flash of pain made her dizzy. She shifted her middle finger onto the lever and squeezed off another blast.

In spite of her kicking, the injured dog bit through her shoe. Teeth pierced her right foot.

Chyna triggered another thick stream of ammonia toward her feet, yet another, and abruptly that Doberman let go of her. Both she and the dog were shrieking, blind and shaking and living now in the same commonwealth of pain.

Snapping teeth. The remaining dog. Pressing toward her chin, under the visor. *Snap-snap-snap.* And the eager hungry whine.

She jammed the bottle in its face, pulled the trigger, pulled, and the dog scrambled off her, screaming.

A few drops of ammonia penetrated the visor through the series of small holes across the center of the pane. She wasn't able to see through the fogged Plexiglas, and the acrid fumes made breathing difficult.

Gasping, eyes watering, she dropped the spray bottle and crawled on her hands and knees toward where she thought the motor home stood. She bumped into the side of it and pulled herself to her feet. Her bitten foot felt hot, perhaps because it was soaking in the bath of blood contained in her shoe, but she could put her weight on it.

Three dogs so far.

If three, then surely four.

The fourth would be coming.

As the ammonia evaporated from the face shield and less rapidly from the front of her torn jacket, the quantity of fumes decreased but not quickly enough. She was eager to remove the helmet and draw an unobstructed breath. She didn't dare take it off, however, not until she was inside the motor home.

Choking on ammonia fumes, trying to remember to exhale downward under the Plexiglas visor but half blinded because her eyes wouldn't stop watering, Chyna felt along the side of the motor home until she found the cockpit door again. She was surprised that she could walk on her bitten foot with only tolerable twinges of pain.

The key was still sewn securely to her right glove. She pinched it between her thumb and forefinger.

A dog was wailing in the distance, probably the first one that she had squirted in the eyes. Nearby, another was crying pitifully and howling. A third whimpered, sneezed, gagged on fumes.

But where was the fourth?

Fumbling at the lock cylinder, she found the keyhole by trial and error. She opened the door. She hauled herself up into the copilot's seat.

As she pulled the door shut, something slammed into the outside of it. The fourth dog.

She took off the helmet, the gloves. She stripped out of the padded jacket.

Teeth bared, the fourth Doberman leaped at the side window. Its claws rattled briefly against the glass, and then it dropped back to the lawn, glaring at her.

Revealed by the light from the narrow hallway, Laura Templeton's body still lay on the bed in a tangle of manacles and chains, wrapped in a sheet.

Chyna's chest tightened with emotion, and her throat swelled so that she had trouble swallowing. She told herself that the corpse on the bed was not really Laura. The essence of Laura was gone, and this was only the husk, merely flesh and bone on a long journey to dust. Laura's spirit had traveled in the night to a brighter and warmer home, and there was no point shedding tears for her, because she had transcended.

The closet door was closed. Chyna was sure that the dead man still hung in there.

In the fourteen hours or longer since she had been in the motor-home bedroom, the stuffy air had acquired a faint but repulsive scent of corruption. She had expected worse. Nevertheless, she breathed through her mouth, trying to avoid the smell.

She switched on the reading lamp and opened the top drawer of the nightstand. The items that she had discovered the previous night were still there, rattling softly against one another as the engine vibrations translated through the floor.

She was nervous about leaving the engine running, because the sound of it would mask the approach of another vehicle in case Vess came home earlier. But she needed lights, and she didn't want to risk depleting the battery.

From the drawer, she withdrew the package of gauze pads, the roll of cloth tape, and the scissors.

In the lounge area behind the cockpit, she sat in one of the armchairs. Earlier, she had stripped out of all the protective gear. Now she removed her right shoe. Her sock was sodden with blood, and she peeled it off.

From two punctures in the top of her foot, blood welled dark and thick. It was seeping, however, not spurting, and she wasn't going to die from the wound itself anytime soon.

She quickly pressed a double thickness of gauze pads over the seeping holes and fixed them in place with a length of cloth tape. By tightening the tape to apply a little pressure, she might be able to make the bleeding slow or stop.

She would have preferred to saturate the punctures with Bactine or iodine, but she didn't have anything like that. Anyway, infection wouldn't set in for a few hours, and by then she would have gotten away from here and obtained medical attention. Or she'd be dead of other causes.

The chance of rabies seemed small to nil. Edgler Vess would be solicitous of the health of his dogs. They would have received all their vaccinations.

Her sock was cold and slimy with blood, and she didn't even try to pull it on again. She slipped her bandaged foot into her shoe and tied the lace slightly looser than usual.

A folding metal stepstool was stored in a narrow slot between the kitchen cabinetry and the refrigerator. She carried it into the short hallway at the end of the vehicle and opened it under the skylight, which was a flat panel of frosted plastic about three feet long and perhaps twenty inches wide.

She climbed onto the stool to inspect the skylight, hoping that it either tilted open to admit fresh air or was attached to the roof from the interior. Unfortunately, the panel was fixed, with no louver function, and the mounting flange was on the exterior, so she could not get at any screws or rivets from the inside.

Under her padded clothing, she had worn a tool belt that she'd found in one of the drawers of Vess's workbench. She had taken it off with the rest of the gear. Now it was on the table in the dining nook.

Unable to be certain what tools she would need, she'd brought a pair of standard pliers, a pair of needle-nose pliers, both flat and rat-tail files, and several sizes of screwdrivers with standard blades and Phillips heads. There was also a hammer, which was the only thing that she could use.

When she stood on the first step of the two-step stool, the top of her head was only ten inches from the skylight. Averting her face, she swung the hammer with her left hand, and the flat steel head met the plastic with a horrendous bang and clatter.

The skylight was undamaged.

Chyna swung the hammer relentlessly. Each blow reverberated in the plastic overhead but also through all of her strained and weary muscles, through her aching bones.

The motor home was at least fifteen years old, and this appeared to be the original factory-installed skylight. It wasn't Plexiglas but some less formidable material; over many years of sunshine and bad weather, the plastic had grown brittle. Finally the rectangular panel cracked along one edge of the frame. Chyna hammered at the leading point of the fissure, making it grow all the way to the corner, then along the narrow end, and then along the other three-foot length.

She had to pause several times to catch her breath and to change the hammer from hand to hand. At last the panel rattled loosely in its frame; it now seemed to be secured only by splinters of material along the fissures and by the uncracked fourth edge.

Chyna dropped the hammer, slowly flexed her hands a few times to work some of the stiffness out of them, and then put both palms flat against the plastic. Grunting with the effort, she pushed upward as she climbed onto the second step of the stool.

With a brittle splintering of plastic, the panel lifted an inch, jagged edges squeaking against each another. Then it bent backward at its fourth side, creaking, resisting her . . . resisting . . . until she cried out wordlessly in frustration and, finding new strength, pushed even harder. Abruptly the fourth side cracked all the way through, with a *bang!* as loud as a gunshot.

She pushed the panel out through the ceiling. It rattled across the roof and dropped to the driveway.

Through the hole above her head, Chyna saw clouds suddenly slide away from the moon. Cold light bathed her upturned face, and in the bottomless sky was the clean white fire of stars.

Chyna backed the motor home off the driveway and alongside the front of the house, parallel to the porch and as close to it as she could get. She let the big vehicle roll slowly, anxious not to tear up the thick grass, because under it the ground might be muddy even half a day after the rain had stopped. She didn't dare bog down.

When she was in position, she put the vehicle in park and set the emergency brake. She left the engine running.

In the short hall at the back of the motor home, the stepstool had fallen over. She put it upright, climbed the two steps, and stood with her head in the night air, above the open frame of the broken-out skylight.

She wished the stool had a third step. She needed to muscle herself out of the hallway, and she was at a less advantageous angle than she would have liked.

She placed her hands flat on the roof on opposite sides of the twenty-inch-wide rectangular opening and struggled to lever her body out of the motor home. She strained so hard that she could feel the tendons flaring between her neck and shoulders, her pulse pounding like doomsday drums in her temples and carotid arteries, every muscle in her arms and across her back quivering with the effort.

Pain and exhaustion seemed certain to thwart her. But then she thought of Ariel in the living-room armchair: rocking back and forth, hugging herself, a faraway look in her eyes, her lips parted in what might have been a silent scream. That image of the girl empowered Chyna, put her in touch with hitherto unknown resources. Her shaking arms slowly straightened, pulling her body out of the hallway, and inch by inch she kicked her feet as if she were a swimmer ascending from the depths. At last her elbows locked with her arms at full extension, and she heaved forward, out through the skylight, onto the roof.

On the way, her sweater caught on small fragments of plastic that bristled from the skylight frame. A few jagged points pierced the knit material and stung her belly, but she broke loose of them.

She crawled forward, rolled onto her back, hiked her sweater, and felt her stomach to see how badly she had been cut. Blood wept from a couple of shallow punctures, but she wasn't hurt seriously.

From far off in the night came the howls of at least two injured dogs. Their pathetic cries were so filled with fear, vulnerability, misery, and loneliness that Chyna could hardly bear to listen.

She eased to the edge of the roof and looked down at the yard to the east of the house.

The uninjured Doberman trotted around the front of the motor home and spotted her at once. It stood directly under her, gazing up, teeth bared. It seemed unfazed by the suffering of its three comrades.

Chyna moved away from the edge and got to her feet. The metal surface was somewhat slippery with dew, and she was thankful for the rubber tread on her Rockports. If she lost her footing and fell off into the yard, with no weapons and no protective clothing, the one remaining Doberman would overwhelm her and tear out her throat in ten seconds flat.

The motor home was only a few inches below the edge of the porch roof. She had parked so close that the distance between the vehicle and the house was less than a foot.

She stepped up and across that gap, onto the sloped roof of the porch. The asphalt shingles had a sandy texture and weren't nearly as treacherous as the top of the motor home.

The slope wasn't steep either, and she climbed easily to the front wall of the house. The recent rain had liberated a tarry scent from the numerous coats of creosote with which the logs had been treated over the years.

The double-hung window of Vess's second-story bedroom was open three inches, as she had left it before departing the house. She slipped her aching hands through the opening and, groaning, shoved up on the bottom panel. In this wet weather, the wood had swollen, but although it stuck a couple of times, she got it all the way open.

She climbed through the window into Vess's bedroom, where she had left a lamp burning.

In the upstairs hall, she glanced at the open door across from the bedroom. The dark study lay beyond, and she was still troubled by the feeling that there was something in it that she had missed, something vital she should know about Edgler Vess.

But she had no time for additional detective work. She hurried downstairs to the living room.

Ariel was huddled in the armchair where she had been left. She was still hugging herself and rocking, lost.

According to the mantel clock, the time was four minutes past eleven.

"You stay right there," Chyna instructed. "Just a minute more, honey."

She went through the kitchen to the laundry room, in search of a broom. She found both a broom and a sponge mop. The mop had the longer handle of the two, so she took it instead of the broom.

As she entered the living room again, she heard a familiar and dreaded sound. *Squeak-squeak. Squeak-squeak-squeak.*

She glanced at the nearest window and saw the uninjured Doberman clawing the glass. Its pointy ears were pricked, but they flattened against its skull when Chyna made eye contact with the creature. The Doberman issued the now-familiar needful keening that caused the fine hairs to stiffen on the nape of Chyna's neck.

*Squeak-squeak-squeak.*

Turning away from the dog, Chyna started toward Ariel—and then had her attention drawn to the other living-room window. A Doberman stood with its forepaws at the base of that pane too.

This had to be the first one she had encountered when she'd gone out of the house, the same animal that she had sprayed in the muzzle. It had recovered quickly and had bitten her foot when she'd been pinned on the ground by the third dog.

She was sure that she'd blinded the second dog, which had shot at her like a mortar round from out of the darkness, and the third as well. Until now she had assumed that her second chance at *this* animal had also resulted in a disabling eye shot.

She'd been wrong.

At the time, of course, she herself had been all but blinded by her fogged visor—and frantic, because the third dog had been holding her down and chewing through the padding at her throat, licking at her chin. All she had known was that this animal had shrieked when she'd squirted it and that it had stopped biting her foot.

The stream of ammonia must have splashed the dog's muzzle the second time, just as it had during their first encounter.

"Lucky bastard," she whispered.

The twice-injured Doberman didn't scratch at the window glass. It just watched her. Intently. Ears standing straight up. Missing nothing.

Or perhaps it wasn't the same dog at all. Perhaps there were *five* of them. Or six.

At the other window: *Squeak-squeak. Squeak-squeak.*

Crouching in front of Ariel, Chyna said, "Honey, we're ready to go."

The girl rocked.

Chyna took hold of one of Ariel's hands. This time, she didn't have to pry the fingers out of a marble-hard fist, and at her urging, the girl got up from the chair.

Carrying the sponge mop in one hand, leading the girl with the other, Chyna crossed the living room, past the two big front windows. She moved slowly and didn't look directly at the Dobermans, because she was afraid that either haste or another moment of confrontational eye contact might spur them to smash through the glass.

She and Ariel stepped through a doorless opening to the stairs.

Behind them, one of the dogs began to bark.

Chyna didn't like that. Didn't like that at all. None of them had barked before. Their disciplined stealth had been chilling—but now the barking was worse than their silence.

Climbing the stairs, pulling the girl after her, Chyna felt a hundred years old, weak and depleted. She wanted to sit and catch her breath and let her aching legs rest. To keep moving, Ariel needed constant tension on her arm; without it, she stopped and stood murmuring soundlessly. Each riser seemed higher than the one below it, as though Chyna were the storybook Alice in the wake of the white rabbit, her stomach full of exotic mushrooms, ascending an enchanted staircase in some dark wonderland.

Then, as they turned at the landing and started up the second flight, glass shattered into the living room below. In an instant, that sound made Chyna young again, able to bound like a gazelle up stairs made for giants.

"Hurry!" she urged Ariel, pulling her along.

The girl picked up her pace but still seemed to be plodding.

Leaping, desperate, to the top of the second flight, Chyna said, "*Hurry!*"

Vicious barking rose in the stairwell below.

Chyna entered the upstairs hall, holding tightly to the girl's hand. She could hear the galloping thunder of ascending dogs louder even than her own heart.

To the door on the left. Into Vess's bedroom.

She dragged Ariel after her, across the threshold, and slammed the door. There was no lock, just the spring latch activated by the knob.

*They're dogs, for God's sake, just dogs, mean as hell, but they can't operate a doorknob.*

A dog threw itself against the door, which rattled in its frame but seemed secure.

Chyna led Ariel to the open window, where she propped the mop against the wall.

Barking, barking, the dogs clawed at the door.

With both hands, Chyna clasped the girl's face, leaned close, and peered hopefully into her beautiful blue but vacant eyes. "Honey, please, I need you again, like I needed you with the power drill and the handcuffs. I need you a lot worse now, Ariel, because we don't have much time, not much time at all, and we're so close, we really are, so damn *close*."

Though their eyes were at most three inches apart, Ariel seemed not to see Chyna.

"Listen to me, listen, honey, wherever you are, wherever you're hiding out there in the Wild Wood or beyond the wardrobe door there in Narnia—is that where you are, baby?—or maybe Oz, but wherever you are, *please* listen to me and do what I tell you. We've got to go out on the porch roof. It's not steep, you can do it, but you have to be careful. I want you to go out the window and then take a couple of steps to the left. Not to the right. There's not much roof to the right, you'll fall off. Take a couple steps to the left and stop and just wait there for me. I'll be right behind you, just wait, and I'll take you on from there."

She let go of the girl's face and hugged her fiercely, loving her as she would have loved a sister if she'd had one, as she wished she had been able to love her mother, loving her for what she had been through, for having suffered and survived.

"I am your guardian, honey. *I'm your guardian.* Vess is never going to touch you again, the freak, the hateful bastard. He's never going to touch you again. I'm going to get you out of this stinking place, and away from him forever, but you have to work with me, you have to help and listen and be careful, so careful."

She let go of the girl and met her eyes again.

Ariel was still Elsewhere. There was no flicker of recognition as there had been for a split second in the cellar, after the girl had used the drill.

The barking had stopped.

From the far side of the room came a new and disturbing sound. Not the clatter of the door shaking in its frame. A harder rattling noise. Metallic.

The knob was jiggling back and forth. One of the dogs must be pawing industriously at it.

The door wasn't well fitted. Chyna could see a half-inch gap between the edge of it and the jamb. In the gap was a gleam of shiny brass: the tongue of the simple latch. If the latch was not seated deeply in the jamb, even the dog's fumbling might, by purest chance, spring it open.

"Wait," she told Ariel.

She crossed the room and tried to pull the dresser in front of the door.

The dogs must have sensed that she'd drawn nearer, because they began barking again. The old black iron knob rattled more furiously than before.

The dresser was heavy. But there was no straight-backed chair that she could wedge under the knob, and the nightstand didn't seem bulky enough to prevent the dogs from shoving the door open if, in fact, the spring latch popped out of the jamb.

Heavy as it was, she nevertheless dragged the dresser halfway across the bedroom door. That seemed good enough.

The Dobermans were going crazy, barking more ferociously than ever, as if they knew that she had foiled them.

When Chyna turned to Ariel again, the girl was gone.

"No."

Panicked, she ran to the window and looked outside.

Radiant in moonlight, hair silver now instead of blond, Ariel waited on the porch roof exactly two short steps to the left of the window, where she'd been told to go. Her back was pressed to the log wall of the house, and she was staring at the sky, though she was probably still focused on something infinitely farther away than mere stars.

Chyna pushed the sponge mop onto the roof and then went out through the window while the infuriated Dobermans raged in the house behind her.

Outside, blinded dogs were no longer wailing miserably in the distance.

Chyna reached for the girl. Ariel's hand was not stiff and clawlike as it had been before. It was still cold but now limp.

"That was good, honey, that was good. You did just what I said. But always wait for me, okay? Stay with me."

She picked up the mop with her free hand and led Ariel to the edge of the porch roof. The gap between them and the motor home was less than a foot wide, but it was potentially dangerous for someone in Ariel's condition.

"Let's step across together. Okay, honey?"

Ariel was still gazing at the sky. In her eyes were cataracts of moonlight that made her look like a milky-eyed corpse.

Chilled as if the dead moonlight eyes were an omen, Chyna let go of her companion's hand and gently forced her to tilt her head down until she was looking at the gap between the porch roof and the motor home.

"Together. Here, give me your hand. Be careful to step across. It's not wide, you don't even have to jump it, no strain. But if you step into it, you might fall through to the ground, where the dogs could get you. And even if you don't fall through, you're sure to be hurt."

Chyna stepped across, but Ariel didn't follow.

Turning to the girl, still holding her slack hand, Chyna tugged gently. "Come on, baby, let's go, let's get out of here. We'll turn him in to the cops, and he'll never be able to hurt anybody again, not ever, not you or me or *anyone*."

After a hesitation, Ariel stepped across the gap onto the roof of the motor home—and slipped on the dew-wet metal. Chyna dropped the mop, grabbed the girl, and kept her from falling.

"Almost there, baby."

She picked up the mop again and led Ariel to the open skylight, where she encouraged her to kneel.

"That's good. Now wait. Almost there."

Chyna stretched out on her stomach, leaned into the skylight, and used the mop to push the stepstool toward the back of the hall and out of the way. Dropping down onto it, one of them might have broken a leg.

They were so close to escape. They couldn't take any chances.

Chyna got to her feet and threw the mop into the yard.

Bending down, putting one hand on the girl's shoulder, she said, "Okay, now slide along here and put your legs through the skylight. Come on, honey. Sit on the edge, watch the sharp pieces of plastic, yeah, that's it, let your legs dangle. Okay, now just drop to the floor inside, and then go forward. Okay? Do you understand? Go forward toward the cockpit, honey, so I won't fall on you when I come through."

Chyna gave the girl a gentle push, which was all she required. Ariel dropped into the motor home, landed on her feet, stumbled on the hammer that Chyna had discarded earlier, and put one hand against the wall to steady herself.

"Go forward," Chyna urged.

Behind her, a second-story window shattered onto the porch roof. One of the two study windows. The door to Vess's office had not been closed, and the dogs had gotten into it from the upstairs hall after the bedroom door had frustrated them.

She turned and saw a Doberman coming straight at her across the roof, *leaping* toward her with such velocity that, when it hit her, it would carry her off the top of the motor home and into the yard.

She twisted aside, but the dog was a lot quicker than she was, correcting its trajectory even as it bounded onto the vehicle. When it landed, however, it slipped on the dewy surface, skidded, claws screeching on the metal, and to Chyna's astonishment, it tumbled past her, slid off the roof, and left her untouched.

Howling, the dog fell into the yard, squealed when it hit the ground, and tried to scramble to its feet. Something was wrong with its hindquarters. It couldn't stand up. Perhaps it had broken its pelvis. It was in pain but still so furious that it remained focused on Chyna rather than itself. The dog sat barking up at her, its hind legs twisted to one side at an unnatural angle.

Not barking, wary and watchful, the other Doberman also had come through the broken study window onto the porch roof. This was the one that she'd squirted *twice* with ammonia, hitting the muzzle both times, for even now it shook its head and snorted as if plagued by lingering fumes. It had learned to respect her, and it wasn't going to rush at her as rashly as the other dog had done.

Sooner or later, of course, it would realize that she no longer had the spray bottle, that she was holding nothing that might be used as a weapon. Then it would regain its courage.

What to do?

She wished that she hadn't thrown the sponge mop into the yard. She could have jabbed at the Doberman with the wooden handle when it attacked. She might even have been able to hurt it if she poked hard enough. But the mop was beyond reach.

Think.

Instead of approaching her across the porch roof, the Doberman slunk along the front wall of the house, its shoulders hunched and its head low, away from her but glancing back. It reached the open window of Vess's bedroom, and then it slowly returned, alternately looking down at the shards of moonlight-silvered glass among which it carefully placed its feet and glaring at her from under its brow.

Chyna tried to think of something in the motor home that could be used as a weapon. The girl could pass it up to her.

She said softly, "Ariel."

The dog halted at the sound of her voice.

"Ariel."

But the girl didn't reply.

Hopeless. Ariel could not be coaxed into action fast enough to be of any help.

When finally the Doberman attacked, Chyna wouldn't be lucky again, either. This one would not hurtle across the porch roof and slide off the motor home without getting its teeth in her. When it leaped at her, she would have nothing to fight with except her bare hands.

The dog stopped pacing. It raised its tapered black head and stared at her, ears pricked, panting.

Chyna's mind raced. She had never before been able to think quite this clearly and quickly.

Although loath to take her eyes off the Doberman, she glanced down through the skylight.

Ariel was not in the short hallway below. She'd gone forward as she'd been instructed. Good girl.

The dog was no longer panting. It stood rigid and vigilant. As Chyna watched, its ears twitched and then flattened against its skull.

Chyna said, "Screw it," and she jumped through the broken-out skylight into the motor home. Pain exploded through her bitten foot.

The stepstool, which she had pushed aside with the sponge mop, was against the closed bedroom door. She grabbed it and dragged it forward, out from under the skylight.

Paws thumped on the metal roof.

Chyna snatched the hammer from the floor and slipped the handle under the waistband of her blue jeans. Even through her red cotton sweater, the steel head was cold against her belly.

The dog appeared in the opening above, a predatory silhouette in the moonlight.

Chyna picked up the stepstool, which had a tubular metal handle that served as a backrail when the top step was used as a chair. She eased backward to the bathroom door, realizing just *how* narrow the hall was. She didn't have enough room to swing the stool like a club, but it was still useful. She held it in front of her in the manner of a lion tamer with a chair.

"Come on, you bastard," she said to the looming dog, dismayed to hear how shaky her voice was. "Come on."

The animal hesitated warily at the brink of the opening above.

She didn't dare turn away. The moment she turned, it would come in after her.

She raised her voice, shouting angrily at the Doberman, taunting it: "Come on! What're you waiting for? What the hell are you scared of, you chickenshit?"

The dog growled.

"Come on, come on, damn you, come down here and get it! *Come and get it!*"

Snarling, the Doberman jumped. The instant that it landed in the hallway, it seemed to ricochet off the floor and straight toward Chyna without any hesitation.

She didn't take a defensive position. That would be death. She had one chance. One slim chance. Aggressive action. Go for it. She immediately rushed the dog, meeting its attack head-on, jamming the legs of the stool at it as though they were four swords.

The impact of the dog rocked her, almost knocked her down, but then the animal rebounded from her, yelping in pain, perhaps having taken one of the stool legs in an eye or hard against the tip of its snout. It tumbled toward the back of the short hall.

As the Doberman sprang to its feet, it seemed a little wobbly. Chyna was on top of it, jabbing mercilessly with the metal legs of the stool, pressing the dog backward, keeping it off balance so it couldn't get around the stool and at her side, or under the stool and at her ankles, or over the stool and at her face. In spite of its injuries, the dog was quick, strong, dear God, hugely strong, and as lithe as a cat. The muscles in her arms burned with the effort, and her heart hammered so hard that her vision brightened then dimmed with each hard pulse, but she dared not relent even for a second. When the stool began to fold shut, pinching two of her fingers, she popped it open at once, jabbed the legs into the dog, jabbed, jabbed, until she drove the animal against the bedroom door, where she caged it between that panel of Masonite and the legs of the stool. The Doberman squirmed, snarled, snapped at the stool, clawed at the floor, clawed at the door, kicked, frantic to escape its trap. It was Chyna's weight and all muscle, not containable for long. She leaned her body against the stool, pressing it into the dog, then let go of the stool with one hand so she could extract the hammer from her waistband. She couldn't control the stool as well with one hand as with two, and the dog eeled up the bedroom door and came over the top of its cage, straining its head forward, snapping savagely at her, its teeth huge, slobber flying from its chops, eyes black and bloody and protuberant with rage. Still leaning against the stool, Chyna swung the big hammer. It struck with a *pock* on bone, and the dog screamed. Chyna swung the hammer again, landing a second blow on the skull, and the dog stopped screaming, slumped.

She stepped back.

The stool clattered to the floor.

The dog was still breathing. It made a pitiful sound. Then it tried to get up.

She swung the hammer a third time. That was the end of it.

Breathing raggedly, dripping cold sweat, Chyna dropped the hammer and stumbled into the bathroom. She threw up in the toilet, purging herself of Vess's coffeecake.

She did not feel triumphant.

In her entire life, she had never killed anything larger than a palmetto beetle—until now. Self-defense justified the killing but didn't make it easier.

Acutely aware of how little time they had left, she nevertheless paused at the sink to splash handfuls of cold water in her face and to rinse out her mouth.

Her reflection in the mirror scared her. Such a face. Bruised and bloodied. Eyes sunken, encircled by dark rings. Hair dirty and tangled. She looked crazed.

In a way, she *was* crazy. Crazy with a love of freedom, with an urgent thirst for it. Finally, finally. Freedom from Vess and from her mother. From the past. From the need to understand. She was crazy with the hope that she could save Ariel and at last do more than merely survive.

The girl was on a sofa in the lounge, hugging herself, rocking back and forth. She was making her first sound since Chyna had seen her through the view port in the padded door the previous morning: a wretched, rhythmic moaning.

"It's okay, honey. Hush now. Everything's going to be all right. You'll see."

The girl continued moaning and would not be soothed.

Chyna led her forward, settled her into the copilot's seat, and engaged her safety harness. "We're getting out of here, baby. It's all over now."

She swung into the driver's seat. The engine was running and not overheated. According to the fuel gauge, they had plenty of gasoline. Good oil pressure. No warning lights were aglow.

The instrument panel included a clock. Maybe it didn't keep time well. The motor home was old, after all. The clock read ten minutes till midnight.

Chyna switched on the headlights, disengaged the emergency brake, and put the motor home in gear.

She remembered that she must not risk spinning the wheels and digging tire-clutching holes in the lawn. Instead of accelerating, she allowed the vehicle to drift slowly forward, off the grass, and then she turned left onto the driveway, heading east.

She wasn't accustomed to driving anything as large as the motor home, but she handled it well enough. After what she'd been through in the past twenty-four hours, there wasn't a vehicle in the world that would be too much for her to handle. If the only thing available had been an army tank, she would have figured out how to work the controls and how to wrestle with the steering, and she would have driven it out of here.

Glancing at the side mirror, she watched the log house dwindling into the moonlit night behind them. The place was full of light and appeared as welcoming as any home that she had ever seen.

Ariel had fallen silent. She was bent forward in her harness. Her hands were buried in her hair, and she was clutching her head as if she felt it would explode.

"We're on our way," Chyna assured her. "Not far now, not far."

The girl's face was no longer placid, as it had been since Chyna first glimpsed her in the lamplight in the doll-crowded room, and it was not lovely either. Her features were contorted in an expression of wrenching anguish, and she appeared to be sobbing, although she produced no sound and no tears.

It was impossible to know what torments the girl was suffering. Perhaps she was terrified that they would encounter Edgler Vess and be stopped only a few feet short of escape. Or perhaps she wasn't reacting to anything here, now, but was lost in a terrible moment of the past, or was responding to imaginary events in the fantasy Elsewhere into which Vess had driven her.

They topped the bald rise and started down a long gradual slope where trees crowded close to the driveway. Chyna was sure that Vess had paused on both sides of a gate the previous morning, when he had driven onto the property, and she figured it couldn't be much farther ahead.

Vess hadn't gotten out of the motor home to deal with the gate. It must be electrically operated.

Gripping the steering wheel with one hand, Chyna slid open the tambour top on the console box between the seats. She fumbled through the contents and found a remote-control device just as the gate appeared in the headlights.

The barrier was formidable. Steel posts. Tubular steel rails and crossbars. Barbed wire. She hoped to God that she wouldn't have to ram it, because even the big motor home might not be able to break it down.

She pointed the remote control at the windshield, pressed the button, and jubilantly said, "*Yes,*" when the gate began to swing inward.

She let up on the accelerator and tapped the brake pedal, giving the heavy barrier time to come all the way open before she got close enough to obstruct it. The gate moved ponderously.

Fear beat through her, like the frantic wings of a dark bird, and she was suddenly *sure* that Vess was going to pull his car into the end of the driveway, blocking them, just as the gate finished opening.

But she drove between the posts to a two-lane blacktop highway that led left and right. No car was visible in either direction.

To the north, left, the highway climbed into a forested night, toward ragged moon-frosted clouds and stars, as if it were a ramp that would carry them right off the planet and up into deepest space.

To the south, the lanes descended, curving out of sight through fields and woods. In the distance, perhaps five or six miles away, a faint golden radiance lay against the night, like a Japanese fan on black velvet, as if a small town waited in that direction.

Chyna turned south, leaving Edgler Vess's gate wide open. She accelerated. Twenty miles an hour. Thirty. She held the motor home at forty miles an hour, but she found it easy to imagine that she was going faster than any jet plane. Flying, free.

Although she was suffering uncounted pains and was plagued by a degree of bone-deep exhaustion that she'd never before experienced, her spirit soared.

"Chyna Shepherd, untouched and alive," she said, not as a prayer but as a report to God.

They were in a rural stretch of countryside, with no houses or businesses to either the east or the west of the road, no lights except the glow in the distance, but Chyna felt *bathed* in light.

Ariel continued to clutch her head, and her sweet face remained tormented.

"Ariel, untouched and alive," Chyna told her. "Untouched and alive. Alive. It's okay, honey. Everything's going to be okay." She checked the odometer. "It's three miles behind us and getting farther behind every minute, every second."

They crested a low hill, and Chyna squinted in the sudden flare of oncoming headlights. A single car was approaching uphill in the northbound lane.

She tensed, because it might be Vess.

The clock showed three minutes to midnight.

Even if it was Vess, and though he would be certain to recognize his own vehicle, Chyna felt secure. The motor home was a lot bigger than his car, so he wouldn't be able to run her off the highway. In fact, she'd be able to smash the hell out of him, if it came to that, and she wouldn't hesitate to use the motor home as a battering ram if she couldn't outrun him.

But it wasn't Vess. As the car drew nearer, she saw something on the roof, first thought that it was a ski rack, but then realized that it was an array of unlit emergency beacons and a siren-bullhorn. Last night, as she had followed Vess north on Highway 101 toward redwood country, she had hoped to encounter a police car—and now she had found one.

She pounded the horn, flashed the headlights, and braked the motor home.

"Cops!" she told Ariel. "Honey, see, everything's going to be all right. We found ourselves some cops!"

The girl huddled forward, snared in her harness.

In response to her horn and the flashing lights, the police officer switched on his emergency beacons, although he didn't use his siren.

Chyna pulled to the side of the road and stopped. "They can get Vess before he discovers we're gone and tries to run."

The cruiser had already passed her. She had glimpsed the words SHERIFF'S DEPARTMENT in the crest on the driver's door, and they were the two most glorious words in the English language.

In the sideview mirror, she watched the car as it hung a wide U-turn in the middle of the road. It came past her in the southbound lane now, and it coasted to a stop thirty feet ahead, on the graveled shoulder.

Relieved and exhilarated, Chyna opened her door and jumped down from the driver's seat. She headed toward the cruiser.

She could see that only one officer was in the car. He was wearing a trooper's hat with a wide brim. He didn't seem to be in any hurry to get out.

The revolving emergency beacons cast off gouts of red light that streamed across the moonlit pavement, and splashes of blue light as in a turbulent dream, while the tall trees by the side of the road appeared to leap close and then away, close and then away. A wind came out of nowhere to harry dead leaves and clouds of grit across the blacktop as though the strobing beacons themselves had disturbed the stillness.

Almost halfway to the car, where the policeman still sat behind the steering wheel, Chyna remembered the files in Vess's study, and suddenly they meant something far different from what they had meant before, as did the handcuffs.

She stopped.

"Oh, Jesus."

She *knew.*

Chyna spun away from the black-and-white and sprinted back to the motor home. In the flashing blue and red light, weighed down by the fat moon, she felt as if she were running slow motion in a dream, through air as thick as custard.

When she reached the open door she glanced toward the patrol car. The cop was getting out.

Gasping, Chyna climbed up into the driver's seat, pulling the door shut behind her.

The officer had gotten out of the cruiser. Edgler Vess.

Chyna released the emergency brake.

Vess opened fire.

11

Sheriff Edgler Foreman Vess, youngest sheriff in the county's history, watches the side mirror as Chyna Shepherd hurries along the shoulder of the highway toward his patrol car, and he wonders if this woman is, after all, his blown tire, the destroyer of his bright future. When she abruptly stops, whips around, and races back through the flashing lights toward the motor home, Mr. Vess's alarm increases.

At the same time, he is enormously taken with her and is not entirely sorry that they met. He says aloud, "What a clever bitch you are."

Getting out of the black-and-white, he draws his revolver, intending to put a round in one of her legs. He still has some hope of salvaging the situation. If he can disable her and get her into the motor home before another motorist comes along, all will be well. What fun he will have when he wraps her in chains again. Ariel won't lift a hand to help this woman, and if she tries, he'll pistol-whip the little bitch into submission; that will spoil the plans he has for her, but he's been looking at her beautiful face for a year, wanting to smash it, and the smashing will be enormously satisfying even in these circumstances.

Although Vess is quick getting out of the car, Chyna is faster. By the time he raises the revolver, she is behind the wheel of the motor home, drawing the door shut.

He can't take any chances now, can't risk merely wounding her to have fun with her later. She has to be wasted. He pumps six rounds through the windshield.

When Chyna saw the gun coming up, she shouted, "Get down!" She pushed Ariel's head below the windshield, throwing herself sideways, half out of her seat, across the open console. She covered the girl as best she could, squeezing her eyes tightly shut and shouting at the girl to close hers too.

Gunshots cracked, one right after the other, as fast as Vess could squeeze them off, and the windshield imploded. Sheets of gummy safety glass crashed into the front seats, spilling over Chyna and the girl, and things split and shattered farther back in the motor home as the slugs found stopping points.

She tried to count the shots. She thought she heard six. Maybe only five. She wasn't sure. *Damn.* Then she realized that it didn't matter how many rounds he'd fired, because she hadn't gotten a good look at the weapon. She didn't know for sure that it was a revolver. A pistol wouldn't have just six rounds; it could have ten or more, a *lot* more if it had an expanded magazine.

Risking a bullet in the face, Chyna sat up, shaking off cascades of gummy-prickly glass, and looked out through the empty windshield frame. She saw Edgler Vess by the patrol car, thirty feet away. He was tipping the expended cartridges out of his piece, so it had to be a revolver.

Already she had released the emergency brake. Now she shifted the motor home out of park.

Standing tall, appearing cool and unhurried but nevertheless nimble-fingered, Vess plucked a speedloader from the dump pouch on his gun belt.

Thanks to her mother's criminal friends, Chyna knew all about speedloaders. Before Vess could reload, she took her foot off the brake pedal and stomped the accelerator.

*Move, move, move.*

Slipping the speedloader into the revolver and twisting it, Vess looked up almost casually when he heard the roar of the motor-home engine.

Chyna drove onto the pavement as though she intended to sweep past the patrol car and away, but she was going to run the freak into the ground.

Vess dropped the speedloader, snapped the cylinder shut.

Afraid that Ariel might look up, Chyna shouted, "Stay down, stay down!" She ducked her own head just as a slug smacked off the window frame and ricocheted back through the vehicle.

She raised her head at once, because the motor home was on the move, and she needed to see what she was doing. She swung the wheel to the right, heading for Vess at the open door of the patrol car.

He fired again, and she seemed to be looking straight down the bore of the barrel when the quick flame flared. She heard a strange hissing-throbbing-buzzing, not unlike the lightning-quick passage of a fat bumblebee on a summer afternoon, and she smelled something hot, like singed hair.

Vess dived into the car to get out of her way. The motor home smashed into the open door, ripping it away, maybe taking off one or both of the hateful bastard's legs as well.

The fragrance of gunfire always reminds Sheriff Vess of the stink of sex, maybe because it smells hot or maybe because there's a trace of the same ammonia odor in gunpowder that is stronger in semen, but no matter what the reason, gunfire excites him and gives him an instant erection, and when he leaps into the car, he lets out an exuberant whoop. The roar of the motor home is all around him, bearing down on him, the headlights blazing, as much tumult as if he were in the middle of a close encounter of the third kind. As he dives for safety, he yanks his legs in after himself, knowing that this is going to be close, damn close, which is what makes it *fun*. Something raps hard against his right foot, cold wind rushes in around him, the driver's door tears off and clatters end over end along the blacktop as the motor home shrieks past.

The sheriff's right foot is numb, and although he feels no pain yet, he believes that it might have been crushed or even torn off. When he sits up in the driver's seat, holsters his revolver, and reaches down with one hand to feel for the expected stump and the warm gush of blood, he discovers that he is intact. The heel was torn off his boot. Just that. No worse. The rubber heel.

His foot is numb, and his calf tingles all the way to the knee, but the sheriff laughs. "You'll pay for the shoe repair, you bitch."

The motor home is two hundred feet from him, heading south.

Because he never switched off the engine when he pulled onto the shoulder of the highway, he needs only to release the hand brake and shift into drive. The tires kick up a storm of gravel that thunders against the undercarriage. The black-and-white lurches forward. Hot rubber shrieks like babies in pain, bites into the blacktop, and Vess rockets after the motor home.

Too late, distracted by his numb foot and recklessly eager to get his hands on the woman, he realizes that the big vehicle is no longer heading south. It's reversing toward him at maybe thirty miles an hour, even faster.

He slams his foot down on the brake pedal, but before he can pull the wheel to the left to get out of the way, the motor home crashes into him with a horrendous sound, and it's like hitting a rock wall. His head snaps back, and then he pitches forward against the steering wheel so hard that all the breath is knocked out of him, while a dizzying darkness swirls at the edges of his vision.

The hood buckles and pops open, and he can't see a damn thing through the windshield. But he hears his tires spinning and smells burning rubber. The patrol car is being pushed backward, and though the collision dramatically slowed the motor home for a moment, it's picking up speed again.

He tries to shift the black-and-white into reverse, figuring that he can back away from the motor home even as it's pushing at him, but the stick first stutters stubbornly in his hand, clunks into neutral, and then freezes. The transmission is shot.

As bad: He suspects that the smashed front end of the car is hung up on the back of the motor home.

She's going to push him off the highway. In some places the drop-off from the shoulder is eight or ten feet and steep enough virtually to ensure that the patrol car will tumble ass-over-teakettle if it goes over the edge. Worse, if they *are* hung up on each other, and if the woman doesn't have full control of the motor home, she'll most likely roll it off the road on top of the black-and-white, crushing him.

Hell, maybe that's what she's *trying* to do.

She's a damn singularity, all right, in her own way just like him. He admires her for it.

He smells gasoline. This is not a good place to be.

To the right of the center console and the police radio (which he switched off when he first saw the motor home and realized that it was his own), a pump-action 20-gauge shotgun is mounted barrel-up in spring clips attached to the dashboard. It has a five-shell magazine, which Sheriff Vess always keeps loaded.

He grabs the shotgun, wrenches it out of the clips, holds it in both hands, and slides left from behind the steering wheel. He bails out through the missing door.

They're reversing at twenty or twenty-five miles an hour, rapidly gaining speed because the car is in neutral and no longer resisting the backward rush. The pavement comes up to meet him as though he's a parachutist with huge holes in his silks. He hits and rolls, keeping his arms tucked in against his body in the hope that he won't break any bones, fiercely clutching the shotgun, tumbling diagonally across the blacktop to the shoulder beyond the northbound lane. He tries to keep his head up, but he takes a bad knock, and another. He welcomes the pain, shouting with delight, reveling in the incredible *intensity* of this adventure.

Chyna was watching the side mirror when Edgler Vess sprang out of the patrol car, slammed into the blacktop, and rolled across the highway.

"Shit."

By the time that Chyna braked to a full stop, crying out at the flash of pain in her bitten foot, Vess was sprawled facedown on the far shoulder of the roadway, three hundred feet to the south. He lay perfectly still. Though she didn't believe that the tumble had killed him, she was sure that he must be unconscious or at least dazed.

She wasn't capable of running over him while he lay insensate. But she wasn't going to wait around to give him a sporting chance either.

She buckled into the combination shoulder and lap belt. She suspected that she was going to need it.

As she shifted into drive and started forward, she became aware of a sharp stinging along the right side of her head, and when she put a hand to her scalp, she discovered that she was bleeding. The passing bumblebee buzz had been a grazing bullet, which had burned a shallow furrow about three inches long and a sixteenth of an inch deep. Any closer, it would have taken off the side of her skull. This also explained the faint smell of burning that she'd briefly detected: hot lead, a few singed hairs.

Ariel was sitting up in a sparkling mantilla and shawl of gummy glass. She gazed out through the missing windshield toward Vess, but she was blank-eyed.

The girl's hands were bleeding. Chyna's heart leaped at the sight of the wet blood, but she realized that the wounds were only tiny cuts, nothing serious. The safety glass couldn't cause mortal injury, but it was prickly enough to nick the skin.

When Chyna looked at Vess again, he was on his hands and knees, two hundred feet away. Beside him lay a shotgun.

She tramped on the accelerator.

A hard *clunk* at the back of the motor home. The vehicle shook. Another *clunk*. Then a scraping noise arose, and a hellacious clatter-jangle, but they gained speed.

Glancing at the side mirror, she saw showers of sparks as ragged steel scraped across blacktop.

The damaged patrol car was behind her, rumbling along in her wake. She was dragging it.

Sheriff Vess's right ear is badly abraded, torn, and the smell of his blood is like January wind rushing across snowfields high on a mountain slope. A brassy ringing in *both* ears reminds him of the bitter metallic taste of the spider in the Templeton house, and he savors it.

As he gets to his feet, all bones intact, choking down the interestingly sour insistence of vomit, he picks up the shotgun. He's happy to see that it seems to have come through in fine shape.

The motor home is angling toward him across the two-lane, about a hundred fifty feet away but closing fast, a juggernaut.

Instead of running off the road into the woods and away from the oncoming vehicle, he sprints toward it in a rightward-leading loop that will bring him alongside as it races past. He's limping—not because he has injured his leg but simply because he is missing the heel on his right boot.

Even with one boot heel too few, Vess is more agile than the lumbering vehicle, and the woman sees that she's not going to be able to run him down. She also sees the shotgun, no doubt, and she pulls the steering wheel to her right, away from him, ready to settle for escape instead of vengeance.

He has no intention of trying to blast her head off through the already shattered windshield or through the side window, partly because he's beginning to be spooked by her resilience and doesn't think he'll be able to do enough damage to stop her as she sails past like a skeet disk. Also, it's far easier to halt and shoot from the hip than to raise the gun and aim, and shooting from the hip means shooting low.

The recoil from the first three rounds, fired as quickly as he can work the pump action, nearly pounds the sheriff off his feet, but he takes out the front tire on the driver's side.

Hardly six feet from him, the motor home starts to slide. Snakes of rubber uncoil into the air from the ruined tire. As the behemoth streaks past, Vess uses his last two rounds to blow out the rear tire on the driver's side.

Now Ms. Chyna Shepherd, untouched and alive, has big trouble.

The steering wheel spun back and forth in Chyna's hands, burning her palms as she tried determinedly to hold on to it.

She tapped the brakes, and that seemed to be the absolute wrong thing to do because the vehicle yawed dangerously to the left, but when she let up on the brakes, that also seemed to be wrong because it yawed even more wildly to the right. The trailing black-and-white stuttered against the back bumper, and the motor home shuddered even as it swayed more violently side to side, and Chyna knew that they were going to tip over.

Half drunk on the deliciously complex smell of his own blood and the pure-sex stink of the shotgun fire, Sheriff Vess tosses the 20-gauge aside when the magazine is empty. With shining-eyed glee, he watches as the aged motor home rises inevitably off its starboard tires, tilting along the night highway on its port-side wheel rims. Virtually all of the rubber has shredded away; strips and chunks of it litter both lanes. The steel rims carve into the blacktop with a grinding sound that reminds him of the texture of crinoline crisp with dried blood, which brings to mind the taste of a certain young lady's mouth in the very moment that she died. Then the vehicle crashes onto its side hard enough for Vess to feel vibrations in the pavement beneath his feet. The flat boom echoes back and forth between the road-flanking trees, like the devil's own shotgun fire.

Hung up on the back of the motor home, the black-and-white is hauled onto its side by the larger vehicle. Then it finally tears loose, flips onto its roof, spins three hundred and sixty degrees, and comes to rest in the northbound lane.

The motor home is far past the car, three hundred feet away from the sheriff and still sliding, but it is slowing and will soon stop.

Everything is screwed up big time: the mess scattered all over the highway, which he will be hard-pressed to explain; the ruination of his plan to deal with Ariel in the methodical manner that has kept him so excited for the past year; and the incriminating bodies in the bedroom of his motor home.

Yet Sheriff Vess has never felt half as buoyant as he does now. He is so *alive*, all of his senses enhanced by the ferocity of the moment. He feels giddy, silly. He wants to caper under the moon and twirl with his arms out like a child making himself dizzy with the sight of spinning stars.

But there are two deaths to be dealt, a lovely young face to be disfigured, and that is fun too.

He reaches to his holster for his revolver. Evidently it fell out when he leaped from the car and tumbled across the highway. He looks around for it.

When the motor home slid to a stop, Chyna wasted no time being astonished to be alive. Instantly she disengaged her safety harness and then the girl's.

The starboard flank of the tipped-over motor home had become its ceiling in this new orientation. Ariel clung to the door handle up there to avoid dropping down on top of Chyna. The port flank, where Chyna lay, was now essentially the floor. The window in the driver's door at her side provided a close-up view only of blacktop.

She struggled out of her seat, turned around, and perched on the dashboard with her back to the windshield and her feet on the console box. She leaned her right side against the steering wheel.

The air was thick with gasoline fumes. Breathing was difficult.

She reached to Ariel and said, "Come on, baby, out through the windshield, quickly now."

When the girl failed to look at her but clung to the door and stared out the side window at the night sky, Chyna took her by the shoulder and pulled.

"Come on, honey, come on, come on, come on," she urged. "It's damn stupid if we die now, after getting this far. If you die now, won't the dolls laugh? Won't they laugh and *laugh?*"

Here, now, comes Sheriff Edgler Vess, battered and bleeding but sprightly in his step, past the roof of the motor home, which is now essentially the vehicle's port flank as it lies half capsized on this sea of blacktop and spilled gasoline. He glances curiously at the broken-out skylight but proceeds without hesitation to the front of the vehicle—where he discovers Chyna and Ariel, naughty girls, who have just come out through the windshield.

Their backs are to him, and they are moving away, heading toward the west side of the highway, where a sheltering grove of pines stands not far beyond the pavement, surely hoping to scuttle out of sight before he finds them. The woman is hobbling, urging the girl along with a hand in the small of her back.

Though the sheriff was unable to find his revolver, he has the 20-gauge, which he holds in both hands by the barrel. He comes in fast behind them. The woman hears the odd squish that he makes limping on one bad boot heel across the reeking wet pavement, but she doesn't have a chance to turn fully and confront him. Vess swings the shotgun like a club, putting everything he has into it, smashing the flat of the stock across her shoulder blades.

The woman is knocked off her feet, the breath hammered from her, unable to cry out. She pitches forward and sprawls facedown on the pavement, perhaps unconscious but certainly stunned immobile.

Ariel totters forward in the direction that she was headed, as though she knows nothing of what happened to Chyna, and perhaps she doesn't. Maybe she is desperate for freedom, but more likely she is stumbling across the blacktop with no more awareness than a wind-up doll.

The woman rolls onto her back, looking up at him, not dazed but white and wild-eyed with rage.

"God fears me," he says, which are words that can be formed from the letters of his name.

But the woman seems unimpressed. Wheezing, because of either the fumes or the blow to the back, she says, "Fuck you."

When he kills her, he will have to eat a piece of her, as he ate the spider, because in the difficult days ahead, he may need a measure of her extraordinary strength.

Ariel is fifty or sixty feet away, and the sheriff considers going after her. He decides to finish the woman first, because the girl can't get far in her condition.

When Vess looks down again, the woman is withdrawing a small object from a pocket of her jeans.

Chyna held the butane lighter that she'd been carrying since the service station where Vess had murdered the clerks. She released the childproof lock on the gas lever and slid her thumb onto the striker wheel. She was terrified to ignite it. She lay in gasoline, and her clothes, her hair, were soaked with it. She could barely draw breath through the suffocating fumes. Her trembling hand was damp with gasoline too, and she figured that the flame would leap immediately to her thumb, travel down her hand, her arm, enshrouding her entire body in only seconds.

But she had to trust that there was justice in the universe and meaning in the redwood mists, for without that trust, she would be no better than Edgler Vess, no better than a mindlessly seeking palmetto beetle.

She was lying at Vess's feet. Even if the worst happened, she would take him with her.

"Forever," she said, because that was another word that could be formed from the letters of his name, and she thumbed the striker wheel.

A pure flame spurted from the Bic but didn't instantly leap to her thumb, so she thrust the lighter against Vess's boot, dropped it, and the flame went out at once but not before igniting the gasoline-soaked leather.

Even as Chyna let go of the lighter, she rolled away from Vess, arms tucked against her breast, *spinning* across the blacktop, shocked by how quickly fire exploded high into the night behind her with a *whoosh* and a sudden wave of heat. Ethereally beautiful blue flames must be streaking toward her across the saturated pavement, and she steeled herself for the killing rapture of fire—but then she was out of the gasoline, rolling across dry highway.

Gasping for air, she shoved onto her feet, backing farther from the burning pavement and from the beast in the conflagration.

Edgler Vess was wearing boots of fire, screaming and stamping his feet as great sheets of flame were flung up from the blacktop around him.

Chyna saw his hair ignite, and she looked away.

Ariel was well beyond the gasoline-wet pavement and out of danger, though she seemed oblivious of the blaze. She was stopped with her back to the fire, gazing up at the stars.

Chyna hurried to the girl and led her another twenty feet south on the highway, just to be safe.

Vess's screaming was shrill and terrible and louder now, louder because, as Chyna discovered when she turned to look back, the freak was coming after them, a pillar of fire, totally engulfed. Yet he was on his feet, slogging through the boiling tar that bubbled out of the softening blacktop. His bright arms stretched in front of him, blue-white tongues of fire seething off his fingertips. A tornado of blood-red fire whirled in his open mouth, dragon fire spouted from his nostrils, his face vanished behind an orange mask of flames, yet he came onward, stubborn as a sunset, screaming.

Chyna pushed the girl behind her, but then Vess abruptly veered away from them, and it became clear to her that he hadn't seen them. He was seared blind, chasing neither her nor Ariel but an undeserved mercy.

In the middle of the highway, he fell across the yellow lines and lay there, jerking and twitching, writhing and kicking, gradually turning on his side, pulling his knees up to his chest, folding his blackened hands under his chin. His head curled down to his hands as though his neck were melting and unable to support it. Soon he was silent in his burning.

On one level, Vess knew the fading scream was his own, but his suffering was so intense that bizarre thoughts flared through his mind in a blaze of delirium. On another level, he believed that this eerie cry was not his own, after all, but issued from the unborn twin of the service-station clerk, which had left its image as a raw pink birthmark on the forehead of its brother. At the end, Vess was very afraid in the strangeness of the consuming fire, and then he was not a man any more but only an enduring darkness.

Pulling Ariel with her, Chyna backed farther from the fire, but at last she was unable to stand one moment longer. She sat on the highway, shaking uncontrollably, pain-racked, sick with relief. She began to cry, sobbing like a child, like an eight-year-old girl, loosing all of the tears never spent under beds or in mice-infested barn lofts or on lightning-scorched beaches.

In time, headlights appeared in the distance. Chyna watched as they approached, while beside her the girl mutely studied the moon.

From her hospital bed, Chyna gave detailed statements to the police but none to the reporters who strove so arduously to reach her. From the cops, in a spirit of reciprocity, she learned a great many things about Edgler Vess and the extent of his crimes, although none of it explained him.

Two things were of personal interest to her:

First, Paul Templeton, Laura's father, had been visiting Oregon on a business trip, weeks before Vess's assault on his family, when he had been stopped for speeding. The officer who wrote the citation was the young sheriff himself. It must have been on this occasion that the photographs had accidentally dropped out of Paul's wallet as he had been hunting for his driver's license, giving Vess a chance to see Laura's striking face.

Second, Ariel's complete name was Ariel Beth Delane. Until one year ago, she had lived with her parents and her nine-year-old brother in a quiet suburb of Sacramento, California. The mother and father had been shot in their beds. The boy had been tortured to death with the tools from a kit that Mrs. Delane had used in her doll-making hobby, and there was reason to believe that Ariel had been forced to watch before Vess had taken her away.

Besides policemen, Chyna saw numerous physicians. In addition to the necessary treatment for her physical injuries, she was more than once urged to discuss her experiences with a psychiatrist. The most persistent of these was a pleasant man named Dr. Kevin Lofglun, a boyish fifty-year-old with a musical laugh and a nervous habit of pulling on his right earlobe until it was cherry red. "I don't need therapy," she told him, "because *life* is therapy." He didn't quite understand this, and he wanted her to tell him about her codependent relationship with her mother, though it hadn't been codependent for at least ten years, since she had walked out. He wanted to help her learn to cope with grief, but she told him, "I don't want to learn to cope with it, Doctor. I want to *feel* it." When he spoke of post-traumatic stress syndrome, she spoke of hope; when he spoke of self-fulfillment, she spoke of responsibility; when he spoke of mechanisms for improving self-esteem, she spoke of faith and trust; and after a while he seemed to decide that he could do nothing for someone who was speaking a language so different from his own.

The doctors and nurses were worried that she would be unable to sleep, but she slept soundly. They were certain that she would have nightmares, but she only dreamed of a cathedral forest where she was never alone and always safe.

On April eleventh, just twelve days after being admitted to the hospital, she was discharged, and when she went out the front doors, there were over a hundred newspaper, radio, and television reporters waiting for her, including those from the sleazy tabloid shows that had sent her contracts, by Federal Express, offering large sums to tell her story. She made her way through them without answering any of their shouted questions but without being impolite. As she reached the taxi that was waiting for her, one of them pushed a microphone in her face and said inanely, "Ms. Shepherd, what does it feel like to be such a famous hero?" She stopped then and turned and said, "I'm no hero. I'm just passing through like all of you, wondering why it has to be so hard, hoping I never have to hurt anyone again." Those close enough to hear what she said fell silent, but the others shrieked at her again. She got into the taxi and rode away.

The Delane family had been heavily mortgaged and addicted to easy credit from Visa and MasterCard before Edgler Vess had freed them from their debts, so there was no estate to which Ariel was heir. Her paternal grandparents were alive but in poor health and with only limited financial resources.

Even if there had been any relatives financially comfortable enough to assume the burden of raising a teenage girl with Ariel's singular problems, they would not have felt adequate to the task. The girl was made a ward of the court, remanded to the care of a psychiatric hospital operated by the State of California.

No family member objected.

Through that summer and autumn, Chyna traveled weekly from San Francisco to Sacramento, petitioning the court to be declared Ariel Beth Delane's sole legal guardian, visiting the girl, and working patiently—some claimed stubbornly—through the byzantine legal and social-services systems. Otherwise, they would have condemned the girl to a life in asylums that were called "care facilities."

Although Chyna truly didn't see herself as a hero, many others did. The admiration with which certain influential people regarded her was at last the key that unlocked the bureaucratic heart and got her the permanent custody that she wanted. On a morning late in January, ten months after she had freed the girl from the doll-guarded cellar, she drove out of Sacramento with Ariel beside her.

They went home to the apartment in San Francisco.

Chyna never finished her master's degree in psychology, which she had been so close to earning. She continued her studies at the University of California at San Francisco, but she changed her major to literature. She had always liked to read, and though she didn't believe she possessed any writing talent, she thought she might enjoy being a book editor one day, working with writers. There was more truth in fiction than in science. She could also see herself as a teacher. If she spent the rest of her life waiting tables, that was all right as well, because she was good at it and found dignity in the labor.

The following summer, while Chyna was working the dinner shift, she and Ariel began spending many mornings and early afternoons at the beach. The girl liked to stare out at the bay from behind dark sunglasses, and sometimes she could be induced to stand at water's edge with the surf breaking around her ankles.

One day in June, not realizing quite what she was doing, Chyna used her index finger to write a word in the sand: PEACE. She stared at it for a minute, and to her surprise, she said to Ariel, "That's a word that can be made from the letters of my name."

On the first of July, while Ariel sat on their blanket, gazing out at the sun-spangled water, Chyna tried to read a newspaper, but every story distressed her. War, rape, murder, robbery, politicians spewing hatred from all ends of the political spectrum. She read a movie review full of vicious ipse dixit criticism of the director and screenwriter, questioning their very right to create, and then turned to a woman columnist's equally vitriolic attack on a novelist, none of it genuine criticism, merely venom, and she threw the paper in a trash can. Any more, such little hatreds and indirect assaults seemed to her uncomfortably clear reflections of stronger homicidal impulses that infected the human spirit; symbolic killings were different only in degree, not in kind, from genuine murder, and the sickness in the assailants' hearts was the same.

There are no explanations for human evil. Only excuses.

Also in early July, she noticed a man of about thirty who came to the beach a few mornings a week with his eight-year-old son and a laptop computer on which he worked in the deep shade of an umbrella. Eventually, they struck up a conversation. The father's name was Ned Barnes, and his boy was Jamie. Ned was a widower and, of all things, a freelance writer with several modestly successful novels to his credit. Jamie developed a crush on Ariel and brought her things that he found special—a handful of wildflowers, an interesting seashell, a picture of a comical-looking dog torn from a magazine—and put them beside her on the blanket without asking that she be mindful of them.

On August twelfth, Chyna cooked a spaghetti-and-meatball dinner for the four of them, at the apartment. Later she and Ned played Go Fish and other games with Jamie while Ariel sat staring placidly at her hands. Since the night in the motor home, that terrible anguished expression and silent scream had not crossed the girl's face. She had also stopped hugging herself and rocking anxiously.

Later in August, the four of them went to a movie together, and they continued to see one another at the beach, where they took up tenancy side by side. Their relationship was very relaxed, with no pressure or expectations. None of them wanted anything more than to be less alone.

In September, just after Labor Day, when there would not be many more days warm enough to recommend the beach, Ned looked up from his laptop next door and said, "Chyna."

She was reading a novel and only replied, "Hmmm," without taking her eyes off the page.

He insisted, "Look. Look at Ariel."

The girl wore cut-off blue jeans and a long-sleeve blouse, because the day was already a touch cool for sunbathing. She was barefoot at the edge of the water, surf breaking around her ankles, but she was not standing zombie-like and staring bayward, as usual. Instead, her arms were stretched over her head, and she was waving her hands in the air while quietly dancing in place.

"She loves the bay so," Ned said.

Chyna was unable to speak.

"She loves life," he said.

Choking on emotion, Chyna prayed that it was true.

The girl didn't dance long, and when later she returned to the blanket, her gaze was as faraway as ever.

By December of that year, more than twenty months after fleeing the house of Edgler Vess, Ariel was eighteen years old, no longer a girl but a lovely young woman. Frequently, however, she called for her mother and father in her sleep, for her brother, and her voice—the only time it was heard—was young, frail, and lost.

Then, on Christmas morning, among the gifts for Ariel, Ned, and Jamie that were stacked under the tree in the apartment living room, Chyna was surprised to find a small package for herself. It had been wrapped with great care, though as if by a child with more enthusiasm than skill. Her name was printed in uneven block letters on a snowman gift tag. When she opened the box, a slip of blue paper lay within. On the paper were four words that appeared to have been set down with considerable effort, much hesitation, and lots of stops and starts: *I want to live.*

Heart pounding, tongue thick, she took both of the girl's hands. For a while she didn't know what to say, and she couldn't have said it if she had known.

Finally words came haltingly: "This . . . this is the best . . . the best gift I've ever had, honey. This is the best there could ever be. This is all I want . . . for you to try."

She read the four words again, through tears.

*I want to live.*

Chyna said, "But you don't know how to get back, do you?"

The girl was very still. Then she blinked. Both of her hands tightened on Chyna's hands.

"There's a way," Chyna assured her.

The girl's hands gripped Chyna's even tighter.

"There's hope, baby. There's always hope. There's a way, and no one can ever find it alone, but we can find it together. We can find it together. You just have to believe."

The girl could not make eye contact, but her hands continued to grip Chyna's.

"I want to tell you a story about a redwood forest and something I saw there one night, and something I saw later, too, when I needed to see it. Maybe it won't mean as much to you, and maybe it wouldn't mean anything at all to other people, but it means the world to me, even if I don't fully understand it."

*I want to live.*

Over the next few years, the road back from the Wild Wood to the beauties and wonders of this world was not an easy one for Ariel. There were times of despair when she seemed to make no progress at all, or even slid backward.

Eventually, however, a day came when they traveled with Ned and Jamie to that redwood grove.

They walked through the ferns and the rhododendrons in the solemn shadows under the massive trees, and Ariel said, "Show me where."

Chyna led her by the hand to the very place, and said, "Here."

How scared Chyna had been that night, risking so much for a girl she had never seen. Scared less of Vess than of this new thing that she had found in herself. This reckless caring. And now she knows it is nothing that should have frightened her. It is the purpose for which we exist. This reckless caring.

A  NOTE  ON  THE  TYPE

This book was set in Janson, a typeface long thought to have been
made by the Dutchman Anton Janson, who was a practicing typefounder in Leipzig during the years 1668–1687. However, it has
been conclusively demonstrated that these types are actually the
work of Nicholas Kis (1650–1702), a Hungarian, who most probably learned his trade from the master Dutch typefounder Dirk
Voskens. The type is an excellent example of the influential and
sturdy Dutch types that prevailed in England up to the time
William Caslon (1692–1766) developed his own incomparable de-
signs from them.

Composed by North Market Street Graphics,
Lancaster, Pennsylvania
Printed and bound by R. R. Donnelley & Sons,
Harrisonburg, Virginia